Horse Barn

art
vuley

This book is a work of fiction. Any resemblance to actual events or persons, living or dead, is entirely coincidental.

"Horse Barn," by Art Vuley. ISBN 978-1-60264-008-5.

Library of Congress Control Number on file with publisher.

Published 2007 by Virtualbookworm.com Publishing Inc., P.O. Box 9949, College Station, TX 77842, US.

Manufactured in the United States of America.

For my mother,

Mary Christmas

So he binds himself
To the galloping mare
And she binds herself
To the rider there
And there is no space
But there's left and right
And there is no time
But there's day and night ...

Now the clasp of this union
Who fastens it tight?
Who snaps it asunder
The very next night?
Some say the rider
Some say the mare
Or the doves, like the smoke
Beyond all repair

Leonard Cohen
Ballad of the Absent Mare

Prologue

The Fifty's heartthrob, Ricky Nelson, was able to find his ideal wherever he stopped – all over the world. I remember watching him sing at the end of random episodes of *The Ozzie & Harriet Show* on our black and white television, his smile obligatory while he strummed a guitar. An occasional seductive blink of his eyes would send a horde of bouncy teenage girls into screaming fits, tugging at their hair. An odd response, I thought; even Kaptain Kangaroo's somnambulant Grandfather Clock was more animate, and no less sincere. The pop star's quest, as a *Travelin' Man*, was for a lovely girl. Unlike others who might share his interest, Ricky, not surprisingly, scored all the time; in old Mexico, in Alaska, in Berlin town, in old Hong Kong, and yet again in Waikiki, to name the places he revealed.

In the case of Ponce de Leon, it wasn't so easy. The famous explorer's ideal was immortality. He searched far and wide for a copious aquifer that promised eternal youth. With no report of any such fountain in the Old World, he set off for the New World in hopes of finding it there. The closest he got was St. Augustine, Florida where, centuries later, I saw far more old people than young. I don't know how old he was when he died but other than achieving a dubious form of immortality in Atlanta, where a busy thoroughfare is named after him, I'm fairly certain he never found his ideal.

While some people believe there's nothing more ideal than their own home, virtually never leaving it, others travel great distances in search of various ideals: the perfect climate, the most exhilarating adventure, riches, fame, or tranquil seclusion.

As one who appreciates art, my ideal, not surprisingly, is beauty. I've traveled a fair amount in search of it. And I have found beauty; in nature, in people, and in more than a few creations of the human hand. To me, Henry Moore sculptures are as beautiful as they are mysterious.

The puzzling cubism of Arizona's Painted Desert, rendered in oil or in watercolor by gifted artists desperate to decipher the message of time's soul, held me in hypnotic sway when I stood there scanning its pastel strata, listening to the silence of eons.

I've seen the teeming beauty of Costa Rica's cloud forests where leaves are elephant ears and parasitic vines manacle mammoth trees from limb to root; where mammals and reptiles dine in Eden while butterflies and birds fly in the eye of paradise.

I remember circling Manhattan in a deadpan night – our plane descending through an artist's trance – when towering stalagmites suddenly sparkled with a shower of lights, like a meteor's secrets shared.

As a traveling man in search of beauty, I've made a lot of stops – all over the world. I've heard the sound of beauty whispering above the roar of Caribbean surfs. I felt it surge through me diving into the aquamarine clarity of the Adriatic. I bowed to its majesty at the foot of snowcapped Mount Rainier, drank its foggy potions of enchantment in the Smoky Mountains, and absorbed its quiet power while lingering on arching foot bridges in the misty gardens of Hang Zhou, China.

And yet, for me, there is no greater miracle, no richer wonder, no spectacle more colorful and vibrant as autumn in Vermont; its ephemeral beauty nature's most profound treasure.

It was early October, 2006. My friend and I stood in the bright sunlight on a high bluff, alone together in our separate but commingled thoughts, looking down the steep slope with a sense of accomplishment at the horse barn we had helped build three decades earlier.

The hills surrounding the wide valley were on fire with the auburn of stately oaks, with the gold and magenta, platinum and scarlet of beech and ash, horse chestnut and hop hornbeam. Combustions of crimson, conflagrations of yellow, and flumes of vermillion blazed from the maples and the elms, from the sumac and the poplars.

Glowing forests undulated under the sweep of breezes; billowing quilts stitched with birches, embroidered with cedar and spruce.

A coltish wind bedeviled our hair. A riot of fragrances – blackberries and chokecherries, rhubarb and crabapple – gamboled about us like mute spirits, like memories dashing across the fields of time.

We watched as young equestrians trotted their horses with wary discipline and awkward grace in the outdoor riding ring. White-gray clouds lounged low in the southeastern sky. A rider ambled out of the barn. Another strode inside to dismount and groom her horse; to clean tack, muck a stall, and feed a pastime's passion with sweetened grain and the consummate nourishment of love.

"We built that barn," my friend said.

"Yes. Yes we did."

"A lot of memories down there."

"I can't believe it's been thirty years."

"I remember like it was yesterday. *You?*"

"Give or take a day or two. I've never laughed so hard, before or since."

"Times have changed. We'd never get away with a lot of that stuff today."

"We wouldn't get away with any of it. You think about it often?"

"Sure do. You?"

"Yes. Yes I do. It was insane; the most bizarre three months of my life."

My friend chuckled. "How about that dunce from Tunbridge?"

"We spoofed a lot of people, but there was one guy we never said a word to."

"Some pretty hellacious dancing, wouldn't you say?"

"I don't know which dance took the blue ribbon, the muumuu romp or the tripe flop."

"What about the pig roast? Pure madness; that's all I can say about it."

"I can't even look at blood sausage without thinking of that day."

"I think about the horse barn every time I see a banana."

"Or a *Zero* bar."

"Loggerheads or intellectuals; what's the verdict?"

"I'd have to say it's a hung jury. Classic case."

"The whole project was lunacy, from the time the footings were poured to the last nail in the roof. Or was it a stable?"

"Doesn't matter. It was the most hilarious time ever; that's what matters."

Inexplicably, my friend's head dropped to his chest. When he raised it, "and the most desperate?"

"There were a lot of desperate moments, I'll grant you that."

He ran a hand through his hair, repressed emotion escaping in a measured breath. "Ever see anything as beautiful as this?"

"No. No I haven't. Not unless it was here."

"Can there be a state as beautiful as Vermont?"

"Not this time of year. Not when the leaves turn."

Nudged by a frisky wind, one of the barn doors thudded against the siding. My friend looked over his shoulder to the west, raising a wistful eyebrow in discovery.

I turned to catch up with his vision, hearing a distant growl. An ominous nimbus rumbled, rolling toward us.

"Vermont's other personality," I said, trying to make light. "Never long before a dark cloud shows up."

My friend was reticent. A glossy glint in one eye suggested humor. The stark opaque of the other looked haunting. "You know," he finally said, "I can't shake loose of it. Not to this very day."

"Shake loose of what?"

"The gun."

"Which one?"

He stared at me for several searching seconds. "Good question."

A shrill whinny carried up to the bluff. A sorrel mare, feisty by nature or startled, was rearing up. The horse hopped clumsily on its hind legs, pawing at the air in defiance, snorting with frustration.

I stepped forward. My friend grabbed my arm.

"*Don't.* She's on her feet. She'll be fine."

The horse cavorted with naughty conceit, hoofing the loamy dirt with petulant pride. Then it clopped away, its dignity restored.

The rider, shaken but not injured, dusted herself off, repositioned her cap, and snapped her chinstrap. She bent down to retrieve her crop. Then she walked with tight-lipped resolve toward the horse – to regain her dignity, to restore her pride.

The horse stood at the other end of the ring looking back at her, snorting and shaking its head with apprehension. Clouds tumbled above, determined to deny the sun.

Dog Soldiers were the military elite of the Cheyenne nation.

"In the band, haughty and obstinate, are to be found
the best representatives of the American aboriginal,
who are still extant."

Henry M. Stanley
War Correspondent,
Missouri *Democrat*
(*Circa*, 1867)

Struggling with confusion, disillusionment too
Can turn a man into a shadow, crying out from pain

Through his nightmare vision, he sees nothing, only well
Blind with the beggar's mind, he's but a stranger
He's but a stranger to himself

Suspended from a rope inside a bucket down a hole
His hands are torn and bloodied from the scratching at his soul

Traffic
Stranger to Himself
"John Barleycorn Must Die"

One

The call came late in the day at the beginning of fall. Walter Birdsong got up from his typewriter at the kitchen table, glanced at the stove where he was cooking up an elaborate rendition of his grandmother's tomato soup, and walked to the phone at the end of a pea green countertop singed along its edges by neglected cigarettes.

"Hello," Walter said, his muffled voice clogged with phlegm.

"Jericho Laramie. Have gun, won't travel."

Walter cleared his throat. "*Jeepers*, if it isn't the cloistered paladin."

"What the hell does that mean?"

"Hermit bounty hunter. Gun-toting troglodyte."

"There it is."

"I haven't heard from you in a while, Jericho. What's happening these days in the bowels of the bug belt?"

"Nothing. Listen, you looking for work?"

"I am working."

"Yeah, but you're starving. What'd you say the newspaper paid you for that stupid article, twenty bucks?"

"I beg your pardon, Mister Laramie. Calling scrupulous attention to the demise of a local brick producer as analogous, albeit in a somewhat myopic sense, to the national problem of big business making a mockery of job creation by destroying the little guy who makes it all happen is hardly a stupid story."

Walter paused to cough and catch his breath.

"This is an issue of monumental significance. I happen to believe my insightful investigative report may be nominated for an award before it's over."

"Before what's over?"

Walter pondered the steam emanating from the soup, concerned that his nutrient-dense nostrum might be cooking too fast. "I'm not sure. Anything. *Everything*, maybe."

"Listen to me, Walter. Your rent's almost a hundred bucks a month. Figure an article a week at the going rate and maybe, just maybe, you can afford that shit-hole apartment you're in. But you can't eat. Either that or you can put a morsel or two into that disease-ridden body of yours and end up getting evicted."

"This apartment's pretty nice. Wait till you see it."

"I don't want to see it. There's no money in freelance writing, Walter.

You've said so yourself."

"My work is beginning to attract attention. I'm learning tenacity."

"You're about as tenacious as a three-toed sloth and twice as ugly."

"The sloth is cute and cuddly, Jericho. I hear they make wonderful pets. Furthermore, they don't try to outwit humans, like cats do. Or chase cars, like dogs."

"That's what I'm saying. Anyway, the job I've got for you is just temporary. You can get back to writing later. It pays half-a-dollar over minimum wage and you'll get plenty of hours."

The long spiraling phone cord slid across the counter top, grazing a set of canisters and bouncing over cracks and blisters in the vinyl when Walter shuffled in his fur-lined moccasins over to the gas range. He gave the inky concoction of vegetables and herbs a gentle stir and lowered the flame, listening with vague interest to his friend from the hills of central Vermont.

"My guess is we're looking at three months, all told. You with me?"

Walter leaned into the steam to savor a labored sniff through stuffed up nostrils. "I'm listening."

"Well, do you want it or not?"

"How'm I supposed to know? You haven't told me what it is yet."

"It's a goddamn job with a regular paycheck. It may be a one shot thing, but it's a sure thing."

"And I don't get to know what the job entails? What if it's painting a tall building? You know I'm afraid of heights."

"You're afraid of a lot of things. But that ain't it. Anyway, it doesn't matter what it is because I got all the guys coming. I'm talking Fritz, Remington, and Gulliver. Box Car and Grumpy too. Even Weepy; he'll keep us entertained while we work."

Walter lit a *Lucky Strike* between coughs. "What'd you do, Jericho, start your own company? The mere thought of it is ridiculous. Tragic, the more I think about it."

"You're pissing me off, Walter."

"With the crew you're assembling, you'll be out of business in no time."

"Anyway, that ain't it."

"What isn't?"

"I haven't started a business."

"Quit beating around the bush and tell me what you're up to."

"We're going to build a horse barn."

"*Whoa.* Are you insane? A work crew with the Swilling brothers and the Bork boys couldn't finish a sober day, never mind a huge building. Call me when you land something rational."

"I don't give a rat's ass about rational. The site is over near Hardwick. It'll be a helluva drive back and forth, but the pay'll be worth it. Listen, I can't fiddle-fart around with you all day. Are you in or not? I have to call the others."

"I'm the first guy you called?"

"I figure you need the work the most."

"The others don't have regular work either."

"That's right. But at least they play music, traffic in pot, gamble, tend bar once in a while. Grumpy hauls gravel when his dump truck's running. You though, all you got is a typewriter and a bunch of rags that don't pay crap for your stories. Here's a chance for a decent paycheck. Thing is, once I finish recruiting, you're either in on it from the get-go or you'll have to wait till somebody quits."

"Sounds like it might be worth the wait."

"Except nobody's going to quit. Know why? Because this is too good to be true. We'll be talking about this horse barn the rest of our lives. Can you imagine all us old whore dogs working the same job? We'll be lucky we aren't kicked out of the state, every damn one of us."

"*Jeepers*, Jericho, this does spell trouble."

"That's the beauty of it, Walter; all the trouble you'd ever want, what with the crew I'm bringing together."

"What if the others don't want in?"

"Once I tell them you're in, they'll be in too. The thought of you doing physical labor; shit, I could sell tickets."

"I don't know anything about carpentry."

"It's bull and jam work, Walter. A goddamn fool could do it."

"Maybe. But I'd like you to recall that it took me half the summer to build a tree house; a place where we could sneak off and get drunk when we were teenagers. The first time I climbed up on it the damn thing collapsed. I must've broken half the bones in my body."

"The only thing that got hurt was your ego, especially after Fritz and me rebuilt it in an afternoon – drunk off our asses. Sturdy as could be after that. We went drinking up there, what, fifty times, all told?"

"I think it was more like ten or twelve."

"Fritz would get wicked shit-faced and we'd jump up and down to that Dave Clark Five song, *I'm in pieces, bits and pieces* ... It's a wonder we didn't all go crashing down, what was it, thirty-feet or something?"

"I think it was more like ten or twelve."

"It's a testament to how good we were with a hammer that it lasted so long. And nobody benefited from it more than you, all those girls you put the screws to up there; what was it, ten or twelve?"

"I think it was more like two or three."

"Horse shit! I can think of six or seven right off the top of my head. What was it you used to tell us? *In her secret heart, every girl wants an albino.* Fritz always said you had that backwards."

"Obviously, Jericho, every albino wants a girl. I'm speaking, of course, of male albinos. Unless, that is ..."

"*No, no, no.* Fritz said girls don't go for pink dicks with white pubes."

"How would he know?"

"I'm just saying what he was saying. Not only that, Fritz says ..."

"It doesn't matter what he says. What matters is that I'd be worthless trying to help you guys build a horse barn. I'm no better with a hammer now than I ever was. I don't even understand how pennies wound up in the definition of nail sizes. I'd be downright dangerous with a saw in my hands. And don't let me near a power tool; there's no telling the injuries I could cause."

"I hear you, Walter. It's true, every bit of it. But you could lug lumber, hand boards up to us once we started on the strapping. Besides, I need you to do it *down-and-dirty* every time some new guy gets hired."

"Dance? You want me to dance?"

"Of course. *Dirty* though, like only you can do it. It's the perfect initiation. Think of it. Whenever some dirt ball out of the unemployment office hires on, we'll stop everything the moment he hits the job site. Everybody'll gather round to watch you climb a stack of boards and go into those hip gyrations you're famous for. We'll have Weepy strike up a little Hendrix and we'll force the new guy to stand right there and watch your filthy gyrations till we figure he's broken in good and proper."

"Makes sense."

"That's the beauty of it. Don't you see?"

Walter snuffed his butt in the ashtray next to his typewriter. "Let me think about it."

"You don't get to think about it. You're in and that's all there is to it."

"I hate to mention this, Jericho, but *jeepers*, did you happen to notice that little scratch in my voice?"

"Don't go telling me you're coming down with another goddamn cold."

"I wish. Most of what I felt this morning was in my sinuses, but then came that scratch in my throat around noontime. Could be a lot worse than the common cold, I'm afraid. It seems to be gaining in intensity. Just to be on the safe side, I'm in the middle of preparing tomato soup like my grandmother used to make. She always said tomatoes have special healing properties. And garlic. Garlic is loaded with selenium, in case you didn't know. Onions too. Come to think, it might be a good idea if I put more onions in. Maybe another bay leaf too. Or cloves. Cloves could be just the ..."

"*Walter, Walter, Walter*. Every time I turn around you've got some strange new virus or bacteria – what's the name you got for them?

"Pathogens."

"There it is. I'm tired of it. We're all tired of it. Fritz says it's all in your head."

It took two strained swallows for Walter to coax a spongy ball of mucous down his constricted throat. "Psychosomatic?" he suggested through a shallow cough.

"That ain't it. He claims you're a *hypo* something-or-other. Anyway, eat as much of that witch's brew as you can stomach and be ready to go first thing Monday."

"I don't know, Jericho. I really am worried about this scratchy throat. I may be getting swollen glands besides. The left one is bulging out like you wouldn't believe."

"I'd believe anything, coming from you. Get over it, Walter. We've got work to do. You haven't been paying attention. I said you have to be on the crew right from the get-go. I don't care if you're sick or not. Every time I get sick I work right through it. Being sick ain't no excuse."

"A half-dollar over minimum wage?"

"That's right."

"And who is it we'll be working for? Who's running the show?"

"I'll be running the show, that's who. What a stupid question. Just to prove it, I'll take out my sweet little Colt .45, give it a couple fancy twirls and pop off a few right between some bastard's feet: *pop, pop, pop*. That'll prove who's running the show, watch and see."

"I'm sure you'll do all of that and then some. But you're not the actual employer, Jericho. I'd like to know who the employer is, the name of the company we'll be working for. I need to be comfortable there'll be a paycheck at the end of the week; something the bank won't bounce back to me."

"You do like to play it safe don't you Walter?"

"I'm just being practical."

"You can throw practical right out the window. Won't be nothing practical about this job. But we'll get this barn built, on time and under budget. We'll do it righteous, watch and see."

"I'm not giving up on this, Jericho. Who is the employer?"

"It's an established company. My friend Rudy owns it."

"Rudyard Appling?"

"That's him."

"You used to play in a band with Rudyard, if I remember."

"That's right. *The Fender Benders*. He was the bass player. Couldn't sing a lick, but we put up with him."

"He's got his own construction company?"

"Yup. He's a pretty respectable guy over in my area. Been a builder for what, ten, twelve years? Built lots of houses around here. Not those cheapie capes and ranches you got in Chittenden County. Nice big colonials. He started out refurbishing old farm houses and went from there."

Walter fired up another *Lucky*. "Impressive."

"This might be his first horse barn, I can't say. Thing is, he's got houses going up in Northfield, Williamstown, and Middlesex. All his regulars are flat out. He didn't think he'd win the bid for this horse barn. It's going to be a big one."

With that, Jericho paused while an invisible trigger to some salacious vision was pulled. Walter could hear it. This was a refrain of intrusive vulgarity that occurred whenever the word big was uttered, a repetitive carnality immediately followed by a demand that someone else share his perverse enjoyment.

"Be big for me," Jericho said with wanton affectation.

Walter knew what came next.

"Say if for me, Walter. *Say it.*"

Walter was not always inclined to oblige. But this time he was eager to get back to the information at hand. "Okay, be big for me."

"*No. No. No.* Say it without okay. I don't want that word in there. It takes away from it. Say it again, goddamnit. But this time, say it righteous."

"Be big for me," Walter wheezed, feigning seductive enthusiasm.

Jericho roared. "Jesus, I like that. Anyway, twenty stalls running down two sides; something like forty in all. Or maybe Rudy said thirty-six, what with the tack room and washroom and I don't know what else. It'll have a riding ring right in the middle of it."

"Who's Rudyard doing the job for?"

"Three state officials pooled their money. To hear him tell it, there's money in renting stalls, charging fees for riding lessons, having shows; all kinds of horse shit."

Walter took a studied drag on his *Lucky*. "Impressive."

"Rudy's over a barrel on this one. Called me as a last resort. He knew I was out of work, what with all the scab electricians running around and the local missing out on that hospital job over in Berlin."

Walter gave the soup a couple of slow stirs, turning up the heat. "Thanks for the background, Jericho. I like Rudy. I always thought he played the bass pretty good."

"I didn't say he can't play a good bass; I said he can't sing. Pay attention, Walter. What other stupid questions you got?"

"How will Weepy get paid if he isn't helping?"

"He'll be helping."

"Come on, Jericho. The only hammer Weepy knows how to work with is the one in his middle pocket."

"One helluva mallet, to hear Fritz tell it."

"Fritz seems to be quite an authority on these matters."

"Weepy won't be helping with the construction part of it. Thing is, we'll need entertainment. He can set up off to the side. We'll have a generator on the site so we can run the power tools. Rudy's got a pneumatic nail gun. Powerful little gadget. Ever seen one?"

"No."

"Throws a ten-penny through a two-by-four slick as the flick of a tongue in a honey-pie."

"What the hell does that mean?"

"Horny toad, thirsty as all get-out, sucking the sweet swamp."

"There it is."

"I'll hook Weepy's guitar and amp into the generator. He can sing and wail away till the cows come home. Can you picture it?"

"It's a rather crude picture. I've never heard of live entertainment on a construction site. Are you sure Rudy will go for it?"

"I don't give a baboon's shiny red ass if he goes for it or not. I'll be running the show, Walter, like I said. Are you going to let me hang up so I can call the others?"

"Sure. Let me know how it goes."

"Look, you pink-peckered pansy, I told Rudy I'd put a crew together. After me, you're the first guy I picked. If you're in, the others will sign up too."

"What have you got against pink, Jericho?"

"What you want is purple."

"I like purple."

"Can I get a straight answer out of you?"

Walter laid his cigarette on the counter, certain he wouldn't forget it, and toddled over to the stove to give the soup another stir. He stroked his throat, his finger tips pushing lightly against the swollen gland. It felt tender, but perhaps it wasn't as large and sore as it was before the phone rang. The soup's soothing aroma filled the kitchen. Walter breathed in. Despite the rattle of fresh phlegm, a sense of well-being welled up in him. After all, he thought, a steady paycheck could cure a lot of ills.

Jericho was at the end of his rope. "You with me?"

"I'm here."

"What's it going to be?"

"Okay, Paladin. I can't believe I'm saying this, but you can count me in. As long as my health doesn't take a drastic turn for the worse."

"You won't regret it. We'll be talking about this horse barn the rest of our lives."

"That's what I'm afraid of."

"Pay attention, Walter. That's the beauty of it."

Two

Mabel Broome had a horse face, vertical and angular. Her canoe-shaped eyes, glancing as much to the sides as to find you straight ahead, appeared and disappeared with solicitous sweeps of heavy eyelids. Mabel's eyes were big, mysterious, and vacuous; like those of a horse. Except for the color. Horses have brown eyes. Mabel's eyes were blue; shimmering pools of blue refracting every hue from cerulean to periwinkle, from baby to navy, from sea to shining see.

The whites of Mabel's eyes were as glossy as polished marble. Thin bands of granite gray encircled each azurite iris. The pupils, suspended like dark planets between cumbersome winks, were black holes where wet mirrors met you at some deceptive bottom, reflecting your distorted presence.

When Mabel looked at you with a sideways tilt of her formidable head you might think she was acknowledging you, verifying your existence, allowing for personal identification. A moment later, you'd realize she wasn't seeing you at all, her focus losing itself, becoming distant, gone for someone or something else. Determining which was either – temporal awareness or infinite emptiness – between the lazy shutter clicks of those stolid eyes could be maddening. Or rewarding, depending upon the purpose of your indulgence.

Her long lashes, tightly stitched and curving into tiny whips, were the color of straw; a pale contrast to the rich eggnog hair that poured in dense swirls over her muscular palomino shoulders. When her eyelids closed with a faint quiver of lolling lashes you would wonder if she was still in there, the answer coming in the huffing heat of her breath. Upon opening, goddess-like, her eyes were two white orbs, lubricous and spacious, the ebony pupils having flown away like swallows to their nests.

Mabel had large teeth. *Horse teeth.* She displayed them proudly whenever she laughed or guffawed. Their alarming size was disarming.

Mabel Broome might have been beautiful if not for the horse that shared her face. The cheekbones rode high and prominent. A graceful ski jump nose had a narrow ramp, flaring at the bottom to accommodate nostrils that opened and closed almost frantically whenever her emotions heated in excitement, argument, confusion, or orgasm. Her cheeks were concave; implosions that might have been unattractive if not for their bellows aspect. Her chin was ordinary, resolutely defined but thankfully lacking ungainly protrusion. Her sinuous neck was long and promising.

If not for her enchanting eyes and thoroughbred form, Mabel was as homely as an old pony. Unless, that is, you laid it all on her lips; rosy as a Macintosh apple and just as sumptuous. Purposed for pleasure, plump with sensuality, glistening with sinful invitation, Mabel's lips might have been inherited directly through the millennia from Eve herself; smiling and pouting, pursing and puckering, tensing and slackening, forbiddingly teasing with delicious temptation.

Grumpy Bork had always wanted to ride a horse, though he was nervous around them and had never seized the opportunity to mount one. Heavy equipment was a horse of a different color. Caterpillars, road graders, dump trucks, bulldozers, skidders, backhoes, were, to the Grump, exquisite beasts. Likewise massive cars adorned with chrome and bulbous motorcycles with leather saddlebags and loud mufflers.

However, as Grumpy would come to know, there was one ride that surpassed the dozer and the mare, the fancy car and the deep-throated motorcycle. Mabel Broome, with her elegant eyes, with the masticating movements of her moist mouth and the surprising reach of her marauding tongue, with the rise and fall of her pendulous breasts and the flex of her muscular flanks in full giddy-up, was a mythical composition of all that was worthy of riding.

It was a crowded Friday night at the Westford barn dance when Grumpy first met Mabel. A popular rock & roll band from Essex Junction was in the middle of its second set when he pulled into the gravel parking lot in his sleek robin's egg 1960 Buick Invicta 322 Nailhead V8 four-door sedan; an automatic with electric windows, electric seats, electric door locks, Hollywood mufflers, and a pair of large Styrofoam dice dangling from the rearview mirror. Grumpy Bork loved his Buick, with the exception of the electric windows which he disconnected in favor of crank handles because the idea of not being able to get the windows down if the electric motors went on the fritz was simply too much to worry about.

There was no place to sit at the bar and no empty tables, so Grumpy stood by the entrance with his hands stuffed in his jeans watching with unconcealed disdain the thirty or forty people on the dance floor mindlessly flailing about. Grumpy disliked disorder. Dancing, to him, was a chaotic exhibitionist activity with sadly ritualistic connotations; a senseless agitation that made him uncomfortable, discomfited, and ornerier than normal.

He had a six-pack on the front seat of his car and was thinking about going back out to pop one when a waitress surprised him, hollering into his ear did he want a drink.

"Get me a Schaeffer," he yelled back to her.

As always, Grumpy was on the prowl for a slut. He wanted nothing to do with proper girls who might try his patience with prudish protestations or thwart his intentions with moralistic arguments rooted in religious fears.

Besides, he had no intentions of establishing a long-term relationship. The extent of his desire was a fleshy rump and a quickie romp, nothing more.

His taste in women was without discrimination. His partner could be passably unattractive, decidedly ditsy, skinny as a swizzle stick, a boisterous porker, or, in the words of his friend, Gulliver, delightfully stupid. The dumber the better, in fact, since he had no interest in high-minded conversations.

Grumpy just wanted to get laid, without any pretence that something serious might come of it. Loose ladies with a hankering for a good old-fashioned roll in the hay, that's what he needed. *Sluts.* Their needs were his needs.

By his estimate, there was at least one slut for every dozen girls, depending on the setting. At a county fair, the ratio was better. At a church sponsored dime-a-dip supper, not so good. At a barn dance out in the country, the odds were as good as anywhere.

Problem was, Grumpy would never be mistaken for Steve McQueen. At nineteen, he looked all of forty. He hated shaving and he hated beards. The compromise was to shave once a week, always on Sunday. His stubble, a wire brush by Tuesday, was speckled with gray. The hair on his head, coal black at fifteen, had streaks of gray and white and was already thinning out.

Growing up in the middle of six unruly brothers and having a shorter temper than any of them predisposed Grumpy's face to disfiguring insults from the time he entered elementary school. Punctuating the mosaic of nicks and pocks was a snaking scar over his right eyebrow where a deep gash required eighteen stitches after one brother or another scored a direct hit with a bottle of milk. The scar might not have been so grisly if the wound had gotten immediate medical attention. However, the assaulting brother went out to play immediately following the incident, leaving Grumpy sprawled on the floor unconscious and bleeding profusely. He was still there an hour later when his mother returned from a visit with one of the neighbors. The deep cut oozed all the way to the emergency room at Fanny Allen Hospital where it was finally sewn up.

Grumpy had two chipped teeth and a nose permanently bent out of shape from more fist fights than he cared to count. And yet, it was his widely set dual-focus eyes that were his most disturbing feature. He had Jack Elam eyes, one askance, the other adrift, giving him the uncanny ability to look in different directions simultaneously. More alarming, he could put one directly on a person, sure as a beam, while the other roamed like a swiveling searchlight. It's entirely feasible that in a previous life Grumpy was an iguana.

The waitress returned with his beer. The middle Bork boy surveyed the crowd from various angles. The old cow barn had been restored for auctions and barn dances three years earlier. One of the auctions, held at the beginning of each month, was for livestock. Cows and bulls, pigs and goats, and an occasional horse would be tagged and paraded through. The other auction, in the middle of the month, was for farm equipment; tractors, hay bailers, mowing machines, and manure spreaders. Grumpy was not in the market for cows or spreaders, but he did appreciate the orderly procedures involved. Each piece of equipment was described in considerable detail in a little booklet handed out when people came through the door. Each animal, an ID tag stapled to one ear, was escorted –

bleating, mooing, squealing, or baying – into the bidding pit, then marched away in a state of trance-like obedience while the auctioneer launched into a breathless finger-pointing hustle for the highest bidder.

Much as he enjoyed the auctions, Grumpy's primary purpose for being there was to scope out the crowd for slutty farm girls, even though his efforts were never rewarded.

With the last swig of his beer, Grumpy spotted an empty bar stool. How about that, he said to himself; the seat is right next to a young lady with perfect posture and long blond hair. Who knows, maybe she's a slut.

Muscling his way through the crowd, his luck held. Grumpy climbed onto the stool and waved his empty beer mug at the bartender. *"Schaeffer."*

The blond, to his left, nudged him with her elbow. "Hey you, that stool is taken."

He looked at the girl, searching for signals. Her eyes were captivating but noncommittal. "You mean it is now," he said.

"My girlfriend was sitting in that chair. She went to the bathroom but she'll be back in a minute."

"Looks to me like she'll have to find somewhere else to sit. I ain't moving."

The blond looked over her shoulder and spotted her friend heading for the dance floor, led by some gawky clod yanking her hand. "Never mind; it looks like my friend decided to dance."

Grumpy nodded. A minute later, "You look familiar."

"Oh don't start."

Grumpy chuckled. "Start what? I'm just saying it seems like I've seen you before. I don't mean nothing by it. Fact is, I don't care if I have or not."

She ignored him. The bartender came with his refill. Grumpy looked at the girl's glass, which was empty, and yelled over the din at the bartender, "Go get another one for the lady here."

The bartender looked peeved, stepping toward him. "Why didn't you ask for two to begin with?"

"Just do your goddamn job, smart ass."

"You don't need to buy my beer," the blond said with curt reproval. "I've got plenty of money."

Grumpy nodded. "Must be nice to be rich. What's your name?"

"I said don't start." Her tone was abrupt, stabbing the air with sharp impertinence.

Grumpy was miffed. "Settle down, lady. I'm just trying to be sociable. If you want to know the truth, I don't give a shit what your name is."

The woman was silent for several minutes. She toyed with her empty glass, spinning it in one direction and then the other, her slender fingers moving with a dexterity that was nimble and playful with left-hand turns, restive and fidgety with spins to the right; not unlike Grumpy's vision. Still staring at the glass with unresolved concern, she finally spoke. "It's Mabel." She pronounced her name with a rhythmic lilt; a caressing emphasis on the first syllable, the second gently fading: *MAY-belle*.

"Thanks for telling me. I'm Grumpy. I live over in Underhill."

"*Grumpy?* Why do they call you that?"

"Goes back to when I was a kid. My folks noticed I'd get cranky when things got out of hand. I've got six brothers. Things get out of hand real quick when that many boys are living together. According to my folks, whenever I didn't get my way I'd get grouchy. Every time I got confused about something, my temper'd get the best of me. Put those two traits together, you end up with grumpy."

"Do you like being called Grumpy?"

"I'm used to it."

"You're kind of old to be coming to a place like this aren't you?"

Grumpy was miffed anew. "How old do you think I am?"

"I'm not good at guessing ages."

"I bet I'm no older than you."

"You're kidding."

"Are you in your twenties?"

"Yup."

"Not me."

"Thirties?"

"You're going the wrong way, Mabel. But there you have it; everybody thinks I'm a lot older than I really am."

"Does that bother you?"

"Shit no. I'm used to it."

Mabel went silent, her mind drifting, absconding with her eyes.

Grumpy broke the silence. "Mind if I ask where you're from, or would that mean I'm trying to start something?"

Mabel smiled. "South Burlington."

"What brings you way out here? There's plenty of entertainment down in Burlington."

"My girlfriend likes this place. I don't know anybody here."

"Is that good or bad?"

"Fine with me. Makes it interesting, I guess."

"How's that?"

Mabel raised her voice, her annoyance button apparently pushed. "It means nobody will bother me. Or so I thought."

The bartender returned with her beer.

Even if she wasn't a trollop, Grumpy didn't take to rudeness. "Hey sister, anytime you think I'm bothering you, get your sweet ass up and go find somewhere else to sit."

Mabel's head snapped away.

"Maybe some guy'll ask you to dance. It damn sure ain't gonna be me. I don't dance."

Mabel took a sip of her beer, silent for a long while. Finally, "I don't either."

Grumpy smiled. Most girls enjoyed dancing, sluts included. That's one thing that made it difficult for him to score.

He couldn't figure Mabel out. Was she the flighty type? Or did she have her feet widely set on solid ground? Certainly her posture was good. The curve of her back was graceful and athletic. Grumpy appreciated her directness. He liked her salty disposition, the sprinkle of pepper in her voice. Maybe she was a Gemini, like Fritz and Walter; a split personality. Certainly she had mood swings. Grumpy studied her in the mirror behind the bar, between the gin and the rum. She wasn't what you'd call pretty, although her face held a certain fascination. It was long, he decided; or maybe it only seemed that way because of all the hair. Her eyes were wicked blue, almost transparent; they seemed to have a remote preoccupied focus.

What Grumpy found most appealing about Mabel were her plucky lips, moist and full, smooth and tender; damn near perfect.

But the conversation wasn't promising, discounting their mutual distaste for the dance floor.

Grumpy took a slug from his mug. "What do you for work?"

Mabel took a slow sip, her eyelids dropping like a couple of *Out to Lunch* signs. She smacked her lips, her eyelids withdrew, and she turned to him with an accusatory tone of voice. "Now you really are starting."

"I was just curious how you got all that money?"

"I didn't say I was rich. You did."

"Hey lady, you don't have to give me an answer. To be honest about it, I could give a shit less what you do for a living."

"I'm a nurse. At the Fanny Allen."

Grumpy ran his fingers though his hair. "I'm familiar with the place. When I was growing up, the emergency room there was like a second home to me. What I didn't like about the place were all those fat little penguins running around."

"I've never seen any penguins there."

"That was a joke, Mabel. I was talking about the goddamn nuns."

That tickled her. "Well for goodness sake, it *is* a Catholic hospital."

"I know. But nuns make me nervous. Especially since I was raised Catholic. I got over that though. Church and me don't mix."

Mabel drained her beer and set the glass down on the bar. "I'm not Catholic. But I said I was on my application."

"Why'd you do that?"

"I was desperate to get a job. The Mary Fletcher and the DeGoesbriand didn't have any openings."

"That's understandable." Grumpy shuffled on the stool. "I mean that you lied to get into the Fanny Allen. Not that I'm calling you a liar."

Mabel closed her eyes, her head abruptly turning, her hair swirling and settling.

"Hey, I understand there are times when you don't have much choice but to lie. That was probably one right there. Anyhow, you got the job, so I guess that proves it. Besides, it doesn't mean being a good nurse depends on you being Catholic."

Mabel turned back, her expression confused. "I don't know if any of that was a compliment or not."

"It was meant to be," Grumpy said. "Look, your beer's finished. I'll order two this time. The bartender thinks I can't be friendly."

"Are you buying again?"

"No problem."

"Thank you. Is it all right with you if I get something different? I don't know why I'm drinking beer. I don't even like it."

"Order whatever you like. Truth is I don't care what you drink, as long as you drink."

Grumpy beckoned to the bartender, who frowned as he approached. "I need another cold one," the Grump told him. "And something for the lady. Tell the man what you want, Mabel."

"I would like a black Russian, please."

"You don't fool around," Grumpy said.

Mabel looked at him and smiled, her eyes closing, her long lashes fluttering against her cheekbones like little feather dusters. "*Fool around?* I don't remember saying I have a boyfriend."

Grumpy scratched his five-day stubble, waiting patiently for her eyes to reopen. When they finally did, "Do you?"

"What?"

"Have a boyfriend."

"Not at the moment."

"I thought maybe you did. One minute you're friendly with me, the next you're not. What's the deal, Mabel; you playing hard to get?"

"My girlfriend said that's what I should practice doing. I'm not very good at it."

"Far as I'm concerned, it's not something to be good at. You're either available or you're not. You either like me or you don't. I'm not into playing games."

"I like you okay, Slumpy."

"It's *Grumpy*."

"Maybe that's what I like, the way you come right out and say things."

"I don't beat around the bush, if that's what you mean."

"What do you do with it?"

"With what?"

"The bush."

"I don't beat around it."

"Oh. Okay. Why don't we just drink and try to be nice to each other?"

"I'm up for that."

Nine beers and four black Russians later Grumpy and Mabel were hitting it off. Grumpy had gone into his most endearing talk-dirty mode, always a winning strategy if a girl laughed instead of getting offended. Mabel's speech was degenerating into a slur.

"Go ahead, Rumpy," she said, laughing with startling snorts. "You tell the funniest *jo-hokes*."

"Okay, here's another. So my friend asks me, 'Are you a leg man, an ass man, or a breast man?' I thought about it for a good minute or so and I finally says, 'Let's see now. What I like best is to squeeze a nice ass with legs wrapped around me and tits in my face; must be I'm all three'."

Mabel laughed so hard she almost fell off her bar stool. "You got a gray sessa humor, Dumpy." Regaining her balance, she sat up straight and thrust out her bosom. "Wha's my mos' prominum feeshur?"

Grumpy studied her exaggerated posture. "Welp, some guys say anything more than a handful is a waste. But I always say two hands are better than one. Looks to me like it'd take two good hands just for one of those babies."

Mabel shook her head from side to side with loud harrumphs. "You don' know how righ'choo are, Lumpy."

"Tell you what, Mabel, when the band goes on break again, let's you and me go out to my car. I got some beer in it, even though it's probably warm by now."

"I don' lipe beer."

"That's okay. Maybe you can think of something to do while I'm drinking them."

"Are we all paid up for deez drinnns?"

"Yup. I paid the man every time."

"Wha're we wainin' for? We're not dassin', are we?"

It was getting late, his sore throat worsening by the hour. The simple act of swallowing brought excruciating pain, as if the tender tissue inside his throat was sponsoring a dart tournament. Walter wondered why it was that he never had to swallow nearly as often when his throat wasn't hurting. He was ready to call it a night, nudging his cigarette into the ashtray to extinguish itself. He yanked the half written sheet of paper from his typewriter, snuggled the dust cover down over the ancient machine, and shuffled toward the bathroom for some *Vicks Vapo Rub* and a handful of aspirins, pausing at the counter to snatch two butts off the edge and toss them into the sink.

Before opening the medicine cabinet, Walter peered over puffed-pastry cheekbones into his bloodshot eyes for signs of hope. He wasn't sure what he saw. He backed off a bit to scan the whites. Sure enough, there was hardly any white at all. Backing off farther, he pondered the purple pouches under his eyes. They appeared to be more pronounced than at the start of the day. If so, the question was whether the change was simply a sign of fatigue from having sat at his *Royal* relic most of the day or, more troubling, if it manifested the encroachment of a dire disease-state.

He opted for five aspirins, letting them partially dissolve in his mouth to savor their bitter taste. He washed down the grainy residue with a glass of water into which he had stirred a heaping tablespoon of baking soda to quell the turbulence in his stomach. After brushing his teeth, rinsing and gargling with mouthwash and brushing his tongue with hydrogen peroxide, he shed his T-shirt and began rubbing his throat and chest with eucalyptus oil, taking special care to thoroughly massage his left gland.

Shuffling back into the kitchen, slumping with justifiable ennui, he ran some water into the tea kettle and placed it over a flaming burner. A cup of pekoe with vinegar and honey right before bed would help him sleep. After pouring his tea, he would empty the kettle into his hot water bottle. Heat radiating from the rubber bladder would be good for the back of his neck, which seemed to be cramping up on him. Once he got some relief there, he would move the hot water bottle to his chest to aid the dispersion of soothing menthol vapors into his nostrils and lungs.

Walter hunched over the stove, waiting for the kettle to whistle. Wouldn't you know it? he mused. Here I am hard at work on an article that any one of a dozen publications would pay top dollar to get the rights to and Jericho calls me right out of the blue. Rather than being tinkled pink about an opportunity to augment my journalism stipends, I'm green around the gills and no doubt in the rapidly progressive stages of yellow fever or the black plague.

In bed, adjusting the hot water bottle under the nape of his neck but unable to get comfortable, Walter closed his burning eyes. He hurt from head to toe. Wouldn't you know it, he muttered. At the worst time, I take deathly ill.

By the time Grumpy had gotten the sleeping bag from the trunk of his car, unzipped it from one end to the other to use as a blanket and climbed into the back seat, Mabel was already naked.

"Wha' took you so long, Bumpy?"

"I had to get this sleeping bag so we could have some goddamn privacy." Grumpy nearly choked on a swig of warm beer when he spotted two pink nipples as big as wine bottle corks. "Holy shit, I wanted to do that."

"Do what?"

"Take your clothes off."

"Okay."

"You already did."

"Das chroo."

"Here, put this sleeping bag over you while I get mine off."

When he'd gotten his dungarees down around his feet, Mabel straddled him, her immense breasts pushing him back against the seat.

Lickety-split, they were off to the races.

Mabel's heavy breathing, sodden with kahlua, trampled across his face.

"*Whoa,* Mabel. Slow the fuck down."

Grumpy was hanging on for dear life when he heard two raps against the window. He ignored them. Seconds later, three more knocks. The distraction was annoying, although it had the benefit of slowing the pace. Angered, Grumpy pulled the top of the sleeping bag down from his head and tried to look through the fogged up window. He could see shadows, then a row of knuckles when the raps resumed.

"Who's out there?"

"Hey Grump, it's Rem. What you up to, man?"

Grumpy reached a hand outside the bag and slammed the door lock down. "Get the fuck out of here Rem! Can't you see I'm busy?"

"Sure can. The old Buick looks like a runaway rocking horse from out here."

"I can't talk right now."

Rem opened the driver's door and jumped in. "Who you got back there, Grump?"

"None of your goddamn business."

"Got blond hair, I can see that. *Mister Man*, she's as wild as a mustang, from my perspective."

"If you don't get the hell out of my car, Rem, I'll flash my badge and write you up the minute I finish up here."

"Sure thing, Grump. You don't have to get so darned huffy about it." Rem jumped out and slammed the door.

Grumpy stiffened and groaned. Mabel bore down harder, lunging and panting. He dug his fists into the seat for balance. Hers was an animal lust; his, hydraulic heaven. The combination was fevered, torrid, slushy with thudding sounds not unlike hooves pounding a muddy track. Reaching a crescendo, Mabel flung the sleeping bag from her shoulders with a long hoarse bray. Her eyes rolled back into her head and her eyelids closed. The pace slowed to a jerky lope. In a series of breathy pants their muscles loosened and they clopped to a sloppy stop, clinging to one another in a cloying sweat.

They were motionless for several minutes. Finally, Grumpy moved. "Okay, sweetheart, you gotta get off me now. I have to go find Rem."

Mabel fell to one side, wrapping the sleeping bag around her. She spoke with a sober voice while Grumpy zipped up his jeans. "Who *was* that?"

"Come again?"

"The guy who got in the car."

"Remington Swilling, a friend of mine. He's the drummer in the band."

"Are you going back in?"

"You mean the barn?"

"If that's what *you* mean."

"Yeah, I'm going back in the barn. I need a cold one."

"Do me a favor, Pumpy. When he goes on break, send him out here."

Three

"Yeah, this is Jericho."

"It's Rudy."

"What's the problem?"

"The horse barn. You said you could put a crew together. I'm calling to find out if you've made any progress."

"It's done. I got eight guys, including me. We'll be on the construction site first thing Monday morning."

"That was quick. What kind of guys are they?"

"That's a stupid question. They're bull and jammers, like I promised. That's what you wanted, right?"

"Any of them know carpentry?"

"Of course they don't know carpentry. You said not to worry about that; all you needed was some muscle, guys who can put in a full day without slowing down."

"Fine, Jericho. That's fine. I was hoping maybe one or two of them might have some experience with carpentry, only because I'm short handed for skilled labor right now."

"You also said you'd have one of your best men on the horse barn with us, a foreman who supposedly knows his shit."

"I will. Everything's fine. You're right, we need plenty of men who can bull and jam, as you call it. It just means I'll have to put Pierre on it full time, that's all. I was hoping I wouldn't have to."

"A Frenchman?"

"What's wrong with that?"

"I've had my share of dumb Frenchmen over the years."

"They're not all dumb."

"Maybe. What'd you say his name is?"

"Pierre. Pierre Toussenant."

"Sounds like a dumb Frenchman to me."

"The man knows what he's doing, Jericho; he's a lot smarter than you might imagine. Been with me a long time. He gets along well with everybody. Something tells me that's a good trait, considering the kind of people you call friends."

"They're a bit rough around the edges, I'll admit."

"But they're good workers, right?"

"Look Rudy, the crew I put together will get the horse barn built and built right, watch and see. There ain't no pussies in this group; that's a personal guarantee. Except maybe Walter. He's an albino. Tends to get sick a lot. But he's smart. As long as he shows up everyday, he'll pull his load."

"An albino?"

"What's wrong with that?"

"Nothing. It's just ... I don't believe I've ever seen one."

"You'll see one come Monday." Jericho chuckled. "It'll be fun introducing you to him. Look at his eyes real good, Rudy. They're dead red. Put the fear of God Almighty right in you."

"You'll have them there at seven o'clock on the button?"

"They'll be there. I ain't saying they'll be right on time the first day. The building site's hard to find. I expect the Grump will be driving; he's got the biggest car. 'Course, he won't know how much time it's going to take driving around picking everybody up. And he won't know how long it'll be from Essex all the way out past Hardwick. I told Walter the drive is a good hour and a half, maybe longer. They'll have to get out of bed long before day break, which'll be a problem to start with. Usually, these guys are just getting into bed around that time. But they'll get used to it. Give 'em a break the first day, Rudy."

"Ten-hour days, Jericho. That's what we agreed to. If they show up late, they'll have to work that much later. We're not on daylight savings time yet, so it stays light pretty late. And don't forget they'll be working Saturdays. Sixty hours a week for thirteen weeks. That's what I put in my bid for the eight men I asked you to get for me, plus the men I'll get from the unemployment office. Are you sure your guys can handle those hours?"

"They can handle anything."

"We'll see."

"You're a worry wart, Rudy, just like Walter. Don't you goddamn worry about the horse barn; worry about the other projects you got going. We'll get the horse barn done. And we'll do it righteous, watch and see. Just leave it to me and that dumb Frenchman. As far as I'm concerned, you don't even have to show up."

"I'll be there Monday morning. And I'll be checking on things from time to time. But I expect Pierre and Richard will alert me to any significant problems."

"Richard?"

"Richard Welter. He's my superintendent. He'll be checking in on the horse barn too, every now and then."

"What's the lowdown on him?"

"Ambitious young man. Excellent with estimates. He's the reason we got this horse barn job. I saw it in the Dodge Report but I didn't intend to bid on it. Richard knows the owners, the government big shots I told you about. It's his opinion this job could provide solid margins, as long as we can bring in laborers we don't have to pay too much over minimum wage. Richard gets a bonus based on profitability."

"That's all a bunch of mumbo jumbo to me, Rudy. All I asked was what this character Richard is all about."

"He's an okay guy, Jericho. On the quiet side. A good man, in my opinion."

"Can he take a joke?"

"Actually, I'd have to say humor isn't his strong suit. He's a serious fellow. Why would you ask me such a thing?"

"These guys I recruited, humor is big with them." Jericho paused. Then, *"Oh, be big for me."*

"What's that?"

"I was saying they like a good laugh. In fact, that's what they live for."

"Fine. I don't see a problem. Might even make the job go easier."

"Thing is, Rudy, a lot of people would say the brand of humor my guys enjoy is a little on the sick side, if you know what I'm saying."

"I believe I do. I played in a band with you, remember? Nobody's sense of humor is any sicker than yours."

"Actually, it's a safe bet these guys are my match. 'Course, that's the beauty of it."

"The beauty of it, Jericho, will be if this horse barn is finished before the deadline, within the constraints of a tight budget."

Four

Fritz banged on the door for the third time. "Wake up you good for nothing drug addict. It's time to go to work."

For a moment, Weepy thought he'd left the TV on. He had passed out on the couch no more than an hour earlier. Opening the only available eye, the other buried in his armpit, he was surprised to see that the television was off.

Bang. Bang. Bang. "Wake up in there, O'Toole, before I kick this door in."

Weepy sat up, leaned forward, and held his head between his hands trying to squeeze it back to normal size. "Hold on a minute." A tinny voice, which he suspected was his, rattled around in his brain.

"Did you say something in there?"

Weepy stood, waited a moment to gain a semblance of balance, and staggered across the room to open the door. "Oh, it's you."

"That's right, it's me. Get your equipment, Weepy. We're headed somewhere over near Hardwick."

"I can't."

"You can't what?"

"I can't get my equipment."

"Why not?"

"I've got my guitar here but my amp and speakers are still at the *Blue Tooth*."

"What are they doing there?"

"That's where I played Saturday night. The cab I took home had a bunch of people in it. I only had room for my guitar."

"You had all day yesterday to get those things."

"I don't go out on Sundays. I stay in the apartment, get high, and work with my pastels. You should see the drawing I'm ..."

"Never mind that," Fritz interrupted. "Grumpy, Rem, and Gulliver are all down in the car. We still need to pick up the Box and that pink and white freak."

"The what?"

"Walter."

"Right."

"After we get him, we can drive out to the job site. Let's get a move on, Weepy. It's a long drive out to the Hardwick area. We're already late.

Wouldn't surprise me if Jericho blows our brains out the moment we arrive."

"He'd be doing me a favor. No sense bringing my guitar?"

"Not if we can't hear it. Anyway, we don't know what's expected the first day. I doubt we'll be doing much more than finding out how the project needs to get done; maybe move some shit around, according to Laramie. We'll get the entertainment going tomorrow."

"Good. If you don't need me till then, I'm going back to sleep."

"Horse shit. Turn the light off. We're out of here."

Outside the apartment of Grumpy's older brother, Box Car was sitting on the curb getting angrier by the minute. "What took you boys so long?" he grunted. "I've been out here for hours. I figure I already lost eight bucks because of your lazy asses."

"Get in the car," his brother yelled to him.

Fritz stared with glaring eyes at the hairy beast who insisted on sitting up front, forced Fritz to sit in the middle, then farted.

"When we pick up Walter," Fritz said, "I'm getting in the back. I can't ride all the way to Hardwick next to this flatulent freak."

Box Car laid his head back on the seat and grumbled in a low raspy voice. "Don't talk to me."

"Why not?" Fritz asked.

"I said don't talk to me."

"And I asked why the hell not."

Box closed his eyes. "Because I'm pissed off and I don't talk when I'm pissed off."

"You're always pissed off at something."

"That's why I don't talk much."

"Good," Fritz said. "I don't talk your language anyway. It's usually nothing but grunts and groans, all sorts of prehistoric gibberish."

"He's the *Missing Link*," Rem said from the back seat. "They've looked everywhere for the connection between ape and man and it's right here in the car with us. Forget about the horse barn. Let's go over to the University of Vermont's paleontology department and turn this creature in. We'll make a fortune."

Fritz laughed. Box Car grunted.

Rem was nominated to knock on Walter's door.

"Are you up yet? Get a goddamn move on; we're late."

Rem waited a minute, then turned to the men in the car and hunched his shoulders. "He's gotta be in there. Where else would he be at this hour?"

Rem gave the door a few rapid-fire raps. He waited. He was about to give the door a shoulder when Walter opened it. The spindly white haired man stood in the doorway in his underwear, his neck and chest glistening like an oil slick. "I can't go to work today," he said in a feeble voice.

"Why not?" Rem asked. "What the hell's wrong with you now?"

Walter's voice was scratchy, barely audible. "I'm pretty sure it's a combination of strep throat and double pneumonia."

Rem turned toward the car again and shouted, "This lollipop is half dead. Could be late stage leukemia by the looks of it. If we make him come with us in this condition, we'll embarrass Jericho."

Box Car got out and yelled to Rem in a gravelly voice over the roof of the car, "Let that sickly albino go back inside and die. He ain't even dressed. We'll be lucky to get there by noon as it is."

Rudy unfolded the plans over two sawhorses, laying a level on one and a tape measure on the other to keep the blueprints from blowing away in the brisk wind. He walked over to Jericho. "Why aren't they here by now?"

"That's the seventh time you've asked me in the last hour. Give 'em time, goddamnit. They'll be here soon enough."

"It's already ten o'clock. You think I can hang around here all day? I've got other projects to check on."

"I'm sure they're close by now."

"I'll give them fifteen more minutes. After that, I'm going to the unemployment office and hire the next seven guys I see."

Jericho looked over Rudy's shoulder and saw a blue Buick approaching the bluff above the construction site. "There they are now. What'd I tell you?"

Rudy turned around. "They're three hours late. That can't happen again."

"They've got the routine down now," Jericho said. "They'll be on time from here on out. Probably couldn't find the place, that's what I figure."

Grumpy parked the car at the top of the bluff alongside three pickup trucks. Box Car, Fritz, Remington, Gulliver, Weepy, and Grumpy piled out of the car and ambled down the makeshift road to the building site.

"I thought you said you recruited seven guys. I see six."

"I was afraid of that. Must be Walter's under the weather."

Rudy gave Jericho a stern look. "We're all under the weather. When you get home tonight, call him up and fire his ass. I won't have any pansies on my payroll."

"Walter's not a pansy, Rudy. Not always. He took sick. That can happen to anybody."

"Find somebody to replace him."

"We need a guy who can do it dirty. Nobody's better than Walter."

"Do it what?"

"Look, Walter's an albino. You said you wanted to meet one. He's a good man for the crew, I promise. Once you see him, you'll be glad we didn't let him go."

Rem and the group stopped in front of Jericho and Rudy in the center of the partially graded area where the horse barn was to be erected.

Jericho greeted them. "I didn't expect you boys till a couple hours from now. You were supposed to be five hours late, not three. What are you trying to do, make me look good?"

Remington extended his hand. "Sorry, Jericho. We had trouble getting going. Plus, we didn't know the last fifteen miles would be dirt roads, most of them in pretty bad shape."

Jericho shook his hand. "How were my directions?"

"Perfect."

"Rem, let me introduce you to Rudy. He used to play in *Fender Bender* with me. Now he wants me to run his company for him on this project, make sure things get done right."

Rudy shook hands with Rem. "Part of what Jericho says is accurate," Rudy said. "We were in the same band a while back."

"Let me finish the thought," Rem said, giving Rudy's hand a half dozen hearty pumps. "You and the others decided to break up the band before Jericho got you all arrested by pulling some stunt that only a man completely out of his mind would pull, like pissing into somebody's beer mug or grabbing the mike and yelling obscenities at the patrons, or maybe slipping out that puny wiener of his and waving it around like he had a reason to be proud."

Rudy scratched his head, giving the last scenario some thought. "Seems to me being able to wave it around is reason enough to be proud. But no, that's not what happened. We broke up the band because nobody wanted to hear us. We sucked."

"Wouldn't have been that way," Jericho said, "if one of us had been a singer." He looked at Rem. "Rudy said he was good at it, but the truth is, he can't sing for shit."

Gulliver, without being introduced, stepped forward. "Let me get this straight, Rude. The band broke up and it wasn't because of Jericho?"

"He wasn't easy to work with. Many's the time he threatened to shoot us for showing up late for practice or if we refused to tear down his drums for him. But no, that wasn't it. *Fender Bender* was actually a pretty serious accident."

Rem finally let go of Rudy's hand and looked at Jericho. "Are you doing the honors or would you like me to?"

"You go ahead," Jericho said, a smirk on his face.

"Rudy, this is my older brother, Fritz. He's a Vietnam vet; Third Marines, Quang Tri Province. He's also an iconoclast."

"What the hell does that mean," Jericho asked.

"Dances to his own jig, looks a lot like Jesus Christ, doesn't respect any opinion that differs from his own, thinks he's surrounded by fools."

"There it is," Jericho said. "Describes the old leatherneck pretty good, as far as I'm concerned."

Fritz said nothing, declining to shake hands by folding his arms chest high, though he nodded in apparent agreement.

Rudy nodded in return.

"Gulliver over here," Rem continued, "is my younger brother. Our folks didn't know this would be the case when they named him, unlike the prescience they showed in naming me, but the man has never traveled anywhere. Whereas Swift's character went everywhere he shouldn't have, our own Gulliver stays in the same place he shouldn't – holding his ground, as he puts it – despite our ceaseless efforts to convince him to leave. Fact is this very place may be the farthest from home he's ever been."

Rudy's expression was pained.

"This may sound like a contradiction, Rudiment ..."

"It's Rudy."

"... but Gully is a verbose man of few words."

Rudy's face twisted.

"He doesn't often speak. But when he does, he fancies himself an elocutionist. He's not above wielding his command of the English language as a tool of intimidation; more to the point, as a deadly weapon. If the tongue was a sword, Gulliver could cut a person to ribbons with the turn of a phrase, dice up an aristocrat with verbal pomposity, carve a politician into little pieces with flamboyant bombast."

"While I am seldom vocal," Gulliver interrupted, "my occasional need for clarification of key points calls for timely summations that, in other minds, sad to say, are convoluted and equivocal."

"This very loquaciousness," Rem resumed, "however infrequently he may brandish it against us, is why we appreciate it when he keeps his mouth shut."

Rudy's face remained gnarled.

"Complicating matters, his disposition is rigid and noncompliant. Fact is the man's as nasty as your typical storm trooper. None of us, by the way, is all that thrilled with the idea of Gulliver having a hammer in his hand. Nevertheless, it was Jericho's decision to hire him, so what in God's relatively holy name can we do about it?"

Rudy shrugged his shoulders.

Rem looked at his younger brother. "Come over here, Gulliver, and shake hands with Rudolph Appleman."

"It's Rudyard Appling."

Gulliver stepped forward, the scowl on his face suggesting he may not have appreciated the description of him, although the absence of a retort seemed to indicate he had no viable argument. "Nice to meet you, Rude."

"It's Rudy."

"It's whatever I say it is."

A look of pain returned to Rudy's face, but since he was tiring of the contest with his name, he let the comment go uncontested.

Rem continued with the introductions, jabbing an index finger toward Box Car Bork. "I happen to believe this guy is the *Missing Link*. Let me ask you a question, Rude. Did you ever see a man with more hair on him than a bear has fur?"

"I don't believe so."

"Box, as you can see, hasn't shaved in years. If he had, the clippings would have provided toupees for half the bald men the world over. You've seen men with hairy chests? The hair on this man's back is thicker than a shag carpet. Nobody knows what he's got for a dink because it's buried in more pubic hair than the annual production of a steel wool factory. He's got hair on his knuckles, hair on his kneecaps, and while we haven't checked, he probably has hair on the soles of his feet. Devil of it is, the women love it. All that hair is an effective aphrodisiac. Box Car gets seduced by strange women all the time, in ways that would make the average woman sick. Millennia ago, the *Missing Link* was a brutish wanderlust. Don't ask a paleontologist. Ask me. I have irrefutable proof right here."

Box Car chuckled with a low rumble.

"Please to meet you," Rudy said.

Box offered a clubby hand covered with black hair. "My pleasure," he growled.

"Next," Rem said, "we have Grumpy Bork. He hates to claim the Box as his brother, as I'm sure you can imagine, which is why we remind him of it at every opportunity. Grumpy is our driver. More importantly, he's a slut chaser *par excellence*. And for that, he has our abiding respect."

"And finally, this here's Wilmer O'Toole. We call him *Weepy*. He's as strong as an ox. Does fifty pushups and a hundred sit-ups every day. Then he runs five miles full tilt in all kinds of weather. An intellectual with enormous musical talent, some would contend he doesn't have the constitution of a half-assed drummer."

Weepy, whose hands were large, gave Rudy an extraordinarily strong squeeze, trying to prove Remington right.

Rudy, as if Weepy existed in name only, asked Remington why the man was called Weepy.

"Because he's a sensitive manic depressive. He cries a lot."

Rudy looked again at Weepy, whose bottom lip trembled – a seemingly involuntary movement that the singer-guitar player actually controlled at will – again proving Remington's statement to be accurate.

Rudy was visibly dismayed by Weepy's eggshell constitution. He turned back to Jericho. "I must say, you've put together quite a crew. But I'm curious where the absent man is. And whether or not he'll be a no-show tomorrow."

Jericho looked at Rem. "Walter couldn't make it?"

"He's sick."

"I suspected as much. On Friday, he told me he might be coming down with something. What do you think it is?"

"Don't know. Since he's white as a ghost in his natural state, it's difficult to narrow it down to a single sickness. Could be anything. By the looks of him a couple of hours ago, he could be dead by now."

Jericho laughed. "I'll give him two days to get over whatever the hell he's got. After that, he works sick. We can't have any malingerers."

After his introduction, Grumpy had walked over to check out the bulldozer. He and the operator, a man of preposterous girth, were shouting and pointing fingers at each other.

Rudy was alarmed. Jericho and the crew followed him to the scene.

"What's the problem over here?" Rudy asked.

The operator shut down his machine. "Is this guy an inspector of some kind?"

"No," Rudy said. "Why?"

"I could have guessed as much. He keeps yelling that he's going to write me up if I can't handle this rig proper. I told him he better lay off or I'll climb down and clock him one."

"Get your fat ass down here," Grumpy shouted up to him. "It's time we find out who gets clocked and who does the goddamn clocking."

The operator got up from his seat. Rudy told him to relax and sit back down. Turning to Jericho, "Have you got an explanation for this?"

"Grumpy's the best dozer operator in Vermont. He'd have this whole area leveled in no time if he was up there running that thing."

Rudy scratched his head. "And what's this about *writing up* the operator? I don't get it."

"Grumpy writes everybody up for one thing or another."

"By what authority?"

Jericho walked Rudy ten or twelve feet away from the altercation and spoke in a hushed voice. "You have to understand, Rudy; Grumpy directs traffic at the Champlain Valley Exposition every summer, come fair time. He gets to wear a badge. If somebody parks in the wrong place he writes a ticket and puts it on their windshield; you know, under the wiper."

"What's that got to do with this?"

"Nothing. But the lesson is, you give some people a little authority and it goes right to their head. That's what happened to the Grump. It's my guess he thinks he's got the clout of a deputy Sheriff. He never turns his badge in after the fair's over; keeps it clipped to the inside of his wallet. He likes to flash it when things get out of hand. Listen, we don't understand it either. But it's the way it is. Let him write the man up, for chrissakes. What harm could it do?"

"Write him up for what?"

Jericho looked back at the Grump. "Why do you need to write this man up?"

"For being a shitty-ass operator, for one thing. Sassing, for another."

The operator yelled down to Appling. "Hey Rudy. I'll tell you what. If this *deputy-something-or-other* thinks he can run this machine better than me, let him try. I don't mind taking a break. I'll head up to the truck and eat a package of donuts."

Rudy wasn't comfortable discussing the idea with Grumpy, so he turned to Jericho. "What do you think? Can your man really handle this dozer?"

Fritz intervened. "Get down from there, fat man. My friend'll take over now."

The operator climbed down from his machine and waddled up to Fritz. "Who you calling a fat man?"

"What the hell do you expect?" Fritz said, staring the man down. "You weigh all of four-hundred pounds. And what do you do when you take a break? You climb into your truck and wolf down donuts."

Fritz shook his head at the operator, thoroughly disgusted. "Donuts are nothing but fats and sugars. My brother has a friend who owns a *Dunkin' Donuts*. I know how they're made. Hear the news, tubby. You don't like being called a fat man? Kiss those greasy donuts goodbye."

The operator could hardly believe what he was hearing. He shook his head and waddled up the road to his pickup truck, craning his head with a troubled look when he heard Grumpy crank up his dozer.

"I'm getting out of here," Rudy told Jericho.

"Hold on a minute," Jericho said. "You haven't seen the best thing yet."

"What's that?"

"Show him, Rem."

"You mean the eyes?"

"Of course I mean the eyes. What else could it be?"

Rem walked up to Rudy, almost rubbing noses with him.

Rudy looked into his eyes. Remington made them go wide. His pupils began to jiggle.

Jericho howled. "Ain't that beautiful?"

Remington's pupils jiggled frantically. Rudy scratched his head.

Jericho was out control with laughter. "Tell me his parents aren't geniuses."

The contractor stared at the dancing pupils. "I don't get it."

"*Rapid Eye Movement*, you dumb bastard. They named him Rem and it turned out he's got rapid eye movement. How the hell you gonna beat that?"

Moments later, a flatbed truck arrived. Rudy told the men where to stack the two-by-fours, two-by-sixes, treated posts and beams, and texture 111 siding, and where to put the boxes of nails and belts for the pneumatic nail gun. Looking back at Grumpy working the dozer blade, Rudy grudgingly admitted to Jericho that his friend was an excellent operator. He instructed the men to work until eight o'clock to make up for lost time and to show up at seven the next morning and every morning thereafter. Pierre Toussenant, he said, would be at the site the next day with tools, tool belts, work gloves, hard hats, and a generator. A mason would also be coming with a backhoe and a cement mixer to dig and pour the perimeter trenches for the posts.

Rudy was only too happy to leave the site. As soon as he was out of sight, Gulliver and Weepy walked back up to the Buick; Gully to grab his camera, Weepy to get his art tablet and pastel crayons.

Weepy perched himself on a rock in an adjacent pasture and drew pictures while Gulliver walked around taking roll after roll of photographs, including several shots of the men stacking lumber.

At noon, Jericho announced a break for lunch.

Crew members looked at each other with mixed expressions of confusion and concern.

"Did you bring a lunch?" Rem asked Jericho.

"Of course I brought a lunch. Do I look stupid to you?"

Rem looked at the others, then back to Jericho. "Guess we weren't as smart as you."

Jericho bellowed with derisive laughter. "You're telling me you guys didn't bring anything to eat?"

Rem looked down at the ground. "Nope. Never thought of it."

Jericho had no pity. "Ain't that a fucking shame! Here's the deal. I'm going up to my truck where I've got a big-ass lunch Deirdre packed for me. *Oh, make it big.* I've got a meat loaf sandwich, thick as you please, a thermos full of steaming beef vegetable soup, an apple, a devil dog, and a bowl of black raspberries she picked out in the back yard. I've also got a Colt .45 under the seat. Any of you sons-a-bitches come sniffing around my truck looking for a handout will get his head blown off."

With that, Jericho marched up the hill to his truck, laughing hysterically.

"Well boys," Gulliver said, rubbing his hands together, "I'm hungry. One of us is going to have to be sacrificed. The rest of us can go into the woods over there and gather up some dry tinder for a fire. I suggest we eat Weepy since he's got the most meat on him."

Box Car was enthralled with the idea, walking up from behind and putting Weepy in a tight bear hug. The *Missing Link* growled ferociously. "I'll hold him while you guys get the fire going."

Weepy, knowing it was a hoax, was compliant. "What part of me do you want, Box?"

"Your ass," the hairy beast grumbled. "I like fat and that's the only fat you got on you."

Helpless in Box's vice grip, Weepy was surprised to see the others trek off into the woods. Rem returned with dry twigs. Grumpy and Fritz carried small limbs. Gulliver dragged a heavy branch.

Grumpy, Fritz, and Gulliver broke up the limbs and tossed them in a pile. Rem came out of the woods a second time with another load of twigs.

"You boys go get another load while I position this wood for a good fire," Remington said. "We'll be having ourselves one righteous feast in no time."

Remington walked over to the saw horses. He needed paper but apparently Rudy had taken the blueprints with him. He walked part way up the hill and motioned to Jericho, mindful of the threat. Jericho stuck his head out of the window and hollered. "You ain't getting so much as a bite."

Rem yelled back. "You got a lunch pail or a paper bag?"

"A lunch pail. Why."

"You got any kind of paper in that lunch of yours?"

"I've got a little piece of white cardboard that came with my devil dog. Why?"

"We're going to cook Weepy."

"Really?"

"Yeah."

Jericho jumped out of his truck. "Hold up a minute. I gotta get in on this."

"No you don't. Just come part way and hand me that paper. We don't get any of your lunch; you don't get any of ours."

Weepy was transfixed between amusement and alarm. He knew it was impossible to wrestle free of Box Car's grasp but consoled himself by rationalizing that his so-called friends couldn't possibly mean it.

Fritz, Gulliver, and Grumpy returned from another trip into the woods and added to the pile. Remington walked back with the tiny piece of stiff paper. Jericho, twirling his favorite pistol with his right hand, watched impatiently from the bluff.

Rem rolled the paper into a small tube, lit one end with Weepy's *Zippo*, which he had dug out of the entertainer's pocket, and poked his arm into the middle of the pile. The wood was dry. Aided by a light wind, the pile quickly smoked and crackled. Within a minute, there was an impressive fire in the middle of the building site.

Weepy tried to run with the Box attached to his back but the hirsute creature simply picked him up several inches off the ground, rendering Weepy's effort – legs pumping in the air – cartoonish.

Suddenly, the Weepy roast was in jeopardy. The fire, dangerously close to a stack of lumber, was raging. Seeing the flames lick the boards, Rem yelled to Gulliver. "Start moving those two-by-fours!"

"Fuck you. It's not up to me to move the goddamn boards."

"Grumpy!" Rem shouted. "Put the fire out."

"How?"

"I don't know."

"Me either."

"Piss on it then," Rem said, and casually walked away.

"That won't do any good," Grumpy said.

"No, I mean to hell with it. There ain't nothing we can do about it."

Jericho entered the fray. "Throw the sonuvabitch in."

Box was still holding Weepy in his arms, several feet from the fire.

"I said throw his ass in the fire. I want to see him burn." Jericho aimed his pistol at Box Car. "Either that or I'll plug your beard full of bullets."

Flames flicked at the boards.

"We probably ought to move that lumber," Rem said to Jericho.

"Okay," Jericho said, slipping the gun back into his pants. "Let that cry baby go. I want three guys on one end of these boards and three on the other. Get your sorry asses in gear. We don't have much time."

"While we're doing that, what are *you* going to do?" Fritz asked.

"I'm going to watch," Jericho said.

The men grabbed the boards three or four a time, tossing them into a haphazard pile a safe distance from the fire. The frenetic effort took nearly ten minutes. With the two-by-fours out of danger, the men watched the fire abate, then gloated over their heroics, wiping the char from their cheeks and foreheads.

Rem noticed something missing. "Where the hell's Weepy?"

"He high-tailed it," Box Car grumbled, "as soon as I let go of him."

"I can understand that. But where to?"

"I wasn't paying attention. I was saving the boards."

"Good thing I didn't see him," Jericho said. "I'da shot him on the run."

"He can run like a deer," Gulliver said. "I've got a ten spot says he makes it home before we do."

"And I'll lay you two to one he gets lunch somewhere," Rem said.

"Too bad it turned out like it did," Box growled. "Rubbing up against his ass with him squirming like a stuck pig was beginning to feel pretty good."

At seven-thirty it was too dark to continue working. The flat bed truck was nearly empty. The crew, except for Jericho, couldn't remember being so hungry.

In Plainfield, they piled out of the Buick and rumbled into the general store, buying slim jims, cans of Vienna sausages, candy bars, bags of potato chips and cheese curls, a pound of raw hamburger for Box, and two cases of beer. Fritz bought only beer, scowling at all the junk food.

Near Middlesex, Grumpy slammed on the brakes for a hitchhiker. It was, of course, Weepy. He'd made it about thirty miles, his pastels and art tablet tucked under one arm, his guitar in the other. For five minutes he refused to get in the car. He finally relented, not entirely convinced that the lunchtime incident was nothing more than a cruel joke. The men gave him profound assurances that they had enough beer and goodies to make it to suppertime without resorting again to cannibalism.

Five

Sibyl was giving her daughter Beatrice a kiss goodnight when she heard a knock at the door. "Sleep tight, Bea. Don't let the bed bugs bite."

"Mommy?"

"Yes sweetie."

"Are there really bugs in my bed?"

"No sweetie. That's just a saying to help you go to sleep."

"But that doesn't help. It scares me."

"I'm sorry. I won't say that anymore."

"But then you'll say I have to fall asleep before the sand man comes and throws sand in my eyes."

There was another knock.

"I won't say that either. Close your eyes, now; Mommy has to see who's at the door."

"You already know it's Wynona."

"It probably is. But I shouldn't keep her waiting."

"Can you read me a story first?"

"Not tonight sweetie. I will tomorrow night, I promise."

"Okay."

Sibyl tucked her daughter in, kissed her on the forehead, and went downstairs to answer the back door off the kitchen.

"Wynona. Hi. Come on in."

"No problem if I show up this late?"

"Not at all. It's barely eight o'clock."

"I know you get up awful early. I was bored. Thought I'd drive over for a short visit."

"Let's go into the living room. You want something? Tea? A soft drink? I've got instant decaf."

"I'll take a coke if you have one."

Sibyl returned with the soda and a glass of water for herself."

"Remington out for the night again?" Wynona asked.

"I wouldn't have thought so. He started work today building a horse barn over near Hardwick. Grumpy will be coming by at five o'clock every morning. From now on Rem'll have to be up by four-thirty."

"That's about the time he usually goes to bed, isn't it?"

"He'll have to get on a radically different schedule. The job's supposed to last three months, according to his friend Jericho."

"What time do you expect him in?"

"I'm not sure. Maybe he worked late. You're getting at something, Wynona. What is it?"

"You act like Rem's going to be responsible about this new job he's got. Getting up at that hour means he's going to have to get to bed early. We both know that isn't him. I'll bet right after work he headed over to that Indian reservation in New York to gamble on those stupid birds. It's an addiction with him. If he gets in at his normal hour, no way is he making it to work. And you know what that means. I'd say it's like *deja vu* except that it's more like a broken record. He can't hold a job because he can't stay away from the cockfights."

"Rem is *my* problem, Wynona. It's nothing for you to worry about."

"I'm worried for *you,* Sibyl. You're my best friend and I hate to see you having to deal with his shit. Those silly roosters are a higher priority to Rem than his own family. It's a sickness. I've never asked you this before – I know it's none of my business – but does he actually make any money at it?"

Sibyl sighed. "Look, Wynona, Rem loves me. And he adores Beatrice; his little honey bee. I knew about the cockfights long before we ever got married. Okay, I'll admit I figured he'd be over it by now, or that I'd be able to convince him to stop gambling on his cock. But his sickness, as you call it, doesn't change how much he loves his family."

"I suppose you put up with it because he throws a pile of money on the kitchen table after he's been gambling half the night."

"I didn't say that. Truth is he loses money cockfighting. We've had more than a few heated discussions about it. I guess what I'm saying is that it would take more than cockfights to ruin our marriage."

"Here you are almost a licensed accountant. You've got a great career ahead of you. Rem contributes nothing. I think you deserve better, that's all."

"I appreciate your concern, Wynona; I really do."

"Must be there's something going on behind the scenes I don't know about, to make you stick with him like you do. I'd have thrown his sorry ass out a long time ago."

"Behind the scenes?"

"I meant that as a joke, Sibyl; you know, like he's hot in bed or whatever."

"If Rem batted me around, that's something I wouldn't put up with. But he's nonviolent, unlike his brothers. Rem's never laid a hand on me. Not a vicious hand, I'm saying. And yes, if you must know, he's an excellent lover."

"Marriage can't last on sex alone. At some point, things cool down. That's when you find out if your relationship is really solid or if it's only about the bedroom, in which case it's doomed; eventually, I mean."

"Maybe eventually can last a lifetime, Wynona. We went out together for a year and we've been married for almost six. Rem turns me on every bit as much today as he did seven years ago. And there's nothing to indicate it's any different for him. If there's any problem as far as sex goes, I'd say it's the opposite."

"I don't get it."

"I mean he's always horny. I could swear he's a regular sex fiend. The man can't get enough. Phew! He wears me out sometimes, Wynona, I have to tell you."

"Wears you out?"

"Look, I'm only human. I'm not always in the mood, but that's never the case with him. Three or four times a week, at least, Rem comes stumbling in at some ridiculous hour and wakes me up out of a sound sleep because he's got this wicked … well, you know what I'm saying; he's ready for action."

"And you submit to it, like you're his sex object?"

"It isn't like that. He can be very romantic. He's tender and passionate, touching and kissing me in all the right places. It never takes long before I'm a willing partner. Can I ask you a personal question, Wynona?"

"Shoot."

"When your husband has orgasm, is that the end of it?"

"I don't know what you mean."

"Does he, you know, go limp?"

"Of course. What kind of question is that? They all do. It's the nature of the beast."

"Not Rem."

"I don't get it."

"That proves it."

"Proves what?"

"That Rem isn't natural."

"Oh, come on, Sibyl, you're not telling me Rem still has an erection after he's had orgasm."

"That's exactly what I'm saying."

"For how long?"

"Until we do it again. Or even three times. I'm not sure he ever does get soft."

"You must be kidding!"

"Even if we're just sitting around watching television, I'll guarantee he's got a hand in his pants playing with himself. If I complain, he says he can't help it; that he's half hard and it needs attention. That's usually when he asks me to take over. I'm telling you, Wynona, the man's got a cock fixation."

"Incredible."

"Maybe I shouldn't complain. I'll confide in you that my real worry is whether or not one woman can keep him satisfied. Maybe someday he'll slow down. But I don't know; it's been like this ever since our very first time. He hasn't shown any signs of slowing down yet."

"You think he runs around? Or might?"

"No, I don't. All I'm saying is …"

"That's okay, Sibyl. Say no more. I think it's great that Rem's such a wonderful sex partner. The point I was making is that he hasn't done a good job holding up his end of the bargain as it relates to what marriage is all about.

It looks to me – and I'm not the only one who thinks this, by the way – like you're carrying the entire load. I know how much he loves you and Bea. But he's never had a steady paycheck. He has no career ambitions. Come on, Sibyl, he's got to show his love for you in other ways besides under the covers. This cockfighting thing is more than a hobby, you realize. It's an obsession."

"It is frustrating. *No.* It's more than frustrating. The money he's lost ... I'm almost to the point of being desperate about it."

"He's an addicted gambler, Sibyl. Has been ever since he and Gulliver first started betting on those birds that crazy neighbor of theirs had. Remember that wild nut with the peacocks and doves and roosters? That's where he got it from, right there."

"Like I said, Wynona; it's my problem, not yours."

"But going back to whether or not he cheats on you – being oversexed and all – I'll bet he gets his share of opportunities when the band's playing. Think of all the groupies."

"Enough about Rem and me, Wynona. How are you and Bud doing?"

"We're IBMers, Sybil. Of course we're doing great. New cars, decent house, nice vacations. It's good with us. Real good."

"And your sex life?"

Wynona gave her friend a wry look. "Now that you ask, I'll admit the frequency has dropped off the last few years."

"But it's still exciting?"

"I can't believe we're talking about this."

"Come on, Wynona, I was pretty darned forthcoming about our sex life."

"Being honest about it?"

"Of course."

"Back when we were going together we'd go parking all the time. Couldn't wait to get each other's clothes off. Those were the good old days. It's nothing like that anymore. When we do have sex, nothing very exotic happens. But I'd rate it so-so. It's not like all he does is climb on top, gets his cookies, then rolls over and starts snoring; you know, leaving me there to cool off without my own fire being put out. I'm not complaining."

"That wasn't very convincing, Wynona. But I understand your point. You and Bud have more important things going on in your marriage than sex."

"*I didn't say our sex life sucks, Sibyl.* But yes, we do. It's a known fact that after a certain number of years of married life the whole sex thing takes a back seat."

"To what?"

"For instance, sometimes Bud cooks dinner instead of me. Or if I ask him to take me for a Sunday drive instead of him watching baseball or football, he shuts the TV right off and out the door we go."

"I wish I could say that for Rem. If there's a game on I can't even talk to him."

"That's what I was trying to say, Sibyl. There are lots of ways a husband can show his love, but Rem doesn't even know about them. Either that or he doesn't care."

"You don't believe Rem loves me?"

"That's not what I meant. Bud shows me a lot of respect, which is just as important as love. Maybe the level of respect is a good gauge of how deep the love really goes. You can't say Rem shows you a whole lot of respect, gambling money away like he does."

"Rem respects me. I don't question that. But I am frustrated with the gambling."

"Did you ever find out where he keeps his bird?"

"At Box's. He thinks I don't know it, but I do. If it was here, I'd ring the damn thing's bloody neck."

"Mommy."

Sibyl got up from the couch and walked to the stairwell. "Yes sweetie, what is it?"

"Is daddy coming home to kiss me goodnight?"

"I don't know, Bea. Mommy'll be up in a little while."

"Will you read me a bedtime story?"

Wynona got up from her chair. "Oh look! It's after nine. I should be going."

Sibyl smiled at her and called up to Beatrice. "Okay, sweetie." Sibyl looked at her friend and shrugged her shoulders. "I can't believe she's still awake."

Beatrice called out again. "But not the story with the wolf and the little girl who wears a red thing. I'm ascared of the wolf, Mommy."

Wynona walked toward the kitchen. "Bye, Sibyl. I can see myself out."

"Later."

"Give Bea a hug for me."

"I will."

"Hello."

"It's Rudy."

"What's the deal?"

"Jericho, that has to be the worst group of social misfits I ever saw. I've been doing some thinking. I don't want them coming back tomorrow. Call them up and tell them they're out of a job. First thing in the morning I'm going to the unemployment office to recruit a whole new crew. You can stay on, but I don't want those crazies working for me."

"Hold on a minute, Rudy. They'll be on time tomorrow, I'm sure of it."

"It's not only that, Jericho. I get the sense these guys are capable of anything. There isn't a sane man in the bunch. My reputation is at risk. They've got to go."

"Hold on another minute. Did you see what Grumpy did with the bulldozer? He had the entire site cleared inside of an hour. That fat man of yours never even had to come back down; happy as all get-out sitting up on the bluff shoveling donuts."

"Grumpy's the one with the car?"

"The old Grump's real proud of his Invicta. Who can blame him? It's a beauty."

"Maybe I'll let this Grumpy fellow stay on."

"What about his brother?"

"Is he the big short man with all the hair?"

"*Oh, be big for me.* Box Car's one of the strongest men in the state; can throw a shot put a country mile."

"Why would I care about that? I'm not holding Olympic tryouts."

"The job's all about bulling and jamming. Wait till you see the Box bull and jam. He can work circles around any three guys you might dredge up over at the unemployment office."

"All right, we'll keep him too."

"But hold up one more minute. Weepy's strong too. You shook hands with him. Any doubt he does fifty pushups every day?"

"He didn't look too swift to me."

"Fact is his IQ's off the charts. Incredibly well read. Guys like him are usually worthless. But he also happens to be big and strong. He's no match for Box, of course. I'm the only one who fits that category. But the important thing is whether or not he can bull and jam. You should have seen him stacking lumber today, Rudy."

"Okay then. But that's it. Those three."

"Thing is, none of these guys will work unless the entire crew is together. You keep a few, you have to keep all of them. There's no way around it. Plus there's the albino. You want to see the albino don't you?"

"You're making things awfully tough on me. How the hell am I supposed to have confidence in a bunch of guys as uncontrollable as the crew you put together? It scares the shit out of me. I've got a reputation to protect."

"As long as you get the horse barn built – built righteous, I'm saying – your reputation will not only be protected, it'll be remarkably enhanced; mark my words."

"The horse barn needs to be perfect, Jericho. These are state officials we're talking about. Besides that, the profit margins my estimator projected have to be realized. That means the project has to be finished on schedule. Black ink can turn red in a hurry when time-lines get out of whack."

"We'll meet your goddamn projections, Rudy. Say what you want about these men, but they can bull and jam with the best of them. They'll be quick about it too; without sacrificing quality. Why is it I always have to be such a salesman with you?"

"Have it your way then. But they're in a trial period. I've got Pierre coming on the job tomorrow. He'll keep tabs for me."

"I thought that's what I was supposed to do."

"You'll be covering for your friends, Jericho. You don't think I'm aware of that? Pierre will give me the straight skinny. I need an objective observer to let me know what's happening."

"So be it. You don't trust me, you sonuvabitch. So be it."

“I’m not saying I don’t trust you, Jericho. Why do you make things so difficult for me?”

“All right, you trusted me to put a crew together; I’ll give you that much. But I want you to trust that my guys will do this job righteous. Can you do that for me?”

“I suppose.”

“I don’t want to hear about no trial period, either. These boys are committed to seeing the job through right to the end. A commitment like that ought to count for something.”

“We’ll see.”

“You bet your ass we’ll see. You finished with this phone call?”

“I guess so.”

“Get some sleep, Rudy. You’ve got other jobs going on that require your close attention. Don’t you worry about the horse barn. That baby’s going up and it’s going up good and proper.”

“All right then. Sorry to bother you.”

“No apologies necessary. You got a right to your opinion.”

“Thanks. I think.”

“Say no more.”

“Good night then.”

“Good night.”

Sybil didn’t need an alarm clock. She awoke every morning at six o’clock on the button. After three years as a bookkeeper, her morning routine was as neatly arranged as an eight column ledger. Precisely at six she’d swing her legs off the bed directly into the slippers positioned there the night before, trudge down the stairs to make a small pot of coffee, open the front door to get the newspaper, go back upstairs to check in on Bea, walk a dozen steps into the bathroom for her morning constitution, grab a quick shower, brush her teeth, run a brush through her hair, slip into her bathrobe to go back downstairs to pour the coffee, and stroll into the living room for a half-hour of alone time reading the paper. At seven, she’d wake up her daughter and help her get washed up and dressed for first grade classes. After picking out a dress and applying a modicum of makeup, she and her daughter would have a quick breakfast together. Then she’d drive Beatrice to the elementary school ten blocks away and continue on to the office, arriving promptly at eight o’clock.

Remington, under normal circumstances, would hear none of the morning commotion. He’d wake up around noon, sit in the tub under a shower-head drizzle for a full hour, then head downstairs to snatch a beer from the fridge, read the sports page at the kitchen table, then call Box or one of his brothers to see what was on tap for the day. The horse barn dramatically changed his routine.

This particular morning the alarm went off at four-thirty. Sybil had set it the night before, just before climbing into an empty bed. She reached over to shut it off, flicked on her bedside lamp, and turned to see if her husband was in bed. Surprise, surprise. He was. She shook him. "Wake up, Rem. It's four-thirty."

Remington did not respond.

She shook him harder.

He groaned.

"Wake up, damn it. Grumpy will be here before you know it."

Rem rolled over and tried to focus her in, squinting his bloodshot eyes. "I can't," he mumbled.

"You have to."

Rem resumed his snoring.

Sybil shook him again. "Please, Rem. We can use the money you'll make on this job."

Rem did not respond.

Sybil got up, went around to his side of the bed, yanked the covers down, grabbed his lower legs and pulled them off the bed. "*Get your ass up.* I'm not putting up with this shit every morning. What the hell time did you get in?"

Rem sat up and rubbed his eyes with two shaky fists. "I don't know."

"You don't know? Why not? Did you go to New York?"

Rem kept rubbing his eyes. "I think so," he mumbled.

"I'm getting back in bed, Rem, but not until you're on your feet. I've got another hour and a half to sleep, if I can calm down enough. My routine is probably ruined, thanks to you."

"I think I've got a hangover."

"Of course you're hung over. And that isn't the half of it. How much money'd you lose last night with that fucking cock of yours?"

Rem groaned. He got to his feet and traipsed into the bathroom, still rubbing his eyes, never answering the question.

Six

"Fritz, why don't *you* knock on his door this time," Remington said.

"Why me? Because I have experience with dead bodies? No thanks. I'm not getting out of the car till we get to the horse barn."

"Gulliver, it's your turn," Rem said.

The youngest of the Swilling brothers rapped on Walter's door, dropping his head in patient commiseration while he waited for some response. There was none. He rapped again, trying to keep his mental temperature on low seethe.

Walter opened the door, once again clad only in his under shorts, his neck and chest glistening with emollients. "I can't go to work today," he said, his voice riding rough over marbles of crusty phlegm.

"We figured as much. Thought we'd stop by to see if you were dead yet. We might check one more day. After that, if you're dead, somebody else will have to discover your foul carcass."

"You think I might die?" Walter asked, deep concern scribbled across his ashen face.

"Yes. Yes I do." Gulliver's voice was devoid of compassion. "In fact, Walter, we're all hoping as much, so we don't have to waste our time like this."

"I think I'll be able to make it tomorrow, Gully. Yesterday, I thought I was getting better. But I took a turn for the worse when I climbed into bed. I plan to make more of my grandmother's tomato soup today. That could do the trick."

"Fine Walter. We're leaving for the horse barn now. Tomorrow, if you're not dead, why don't you come with us? You may wish to consider bringing some of that tomato soup. That way, if Jericho gets pissed off about your condition and shoots you, the rest of us will have something to eat."

"Thank you Gulliver."

"Think nothing of it, Walter." Gulliver turned and walked back to the car, eyes to the ground, intensely focused on keeping his anger in check.

It took all four barrels of the Buick's thirsty carburetor, along with some daring-do on dirt roads riddled with pot holes, but the crew made it to the work site one minute after seven o'clock, by Rudy's watch.

The owner of the construction company congratulated Jericho.

"Told you. These boys will do it righteous, mark my words."

Grumpy walked directly up to Rudy. "I'm done with the dozer."

"Yes, I can see."

"So get it to hell out of here." Grumpy looked over at Jericho. "If that dozer's still here come noontime, I'm writing somebody up for it; probably the donut man. He's got it coming."

Jericho nodded. "We'll take care of it, Grump. Relax."

Rudy gave the crew the once over. "You boys get cold yesterday?"

"Nope," Rem said. "It was just about perfect, weather wise."

"What's that pile of ashes, then?"

"Oh that. Thing is, we didn't bring anything for lunch yesterday. We figured we'd cook up Weepy."

"But the cry-ass ran off," Fritz said.

Rudy looked at Jericho, scratching his head. "They were going to … *never mind.* You've got your instructions. I'm off to Williamstown. Pierre's there now. Once I get an update from him on our other projects, he'll head over here. Expect him by around ten. He'll go over the plans with you." Rudy paused and scanned the crew. "Can anyone here read a set of blueprints?"

The question was met with blank stares.

"Won't take us long to get a handle on it," Rem said.

"Right. Well, I guess that tells me Pierre will have to be here every day. He'll walk you through the plans and answer any questions that might come up. Please pay special attention to what Pierre has to say."

Rem put a nasal gruffness in his voice, repeating the name with condescending exuberance. *"Pee-ehhhr? Ohh Pee-ehhhr. My leetle leetle pee-pee Pee-ehhhr."*

The crew had a good laugh over Rem's imitation of a Frenchman, then strutted around like a brood of mud hens, unmercifully mimicking Rem's back-of-the-palette elongation of the foreman's name.

Rudy had seen as much as he cared to see. "Okay, Jericho, I'm out of here."

Jericho adopted the others' throaty emissions. *"Wee wee, Moan Sewer rooty tooty Rudy. Wee wee."*

No sooner had the dust from Rudy's fleeing truck settled than Grumpy walked back up the hill to drive the Buick down for Weepy to unload his speakers, amplifier, and guitar from the trunk.

Rem, with full appreciation that Weepy's chronic ennui was nothing more than abject laziness, agreed to help him set up. "A backhoe is coming in to dig a trench for the perimeter of the barn, Weepy. We'll have to haul this equipment off yonder."

"Off yonder?"

"Yeah, I figure we're way the hell out here in the middle of East Bumfuck, I ought to start sounding like the folk living in these here parts."

"Nobody uses that expression in Vermont, Rem; even way out in the country like this. *Off yonder* is more in keeping with the southern vernacular; say the Carolinas, or maybe Alabama. Why don't you keep practicing your French and simply tell me where off yonder is? I'd like to begin tuning up. And by the way, did anybody think to bring a folding chair? I'm not playing my guitar sitting on the cotton pickin' ground all day."

"We'll have one for you tomorrow. For now, climb up on that stack of texture 111. It's better if you're inside the footings for the time being. With the generator and the backhoe going at the same time, we wouldn't be able to hear you anyway if you set up off yonder. *See voo play?*"

Pierre Toussenant drove a black Volkswagen beetle. He parked his bug at the top of the hill next to Grumpy's massive Buick. When Pierre turned off the ignition, he thought the car next to his had its radio on. But when he opened the door to get out, it sounded more like live music. Sure enough, the Hendrix guitar riff was coming from the construction site. Pierre stood by his car for a moment, wondering if he had screwed up the directions Rudy had given him and wound up at some poorly marketed outdoor rock concert.

But wait, a dozer was down there, along with an empty flatbed and more than a dozen large stacks of lumber. This had to be the place. Had Rudy, a musician in his own right, hired somebody to entertain the work crew to kick off what was sure to be a grueling job? A fantastic idea, but it didn't seem like something his tight-fisted boss would do. It made no sense. Then too, Rudy had warned him that the group of men he was going to be working with was unusual in many respects. *Escapees from the loony bin* – that's how he referred to them.

Pierre went around to the front of his car to open the trunk. The small compartment was crammed with tool belts, a wide assortment of tools, and about a dozen nail pouches. There was too much to carry in one load. He closed the lid, deciding to drive down to the site.

A third-generation Frenchman whose grandparents had migrated from Quebec in the early part of the century, Pierre was not the craftsman that his father and grandfather had been, but he was a first-rate carpenter. He had worked his way up over the years to the position of foreman with Rudyard Appling's construction company. A bookworm by nature, he had gotten his Bachelor of Arts degree taking night courses and would soon have his masters, after which he planned to teach.

Quiet to a fault, Pierre was a man with solid values. He was a good Catholic, had a strong work ethic, and had never been at odds with the law. He was affable, could take a good ribbing, and was exceptionally tolerant of people of all stripes. He didn't know it at the moment, but his tolerance was going to be severely – and frequently – tested.

Pierre parked his car next to a stack of two-by-sixes just inside the perimeter of the envisioned building. Jericho greeted him. "You're Pierre?"

"That's me. And you would be?"

"I'd be sane if I wasn't so fucking crazy."

That got a chuckle out of Pierre. "That's great. What's your name?"

"Jericho. Jericho Laramie."

"You're Rudy's friend."

"If that's what he alleges. I'd introduce you to the crew, Pierre, except that I've decided to have my friend, Remington, do the honors. Rem, get your ass over here."

Remington acted like a soldier called front and center, dutifully snapping off a crisp salute.

"At ease," Jericho said. "This man's name is Pierre Toussenant. Please introduce the men who'll be in charge of him while he's on this job."

That got another chuckle out of Pierre. *"In charge of me?"*

"That's what I said, Pierre. You got a problem with that?"

"According to Rudy, there was reason for me to believe that I'd be the foreman on this job."

"I don't give a rat's ass what he led you to believe," Jericho said with startling arrogance. "Everybody on this crew is in charge of *you*."

Pierre squeezed his second chin with nervous fingers, pondering the situation.

"We realize you know what you're doing based on your experience in the trade," Jericho continued, "Whereas we don't have the foggiest notion what we're doing. But that doesn't mean a thing. Problem is nobody's ever been in charge of these boys before. They won't allow it. You're just going to have to submit to these conditions. Why? Because that's the beauty of it."

Pierre again wondered if he'd shown up at the wrong place.

"Do I make myself clear?" Jericho inquired.

"Not really."

"You'll figure it out eventually. For now, I'm calling on Remington here – Rem this is Pierre; Pierre this is Rem – to introduce you to the group I put together for the purpose of building the most righteous horse barn this state will ever have."

Rem snapped back to attention and addressed Jericho directly. "Request permission, Herr crew assembler, to call upon the eloquent Nazi to perform this particular round of introductions."

Jericho snickered. "I might have thought as much, you yellow-bellied wimp. All right then, tell Gulliver it's his turn."

Rem motioned his younger brother to come forward. "Gulliver," he said with uncommon respect, "if you should be so kind, please identify the esteemed members of the crew to our new friend, the pudgy Frenchman."

"It would be my distinct pleasure," Gulliver said, turning to face Rudy's abruptly demoted foreman. "*Pee-ehhhr*, let me be among the first to welcome you to this hallowed ground, the site upon which we will endeavor to erect the most magnificent equestrian edifice in the entire Green Mountain State. With that, let me point out to you the individuals with whom you will have the sublime honor of working side by side during the weeks and months ahead, a time that will no doubt be recorded in the annals of this great state as … let us say, *unique*. Nothing other than a cursory nod of the head in subdued and respectful acknowledgement is necessary on your part. Is that acceptable, Mister …"

"Toussenant."

"Ah yes, *Moan Sewer* Toussenant. Thank you. Well then, the tall man with the long wiry hair, the scraggly beard, the dark bags under his eyes, and the unnerving stare of a relentless president-stalker is none other than the eldest of the reviled, oft-defamed, and incredibly talented Swilling boys. As you can see, Fritz actually resembles, in appearance, the rogue iconoclast of desert fame, quite in keeping with the man's high-minded propensity to pontificate. Moreover, Fritz harbors the exalted belief that he possesses the nearly incomparable ability to save us all from certain doom."

Fritz and Pierre nodded at one another, Fritz with an icy countenance and piercing glare, Pierre with squinting eyes and a forced smile.

"Fritz, I might add, is a Vietnam veteran. We don't know how many people he's killed, partly because he won't say and partly because we don't want to know, since he may not be finished. Suffice to say, my wary Frenchman, that Fritz is sufficiently dangerous. He could, at any time, grab one of Jericho's weapons and attempt to wipe us all out as if reenacting some horrific experience in the jungles of Quang Tri Province. Is there anything else, my solemn French friend, that you'd care to know about the eldest Swilling?"

"I don't think so," Pierre said.

"Fine. Let's move on then. To Fritz's right is the *Missing Link*, a large and largely rectangular being otherwise known as Box Car. Should be easy to remember; Box Car Bork, the *Missing Link*. As you can see, few creatures on earth are either as ugly or as forbidding as this one. Box is a sexual enigma, as you may have surmised by my reference to his being the answer to Darwinism's most perplexing riddle, that homo sapiens were, at one time, kin to the common gibbon. Since the answer is no doubt sexual in nature, let me duly note that procreation, in Box Car's mind, is nothing more than a freak of desire that somehow unites uncommon species; that is, fails to distinguish between species, or, for that matter, between organic and inorganic. The Box, to be blunt, is as much aroused by machinations – generators, compressors, pistons, cam shafts, sump pumps and the like – as he is by tongues, labia, smegma, tight buttocks, and so forth. That said, let me suggest you keep a close watch on your leetle beetle, since I've already noticed that Box has been eyeing its dandy tailpipe with unmasked salaciousness. Is there anything further that you would care to know about the *Missing Link*, my leetle *Pee-ehhhr*?"

"Not really. But I would ask that you not pronounce my name like that."

"Asking won't do any good. Rem's already decided how your name is to be pronounced."

"What's that?"

"Moving on then, let us go next to the ornery one standing beside the bearded rectangle. This man's name is Grumpy. He is the crew member responsible for getting us here on time every day. That's his pride and joy up there on the hill; the Buick Invicta. You can see that his car is quite old. On that note, Pierre, let me ask the age you would guess Grumpy to be?"

"How old is he?"

"I wasn't expecting an echo, *Moan Sewer* Toussenant. Just answer the question."

"I don't know. Let me think." Pierre looked at the Grump and pulled on his lower chin. "I'd have to say late thirties, maybe early forties. But that's just a guess. I'm not real good when it comes to somebody's age."

"I should say not. In fact, I'm afraid you've offended a young man who, when offended, is capable of the most contemptible offenses. This could very well mean that from this day forward, Grumpy is unlikely to be especially friendly toward you. I would not, if I were you, go so far as to offer him any advice regarding how he might proceed with a particular task. The result could be troublesome, to say the least. In any event, Grumpy is nineteen-years old."

"Can't be," Pierre found himself saying.

"Not only can it be, the man-child you see here is nothing more than a child, yet very much a man. Obviously, you let the scars and the gray hair fool you. There's one more thing I should alert you to as it pertains to crew member, Grumpy Bork. He is, shall we say, a man of assumed authority."

"What does that mean?"

"It means that Grumpy is, certainly within his own befuddled mind, the final authority when it comes to whatever he considers to be an infraction, miscue, flaunting of rules, inappropriate behavior, and the like. *See voo play?"*

"What's that?"

"Do you understand what I said?"

"I'm not sure."

"That's fine. I'm sure you'll understand in due course. Let us proceed to the next crew member. This introduction requires special enlightenment, as it pertains directly to whether or not you, *Moan Sewer* Toussenant, are allowed to live for the duration of this project."

"What's that?"

"*Tut-tut*, don't get nervous. I'm simply stating an important truth. Unbeknownst to Mister Appling – the man you, and you alone, take to be your boss – the uncommon laborers who comprise this crew require entertainment. We happen to favor rock & roll. And we like our music live; no eight-track tapes or reel-to-reel bullshit with this group. We'll work long hard hours, to be sure, and we'll do more work and far better work than *common* laborers twice our number, so long as we're entertained in the process. Therefore, this individual, while seldom engaging in the horse barn's erection – notwithstanding the magnificent evidence of his own – is an essential member of the horse barn crew. Allow me, without further adieux, to introduce to you Vermont's most talented singer-guitar player – who, by the way, once accompanied Edgar Winter, the world's second-most revered albino – our very own manic depressive, Wilmer … *Weepy* … O'Toole."

With that, the entire crew exploded in uproarious applause. So struck was he by the glorious adulation that Weepy himself was inspired to stand and engage in a near embarrassing display of self-approbation, hooting and clapping louder than anyone.

"You see, *Ohh Pee-errrh*," Gulliver continued, "This crew is being paid – one would hope – to get a job done. The owner of the company has every right to expect us to do a good job. I assure you there is nary a doubt that the men herewith assembled – minus the colorless man who you may soon meet if he is able to rise from his death bed to join in this undertaking – possess every capability requisite for success related both to the integrity of the horse barn's construction and to the honorable pursuit of ungainly profit. While it may appear, from a distance, that eight men are doing the work of eight men, you, the ninth man, will know, since there's no way to hide it from you, that, in fact, seven men are doing the work of eight men, given Weepy's divergent activities. The math is not as complicated as it may seem. Stated another way, seven men will be covering for one man, who, rather than sawing and hammering, will be singing and strumming, entertaining the seven, or eight, should the eighth man also enjoy his good work. All of which is to say that you, my rotund Frenchman, are hereby commanded never to reveal this unspeakable travesty to the man you call your boss. In return for this kind concession, you will be allowed to deny your family the possible distaste of attending your funeral any time soon. Is that understood, my trembling French person?"

"You're saying the man you call Weepy will be playing music instead of working. And as long as the job is getting done there's no reason Rudy has to know about it."

"*Ohhh Pee-ehhhr*, well said; well said indeed. Except, perhaps, for the less than trifling neglect of the troubling consequences should you not be able to keep your fucking mouth shut."

"Right."

"Excellent. Finally then, to the man who was so kind as to abrogate his responsibilities – to the great disgust of the gunslinger that I decline to introduce, lest I put myself at great peril – it is my profound pleasure to introduce you to Remington Swilling, the brother between Fritz and me. Rem is capable of awesome feats, not the least of which is to get inside a man's brain and turn it into Jell-O. More on that in due course. Remington, as you'll soon discover, is a superb imitator. If Lyndon Johnson had also been assassinated, Remington could have taken his place and no one would have noticed the difference, including Lady Bird, assuming the size of the president's genitals matched his Texas ego. Most remarkable of all, perhaps, is Rem's jittering eyes. Remington, if you please."

Rem approached Pierre, putting his nose within an inch of the Frenchman's face and making his eyes go wide. Within seconds, his pupils were cavorting in wildly erratic gyrations.

Pierre hardly knew what to make of it, but he was gracious enough to smile for a moment. Then he moved back a half step and nodded his head toward Gulliver in apparent appreciation. "Never seen anything quite like it," he said. Pierre turned to walk back to his car.

Gulliver moved quickly to stop him, grabbing Pierre by the arm. "Not so fast, *Moan Sewer*. He's not finished."

"What's that?"

"When Rem's eyes are dancing like this, you have to watch until the dance is over."

"How long will that take?"

"Nobody knows. Not even Rem. Stand in front of him again please and look into his eyes until the pupils stop jiggling."

Trying his level best to keep his growing frustration from boiling over, Pierre acquiesced. The pupils of Rem's eyes jiggled as if their owner was merely a prop, having no control whatsoever over their frenzied action or its duration. Finally, after a couple of unnerving minutes, the pupils came to rest.

"There," Rem said. "How'd you like them apples?"

"Great," Pierre said. "Just great." He looked back at Gulliver. "Is it okay if I get the tools out of my car so we can get to work?"

"Of course, my pleasant Frenchman. Don't let me stop you."

Seven

Beatrice Swilling was a bright little girl. Most of the other kids in her class were still learning the alphabet, but she had known its twenty-six letters by heart ever since kindergarten. She could read lots of words already, and not just "mom" and "dad" or really easy words like "dog" and "cat" or "run" and "see". She could recognize the word "house" or figure out a word like "carpet", which she thought was a funny word because it had two words in it that meant different things when they were apart but something completely different when they were connected. She wondered how many words could do tricks like that.

Some of the other kids knew their numbers, but not as well as Bea. On the first day of school a few weeks earlier, Bea counted all of the chairs in her classroom. Then she subtracted four empty chairs to determine how many students were in her class without counting all of the kids, which was harder because they were almost never in their seats all at the same time.

It made sense that Beatrice would be good at numbers because her mommy was. That's what her mommy did at her office every day for just about the whole day, write numbers on weird looking paper with thin lines and make them add up just perfect. A long time ago when Bea was just little, her mommy taught her how to count up to anything.

Bea was smart even when she wasn't in school. She knew how people were feeling inside, even though she kept this special ability a secret only to herself.

She could tell when her mommy was sad or worried, or if she was trying not to get angry when her daddy didn't come home when he was supposed to and they would eat their supper without him, which happened a lot. His plate looked lonely with no food on it, but it was really her mommy that was lonely, and a little bit angry too, and that made Beatrice feel sad for both of them.

Even when her daddy did come home, sometimes it showed on her mommy's face that she was mad because her daddy had a problem talking right. That's when her mommy would send her up to her room. She would tell her to close the bedroom door so she could talk to daddy and not have to worry about Bea getting nervous or scared. Mostly, the arguing was about gambling, which had something to do with money.

Her mommy didn't know it, but Beatrice could hear the arguments from her room even with the door closed. They argued most of the time, it seemed like. Maybe that's what parents do, she thought.

At the end of the arguments, her mommy would run upstairs and go into her bedroom and slam the door. She would not come out for a long time.

That's when her daddy would open Bea's door and peak in. She would smile at his smile and he would walk in real softly to talk with her. Bea would be sitting on her bed holding her favorite stuffed animal; *Purry*, the white kitten that had one eye fall out and nobody could find it. Her daddy would sit on the bed right beside her and stroke her hair or use the back of his hand to brush her cheek.

Bea didn't know who was to blame for all the arguments. She didn't want to know because that might make her angry at one of them and she didn't want to do that because she loved them both the same.

Her daddy would always kiss her. Beatrice liked that. It made her tummy stop its grinding noises. But she didn't like her daddy's breath, even though she never told him. His breath smelled like the waste basket in the kitchen when it got too full and the cover wouldn't close all the way.

They would talk about school and then about her friends and then he would ask her if she had heard him talking to mommy when their voices were loud. She would always say no, even though she had. That's when her daddy would smile again and say something like, "I'm glad about that, my little honey bee." Then he would tell her that he loved her very much and he loved her mommy too, and that's when a big smile went all through her body.

Beatrice wanted these visits to end happy. That's why she always asked, "Will you make me laugh before you leave, daddy; please?"

He would look at her close and open up his eyes real big and make the brown circles with the black dots inside go jumping up and down and all around. They would do that for a real long time. It made her laugh and laugh, it was so funny. Her daddy was the only person who could do that trick. It wasn't the only reason she loved him. She loved him for reasons she didn't know how to say, but mostly because he was her daddy.

When he got up from her bed he would tell her again, "I love you, my little honey bee."

"I love you too, daddy," she always said.

And he would kiss her on the forehead with his breath making an invisible cloud around her head. Then he would leave her room and instead of laughing because he walked a little bit silly, Beatrice would be sad because she knew that was one of the reasons her mommy was mad at him; besides the gambling thing, which had something to do with bird watching.

On the third morning it was Fritz's turn to knock on Walter's door. When the nettled leatherneck raised his fist for a ferocious pounding, Walter opened it.

"I'm ready," Walter said in a voice deferential enough to disarm the eldest Swilling. "Can you help me with some of this stuff?"

"What stuff?"

"Here, hold these. I'll be right back." Walter handed Fritz a paper bag and a brand new lunch pail, its color remarkably red even in the darkness before daybreak. Walter returned with a thermos and a cup of black coffee that was steaming despite the mild temperature outside.

Remington and Box were sitting up front; Rem in the middle of the Borks. Fritz climbed into the back seat after Walter, who sat next to Weepy. Gulliver was at the other end, behind Grumpy.

"What'cha got there?" Box asked Walter in his raspy morning voice.

"Coffee."

"Yeah, I can smell it. I mean what's all that other shit?"

"I was beginning to feel better yesterday evening so I drove out to Gaynes Shoppers World and I bought a lunch bucket, among other things."

Rem craned his head around to see it. "Looks pretty fancy," his tone admiring. "The rest of us carry our lunches in paper bags."

"When it gets a little lighter," Walter said, "you'll see that it's bright red. It's shaped like a barn, which I thought would be apropos."

Box Car laughed. "That's good thinking, Walter. We wouldn't want you showing up on the job without a lunch bucket that's apropos. Tell me, does it have compartments?"

"*Jeepers*, Box, I'm glad you asked. It's got a spring-loaded wire that holds the thermos inside the cover. And there's a large area for sandwiches and fruit and whatever snacks I may wish to bring."

"And what kind of snacks did you wish to bring this morning?" Box asked with a gruff chuckle.

"Goddamn it, Birdsong, I hate the smell of coffee," Fritz said, interrupting the jovial banter.

"Sorry," Walter said. "I'll try to drink it fast."

Fritz rolled his window down in total disgust.

"I want to know what Walter's got in there for snacks," Box said, his sandpaper voice raised several decibels.

"It's none of your business," Walter said. "You'll find out when we have our lunch break."

"Fritz! Open up that fancy lunch pail of his," Box demanded.

Fritz grabbed the pail and opened it, the snaps rapping with metallic thuds. "I can't see anything," Fritz said. "It's too dark."

Box grumbled loudly across the front seat to Grumpy. "Turn on the inside light so we can make sure Walter's lunch is apropos."

Grumpy grudgingly obliged, saying nothing.

The dome light revealed two sandwiches tightly wrapped in cellophane, three figs, a small bag of *Wise* potato chips, a napkin, a neatly folded piece of paper, and a *Zero* bar.

Box leaned his hairy bulk over the seat. "Gimme those chips, Fritz."

Walter, having to hold his coffee in both hands to prevent it from spilling, was helpless to prevent the theft.

Fritz grabbed the candy bar and held it up to the light. "What the hell is this, Birdsong, a fucking *Zero* bar?"

"Yes. Yes it is."

"Nobody eats *Zero* bars, you dumb shit. The chocolate on it is white, for chrissakes."

Rem was incredulous. "Walter's got a goddamn *Zero* bar?"

"He sure as hell does," Fritz said. "No way Jericho's going to let a guy who eats *Zero* bars work on the horse barn."

Everyone howled with laughter except Walter – and Weepy, who was sleeping. Box snorted, munching on the chips.

"Put that candy bar back in my lunch bucket," Walter told Fritz.

"Gladly," Fritz said, tossing the bar on top of the sandwiches. He pulled the hinged cover down and closed the snaps, keeping the lunch pail on his lap.

Gulliver leaned forward to send his voice past the snoring Weepy. "Why do you have two thermoses?"

Walter sipped his coffee. "I can't quite believe all this interest in the lunch I packed. The thermos I'm holding between my legs, if you have to know Gulliver, has coffee in it. The thermos in my lunch pail is filled with tomato soup. I'm still recuperating from pneumonia and it just so happens tomato soup is very nourishing; it strengthens my immune system and gives me energy. It isn't *Campbell's* I'm talking about. It's a very special recipe handed down from my grandmother on my mother's side. She was raised on a farm, as was my mother. She knew all about the healing properties of various vegetables and herbs. I'd like to inform you, Gulliver, that if it wasn't for this tomato soup, there's no way I could be joining the crew today."

"Are you going to drink coffee on the drive to work every day?" Fritz asked.

"Of course. I'm a journalist. All reporters drink coffee. It helps them gear up to deal with the stress of meeting deadlines. Caffeine stimulates synapses."

"You make me sick," Fritz said. "And I'll be goddamned if I'm going to sit next to you every morning while you drink that foul smelling sludge, especially after it gets too cold to roll the windows down."

"But I have to drink my coffee, Fritz."

"Why don't you drink that horse piss before we get to your apartment?"

"That would require me to get up even earlier. If I did that, it would take even more coffee for me to get going."

"Damn it then, drink a cup while your making your lunch – that's gotta take half an hour right there – then pour yourself another cup once we get to the horse barn. That's a fair enough compromise, isn't it?"

"I'm capable of compromise, Fritzy, you know me well enough to know that. But coffee is one thing I don't compromise on. *Lucky Strikes* either. Mind if I light one up now? A good smoke goes great with coffee."

"You light up a cigarette Birdsong, you bleached excuse for a human being, and I'll reach over and put it out in your ear."

"Hand me that *Zero* bar," Box growled toward the back seat.

Rem was appalled at the request. "You want Walter's *Zero* bar?"

"I've never had one."

"They look like dried bird shit," Fritz said. "Save your health, Box. You don't want anything to do with that *Zero* bar."

"There weren't six potato chips in that little bag. I'm still hungry. Throw that *Zero* bar up here."

"You really want Walter's *Zero* bar," Rem asked again.

"That's right."

"Well that damn well proves it. You *are* the *Missing Link*, aren't you?"

"Just because I want Birdsong's *Zero* bar?"

"Humans don't eat *Zero* bars, you idiot."

"You're saying Walter isn't human?"

"Look at him. Does he look human to you? When's the last time you saw a human being with no skin pigment?"

"I never have, except for Walter."

"Well there you go. Listen, Fritz already said it; we're talking about a candy bar covered with white chocolate. That explains a lot of things, don't you think?"

"Like the fact that I'm an albino?" Walter asked, not especially amused by either the grab for his *Zero* bar or the discussion regarding his condition, although he was used to it.

"Precisely," Rem said. "And if you weren't, you'd be a human being."

"Let me see if I've got this right," Gulliver said. "Any creature that eats *Zero* bars is either sub-human or non-human. Is that what you're saying, Rem?"

"That's exactly what I'm saying. And to settle it once and for all, I want to suggest that the *Missing Link* and the bleached cadaver split the christly *Zero* bar."

"How does that sound to you, Walter?" Box wanted to know.

"Had I known this would happen, I might have brought two *Zero* bars. As it is, I fully intend to eat the entire *Zero* bar myself, come lunch time."

Box wasn't happy. "Why you selfish sonuva …"

"Hold up," Rem said, stretching out his arm to block the Box from catapulting over the seat.

Rem stared at Walter while Grumpy maneuvered the Buick along twisty Route 2 through Jonesville toward the Bolton flats. "How many *Zero* bars do you have?"

"I've got a whole box back in the apartment."

"How many in a box?"

"Twenty."

"You mean to tell me you've got twenty *Zero* bars and you don't want to give this hairy freak so much as half of one?"

Walter pondered the question for a moment, then turned to Fritz. "I'm empty; would you mind holding this cup for me while I pour from my thermos?"

Fritz looked at Walter with glaring contempt. "I'd sooner jump off a bridge into the raging waters of Purgatory."

"*Whoa,*" Rem said. "Tempers seem to be flaring all of a sudden."

"That's interesting, Remington," said Walter. "Here we are headed for a horse barn and you talk like you're riding a horse. I like that. It's apropos."

Grumpy slammed on the brakes. All four of the back seat passengers slammed into the back of the front seat. Rem and Box Car crashed into the dash, their forearms crossed in front of their heads to take the brunt of the impact.

"What the fuck?" It was Weepy. "Did we have an accident?" His voice quavered with curiosity and panic.

Grumpy shut the car off, turned his torso to lean back against his door, threw his left arm over the steering wheel like it was his partner, and jabbed an index finger at the group. "How do you expect me to drive listening to this shit? Here I am trying to relax before a hard day's work, maybe catch a little shut-eye on the flats, but instead, you sons-a-bitches rattle my nerves to the point where I'd just as soon run this rig into the next big tree as listen to you. You're getting written up, every damn one of you."

"I had nothing to do with it," Weepy said. "I was sleeping."

"I'm citing you for being able to sleep through it," Grumpy said.

"We don't even get a warning?" Rem wanted to know.

"I don't give out warnings and you know it. I write up offenses when they happen."

"Mind if I ask Walter what he's got in the bag?" Rem asked. "I think we'd all like to know."

"No you can't! That would start the whole thing right back up again. I've had enough of it. Besides, I don't give a damn what he's got in that bag. Could be explosives, for all I care."

Small talk was held to a minimum during the remainder of the drive, Grumpy's passengers holding their collective breath every time the Buick roared past great white oaks and rugged elms.

A few miles before Grumpy turned onto the first dirt road, Walter tapped the Box on the shoulder, having surreptitiously cut his *Zero* bar in half with his pocket knife. Box happily accepted his half, a glisten in his beady eyes acknowledging the albino's act of contrition.

Despite the Jonesville incident, Grumpy got the crew to the horse barn just as Jericho was pulling in.

Pierre was waiting for them. "Good morning," he said to the group with a note of cheer in his voice.

"Bone-sure, my leetle leetle pee-pee Pee-ehhhr!" Rem said.

"Is that supposed to be French?" Pierre asked with some annoyance.

"You should know; you're the goddamn frog," Jericho butted in.

Pierre ignored the comment. "Okay, gather 'round please."

"Are you going to explain the blueprints?" Fritz asked.

"I'd like to give everyone a general overview of the project."

"I don't care about overviews," Fritz said. "If I'm going to be a carpenter – and I recognize this could be one of my many callings – I'd like to know how to read a blueprint."

"That takes some time," Pierre said. "For the moment, I think it's important for everyone to have a general idea of how this barn will go up."

Fritz glared at the Frenchman with grudging acceptance.

Pierre continued. "Yesterday, we got the corner posts set. You men did a good job helping with that. The posts are exactly the right height and they're plumb. Today, we'll begin setting posts for the walls. Now then, so that you have a ..."

"Hold up," Rem said, both arms raised, palms opened in a presidential way. "Aren't you forgetting something?"

"I don't believe so," Pierre said, visibly annoyed by the interruption.

"Oh but I think you have," Rem said. He stepped forward and turned to address the crew. "Can anyone tell me what the flustered Frenchman has forgotten this morning?"

Crew members looked at one another, agog.

"Are you shitting me?" Rem asked. "Do I have to do this myself?"

Rem turned to Pierre. "You didn't notice anything unusual about the group this morning, *my leetle pee-pee*?"

"You've got a new member with you."

"And not just any new member," Rem stated with brusque pomposity. "We have with us today, my rather likeable Frenchman, an individual of uncommon attributes. Here is a man – or perhaps *riddle* is more precise – who becomes invisible when naked in a blizzard, whose eyes are as pink as swollen tonsils, whose pubic region could be mistaken for a lab mouse, and whose slow pace, idiomatic circumlocution, and chronic ills can put the measure of any man to the supreme test. This skeletal creature you see here happens to be a dancer of unusual skill, rather like a snowshoe rabbit hippity-hopping to avoid a rain of bullets. If you've been wondering how it is that my jiggling eyes got that way, my curious Canuck, wonder no more. It happened the very first time I saw this blanched abnormality dance. Contrary to his lily-white appearance, this man can do it dirty. *Moan Sewer* Toussenant, my wide-mouthed bull among frogs; allow me to introduce to you everybody's favorite albino, Walter ... *Birdsong*."

The crew erupted in giddy delight. Pierre pulled on his chins and forced a smile for the waxen one. When the cacophony subsided, Pierre walked over to Walter and shook his hand, making special note of the man's weak grasp and clammy skin.

"May I proceed?" Pierre asked with polite derisiveness.

"You may indeed," Rem said, shuffling back into the group.

Pierre held up the blueprints for everyone to see. "Okay then, as you can tell by the length and width of the footings, this is going to be a big horse barn."

"Oh, be big for me," Jericho interrupted. "Say it for me, Fritz."

Fritz chuckled. "Be big for me," he said.

The Marine's response was only mildly enthusiastic, but Jericho seemed satisfied.

Pierre watched the exchange, shook his head in dismay, then continued. "We have reason to believe this structure, when completed, will be the largest horse barn ever built in the state of Vermont. I think we can all take pride in its grandeur."

"That's French," Jericho said.

"Excuse me?"

"*Grandeur*. I'm pretty sure that's a French word. You seemed to indicate that you can't recognize French, yet here you are using it."

"Of course I can recognize French," said Pierre. "English borrows from a lot of languages, Jericho; French primary among them. Grandeur is, of course, a French word. But since it appears in the dictionary without italicization, it is, by virtue of its longstanding usage by the English, considered to have been fully incorporated into the English lexicon."

"*Oh Pee-ehhhr*, you are so eloquent," Jericho said with a complimentary backhand.

Pierre looked again at the ground, shaking his head. "Now then," he said, "in block or frame construction, such as we have here, poles are set on a continuous concrete footing. We'll be using rough-sawn eastern white pine boards for the framing and to cap it off. Then we'll have a crane brought in to position the trusses, starting and finishing with the gable ends. On the outside walls, we'll use a type of siding called texture 111. We have four stacks of it on those pallets behind you. When the trusses are nailed and braced, we'll lay down the sub-roofing – in this case, regular plywood – then we'll tack down rolls of asphalt insulation. On top of that we'll install the metal roofing. As that's being done, I'll build the cupola. When I put the weathervane on the cupola, the horse barn will be finished. In a nutshell, that's how this project gets done. Are there any questions to this point?"

"I believe I have one," Walter said.

"And what would that be?" Pierre asked the newest crew member.

"Would you mind explaining the fenestration, please?"

"I would, if I knew what it meant."

"Walter's just trying to be a big shot," Fritz said. "Don't let him fool you. He probably looked that word up when he got home from his shopping spree last night."

"I did not," Walter said without hesitation. "I happen to be quite familiar with the word. For your information, Mister Swilling, it means the arrangement of windows and doors on the elevation of a building."

"Fritz is right," Jericho said to Pierre. "Walter doesn't know shit. You don't have to answer him if you don't want to."

"Let me have a crack at it anyway," Pierre said, giving the blueprints a studious look. "The doors will be at each opening of the barn, arranged high and wide enough for the ingress and egress of beast and burden. The windows will be placed where the horses can look out from their stalls."

The crew was jubilant, hooting and howling at Pierre's sarcastic answer.

"Construction of the stalls," Pierre went on, "requires two-by-sixes. I don't know why we had those particular boards delivered this early, but as you can see we've got more than twenty tall stacks of them. We can look forward to a lot of laborious effort on the inside of the barn once the outside is completed. As with everything else, but perhaps more so when it comes to the stalls, accurate measurements will be absolutely essential. Bolts and hinges, handles and latches, have to fit perfectly. Also, with big animals jostling around, they'll have to withstand a lot of wear and tear. Only the highest quality hardware will be used."

Pierre noticed one of Walter's clammy hands weakly waving at him. "You have another question?"

"I do," Walter said, happy to be recognized. "The Pennsylvania Dutch painted cabalistic signs on their barns to scare away witches. What do our plans call for in that regard?"

Pierre was stumped for a moment; not in search of an answer, but because such a question would be asked in the first place. "Actually Walter, I didn't notice any instructions for a cabalistic sign in either the estimate or in the blueprints. Maybe it's something we can give some thought to if we build another barn after this one."

"We've got a couple of excellent artists in the group," Walter said. "If the powers-that-be should change their collective minds, perhaps this is something they might agree to do."

"Thank you, Walter. Consider the matter under advisement."

Gulliver had his hand raised.

Pierre was careful to temper his patience. "Yes Gulliver, what is it?"

"Please tell Walter that if he asks any more stupid questions he's fired."

"I'll take that under advisement as well."

Gulliver nodded his head with gratitude.

"And finally," Pierre said, "I should mention that we face a strict deadline. Rudy needs to see a profit on this project. Nothing puts profits in jeopardy more than having a job take longer than anticipated. Material costs are easily determined. On the other hand, the cost of labor for any days that were not anticipated in the estimate can be the kiss of death. That's especially true with this project because it happens to be labor intensive. In addition to the crew that Jericho has assembled, we'll be hiring a number of additional laborers. We're hoping to recruit some men with carpentry experience but, of course, you never know what you'll get when you hire off the unemployment line. I bring this up because I need to ask that you treat any person who comes onto this job with decency and respect. The unemployment office is a state agency, as you know, and the owners of this barn are state officials. Therefore, it's important that you show new hires every common courtesy."

Everyone in the crew nodded at Pierre. "No problem," said Gulliver. "Wouldn't have it any other way," Fritz concurred. "Your point is well taken," Rem said. "Courtesy is our policy," Box said. *"Pop, pop, pop,"* Jericho shouted.

Pierre was pleased with their response. As time would tell, however, his pleasure could not have been more ill-founded.

Eight

Day three at the horse barn called for more repositioning lumber. Four stacks of two-by-fours had to be reassembled into sixteen smaller stacks, two near the four corners and two along each wall. Metal straps binding large bundles of texture 111 were snipped and each vertically grooved four-by-eight sheet was hauled from inside the barn's perceived dimensions and stacked on pallets along the outside, then covered with tarps until needed.

Fritz, annoyed by the paltry output from the albino's pained exertions, stopped stacking to help Pierre and Jericho hoist posts into position and brace them.

Walter was still weak from his various illnesses, essentially worthless at any activity. While each man was able to carry several boards at a time, Walter could carry only one of the smaller boards and none of the larger ones. That prompted Grumpy to write him up for slovenly effort. When the crew broke for lunch, Grumpy suggested to Pierre that Walter's pay be docked, commensurate with the albino's marginal production. Pierre explained that he could only reduce the hourly rate to the minimum wage mandated by the state, telling Grumpy that he was more inclined to simply terminate the sickly one if his production continued to be lackluster. Grumpy said he thought it would be wiser to write him up, thereby avoiding a possible revolt by the crew, pointing out that Walter was Jericho's hire; therefore, only Jericho could fire him – an unlikely event.

Negotiations between Pierre and Grumpy over Walter's fate broke off during the lunch break when Pierre climbed into his bug. Jericho jumped in his pickup, quick to lock both doors. In the Buick, members of the crew opened their respective lunches and pulled out sandwiches. Walter snapped open his bright red lunch pail and unraveled his first sandwich. Instantly, the stench of egg salad overwhelmed the peanut butter and jelly, deviled meat, and bologna sandwiches the others had brought.

"That's it," Fritz said. "I won't live with this torment. I'm eating in Jericho's truck."

Fritz climbed out of the back seat. Gulliver got out of the other door and asked his older brother if it might be okay by Jericho for him to join them. "I can't sit there smelling Walter's rotten eggs any better than you can."

Remington was disgusted too. "Why'd you have to make egg salad sandwiches, Walter?"

"Eggs are Mother Nature's most perfect food, except, possibly, for bee pollen. Their composition of amino acids creates exceptionally high quality protein, absolutely vital to one's health."

"I hear they can give you a heart attack," Rem said, sneering.

"Pure propaganda promulgated by the cereal institute", Walter said with flippant disdain.

"Maybe, but eggs stink all the same, even with the windows down."

"It's the sulfur content. The amino acid cysteine, critically important to proper metabolic function, is heavily concentrated in the yoke. Personally, I don't find the odor offensive."

"The rest of us do," Rem said. "From now on, Walter, no eggs. Get your protein from something else. Ain't that right, Grump?"

"Rem's right," Grumpy said. "I don't usually give out warnings, Walter. But since this is your first day on the job, I'll make an allowance. You ever bring egg salad sandwiches again, you're going to be written up for it. Fair enough?"

Walter finished his first sandwich without responding, then unraveled the cellophane from the second.

"You're going to eat two sandwiches?" Rem asked.

"Excellent observation," Walter said.

"How can somebody as skinny as you – sick besides – eat so damn much?"

Grumpy watched in disbelief. "He didn't get that appetite from working."

Gulliver opened the door to the Buick and climbed back in. "Jericho won't let either one of us sit in the truck with him. Says he doesn't want to set a bad precedent."

"Fritz climbed into the cargo bed," Box said. "He's eating his lunch on the tool box."

Gulliver's hands twitched nervously holding his deviled meat sandwich."

"What's the matter?" Rem asked.

"Jericho pulled a gun out from under the seat when Fritz started banging on the window to let us in. The look in that lunatic's eyes while he was chomping away on a fat meatloaf sandwich was beyond intimidating."

"I don't think he'd go so far as to shoot you," Box said.

"I wouldn't chance it," Remington said. "Remember that time outside Al's French Fries when Jericho dragged some guy across the road into the graveyard and tied him to a gravestone? Poor bastard was so frightened he actually gave Jericho his lighter. And what does Jericho do with it? He set the guy's shirt on fire. Then he walked away howling with laughter, with every intention of letting the guy burn to death. The only thing that saved that boy was a friend of his hiding behind another grave stone who ran over and put the fire out with his jacket. Think again, Box, about whether or not Jericho would shoot somebody."

"I believe he would," Weepy said. "I'd be shocked if he doesn't fire that pistol at somebody long before this barn gets built."

Box thought about it, shook his head, then asked Walter for the other half of a *Zero* bar.

Walter ignored the request, reaching into his paper bag to extract a bottle of aspirin, *Vicks Vapo Rub*, and a box of *Smith Brothers* cherry flavored cough drops.

"So that's what you had in the bag," Rem said.

"Medicinals," Walter responded.

When Walter had finished his second sandwich, he washed down a handful of aspirins with tomato soup, rubbed gunk all over his scrawny neck, and placed the bottles back into the bag. Curiosity turning to disgust, Rem watched the albino put a handful of cough drops in his shirt pocket, rub eucalyptus ointment under his nose, wipe his hands with a napkin, unfold a blank piece of paper, and withdraw a ballpoint pen from his pocket.

"What's that for?" Rem asked.

"Notes."

"What notes?"

"I thought I'd start a journal of our activities. Who knows, there might be some news value in this project. You heard Pierre. This will be the largest horse barn ever built in the history of the state. Sounds like a story to me."

"You know, Walter, we've been close friends since grade school. In fact, I've always considered you to be my very best friend."

"I appreciate that. The sentiment is mutual, I'm sure."

"I mean, there are things about you that I find interesting. Alarming might be a better description, but I'll be kind. Can you understand, though, why it is that a guy like Fritz, battle hardened and all that, considers you to be so repulsive?"

"No, I cannot. Fritz and I are very good friends. I cannot imagine those are his true feelings."

"I'm not denying he's a friend. And look, we all get under Fritz's skin occasionally; it can't be helped. But nobody gets any deeper than you do. He's a dangerous man, Walter. In some ways, he's even more dangerous than Jericho. Remember that time he threw a full bottle of Budweiser at Gulliver? His own brother, for chrissakes! You were there. Gully took a direct hit just above the hair line. It could have killed him. Took more than thirty stitches to sew him up. Ain't that right, Gulliver?"

"Forty-four, to be exact. I remember because that's Hank Aaron's number."

"Willy McCovey," Grumpy said.

"Johnny Roseboro," Box added.

"Of course I remember. It was an ugly episode." Walter slipped the pen back into his pocket and folded up the piece of paper. "I guess it's unlikely I'll be able to begin my journal during our lunch break. What is your point, Rem?"

"The point is you haven't seen much of Fritz since he got back from Vietnam. He's a changed man, Walter. He's jumpy. The most trivial things irritate the shit out of him. And let's face it; most of what comes out of your mind is trivial."

"I wouldn't say that."

"Listen to me. Fritz can go on the attack at any minute. A word to the wise, my little Q-tip."

"If you must call me names, I'd prefer something more wholesome than cotton swabs intended to collect ear wax."

"Okay, my little egg-white buddy. How's that?"

"I'm thinking about it."

"Anyway, take it for what it's worth; fair warning."

"That's the second warning I've had during my very first lunch break."

"You're not paying enough attention to my advice. Listen to me. You've been as reclusive as a ghost ever since you decided to try your hand at journalism. We've been around Fritz a lot more than you have since he got back. I'm telling you, the least little thing pisses him off. And nobody pisses him off more than you, given all your little quirks and complaints."

The men climbed out of the Buick and ambled down to the work site. Remington and Walter lingered by the car. "What quirks?" Walter asked.

"Your sudden fascination with being a reporter, for one thing. Fritz doesn't believe you're cut out for it. I'm not saying you are or you aren't; I'm just saying that's what he says. And hey, maybe I'm reading it all wrong; maybe the man loves you so much he doesn't want to see you get hurt if it turns out you're not journalist material."

"I happen to know that I am, though."

"Fair enough. The point I'm trying to make is that Fritz has changed. Vietnam can do that to a man. He wasn't exactly mild-mannered before he went off to war, but he's far more volatile now. One minute you think everything's hunky-dory and the next thing you know you've stepped on a land mine. Don't push that crazy leatherneck too far. Especially when it comes to junk food; that seems to be his hot button."

"Fine."

"This isn't advice for you alone, Walter; we're all leery of him these days."

"You're a worry wart, Rem; always paranoid about one thing or another."

"Fair enough. Make light of my advice at your own peril."

"Fritz is no doubt suffering from battle fatigue. It's true I haven't spent much time with him since he got out of the Marine Corps. I've been honing my journalistic talents, adjusting my writing skills down to the eighth-grade level, developing tenacity. I'm sure Fritz had some harrowing experiences during his thirteen months in combat. But I wouldn't necessarily translate from his touchy behavior that he's a powder keg ready to blow sky high at any moment. He's having a problem getting his bearings, that's all. Time heals a lot of wounds, Rem, especially those that are emotional in nature. Fritz needs our sympathy, some handholding. Speaking strictly for myself, I'm not any more concerned about his violent tendencies now than I ever was."

The two men walked down to the construction site. "Have it your way," Rem said. "But I suggest you not let naïveté set a trap for you. In addition to your chronic illnesses and the weird idiosyncrasies that drive us all batty, Fritz is of the unshakable opinion that your ideas for news stories basically suck. He thinks you ought to give up on the journalism thing altogether, find work as an orderly at the hospital maybe; that way you'll never run out of aspirin."

"Aspirin is cheap and plentiful, Rem; not that I wouldn't make an excellent orderly. As far as stories go, Fritz has only heard a few of my ideas. I've got plenty more that seem quite promising."

Rem and Walter carried boards from one pile to another. Satisfied he had provided ample warning about the jarhead's temper, Remington turned his attention to his friend's psychosomatic proclivities. "How many aspirins do you consume on a good day?"

"I've never counted."

"I want to know how many. Take a guess."

"I'd say a regular size bottle of *St. Josephs* lasts me an entire week."

"How many come in a bottle?"

"Sixty."

"*Mister Man*, that's almost ten aspirins a day."

"Doesn't sound like so many when you break it down like that."

"Are you kidding? You're wolfing those things like *Goobers* at the Flynn Theater. But you're still sick all the time. Obviously, they're not doing the job."

"Given that analysis, it strikes me that perhaps the efficacy of aspirin diminishes after a certain number of years of consistent usage. Maybe I should be increasing rather than decreasing my intake in order to maintain or perhaps boost their effectiveness."

"You take too many aspirins as it is, Walter. It's a dangerous practice. And why the hell can't you carry more than one board at a time, for chrissakes?"

"I shouldn't have to remind you that I'm only beginning to get my strength back after being stricken with double pneumonia, to say nothing about a lingering case of strep throat. *Jeepers*, Rem, you've been giving me warnings or criticizing me for one thing or another all day. I don't criticize you for betting the birds, do I?"

"And you shouldn't. My cock performed quite admirably on the reservation a couple nights ago."

"I can't understand what you get out of it, other than the thrill of gambling your money away."

"Cockfights are therapeutic. They take my mind off a lot of troubling issues."

"You're placating yourself; it's an awkward attempt to convert emotional disquietude into a harmless byproduct of intellectualization."

"You're pissing me off, Walter."

"We both know you got hooked on the birds as a little boy when that nutcase neighbor of yours who wore a mink coat to St. Mike's basketball games pitted rooster against peacock, dove against pigeon. I don't even consider it sport. And there's certainly nothing intellectual about it."

"Cockfighting happens to be a recognized sport."

"Sure; recognized by the authorities as being illegal."

"It's legal on the reservation. And gambling, for your information, is far more intellectual than you might imagine. Betting on a violent sport is both an emotional release and a cerebral challenge. It's good therapy. It helps me cope with the burden of what I know."

Walter slid a board into place on the new pile and paused for a shallow breath. "Sounds like emotional intellectualizing to me. Did you happen to win any money the other night?"

"I was way up when it was my cock in there. I gave some of it back in the fight that followed. Then I mopped up on the next one. But I lost the last three and wound up down a ten spot."

"In other words, the weight of your wallet was a little less burdensome come the end of the night."

"You'll be less burdened, I swipe that lump of sour cream off your shoulders."

"I've been giving some thought to the idea of doing an investigative report on cockfights, provided I can stomach watching them."

"Once those birds get to squawking, you can't help but be engrossed by it."

"Or grossed out."

"The feathers fly, *Mister Man*, once they're digging their spurs in, kicking and pecking at each other in good shape."

"Spurs?"

"Yeah. In some of the fights, sharp spurs are strapped to the birds' legs."

"How barbaric!"

"Laying money on your favorite rooster takes the experience to an entirely different level, especially after the boys have been drinking up a storm. I can't get enough of it."

"Think you'd want to take me along with you one of these nights?"

"I wouldn't dream of it."

"Why not?"

"For one thing, I'm not keen on the idea of being quoted in a newspaper article about cockfighting. For another, I'd have to explain everything to you. That would destroy my concentration. I'd lose my shirt. For yet another, you do not, in fact, have the stomach for it."

"Perhaps I could write the story vicariously. I could study up on cockfights and then interview you, a practitioner, for all the gory details."

"I just got done telling you I don't want to be quoted in a report about it."

"How about if your cock is featured? What's its name?"

"*Jim Dandy*, from the Black Oak Arkansas song."

"Impressive."

"Here's a thought, Walter. Why don't you write the story from the bird's perspective?"

Walter slid a board into place, pausing to consider a violent cartoonist personification. "*Jeepers*, Rem, that's not half bad. *A Bird's-Eye View of Cockfighting*. How does that sound?"

"Damn near plausible. Run it by Fritz; see what his take is."

"I will. It might even change his mind about my potential as a journalist."

"You're intellectually emotionalizing, Walter. It's best to expect ridicule and scorn from Fritz. That's what I do. I'm never disappointed."

Nine

Marsha Leeks wasn't the type to seriously consider suicide, although the notion had played tongue-in-cheek with her psyche in recent months. She was young and attractive, had a degree in political science, and was, generally speaking, emotionally sound. A native of Barrington, Rhode Island, the only child of wealthy, albeit estranged, parents, Marsha, superficially at least, lacked for nothing. But beneath the surface of her secure station in life, loneliness, boredom, and a creeping lethargy regarding her profession plagued her day-to-day existence.

Marsha was a beat reporter for the Washington County *Chronicle*, a weekly newspaper in north central Vermont. In fact, she was the paper's sole reporter. The only effort the owner-editor contributed each week was a tepid gossip column that Marsha had difficulty believing anyone other than its victims actually bothered to read.

Given her father's status as a senior partner with a prominent law firm in Manhattan and the substantial influence her mother wielded as a member of the Board of Directors of a Fortune 500 company, she could have attended an Ivy League school despite missing the honor roll five of six semesters during her senior year in high school. Instead, somewhat defiantly, she chose the University of New Hampshire. She could have selected a lucrative career path but decided, instead, to become a journalist. And what did this mildly rebellious independence get her at the ripe young age of twenty-five? It got her a drab apartment in Barre, Vermont; a small city in a rural state where nothing of importance – from a reporter's perspective – ever happened. It took her away from the camaraderie of peers and an occasional nightlife. It produced a dead-end job. It guaranteed a dearth of romantic relationships. And it brought her to the edge of regret for not having leaned on her parents to get a better head start in life.

What Marsha needed was a break in the lack of action; a tip on a juicy story, the prince-like appearance of a charming suitor, or, perhaps, a compelling reason to abandon her stymied journalism career for an entirely different challenge. On this drizzly September day, mired in detestable self-pity, her work week winding down, her mind waylaid in a labyrinth of frustration and malaise, Marsha Leeks had no way of knowing that events brewing not more than twenty miles from the *Chronicle's* cramped and cluttered newsroom provided the ingredients for an investigative report, a pithy beau with a frothy philosophy, and the heady excitement of a unique business concept.

She worked the remainder of the afternoon putting the finishing touches on a piece showcasing the beginning of another of Vermont's glorious autumns. One positive aspect of having been a Jill-of-all-trades for three years at a weekly paper was the opportunity to develop her talents as a photographer. This particular article featured six spectacular shoots of bucolic farms and sun-dappled country lanes meandering beneath canopies of early fall foliage.

Satisfied with her work, Marsha type-set the obituaries, sized the Dear Abby column and the latest Van Buren bridge hand to their respective pages, and organized the want ads from antiques to yard sales, from birthday greetings to a free zodiac reading promoted in every issue by some kook operating from a park bench in Cabot.

Marsha went into the editor's office to inform him that the latest edition was ready for bed. Pleased that the issue contained no hard news or controversial stories, he bid her goodnight. She strolled back to her desk, picked up the book, *Let's Eat Right* by Adele Davis, and walked out of the little brick building into the dreary weather to drive home in her little Chevy Nova to her dreary little apartment.

Ten

At the end of the workday on Saturday, Jericho climbed into his truck, Pierre squeezed into his bug, and the crew from Chittenden County piled into Grumpy's Invicta, everyone pleased that the first week at the horse barn had ended on a positive note. Weepy, waking up from one of his afternoon naps, played an electrifying rendition of the Stones' *Satisfaction*; chorus gratuitously provided by the hoarse vocals of Jericho and Box.

"Not to be redundant, but what I need about now is to slam down a couple of Jack Black doubles," Rem said. "That oughta pave the way for a steady six or seven hour flow of the King of Beers."

Grumpy had similar thoughts. "I'm so dry I could tap a half-keg and stretch out under the spigot with my mouth wide open. How about you, Weepy?"

"Indeed. I'm looking forward to cleansing my soiled soul in a rapid of suds. This job, I'm sad to say, is one of the most sobering gigs I've ever been on. After a week of it, I find myself suffering from far too much mental clarity. Had I not been remiss this morning, I might have slipped a tab of Purple Haze into my shirt pocket as a dividend for my afternoon tea. However, given the incessant honking of a horrifying horn outside my door long before the soft mouth of the new day could suckle the pulp of my senses, I plum forgot."

Fritz leaned forward to look past Walter and Gulliver at the lyrical hedonist. "It's a good thing I enjoy your singing, Weepy; otherwise, I'd slit your fucking throat."

The Buick was the first to peel out. Jericho was right behind. Pierre followed, glancing back with favor at all the vertical posts that had gone up during the week.

Box Car wanted to know if the albino was ready for some serious drinking. He turned around from the front seat to look for Walter, the frail one nibbling the last of his portion of the *Zero* bar. "Once we find us a proper watering hole, what's your preference, tweety-bird?"

"It's Birdsong. *Mister* Birdsong to you."

Box grumbled behind a devious smile. "It's been a long time since I've seen you get good and drunk, Walter. Once we belly up to the bar, are you going to be putting the booze to you or am I going to have to force it down your scrawny gullet?"

"That won't be necessary, Mister Bork. We've all had a long week of rather taxing labor, therefore ..."

"Not in your case," Gulliver corrected. "You didn't show up till the middle of the week."

"I missed the first two days, Gully, when nothing in the way of physical effort was required. The real work started when I arrived, as I might have expected."

Grumpy slammed on the brakes at an intersection of dirt roads with no stop signs in any direction, not because of the senseless chatter or an impending collision but because Jericho was laying on the horn thirty feet behind him. The callous man from Calais was flashing his headlights and waving frantically through the windshield. Both vehicles skidded to a snaking stop on loose gravel, Jericho's pickup nudging the Buick's back bumper.

Jericho jumped out of the truck and walked up to Grumpy's window, bending down to survey the group. "Any of you men thirsty?"

A chorus of affirmation filled the car.

"Let me take the lead," Jericho said. "I know a decent place on the other side of Waterbury. It's on your way. They've got a three-hour Happy Hour that starts in twenty minutes. I can get us there quick."

Jericho got back in his truck and tore off in front, spitting small stones at the Buick and making Grumpy furious. "If that wild-ass gunslinger ruins my brand new paint job, he's paying for all my drinks. He's lucky I don't write him up."

Box Car resumed his query. "I want to know what your preference is, bird man."

"I believe I'll order a bloody Mary."

"Just one?"

"We'll have to see how good the bartender is at crafting the drink. I won't accept any commercially prepared mix, understand. Furthermore, tomato juice from a can tastes a bit tinny; a bottle is much better. I like a rounded teaspoon of horseradish – one hundred percent natural horseradish, mind you – as well as a half-dozen liberal splashes of *Lea & Perrins* Worcestershire sauce. Then of course, garlic powder, a squeeze of lime, a dash of salt, a lavish sprinkling of fresh ground pepper, a drop of Tabasco, and a touch of celery salt – not as a replacement for, but in addition to a leafy heart of celery stalk. Oh, and should they have it, a fresh scallion for some added zip."

"You're disgusting," Fritz said.

"Don't be so polemical," Walter said.

"What the hell does that mean?" Box asked.

"Disputatious," Walter said, "though more in keeping with Fritz's chronically contentious verbal aggression."

"There it is."

"I was merely stating my preferences." Walter added. "It was none of Fritz's business."

Fritz frothed. "You're a dweeb, Walter; a timid, vigor-deprived dweeb, hopelessly stricken with the colorless pallor and social repugnance of a pucker-mouthed bottom feeder."

"*Jeepers*, that's quite endearing, Fritzie. And here I thought you might not like me."

"Let me see if I've got this right, Walter" Gulliver intervened, intrigued by the elaborate particularity of the albino's choice of alcoholic beverage. "You're going to order a bloody Mary, but if the bartender can't come up with all the right ingredients, then it's simply not possible to make the *perfect* bloody Mary; therefore, you're going to limit yourself to one, if indeed you even drink that one."

"Correct."

"And do you require a special brand of vodka or will anything off the shelf do?"

"I don't drink a bloody Mary for the vodka, Gulliver; I drink it for its vegetable content. If you're going to consume alcohol, a bloody Mary is the only healthy drink there is."

"And I suppose it has to be *Lea & Perrins*. No other brand of Worcestershire sauce will suffice."

"I'll accept *Heinz*, although I must say it's a decidedly inferior product. I will most certainly not, however, abide by any generic concoction."

"And I suppose," Gulliver pressed, "that the garlic must be in the powdered form, as opposed to salt."

Grumpy had heard enough. "*Look you sons-a-bitches*, I'll head right for the nearest tree if you keep it up. I'm trying to stay on Jericho's ass so he won't lose me in this Barre-Montpelier traffic. He's driving as if he forgot about me being behind him, gunning it through yellow lights every chance he gets. By the time I go through, the light's turned red. I ain't putting up with this horse shit another minute."

Weepy thought he'd make light of the situation, possibly diffusing the driver's angst and prompting the Grump to think twice before running any more red lights. His comment, though riding on a well-intentioned chuckle, evoked an unnerving specter. "You talk like killing us is a viable way to rid yourself of a nuisance."

Grumpy plowed through a red light two blocks past the gold-domed capitol. A gaggle of cars honked. "Listen, acid head; I don't give a flying fuck for your life or mine either."

The *Hounds Tooth Lounge* was filling up with Happy Hour patrons when the truck and the Buick whipped into the parking lot. Grumpy jumped out of the car in great haste to inspect any damage from the rain of pebbles. As he ran his hands lovingly across the nose of the hood and along the grill, Jericho and the crew rushed into the bar.

The men hunted down two empty tables, pushed them together, and yanked chairs into place around them. The eldest Swilling marched directly to the juke box, yanked the cord out of its socket, and turned to the dozen or so customers to make an announcement.

"*I hate country music.* Anybody who likes this shit should be dragged outside and riddled with bullets. When I plug this thing back in, I'm playing rock and roll. If any of you care to put your hard earned money into this machine that's fine with me. But if you play any country crap, you're risking your life."

With that, Fritz reinserted the plug, fed several quarters into the slot, and selected The Doors, Canned Heat, Joe Cocker, Led Zeppelin, Traffic, and The Who. Out of coins, he stormed over to the tables where the crew was standing in furious applause, thrilled with the jarhead's justifiable outburst.

When the waitress came by to take their order, Walter went to negotiate with the bartender. The waitress returned with an immense tray filled with mugs and pitchers and mixed drinks. Walter stepped away from the bar holding his bloody Mary high in the air. With his other hand he flashed a thumbs-up to his buddies. Half way across the dance floor, the guttural vocals of Jim Morrison filled the room. *Love Me Two Times* blared from the machine. Walter's hips began to gyrate, his shoulders quivered, his head shook violently from side to side, his feet skittered in a spastic frenzy, and his knees bowed and snapped, bowed and snapped.

Not a drop of his drink spilled while the bony albino convulsed in a half squat, driving his pelvis backward and forward in rhythmic jolts. The regulars and the staff were appalled. The crew stood as one and sang along lustily. Jericho banged his beer mug on the table, yelling, *"That's the beauty of it, Walter; that's the goddamn beauty of it."*

During four hours of heavy drinking, Walter averaging one bloody Mary every forty-five minutes, the crew gave scant notice to a Saturday night crowd that had expanded to standing room only.

Remarkably, not one country music song played the entire time. But Fritz's luck was bound to turn bad sooner or later. At eleven o'clock, a Waylon Jennings' platter settled onto the turntable. Fritz rose to his feet the instant the twang of the singer's voice could be heard through the din. Incensed, the ex-Marine shoved the table out of the way, beer and mixed drinks trembling in their containers, and marched in an awkward but determined gait to the juke box. Rather than yank the cord, Fritz gave the machine a ferocious kick, its neon pink and green lights fading away, glass shattering, and the music abruptly ending. Three men, then two more, then four more, descended on the eldest Swilling before he could grasp the consequences of his rage.

Jericho was the first to respond, followed closely by the rest of the crew.

Walter engaged the fray still holding his bloody Mary. He was immediately punched in the stomach, dropping to his knees in the certain knowledge that he would never breathe again.

Fists were flying, bottles were smashed, tables were overturned, waitresses screamed, Walter was puking his guts out, and the bouncer was banging heads together when someone grabbed the albino by the arm and dragged him on his back away from the altercation. It was Jericho. "Get up you dumb shit. We're gettin' t'fuck out of here."

Walter climbed an invisible rope ladder to his feet and staggered out of the bar clutching his stomach. In the parking lot, he could see the other crew members piling into the Buick, although he was unable to count them to make sure they were all accounted for. Jericho shoved him into the truck and slammed the door. Seconds later, Jericho was hugging the Buick's rear end, the blue bomb fishtailing onto Route 2 and heading for Richmond.

Jericho hooted and sang his own raunchy version of *Sink the Bismarck* at the top of his lungs.

Walter looked through the back window, which was awash with myriad pairs of onrushing headlights. "Get around Grumpy," he yelled. "Get around the Buick, Jericho. I know a detour."

"That ain't gonna be easy; he's driving like there's no tomorrow."

"There may not be, if you don't get around him."

Along the Bolton Flats, Jericho buried the accelerator, the truck's speedometer inching past the one-hundred mile per hour hash mark. Grumpy must have thought the gunslinger had a death wish. He backed off to let the truck pass him.

"Keep up the speed all the way to the end of the flats," Walter shouted. "Grumpy will keep up but the rest of them will be too scared to stay real close."

"We've got a bunch of tight curves straight ahead," Jericho yelled.

"That's right. Hit 'em hard. When you see the bridge in Jonesville, hang a left across it and slam it to the floor. It's a dirt road but it's in good shape and pretty soon it straightens out and stays that way for about two miles."

Jericho followed Walter's instructions, amazed at the sallow one's *take charge* lucidity.

The left onto the bridge was at a forty-five degree angle. Jericho came into the turn too hard and the truck bounced lightly against the side of the bridge. Jericho floored it again with cowboy yelps at the top of his lungs. Through the dust behind him, he could see that the Buick was following close behind. He had no idea whether or not the others were still in pursuit.

Several miles down the road, Walter shouted. "There's a graveyard up ahead on the left. Hit the brakes as soon as you see it. On the other side of the graveyard there's a logging road that goes way up into the woods. It's probably covered with high weeds nowadays, so you may not see it real well. But it's there. Trust me."

Jericho went with his gut. Sure enough, there was no discernable road past the graveyard. The truck skidded to a stop and Jericho yanked it into a small header, hitting the gas pedal hard. The truck bounced and lunged through a narrow clearing, zigzagging at breakneck speed another hundred and fifty yards. Suddenly, a thick stand of trees appeared out of nowhere and Jericho slammed on the brakes.

"Shut off the lights," Walter yelled.

Jericho hit the lights and killed the motor. Both men jumped out of the truck. Walter ran back down the path. A pair of bouncing headlights raced toward him. Walter held up both hands. The Buick slid and swerved to a stop less then two feet in front of the frozen albino.

"The lights. *Kill the lights*," Jericho hollered.

The men spilled out of the car in uproarious laughter. Less than a minute later, a stream of cars could be heard racing along the dirt road below.

"Dumb bastards went right by," Box howled. "That'll teach those yellow-bellied redneck green horns."

Weepy lit an *Old Gold*. "Colorful, Box. Like your shirt. What happened, somebody pop you in the nose?"

"It's not my nose that got bloodied, you asshole. That's somebody else's blood you're looking at."

"Some fat farm hoss hit me with all he was worth," Remington said through the flame of Weepy's *Zippo*. "My right eye's almost swelled shut."

"I took a few good shots," Grumpy said. "But I dished out a lot more than I took. By the time I got to Fritz, there must have been ten guys on him."

"I'd say ten more piled on after that," said Gulliver.

Fritz had welts on his neck. A bulbous lump nested on his forehead where he had taken an elbow during the mêlée. Though his face was saved by mimicking Ali's rope-a-dope, Fritz's ribs had been heavily pummeled. And yet, in the glow of the moonlight, the trace of a smile was visible.

"What's that shit-eating grin for?" Grumpy asked him.

"I was just thinking, what if I'd had my weapon? We could have set up a road block. Two clips and fourteen seconds; that's all it would have taken for me to mow them down."

Rem walked over to his big brother and put a hand on his shoulder. "Fritz! Fritz, 'ol boy. Snap out of it. This isn't Vietnam. You don't have an automatic rifle that can burst an entire magazine in a matter of seconds. Furthermore, we're talking about a pack of local rowdies, not a North Vietnamese Army platoon."

Fritz's chuckle was too purposeful, like he was concealing something. He turned to Jericho. "You still got that pistol in your truck?"

"I don't go anywhere without it. I happen to have two with me tonight."

"Good," Fritz said. "I say we run back down to the road; just you and me. When those cocksuckers figure out we lost 'em, they'll come back this way hoping to spot us. You and I will lay low on the side of the road. When the time is right, we'll ambush them. I'll fire the first shot. A few of them might have guns themselves, but in the dead of night they won't know where the fire is coming from till it's too late."

Rem looked at Weepy. "I think he's serious."

"Can there be any doubt?" Weepy asked.

The pursuers stopped at the Old Round Church less than three miles down the road, slamming on the brakes when they realized their prey could have gone in any one of three directions; straight ahead toward Huntington, right into Richmond the back way, or onto the Hinesburg road. Baffled, they turned around and headed back to Jonesville the way they had come.

Twenty seconds after Fritz had laid out his strategy, Jericho rummaging behind the seat for the second pistol, the befuddled ruffians from the *Hounds Tooth Lounge* went roaring by in the opposite direction. Fritz banged the roof of the Buick with his first. "Fuck, fuck, fuck! We had our chance and we blew it."

"Don't pound my car like that, you deranged war criminal," Grumpy said.

"They had their chance and *they* blew it," Gulliver said. "I say we pull out of here, continue on into Richmond, get back on Route 2, take the River Road, and hit *The Man's Bar* for a couple of victory drinks."

At one-thirty in the morning the bar in Essex was still crowded; not unusual for a Saturday night. The crew split up. Gulliver and Fritz found empty chairs at a table with some friends. Box Car stood by the door in his blood-stained sweatshirt ordering the bouncer to get him a beer. Jericho shouted drink orders for himself and Walter to a passing waitress. Grumpy slid onto a bar stool to hit on a chain-smoking brunette. Remington latched onto a pin ball machine, curious if he'd be on his game with only one good eye. Weepy stayed out in the Buick, telling the others he'd be in as soon as he finished another joint.

At quarter-after-two the bar was thinning out. Crew members remained in their original positions. Weepy had passed out in the car.

Rem, a pinball wizard, found that his disability did not diminish his extraordinary skills. He owned the machine, having racked up a healthy backlog of free games. He was masterfully directing the last ball of the current game through a carnival of glitzy pulsations when someone behind him squeezed his sides with sinewy fingers. Rem twitched but kept his focus on the right flipper, slapping the ball back to the top of the gaily lit obstacle course where it temporarily lodged in a hole. Points tallied and a distinct pop resounded from the bowels of the machine, signifying another game won. The ball was ejected toward a game-ending side shoot but Rem gave the machine a gentle nudge, just enough to influence the ball's course to keep it in play without a disqualifying tilt. His left flipper sent the silver ball back to the top of the course. "Who's that?"

"Guess," said a purring voice, delicate hands closing over his eyes.

Remington did not appreciate the distraction. "I can't. Please remove your hands; you're fucking up my game."

The hands uncovered his eyes, moving to the back of his neck for a gentle massage. Rem's trigger-quick agility avoided disaster. His right flipper fired a vicious shot against a left-side bumper at a thirty-degree angle. The shiny spheroid ricocheted its way up the slope to ding an iridescent disk that flashed with triumphant brilliance in concert with a cacophony of bells and sirens. Digits in the scoring apparatus flew by like icons in a slot machine. *Pop, pop, pop.* Remington took a deep breath as the ball rolled and bumped its way back down toward the flippers, mentally calculating the number of games he'd added to his tally.

"You feel really stiff, Rem. Are you always this hard?"

Rem took fifteen frantic swipes at the pinball with both flippers but the fifth and final ball slipped between them, rolling right and coming to rest against the other balls with a metallic tick. Game over.

He turned to confront his would-be seducer. Wynona, seriously drunk, smiled and batted her eyes like a saucy hussy.

Rem put his hands on her shoulders and moved her one step back. "You can't come on to me, Wynona. I haven't had to say that to you since high school."

"But that's before I found out you could ... *Oooh, Remington.* What the heck happened to you?"

"Oh this," he said, touching his swollen cheekbone. "The boys and I got into a little tussle earlier."

"I thought you were a lover, not a fighter."

Remington looked around the room. "Where's your husband, Wynona?"

"He's home, dead to the world by now. I'm here with friends. They want to stay but I'm ready to leave. Will you take me?"

"You know I can't do that. What would it look like, you and me leaving this place together?"

The corners of Wynona's glossy lips turned down in disappointment. She walked away with a seductive pout toward her friends at the bar, one of whom was wagging a finger of warning in Grumpy's face.

Eleven

Jericho woke up at ten am sprawled on the couch in Walter's apartment. Grumpy had dropped them off around four o'clock. The gunslinger sat up, disoriented, head pounding, nauseous, his bladder about to explode.

At Jericho's house in the sparsely populated hills twenty miles northeast of the state's capital, *yard pissing* was always in effect. He rubbed his eyes and groaned in misery, debating whether to go outside or lie back down and pee his pants. The thought of going into the bathroom never occurred to him. He decided there might be enough time to make it out the door.

Walter lived on the ground floor of a three-story apartment complex in Essex Center. The building had four apartments on each floor. One of the tenants, a single lady in her mid-thirties who Walter knew only as Christie, was pulling into the driveway after attending Sunday mass when Jericho stepped onto a brick walkway lined with marigolds. Christie got out of her car, reached back in for her purse, closed the door, and walked toward the building. She froze in her tracks three steps along the walk when she heard a hissing sound and glanced up to see an arcing yellow stream barely clearing the flowers not six feet in front of her.

The sound of her purse hitting the bricks caught Jericho's attention. "Good morning," he said, peering through a bright sun in Christie's direction but unable to discern whether the intruder was male or female.

Christie was speechless for several seconds. When she found her voice, it was filled with alarm and disgust. "Who *are* you? And what the hell do you think you're doing?"

"I'm Jericho. And I think I'm taking a piss."

Shocked and humiliated, she shrieked. *"I can't believe what I'm seeing.* You can't do that here."

Jericho displayed the affect of a garden hose, waving the sprayer from side to side and making a wavy pattern over the marigolds. "Sure I can. A man has to drain the lizard once in while, know what I'm saying?"

"No I do not. I'm going inside and I'm calling the cops."

The intensity of the stream abated and Jericho took two steps forward to keep the spray on the flowers. "Go ahead," he said, shaking out the last few drops directly over the yellow and orange blooms. "I'm just trying to be neighborly."

"Let me past this instant," Christie demanded.

Jericho zipped up, walked back in the front door, staggered around the common area getting his bearings, then stomped back into Walter's apartment. Splashing his face in the kitchen sink, he heard a door slam. High heels hammered the stairs. Leaving the apartment, he heard another door slam two floors above.

Outside, he looked around in a confused state. Then he remembered he'd parked his truck on the front lawn. Within minutes, he was at the intersection of Sand Hill Road and the River Road. He turned left toward home.

At ten-thirty, Walter was awakened by two policemen and a vaguely familiar woman with murderous eyes standing in the doorway of his bedroom.

Deirdre wasn't pleased. "Where the hell have you been?"

"Sorry, babe. The boys talked me into going out with them after work. I thought it was the least I could do, this being their first week on the job."

"I had dinner waiting."

Jericho stepped toward his wife with his arms outstretched. "I'm sorry. It won't happen again."

"I've heard that a thousand times. Where did you stay last night?"

Jericho was a different person around his wife. She was strong and athletic, his equal physically and nearly his equal temperamentally. If push ever came to shove, he might find himself on his keister.

They had met in eleventh grade at a school dance. When he'd mustered enough courage to ask her to dance, she turned him down. But he persisted. On the fourth try his tenacity paid off. They were doing the *Mashed Potato* when he moved in and asked for her name. The music was loud. He couldn't make it out but he smiled anyway, not wanting to disappoint her. He vowed to find out her name some other way. She asked for his name. He yelled it back to her. Later in the evening, when they were slow dancing, she whispered into his ear, "I like the way you hold me, Jericho." He was elated.

Deirdre had danced the *Mashed Potato* much better than him, bending her knees low and whisking them from side to side. He had no idea until they danced a slow song that she stood three inches taller. Her height was intimidating. He had to rise up on his tiptoes to bury his nose in the crook of her neck. When he found out her name from his friend Walter the next morning, he looked her up in the phone book and telephoned.

Several months after dancing the *Mashed Potato*, he was in her gravy. A few summers later they were married.

"Jericho! Are you listening to me?"

"No, sweetie. I mean *yes*, of course I am."

"Either you were daydreaming or you're hung over. Which is it?"

"I thought that's what I heard you say."

"That's not what I said. I asked you where in holy hell you spent the night?"

"Right. I was at Walter's."

"Why couldn't you have called? Is that too much to ask? After nine o'clock, I was worried sick. While you were snoring up a storm at Walter's, I hardly slept the entire night. Damn it, Jericho, you piss me off."

"I know. It won't happen again."

"Of course it will. It always has and it always will; unless I decide to give you the heave-ho."

"But I promise."

"I've heard it too many times."

"Come on, babe; let me make it up to you."

"You can't. The damage is done."

"I bet I can."

"I said you can't."

"But I want to bet."

"Bet what? That cold plate of food sitting in the fridge?"

Jericho gave his wife a hug. "Something a lot better than that."

"I made you a nice supper, darn you."

"I know. Let me make it up to you."

The ice was thawing. Deirdre returned his hug. They embraced for half a minute. He grabbed her hand and led her into the bedroom. Last night's supper could wait.

It was one o'clock in the afternoon when the phone rang. Deirdre kicked the blankets away. "I'll get it," she said, sliding off the bed.

Jericho thought he was reliving a bad dream. He sat up, disoriented, head pounding, nauseous, his bladder about to explode.

"For you," Deirdre yelled into the bedroom. "Walter."

Jericho staggered out of the bedroom rubbing his eyes. He grabbed the receiver. "This better be good, Walter. I was sound asleep."

"It isn't good. You wouldn't believe what hap …"

"Hold on a minute."

"What?"

"*Yard pissing's* in effect. I'll be right back."

Jericho came back into the house several minutes later. "Did you say my supper is in the fridge, babe? I'm starving."

"Walter's still holding for you, Jericho. I'll warm it up while you talk to him."

"Oh yeah. I forgot." Jericho picked up the receiver. "Go ahead. I'm back."

"This is a long distance phone call, Jericho."

"I don't want to hear any bellyaching. What's your problem?"

"I got arrested."

"For what? You hit the sack the same time I did. What'd you do, go back to *The Man's Bar* and get in trouble?"

"No. I don't even remember getting home or going to bed or anything else. All I know is two cops were standing over my bed a few hours ago reading me my rights. I thought I was dreaming until I heard Christie describing some guy's lewd behavior. I knew she had to be talking about you. I mean, who else would do something like that?"

"Like what?"

"Oh come on, Jericho. Are you telling me you don't remember?"

"Remember what?"

"Peeing in front of my neighbor."

Jericho roared.

"That was inexcusable. I'm in a heap of trouble because of you."

"How could you be in trouble? You didn't have anything to do with it."

"Of course not. I would never be a party to such despicable behavior. But you were my guest, Jericho. Christie described you perfectly. I can't believe you would offend one of my neighbors so egregiously. They call that *indecent exposure*, you know."

"That's the beauty of it; the most decent exposure that lady's seen in a while. I'm surprised she let me leave."

"You're lucky she did let you leave. You got away free as a bird. I'm the one who has to face the consequences."

"What consequences?"

"I was taken to police headquarters at the Five Corners and officially charged. I'm surprised they didn't lock me up and make me post bail."

"There's no jail in Essex. What the hell did they charge you with?"

"Abetting lewd and lascivious behavior."

"They can't prove anything, Walter. Tell 'em to piss up a rope."

"My goodness, why didn't I think of that?"

"I mean it, Walter. The marigolds were all dried out by the time the fuzz got there, sun beating down like it was. It's her word against nobody's. Did you tell them where I live?"

"Of course not. I utilized Socratic irony."

"What the hell does that mean?"

"Playing dumb as a diabolical means of usurping your opponent's predication by exposing the fallacies of an assumed logic."

"There it is."

"It was amazing I could think so fast, waking up to a crippling hangover with two cops glaring down at me."

"I thought you said you played dumb." Jericho roared again. "That doesn't call for quick thinking."

"Accolade accepted."

"Think nothing of it. Did they give you a court date?"

"Not yet. They told me to expect a notice in the mail. This might make the papers, Jericho. I'm on the police blotter. With my luck, I'll have a by-line on the front page for the story I'm working and on page thirteen my name will show up again in the police round-up."

"Could be worse."

"Thanks for the show of empathy."

"Think nothing of it."

"How am I going to face Christie again? I actually believe she may have been sweet on me. Thanks to you, I can kiss that relationship good-bye."

"She's what, ten, twelve years older than you?"

"I'd say half that. Anyway, I prefer a woman who's been around the block a few times."

"Here's something that'll put her on the right block: tell her you're hung like a horse, just like that degenerate friend of yours. She'll be on you like a confused horse fly on a cow's ass. Be sure to get her dead drunk first. That way she won't know if you're big or not when it comes to crunch time. *Oh, be big for me.* Say it, Walter."

"No. But on that note, are you hung over?"

"I wouldn't be if it wasn't for the thirty-two piece orchestra in my head, everybody looking at different sheet music. You?"

"I had to excuse myself twice at the police station to go into the john and throw up."

"I'm sorry to hear that, Walter. I hate puking. You'll feel better tomorrow. That's the beauty of hangovers; they feel like they're going to last forever and the next thing you know you're aching for another one. Tell you what; to square things between us, I'll bring a fresh bottle of aspirin to the horse barn for you.

"You're a real friend, Jericho."

"Think nothing of it."

Sibyl shook Remington's shoulder again. "Do you think I'm going to let you sleep all day? *Get up.* It's Sunday. You promised Beatrice you'd take her to the park today. She's been sitting at the kitchen table waiting for you ever since breakfast. That was hours ago."

Rem felt like he was in someone else's nightmare. He sat up, disoriented, head pounding, nauseous, his bladder about to explode.

"I put some coffee on for you. You need to get your wits about you. I'll tell Bea you'll be downstairs in five minutes."

Rem sat on the edge of the bed and rubbed his eyes. "Which park?"

"If you're too hung over to drive out to Battery Park – you know how much she loves Beansie's French fries – the two of you can walk over to Fort Ethan Allen. Bea would enjoy that almost as much."

"Okay," Rem said, achieving a precarious balance when he'd made it to his feet. He yawned, gave his chicken skin a scratch with one hand and his chest a stroke with the other, then staggered into the bathroom. Sibyl watched her depraved husband with a smirk on her face, wondering how she ever fell in love with him.

Beatrice was pretending to read the funny papers, nervous about the result of her mommy's attempt to wake up her daddy. "Come on little lady," Sibyl said. "Daddy's up now. He'll be down in a few minutes. It's chilly out today. I want you to put your jacket on."

"It's sunny, mommy. I don't want to wear a jacket."

"You heard me."

Beatrice jumped out of her chair and ran to her daddy when she heard his footsteps on the stairs.

Horse Barn

Remington sipped his coffee and held his daughter's hand while they strolled down the sidewalk and turned onto North Avenue, their destination only a few blocks away.

Fort Ethan Allen was a large park with magnificent oaks and maples, spacious lawns with wending walkways, and a paved road that forked half way around it. One road went to the playground area and dead-ended. The other twisted up a steep hill to a stone tower where the famous *Green Mountain Boys* had looked out for British vessels on Lake Champlain.

Bea and her dad cut cross-lots directly to the swings and the teeter-totters. This was a special moment for both of them. Remington adored his little honey bee. He cherished their time together. On this dazzling September morning, he cursed himself for allowing his *bird-watching* hobby to cause him to miss spending more time with her.

Remington was like a giant to her; a funny giant with a beard, soft hugs, and eyes that could do tricks. He was her very own giant and she didn't have to share him with anybody. Except, of course, her mother – sometimes. She wondered why her mommy never asked him to make his eyes dance. Maybe he had already done it so many times for her that she thought it was silly by now. But Bea didn't. She loved it when he made his eyes jiggle. And he did it every single time she asked him to.

"Teach me how to pump, daddy, like the big kids do. If I can make the swing go all by myself, you won't have to push me. You can lie down on the grass and take a nap. I know you're tired."

"I'm not tired, Bea."

"You yawn a lot."

"I was yawning a while ago but I drank all my coffee and now I'm wide awake. Besides, I enjoy pushing you."

"Do you think I'm too little to get the swing started by myself and pump real high?"

"I don't know. Tell you what. You sit on a swing and I'll sit on the one next to it. You can watch what I do and try it yourself. How does that sound?"

Beatrice jumped up and down, laughing and clapping her hands. "Okay, daddy. I'll do everything exactly the way you do it."

Remington let his daughter take her jacket off while the sun was high. Bea sat on the edge of the swing and walked backwards in tiny steps with the board under her bum. She held onto the metal chains just like her father. But when she let go, like he did, her swing slowed to a stop after going back and forth only a few times.

Her father was swinging high, telling her to try it again. She did. But it was no use. She couldn't make the swing keep going.

Remington dragged his feet on the ground and came to a stop. "Here honey bee, watch how I do it. Kick your feet out straight when you're going forward and then tuck them under the swing when you go back. Like this. You see? Feet out, tucked under … feet out, tucked under. Okay, you try it."

Beatrice took tiny steps, sitting on the edge of the seat. She let go and went forward, kicking both legs out. She tucked them under on the way back and kicked them out when she went forward. The swing went back and forth more times than before but it still kept slowing down no matter what. Bea put her head down and tried not to cry. It wasn't working. Her daddy couldn't teach her it. She was sad for both of them.

Rem slowed to a stop. "Try it one more time, Bea. This time, when you kick your legs out, lean back with your arms out straight, holding the chains tight. Okay?"

"Okay, daddy. I'll try it again."

Bea kicked with all her strength. Her arms could barely hold on when she leaned back. Her daddy yelled encouragement and instructions. She got confused. Once, she forgot to tuck her legs under. The swing slowed. She kicked and strained her arms. But the swing slowed down. When it stopped, Bea wrapped her arms around the chains, dropped her head into her hands, and cried.

Remington dragged his feet and came to a stop. He pulled his daughter from the swing and held her tight. "There there, Bea. It's all right. You'll be doing it just like the big kids real soon, I promise. It takes practice, that's all. You'll see."

"I don't want to practice anymore," Bea whimpered. "Look, daddy." She held her hands open in front of his face. "My hands hurt from the chains." She looked at them herself. They were red. The sight of them made her cry again. Her daddy hugged her but it didn't make them feel better until at least a minute.

"Let's put your jacket on now, honey bee." He squatted down and helped her. "Would you like to teeter-totter now?"

"No, daddy."

He stood up. "Do you want to walk back home already?"

"No."

"Do you want to hike up to the fort?"

"Not really. We can do that a different time."

Remington squatted down again, eye level with her. "What do you want to do?"

"Can we walk on a path for a while and find a place to lie down on the grass? We could look up at the sky and talk about stuff."

"The ground might be cold. But sure. Sounds like fun to me."

Rem and Bea clasped hands and walked along a path at a leisurely pace. They strolled past families enjoying picnics. Bea found a spot she liked and they sat on the ground side by side, still holding hands.

"Do you love mommy, daddy?"

"Of course."

"Does she love you?"

"I hope so."

"Does it bother you when she gets angry?"

"Sometimes."

"It seems like it happens a lot."

"Does that bother you, Bea?"

"I think so."

"I'm sorry. It's mostly my fault."

"I know. Mommy only gets mad if she has a reason, even with me."

"That's true. Why do you think your mother gets upset with me?"

"I don't know."

"You don't?"

"Well, maybe it's because of your hobby?"

"Bird watching?"

"I think so."

"You're a smart little girl, Beatrice Swilling. There's no hiding anything from you is there?"

Bea smiled. "Nope." She stretched out on the grass and looked up at the sky. "I heard mommy call it a hobby when she was talking to Wynona. Mommy said you pay too much attention to your cock. Is that true, daddy?"

Remington could not hold back a chuckle. "You could say that."

"Does your hobby cost a lot of money?"

"You could say that. But I don't mean for it to."

"Can you stop bird watching someday, if it makes mommy so angry?"

"I'd like to think it's something I could stop doing someday."

"When, daddy?"

"I don't know. When I've had enough of it, I suppose. I wish it didn't bother you so much."

"I doesn't bother me, daddy. It bothers mommy. And it bothers me that it bothers her."

"Wow, you really are a precocious little lady. Sensitive too."

"I don't know those words, daddy."

Remington gave her a big kiss on the cheek. "It's getting late, honey bee. We should be going home now. We don't want to give your mother something else to be angry about do we?"

"Wait, daddy." Bea sat up. "Will you make your eyes dance for me first?"

Remington sat up and put his face close to hers. "Ready?"

Beatrice giggled and clapped her hands. *"Yes."*

Rem opened his eyes wide as saucers and his eyes began to jiggle. Up and down, side to side, and in jagged little circles they danced for almost two minutes. Bea laughed, her own eyes wide with delight. She loved it when her dad did that. When his eyes stopped dancing they looked at her with sparkling smiles inside. Something warm settled in her belly. She smiled back at him. Then she threw herself into his arms. Remington hugged her tight, his soft voice warm inside her ear. "I love you, my little honey bee."

Twelve

Two hours before lunch break Monday morning, a laborer from the Washington County unemployment office arrived at the horse barn.

Fritz saw the man park his Ford Falcon near the other vehicles at the top of hill. He yelled to Pierre. "Is that guy joining the crew?"

Pierre saw a man saunter down the hill wearing the kind of dark green pants and shirt favored by workers on road construction. "Looks like it."

Fritz shouted to the others. "You know what that means boys."

The crew stopped working and gathered near a stack of boards at the perceived entrance to the barn.

"What's going on?" Pierre asked.

"You'll see," Fritz said, walking toward the new hire.

"You the foreman?" the man asked.

"We all are," Fritz said, sweeping an arm behind him at the gathering work crew. "The only one who isn't is this guy. His name's Pierre. He's the only carpenter on the job."

Pierre extended his hand. "I'm Pierre Toussenant. I work for Rudy Appling. And you are?"

The man shook the Frenchman's hand. "I'm Willie Roaf. Pleased to meet you."

"Do you happen to know anything about carpentry?" Pierre asked.

"Not really. I was working the Interstate, driving dump. The company I was with lost the bid for the next section and I got laid off. The new company already had enough dump truck drivers. I've been drawing unemployment ever since."

"Here's a nail bag," Pierre said, handing the man a cloth pouch to tie around his waist. "Nails are in that wooden box. Pick yourself out a hammer from the tool box next to it."

"Hold on a minute," Jericho said. "Willie ain't been properly sanctioned for this crew. Step right over here next to this stack of boards, Mister Loaf."

"*Roaf.* The name's Roaf."

Jericho beckoned to Walter. "Get that scrawny ass of yours up on those boards and do it dirty for the man."

Walter climbed onto a stack of two-by-sixes. Weepy took a moment to tune his guitar, then lit into Hendrix's *Foxy Lady*. From his invisible *Go-Go* box five feet off the ground, the albino moved his hips seductively.

Willie looked at Pierre, perplexed. "What's this all about?"

Jericho yelled at Willie over Weepy's singing. "It's a welcome rite. You're being initiated, Loafer. Enjoy it while it lasts."

Willie looked up at the skinny man with the white hair and pink eyes whose hips gyrated in wide circles. Remington slapped a drumbeat on the boards. Gulliver's low voice provided the bass. Weepy sang. Walter spread his feet, bent his knees, and thrust his hips back and forth in exaggerated vulgarity. Weepy turned up his amp, his guitar licks becoming deafening.

Pierre looked down at the ground and shook his head in disbelief.

Willie considered hightailing it out of there. It was the strangest spectacle he had ever seen.

His perspective of the job did not improve after the grotesque exhibition. No sooner had the creamsicle man climbed down from the pile of boards when Fritz began bossing Willie around. Jericho and Remington barked orders at him too. Pierre knew he should say something. At the moment, however, he was at a loss for words.

"Bring over a dozen of those two-by-fours; we'll need them to start strapping in the far corner," said Fritz.

"I hope you're good with a hand saw," said Jericho. "These rough cuts look to be an inch or so too long and we ain't got the generator here yet for the skill saw."

"We've been lugging lumber all over this place for a whole week," Rem chimed in. "Now it's you're turn, Gopher."

"I keep telling you people my name is Roaf. It ain't Loafer or Gopher or anything else. It's Roaf. It's been Roaf for forty-two years. Willie ... *goddamn* ... Roaf, goddamnit."

"The names we got for you are better," Jericho said. "Let's get those two-by-fours over here like the man said. You ain't none too speedy, by the looks of it. Maybe you're too old for this kind of work."

Willie dropped the boards he was carrying and strode over to Pierre. "Why are these characters calling the shots? Near as I can tell this job's got too many chiefs and not enough Indians. Who's the actual foreman around here anyhow?"

"I am," Pierre said.

"Okay then, tell these young whippersnappers I ain't takin' no more of their crap."

"Oh Pee-ehhhr," Jericho called out. "Tell Roaf he can pinch a loaf, but he can't be standing around shootin' the shit. We're running behind schedule as it is."

Pierre looked at Willie, then at Jericho, then back at Roaf, speechless.

"Is he talking to you?" Willie asked the foreman.

"Sounds like it," Pierre said.

"Well doesn't that just about take all?" Willie said, untying his nail pouch and tossing it to the ground. His hammer landed next to it. "I ain't never been on a job where the workers tell the foreman what to do. And I ain't stayin' on one neither."

Willie stomped off toward the hill.

"Where the hell do you think you're going?" Fritz yelled.

Willie ignored him.

Jericho drew his pistol and hollered after him. "Get your ass over here with those two-by-fours, Oaf."

"Come on back," Rem shouted. "We'll have 'ol pink-eye do another dance for you."

Willie got in his Falcon and drove off.

The crew exploded in heartless laughter.

Pierre sat on the tool box and buried his head in his hands, talking to himself. Didn't the men agree to treat new hires with courtesy and respect? These guys are even crazier than Rudy thinks. This project is turning into a disaster.

"Are you taking another break, Frenchman?" Jericho yelled to him.

Pierre did not look up, his mind racing, muttering to himself. Okay, I'll hit the books harder. I'll get my Masters. I'll get a teaching certificate. I'll leave construction for the relative calm of a classroom.

A collective moan filled the inside of the Buick when lunch break started.

"What the fuck is that horrid smell?" Rem asked Walter.

"Kipper snacks."

Fritz was annoyed. "I just watched this skeletal freak roll back the cover on a tin can with a pretend key. I'll be damned if it isn't crammed with greasy fish."

"Kipper snacks are good for you," Walter said, forking a bite of his salty delight into his gaping maw.

"They smell like raw sewage," Fritz said.

Walter stabbed another chunk of smoked herring with a plastic fork and held it up to his friend's face. "Once you get past the smell, it tastes pretty good."

Fritz turned his head, sneering in disgust.

Walter offered the bite to Remington.

"Let me put it this way," Rem said, "I'd sooner stretch my bag over an anvil and beg some deranged smithy to jab a red hot poker directly into my throbbing testes than allow one slimy morsel of that overgrown minnow to so much as touch the end of my tongue."

Walter was bemused. "*Jeepers*, I think these little babies are fabulous. They're packed in olive oil. You guys don't know what you're missing. They go great with saltines, which I happen to have right here in my lunch bucket." Walter laid a slab of cured fish on a cracker and shoved it into his mouth, a flurry of crumbs falling onto his shirt while he chewed.

Fritz stared at him with eyes vacillating between hatred and pity. "You're the most pathetic person on the planet. Sometimes I think you do these things on purpose, just to see how far we'll let you go before we give Jericho the go-ahead to blow your worthless brains out."

Walter opened his thermos and poured piping hot tomato soup into the top, which served as a cup. He blew wrinkles across the surface to cool it down and braved a sip. Fritz, Rem, Gully, the Box, Weepy, and Grumpy stared at him in anticipation of a direct response. It was slow in coming. The pallid one rummaged in his lunch pail for another cracker, carefully placing it on his knee. He forked out a kipper snack and laid it on the cracker. He placed a second saltine on top of the fish to make a small sandwich. He shoveled it into his mouth. Flakes of cracker fluttered from the sides of his mouth. He raised the red plastic cup to his lips and sipped his soup with bubbly slurps. He glanced around at his friends, chewing and slurping. All eyes were on him. He paused between gulps. "This steaming thermos is brimming with health-giving nutrients. It's the perfect compliment to the high quality protein provided by this particular cold water fish, to say nothing of the important glycerol esters intrinsic to extra virgin olive oil." Walter took another gulp and smacked his lips, his tongue making a wide arc to catch a tumble of crumbs. "May I suggest you redirect your attention to your own lunches? I don't mind sharing a few kipper snacks, but you're not about to get any of this soup."

Fritz opened his door. "That does it. I'm eating my lunch in Jericho's truck." Before he slammed the door, "I don't know what makes me sicker, smelling putrid fish or listening to this cream puff preach about his sacred soup."

Jericho, surprisingly, let Fritz get into the cab.

"What's the problem this time?"

"Birdsong."

"Egg salad?"

"A can of fish."

"Sardines?"

"Bigger. They stink even worse."

Jericho laughed. "The bird man will eat anything."

"His diet is corrosive." Fritz eyed Jericho's black lunch pail. "What'd Deirdre make for you?"

"Meatloaf sandwich. That's what I always get. I love a meatloaf sandwich. What do you have?"

"Cucumber sandwich. And a peach."

"Don't tell me you're turning into a vegetarian."

"Thinking about it."

"You don't mean it."

"Matter of fact I do. I realize humans are omnivores. And I can savor a juicy tenderloin as much as the next guy. But the meat in this country is tainted."

"What makes you think?"

"I read an article that said the beef in feedlots out in the Midwest is shot up with growth hormones. Eleven year old girls are getting tits because of it."

"What a shame."

"Not only that, they put cement in the feed."

"Why would they do that?"

"Makes the steers weigh more. They get paid by the pound don't forget."

Jericho took a shark's bite out of his inch-thick sandwich. "You believe that shit?"

"Bet your ass I do." Fritz crunched his cucumber sandwich, nodding his head with conviction. "It was an investigative report; an exposé." A large drop of mayonnaise plopped onto the seat.

"*Be careful*, you sloppy bastard," Jericho said. "Are you talking actual cement, like we used for the footings?"

"That's what the article said."

"Hard to believe."

"Food and Drug Administration can't do a thing about it."

"Why not?"

"Cement isn't classified as food."

"I don't taste cement in this meatloaf."

"Maybe the hamburger Deirdre buys isn't from the Midwest. You wouldn't know it anyway; there's probably no taste to cement."

"If there is, I like it."

"They're killing us, you know."

"Who's killing us?"

"The food industry."

"Be pretty stupid of them, wouldn't it? How would we buy their food if we're all dead?"

"I'm telling you that's what it's coming to. The ultimate benefactor is the government sanctioned drug cartel. *Poisons*, Jericho. It's all about poisons."

"What kind of poisons?"

"Pesticides. Dyes. Preservatives. Processing methods that leech nutrients and replace them with all sorts of chemicals our bodies don't recognize and can't begin to tolerate. All to ensure a bigger crop, a more marketable appearance, longer shelf life."

"You sound like Walter. He's a food freak too."

"His information is suspect."

"It might be something he can write about."

"Forget about Walter becoming a journalist. He's too plethoric."

"What the hell does that mean?"

"Effusive, loquacious, given to grandiloquent blather."

"There it is."

"Take *Cheerios*."

"I always thought *Cheerios* were good for you; no sugar, like you get with *Coco-Puffs* or *Trix*."

"Think about what an oat has to go through to end up in a toasted circle."

"They stay crunchy in milk for a long time though."

"I'm telling you, Jericho, something has to be done to stop the food industry. And the pharmaceutical industry too. They're in cahoots. It's all a plot. First they make us obese and disease-ridden. Then the drug companies will fill us full of pills so they can stuff their pockets with big fat profits."

"*Be big for me.* Say it, Fritz."

"I don't want to say it."

"What kind of pills?"

"All kinds. They'll cause more problems than they stop, mark my words."

"You're dripping peach juice all over my seat."

"Sorry."

Jericho put his empty sandwich baggy in his lunch bucket. "Time to get back to work."

Fritz put his peach pit in the ash tray.

"Not in there," Jericho told him.

"Why not?"

"Because I like a clean ash tray. Throw that thing outside somewhere."

Fritz tossed the pit out the window. "Okay, let's go."

"Hold up a sec." Jericho reached under his seat. "Check this out. It's my new Colt .45. She's a beauty, ain't she?"

"Is it loaded?"

"Of course it's loaded. What good's a gun if it ain't loaded?"

"Was your gun loaded the other day when you pointed it at Roaf and pulled the hammer back?"

Jericho stuck the gun down the front of his pants. "Absolutely."

"You aren't worried about that thing going off accidentally? You could shoot your dink off."

"It's a risk you have to take if you're going to carry a loaded gun. Let's get down there."

"Hold up a minute. Did I ever tell you about *my* gun?"

"You've got a gun with you?"

"Not with me. It's a rifle."

"A hunting rifle?"

"Not in the traditional sense. But I could take out a herd of deer with it. In a matter of seconds."

"What the hell is it, a machine gun?"

"Close. It's an automatic rifle."

"Can't be. They ain't legal."

"You think I give a shit about the fucking law?"

"How the hell'd you get an automatic rifle?"

"I smuggled it out of Camp Pendleton."

"An M14? Is that what we're talking?"

Fritz chuckled. "Not a soul knows about it. Don't you say one word."

"I won't say shit. But I want to know how you got that weapon off a military base."

"We had a situation one time where half the guys in our company got food poisoning. Must have been something in the jelly they pack with the beef in those huge cans. I refused to eat it and I never got sick, so I figure the toxin was in the jelly."

"All I asked was how you smuggled out the rifle."

"Don't be so impatient."

"Deirdre says I've got a hair trigger."

"Referring to what, your temper or your performance?"

"Good question. Continue the story."

"The mass poisoning happened just before bivouac. All three of the supply guys were puking their guts out. That's when I volunteered to hand out gear, including rifles."

"Now you're talking."

"Everybody gets assigned their own rifle. At least twenty men were too sick to go out. I took two weapons; my own and a rifle that I broke down and hid in my gear. It belonged to some guy from Jersey City who hadn't been to Nam yet."

"I'm listening."

"I spread the parts around in three different trucks; behind the seats, under canvas. After bivouac, it was a matter of recovering the pieces and scuttling between the motor pool, the supply building, the barracks, and out to my car. It took me a while, but I got away with it."

"The rifle never showed up missing?"

"Sure it did, after the supply guys went back to work and took inventory."

"And the guy whose gun was missing; anything happen to him?"

"Poor bastard got a summary court martial. But the charges didn't stick because he was one of the guys who stayed back sick. He'd never signed for his rifle. Of course, hardly anybody did since I was the one who unlocked the racks and handed out the pieces."

"Nobody suspected you?"

"I was under some scrutiny. I told the brass that I thought signing up for rifles was voluntary. When they weren't too thrilled with that response I suggested the missing rifle was probably still out where we did our maneuvers, that the best thing for them to do was ask for volunteers to go back out and look for it."

"I'm surprised you didn't get promoted. What if they'd searched your car?"

"It wouldn't have been there."

"What'd you do with it?"

"I used to go to this fast food place; something like an A&W except they couldn't make a root beer float to save their ass. That's were I met this girl. She was a car hop."

"You're getting away from the story."

"Hold your horses, for chrissakes. This is where it gets good."

"Go ahead."

"This little lady wasn't the cutest thing you ever laid eyes on but she had great legs; wore a black leather micro-skirt. I used to go over to her house when she was off and her parents were gone."

"And you're accusing Walter of being verbose?"

"I'm giving you the complete story so you'll appreciate it all the more."

"I'll appreciate it when I get to shoot that M14. All this background bullshit doesn't mean anything to me."

"Anyway, one night at her place, every time she went to the bathroom I'd go out for a few parts and stick them up between the slats under the box spring on her bed. Keep in mind I did this when I only had a few weeks left before my hitch was up."

Jericho opened his door to get out of the truck. "Let's start walking down. You can tell me the rest on the way. That ought to make it go quicker."

Fritz stepped out of the truck. "After I had my walking papers I got a motel room and hung around for a few days till her folks went out the same night she wasn't hopping. I put the beer right to her. Pretty soon she was getting up to take a piss every fifteen minutes. That's when I'd run into her bedroom, grab a couple of parts and run them out to my car. Once I had them all crammed under the spare tire in my trunk, I was out of there."

Jericho stopped twenty feet short of the work area. "Did you give her one last plug before you split?"

"I'd already taken care of that back in the motel room. Several times. That was the tricky part."

"What's so tricky about that? You yank her panties down and ..."

"There you go with the impatience thing again."

"Go ahead and explain it then. Half the afternoon's shot anyway, all because I was dumb enough to let you get in my truck. See if that ever happens again."

"You don't like this story?"

"Is it true?"

"Yes."

"Swear it?"

"I swear."

"Let's see how it ends."

"After a couple of torrid sessions at that clap trap I was staying in, she didn't see any reason for me to come to her house. She even put up a bit of a protest; said she was too sore. I had to pretend I wanted to spend a little more time with her before I had to get on the road to Vermont."

"Aren't you one soave sonuvabitch! And now you're telling me you've got this army rifle in your apartment."

"I didn't say where it is. And look, it's not an army rifle; it's a Marine rifle.

"I guess all you jarheads let the army borrow a few of them."

"Something like that."

"Sure as shit you've got an automatic M14 hidden away somewhere?"

Fritz tied his nail bag behind his back, smiling like a kid who's got enough Halloween candy to last through November. "You bet your ass I do."

"*Bullets.* What about bullets?"

"I stole six ammo clips too."

"Loaded?"

"Empty."

"What the hell good's a gun if you ain't got bullets for it?"

"It isn't. I need bullets. Lots of them."

"An M14 takes .308 rounds."

Fritz's jaw dropped. "It does?"

"Sure as shootin'."

"Can you get me some?"

"Matter of fact I've got about twenty boxes tucked away in my garage."

"I need all of them."

"Sounds like you're planning to do some serious firing."

Fritz stared at Jericho with steel gray eyes and an ominous grin. "What good's an automatic rifle if you don't intend to use it?"

Thirteen

Midway through the second week, more than half of the posts had been set. Four feet on center, 50 posts were required for each lengthwise side. Each width required 20 posts, leaving room for large doors front and back.

The dimensions of the building were 200 feet by 100 hundred feet. Each post was 32 feet long, eight feet sunk in cement and 24 feet to the roof's edge lines. When the trusses were installed, the peak of the roof would be 40 feet. Plans called for a cupola at the center of the roof. The topping off ceremony would occur when a stately weathervane could be affixed to the cupola, a rooster perched on an east-west arrow and a horse, under the cock, pointing north-south.

With a perimeter of 20,000 square feet and 480,000 cubic feet inside, the horse barn would indeed be a massive structure. It would feature 36 box stalls ten-feet squared, a large tack room, a bathroom, and plenty of space for mounted set tubs and an assortment of hooks for equine accoutrement.

The posts were supported, at this stage, by rough-cut pine boards nailed part way up the posts. The bracing boards were anchored to stakes sledge hammered deep into the ground. The horse barn was beginning to resemble a structure that, with imaginative license, looked like it could actually become a horse barn.

But there was a problem. Only 80 of the 140 beams were in place. The math didn't work. Nearly 75 percent of the time allotted for setting the posts had elapsed, but less than 60 percent of the posts were up. Given the present crew, erecting the remaining posts by the end of the workday Saturday appeared to be an impossible task.

It didn't help that one of Pierre's uncommon laborers did no work whatsoever; he just sat in a folding chair picking his guitar and singing songs while smoking an unconscionable amount of pot. If that wasn't discouraging enough, another worker, as frail as a severe arthritic with late-stage Parkinson's disease, trudged around complaining about the thick mud caused by Monday's heavy rain. Meanwhile, the guitar player and the albino argued incessantly about whether or not it was hypocritical of Christians at odds with Jews still looking for their savior to idolize the most famous Jew in history. Listening to their inflammatory religious diatribes was unbearable enough without having to contend with their combined drag on productivity.

The past Sunday, faced with an obvious dilemma created by a shortage of men, Pierre had called Rudy for help. Pierre held the phone six inches from his ear while Rudy vented his anger over the fact that none of the three new hires from the unemployment office had lasted more than a day on the job. The general contractor said each of them had stopped by his office to allege that they had been ridiculed, intimidated, and threatened by the horse barn crew; allegations Pierre understood only too well. By the end of the one-sided conversation, however, Rudy pledged to redouble his recruiting efforts. Further, he promised that his superintendent, Richard Welter, would lend a hand despite his right-hand man having to put in long hours at the office when he wasn't traveling back and forth between three new homes under construction in Williamstown, Adamant, and Northfield. And yet, here it was the middle of the week and not only had no fresh laborers arrived, but Welter hadn't shown up either. Rather than eat his lunch at the site, Pierre wolfed it down driving to the nearest phone. He had to get in touch with either Rudy or Welter in the hope that one of them would be able to rectify the situation.

The crew erected seven more posts in the afternoon despite being severely impeded by the muddy turf. Pierre, unable to get in touch with either of his superiors, was pleased with the progress. He had hoped that two or three more posts would go up; seven was a remarkable feat.

At the end of the day, aware of Pierre's surprise, Jericho pulled him aside. "History tells us the *dog soldiers* were known for their noisy songs and effusive dances. Dog men, wolf men, crazy dogs; by any name they were awesome warriors, defiant and proud. These men are no different. Like I told Rudy, they can bull and jam like nobody's business."

Pierre climbed into his beetle and stared through his windshield with the distant and slightly twisted expression of a stroke victim, scratching the stubble on his cheeks and listening to his mind echoing Jericho's mysterious remark. His confused musing was interrupted by the Buick tearing off down the road, its riders hooting and hollering like a band of Indians on the warpath.

Taking a route home through East Montpelier, Grumpy's throaty Invicta pulled up at a general store for supplies of beer, candy bars, and a variety of packaged snacks.

But there was a problem. Jericho's dog soldiers had gone so long without a paycheck that the first week's wages had already been eaten up, pissed away, or otherwise flushed through northern Vermont's microeconomic system. The only one with money on him was Box Car, who not only declined to disclose the extent of his largesse but squarely refused to contribute any more than the sum total that everyone else could put toward the collective purchase, which was less than two dollars.

"I've got an idea," Remington said. The comment halted the berating and shoving behind a tall rack of potato chips, popcorn, and cheese twists. "Pick out your stuff and follow me," said Rem.

Minutes later, more than thirty dollars worth of merchandise was piled onto the counter. The aged proprietor, a bespectacled curmudgeon in a yellow and green John Deere cap, vaguely remembered a rowdy construction crew having been in his store a couple of times recently. He had to wonder if this wasn't the same group.

"How good are you at guessing ages?" Rem asked him.

"As good as I need to be," the man said, his voice testy.

Rem gave the man a wily glare. "Tell you what, old fella…"

"*Old fella?* Is that what you're calling me?"

"Okay then, young fella," Rem said, his voice demurring. "Most long-time Vermonters, even if they're young like yourself, are pretty gosh darned perceptive when it comes to judging people; you know, their character, their gender, and especially their age. You might claim to be one of them but I'll bet you're not half as good as you think you are when it comes to guessing a man's age with the kind of accuracy true Vermonters are noted for."

The old man slid a pile of beef jerky toward the cash register and rang it up. "Try me," he said.

"All righty then," Rem said, his combative smile filled with mirth, "how old do you think I am?"

The store owner answered without looking up. "27, I'd say. 28, maybe; give or take."

"Give or take what?"

"Give or take two years on either side."

Rem took out his driver's license. "Well lookie there! Hard to believe. Looks like you got me on that one, young fella." Rem held his license in front of the man's thick glasses. "Take a gander; I'll be gosh darned if I didn't turn 28 just last month."

The storeowner glanced at the license, snorting with disdain. He inspected another item and punched a few keys on the register. "Told you."

"Mighty impressive," Rem said. He put his arm around Grumpy's shoulders. "Too bad for you we didn't lay an honest bet down on it. But I'll wager a tidy sum you can't guess this old fella's age anywhere close."

The elderly proprietor paused, his hand resting on a devil dog. He adjusted his glasses and leaned over the counter to study the Grump.

"You're squishing my devil dog," Weepy complained. "I hate it when it gets squished; I can't hold it out straight and lick the cream from around the edges."

Gulliver tapped Weepy on the shoulder. "If that's what you enjoy, I've got a devil dog you'd appreciate a lot more than that one."

Weepy feigned a punch at Gully's midsection.

"Quit horsing around in my store," the old man shouted, removing his hand from the devil dog. He looked again at Remington. "Give or take how many years?"

"Now hold on a minute," Rem said.

"For what?" the storekeeper asked.

"How much leeway you figure you have to have to make a bet?"

"Depends on the bet."

"Here's the deal then," Remington said with an air of supreme confidence. "No matter how big the bet, I'm saying you're off by more than 10 years."

The old man stepped back with a loud harrumph, obviously insulted. "Ain't no way I'm off by ten years. I already proved I'm pretty good at this sort of thing."

Rem leaned forward with cunning in his eyes. "That you did. That you did, young fella."

The old codger dragged another six-pack toward the register to ring it up. "Then again," he muttered to himself, "ten years ain't so long as it used to be."

"How much you willing to wager on guessing this man's age to within ten years, you blind old geezer," Rem said with a chuckle.

"Blind old geezer is it?"

"I'm just joshing you," Rem said. "Don't get all riled up."

The old man slapped his hand hard on the counter and shouted at Remington through a raspy rattle. *"You need to learn to talk to me proper."* Spittle oozed from the corners of his mouth.

"Calm down now," Rem said. "Fifty bucks says you can't guess this man's age even if you get ten years to play with on either side. How's that for proper? If you do the math, you'll see I'm giving you twenty years total leeway. How you gonna turn down those odds?"

"I ain't a bettin' man to begin with, but fifty dollars … *whoa* … that's too rich for my blood.

"How much will it be then?" Rem asked. "Remember now, you guessed my age right on the money."

"I'm thinking about it."

"Tell you what. Make it fifty and I'll give you *fifteen years* to play with."

The crotchety storekeeper pursed his lips and leaned over the counter to corral an assortment of merchandise. He carefully inspected two bags of big-stick pretzels, a bag of pork rinds, a *Three Musketeers* bar, a *Zero* bar, and a *Payday*, pausing after ringing up each item to study the Grump. "Ten years is plenty leeway," he finally said.

"Fifty it is then," Rem said.

"I told you I ain't about to bet a sum like that. Cut it in half and I'll have a go at it."

Rem was tough. "Come on now. Go at least thirty. That's chicken feed for a successful store owner like you."

"Put your money on the counter and thirty it is," the man said, his voice rattling loudly.

Rem looked at Box Car with a hound dog's wordless beg.

Box pulled out his wallet, yanked out a twenty and a ten, and tossed them onto the counter.

The old man stared at the bills. "That ain't the money you was going to use to pay for all this stuff is it?"

"Of course not," Rem said. "You know good and well we've been in here twice before. Did you have to chase us for our money either time? No sir. You're looking at a group of working men here. Proud working men, that's what we are. The way I see it, talking proper is a two-way proposition."

The cagey proprietor took his time ringing up the last few items. He ignored Rem's prattle, studying the Grump long and hard. The irascible scar-face moved his head from side to side, staring at the old man with indifference in one eye and intimidation in the other.

"You got ID on you?" the man asked.

"Vermont driver's license," Grumpy said, the chipped marbles in his voice not unlike his counterpart's.

The old codger's eyes went again to Remington. "Ten years? You're giving me ten years?"

"That's right," Rem said. "Take your time. This may not be as easy as you think."

The store owner pursed his lips, splayed his hands on the counter, drummed his fingers, and took long breaths through his spider-veined nose, surveying the topography of Grumpy's face. "I know for sure this man's a helluva lot older than the rest of you fellas; might even be the father of one of you."

"Ah yes, but how much older?" Rem asked, quiet provocation in his voice. "Or for that matter, how much younger? Take your sweet time about it. Workday's over for us. We got no place to be."

Almost a minute went by. "Alrighty then, I'd say I got my mind made up," the shopkeeper finally said. "This here fella is forty-five years old, give or take a year or two at the outside."

The crew erupted in laughter.

Box reached out for the money but the storekeeper slapped a hand over the bills first. "You boys can laugh all you want," he said with nervous resolve, "but I ain't seen no proof I'm wrong; not by no ten years."

Grumpy handed him his driver's license.

The old man brought it close to his eyes.

"I'm nineteen years old," Grumpy said. "Give the man his money, old-timer."

"You just hold on right there, all of you," the storekeeper said sternly. "I get fake drivers licenses in here all the time, mostly young whippersnappers trying to buy beer. How do I know this one ain't fake? You look like the kind of boys who'd pull the wool over the eyes of a decent fella like me, given half a chance."

Rem looked at the Grump. "You got any other ID?"

Grumpy searched his wallet and pulled out a folded paper. "Birth certificate good enough?" he asked, unfolding the paper and handing it to the store owner.

The baffled proprietor took his time looking it over. He compared it to Grumpy's driver's license. Another moment passed and he handed both documents back to the Grump, shaking his head in defeat. "I'll be darned if you ain't the oldest looking teenager I ever seen." Then he looked at Rem. "I have to admit I lost the bet, fair and square."

"I was worried though," Rem said. "Ten years is more than half this man's actual age. That's a lot of leeway to give somebody on a bet this big. I don't usually do that."

The old man finished bagging the beer and snacks and checked the tally. "It comes to thirty-two dollars and three cents. Give me two bucks and I'll call it even."

Rem looked around at the group. "Anybody got two dollars?"

Box Car snatched a twenty from the counter, leaving the other bill. "Use the ten."

The old man hit a key that opened the cash drawer. He deposited the money and handed Box a five and three ones. Shoving four large paper bags across the counter he asked his victor, "How old would you guess me to be?"

"Somewhere between sixty-eight and seventy-two," Rem said.

"I wish t'heck we'd made another bet," the man said. "I'm every year of eighty-seven."

"That's good to know," Rem said. "Next time in here, we can do this all over again."

"How's that?" the man asked.

"Never mind," Rem said. "We'll see you in a couple of weeks."

Aware that everyone was penniless except for Box, there being scant chance the *Missing Link* would pony up for beer for the long ride home, Fritz never bothered going into the store. He was surprised, therefore, to see the men carrying large grocery bags out to the Buick.

Never one to glorify the success of others, the eldest Swilling said nothing when the crew piled into the car. Grumpy was so excited about the virtual heist he laid down twenty feet of rubber yanking the blue bomber out onto the road.

Remington, perched triumphantly between the Bork boys, opened a beer and handed it to the Grump. He popped two more and turned around to pass one of them to Fritz. "Got some suds for you, big brother."

Fritz grabbed the cold can, his curiosity finally getting the best of him. "How'd you get Box to fork over the cabbage for all this beer?"

"He coughed up two bucks, which is a good bit less than his share of the take. I came up with the other thirty."

"I thought you were broke."

"I am. I got the storeowner to bite on Grumpy's age. I could've allowed the old fart twenty years leeway instead of ten. *Mister Man*, the 'ol Grump here is a fucking gold mine. I don't take advantage of him near as often as I should."

Fritz tipped his head back and quaffed his brew. "*Budweiser.* It's always Bud with you."

"It's my favorite beer," Rem said. "You know that."

"You have no idea what your favorite beer is."

"I don't?"

"That's right. You don't."

"I don't mean to be redundant but would you mind explaining to me how it is I don't know how it is Budweiser's my favorite beer?"

"Simple. Guys like you are victims of compulsion-oriented advertising."

"*Guys like me*?"

"That's right; guys who can't think for themselves, guys whose buying habits are determined by Madison Avenue ad agencies, guys who'd eat shit if some tanned bimbo with D-cups said she goes hog wild over guys who eat shit."

Rem glanced at Walter. "Nothing dangerous there, I suppose."

"That *is* the danger," Fritz said. "It's a form of mass hypnosis. The real reason you drink Bud is because Anhauser Busch has a trillion dollar advertising budget."

"That's a lot of money," Box said.

"I'm not sure of the exact number," said Fritz.

"But you figure it's somewhere near a trillion," Box said.

"In the neighborhood, Box; trust me, it's in the neighborhood."

"I'll admit they've got some entertaining ads," Rem said. "But I'm here to tell you I wouldn't drink their beer if it tasted like skunk piss, no matter what the ads say."

"I happen to believe you would," Fritz said. "That's the power of advertising. It can turn ordinary people into compulsive robotic purchasing machines. Something needs to be done about the wholesale exploitation of the mindless bourgeoisie at the retail level."

"What the hell's got you all riled up?" Rem wanted to know. "I go into a store without a dime to my name and come out with a shit load of beer for all of us, including you, and this is the thanks I get for pulling off a perfectly outrageous flimflam?"

"I didn't say you aren't to be congratulated for your canny ability to bamboozle an old man out of his merchandise. I'm merely pointing out that you're one among tens of millions of numbskulls in this country whose behavioral patterns are molded by the unscrupulous tactics of the food and beverage industry."

Rem glanced at Weepy. "Only Fritz can kiss you on the cheek at the same time he's twisting a dagger in your liver."

"It's an observation, Rem. Don't take it personally. You're no different than the rest of the imbeciles out there who think they're making informed decisions when what they're really doing is being blindly obedient to the contemptible consumption deities."

"And you're not?" Rem asked.

"That's right. The purchasing decisions I make are independent of any diabolical influences that attempt to control my behavior. Unlike you, I'm aware of and therefore wary of their diabolical mind games. And I'm not playing."

"Whose mind games?"

"The collusive food and beverage cartel, you fucking idiot. You're just like Walter, never paying attention. The lords of the junk food frenzy and the fast food craze are killing people with their lard-laden, sugar-coated poisons. They're destroying humanity with chemical cocktails engineered to increase shelf life. They're undermining our health with phony fats, aluminum containers, artificial flavors, and a veritable rainbow of toxic dyes."

"That's quite an indictment," Rem said.

"Case in point." Fritz said, "Take a look at Weepy back here chomping on his cheese curls. *What the hell are those things?* He's digging his grubby paws into a brightly colored package of puffed up pellets sprayed with orange cheese dust. Read the ingredients, O'Toole. I'll bet even a super literate like you can't pronounce half the words in the list. I'm telling you it's all a deceptive ploy to push profits, boost stock prices, and reward shareholders – primarily the lords themselves – with big fat quarterly dividends."

"Are you listening to this man?" Rem asked the crew.

"I'm trying not to," Weepy said.

Walter sipped a root beer, put the bottle between his legs, and opened a bag of pork rinds. A rush of gasses evocative of flatulence hit Fritz in the face.

"Goddamn it, Birdsong, a herd of sheep cutting farts at the same time couldn't possibly smell that foul. It's hideous the things you'll eat."

"Allow me to remind you yet again, Fritzie; once you get past the smell, it's pretty good eating."

"I might have expected you to be different, Walter. You're always prattling on about the importance of eating nutritious foods and yet you stuff your mouth with crackled pig skin. It's nonsensical, incongruent, hypocritical."

"It's a challenge."

"It's a challenge all right, for your beleaguered digestive system."

"The challenge I refer to is swallowing. You can chew pork rinds as long as you please but you can't swallow without washing them down with something to drink. It's impossible." Walter held the bag out to Fritz. "Try it."

Fritz slapped at the bag. "Get that shit away from me."

"The best thing to drink with pork rinds," Walter prattled on, "is root beer. Somehow, root beer is capable of taking these airy balls of skin down with it no problem. I've tried everything; orange juice, cranberry juice, even beer. But what works best, far and away, is root beer. It doesn't matter what brand, either. *Hires, Cott, A&W*; they're equally effective."

Something Walter said intrigued Gulliver. "You mean to tell me you drink cranberry juice?"

"Occasionally. It happens to be a marvelous cleanser of the urinary tract."

"Taking a page from Rem's book," Gully said, "I want to go on record as saying, without equivocation, that I'd sooner piss a chunky stream of jagged-edged kidney stones like they were coming out of a pee shooter – better yet, a bazooka – than take one tiny sip of cranberry juice."

Box Car wheeled around at Fritz. "What'd you get to wash down with your beer?"

"Nothing," Fritz said.

"It's been more than six hours since we had lunch," Box said. "Come quitting time, I could eat a fucking horse. You ain't hungry?"

"Of course I'm hungry. But I'm not Pavlov's dog."

"What the hell does that mean?" Box asked.

"Habitualized, conditioned, compromised, snookered, duped; dangling like a puppet at the end of the marketeering strings of the food giants. Case in point: what are you munching on up there? Sounds like potato chips."

"Good ear."

"Any particular brand?"

"*Wise.* I only eat *Wise* potato chips."

"Why *Wise*, Box?"

"About a third of their chips are toasted till they're dark brown, incredibly crispy. I love 'em like that. No other brand toasts their chips as long."

"I like them that way too," Weepy said. "How about a handful, Box?"

"Keep those grubby paws of yours away from my bag, O'Toole!"

"It's my belief," Fritz continued, "that you prefer *Wise* because all those potato chip trucks driving around are owned by *Wise*. That big-eyed owl gives you a sagacious wink and you're had. Almost unconsciously, you pull into the next store and go straight to the chip rack. You can't get through the day without a fistful of potato chips. And not just any potato chip. They have to be *Wise* potato chips. All it takes are a few episodes like this and you're a loyal *Wise* potato chip man for the rest of your sorry life, right up to the day all that grease has contributed mightily to your fatal heart attack."

Box had no quarrel with the scene Fritz depicted. "How much you think *Wise* spends on advertising?" he asked.

"I don't know," Fritz said. "Don't get hung up on the precise dollar amount being spent on marketing and advertising. Their effect on you; that's the critical issue."

"And I suppose none of it effects you," Rem said with biting disparagement.

"I wasn't always immune to it. But I'm a thinking man. Like I said, I don't allow my decisions to be unduly influenced by Madison Avenue; or for that matter by politicians or cult figures either."

"Cult figures?" Weepy asked.

"That's right. Marilyn Monroe, Muhammad Ali, Frank Zappa, Jesus Christ, Marlon Brando, Popeye – the list goes on."

Gulliver looked past Weepy and Walter to fix his eyes on his oldest brother. "Let me see if I understood you correctly. Your position is that Popeye is a cult figure?"

"You heard me. Think of all the kids who wouldn't eat spinach until Popeye came along. Now there's a whole generation of spinach eaters. Why? Because every time Bluto tries to diddle Olive Oil, Popeye gets a hard-on over it and out comes the spinach. His forearms get monstrous, suggesting to children that spinach will make them strong. Then he proceeds to kick the shit out of that sex-deprived oaf."

"What's the crime in that?" Rem asked.

"It's false advertising. Wouldn't surprise me if the creators of Popeye are getting kickbacks from the spinach merchants."

"But spinach is good for you," Rem said. "Your argument is loosing traction."

"He's not talking about *fresh* spinach," Walter said.

"That's the problem right there," Fritz said. "Everything would be hunky dory if the ol' sailor man's preference was for fresh spinach. But he eats it tumbling out of a tin can, probably rusted by the salty seas. Remember, Popeye was created long before aluminum cans. Spinach from a tin can is a soggy lump of spoliated dross, totally depleted of any nutritional value. So now we've got a whole generation that stuffs its collective gut with tangled lumps of worthless spinach to go with the hot dogs and potato chips they gulp down with colas or some other carbonated syrup. It's all a gigantic hoax being perpetrated on a nation of sapheads by slick compulsion-prompting propaganda bankrolled by the profiteering food giants." Fritz had worked himself into a seething lather. *"The bastards shouldn't be allowed to get away with it."*

Box Car fished around the bottom of his potato chip bag but came up empty. He tipped his head back over the top of the seat and poured the last of the salty crumbs into his mouth. He chewed and swallowed and took a swig of his fourth beer as the Buick turned onto the River Road. "When you say bankrolled, are you suggesting …?"

Grumpy hit the brakes hard, swerving to a dusty stop in a patch of noisy gravel on the side of the road and jamming the shifter into park a bit too soon, jolting his passengers half out of their seats. Without saying a word, he got out of the car, slammed the door, and walked ahead at a brisk pace.

Rem reached over and yanked the keys from the ignition to short circuit a likely brouhaha over who would take the wheel. He realized the spectacle of Grumpy stomping off was all about the man's need to straighten out his disheveled sensibilities. After a mile or so he'd come back, demand better behavior, and they'd be on their way again. While there was no shortage of dangerous men in the group, Grumpy took a back seat to none of them.

"At least he didn't hit a tree," Rem said to the others. "Let's get out and stretch our legs."

The men obliged, there being plenty of beer to wait out Grumpy's cooling off period.

Walter and Weepy sauntered over to a large flat rock and sat down together. Walter lit up a *Lucky Strike*. Weepy tapped a fresh pack of *Old Gold* straights against the rock, unraveled the cellophane string, tore away a corner of aluminum wrapping, and held the pack in one hand as he whacked it against the other until three or four sticks popped out. He snatched the one that protruded the farthest, stuck the other end of it in his mouth, flipped open his *Zippo*, torched the unfiltered cigarette, and joined his friend inside a dense cloud of carcinogens.

Box Car got out of the car to let Remington out, then climbed back in, growling like a pit bull about his brother's abrupt departure, a beer in one hand, a candy bar in the other, a bag of pretzels between his stubby legs.

Fritz and Gulliver walked up the road in the direction they'd come from, heavily engaged in a futile argument about who was the better drummer, Keith Moon or Ginger Baker.

Rem, a nonsmoker, joined Walter and Weepy, this being the least toxic among his choices.

"Think he'll write us up?" Weepy asked.

"Of course he'll write us up," Rem said. "That's what he does. It's his way of imposing order. The man's neurotic about it."

"I don't get it," Weepy said.

"At heart, the man's a heavy equipment operator. Guys like him hate to see things out of order. Think about it. They spend all day moving this pile over to that pile, scraping and flattening, leveling and smoothening, grading and feathering. Or, if they're not otherwise scooping and dumping, they're using their buckets or blades to tidy up. It's all about achieving an orderly setting. You'll notice that before any operator shuts down his machine he makes damn sure everything is perfectly balanced, that the weight is properly distributed and all the controls are set in their precise positions. Furthermore, at the end of the day, every machine takes its place in a predetermined row that couldn't be straighter if you'd snapped a line for them."

"I've never noticed," Weepy said. "Then again, I don't spend a lot of time watching heavy equipment operators in action."

"This horse barn project is difficult for the Grump. Not because he can't handle a hammer but because he's not commandeering big-ass earth moving machinery. The next best thing for him, other than wheeling his Buick around, is to bust our balls for what he perceives to be disorderly conduct."

"I don't get the connection," Weepy said.

Remington, a man of innate psychoanalytical powers, was happy to bring metaphor to his explanation. "We, you understand, are like an assortment of knobs and levers that are constantly performing the wrong function, at least in Grumpy's mind. Not being able to control our actions directly, as with a steering wheel or a foot pedal, he has to call us to task the only way he knows how, by filing phantom reports regarding our individual or collective malfunctions. If, with us, he is unable to create order out of chaos, as he does by deftly maneuvering a large machine, he can at least derive a modicum of appeasement from the simple act of documenting our outrageous behavior. By calling attention to it in some recitation, log, or critique, he's able to remove himself from the problem. You with me?"

"Strangely enough."

"In other words, powerless to exert direct control, extrication by documentation is the next best thing."

"Sounds like a mental condition to me."

"Don't be self-righteous, Mister O'Toole. We all have one."

"He must have a ream of offenses documented by now," Weepy said. "What does he intend to do with them?"

"Oh he'll identify some authority figure at long last, hand them over, and consider his duty done."

"What does that mean to us?"

"Nothing."

"Nothing?"

"That's right. Nothing. You see, in the final analysis, it's not about us or what can be done for us; it's about Grumpy's subliminal need to keep a grip, to maintain some sense of mental stability. Remember this, my sullen friend. The confused and disgruntled man values his sanity above all else, whereas mad dogs like us cling to hopeless insanity as the clearest rational value."

Fourteen

Pierre was showing the superintendent, Richard Welter, around the construction site when the crew showed up Thursday morning at eight o'clock.

"Who's that guy?" Fritz asked no one in particular as they piled out of the car.

No one had an answer.

Fritz continued speaking to no one in particular. "Those look like blueprints he's holding. He struts around like he's some kind of important bad-ass."

Jericho pulled up in his *Chevy* pickup. Fritz, able to redirect his question to someone in particular, nodded toward the horse barn, which had the appearance of a large-scale failure, a mingle of giant tinker toys and pieces of a wooden erector set. "What do you know about that highfalutin whiz banger who showed up this morning?"

Jericho looked down from the bluff at the man standing next to Pierre, who was obviously inspecting the project. "That's Richard Welter. He's Rudy's top dog."

"Get him out of here," Fritz shot at him.

"Must be you don't care for the man," Jericho fired back.

"I don't," Fritz said.

"You haven't even met him yet."

"That has nothing to do with it."

"Mind if I ask what it is about the man that's got you in such a tizzy?"

"He's putting on the dog."

"What the hell does that mean?"

"Pretentious swagger, foppish conceit, conspicuous self-obsession. He's a prissy poodle prancing in a parade of one."

"There it is."

"I want him out of here."

"He won't stay long," Jericho said, traipsing down the hill with the crew. "We're behind schedule. Welter came by to see what can be done about it. I want to suggest that Weepy keep his equipment under the tarp, though. *Oh Pee-ehhr* has kept his mouth shut about our live entertainment. But if Welter finds out about it, he'll go right to Rudy."

O'Toole grabbed Jericho by his shirt sleeve. *"You're not expecting me to work I hope."*

"You might have to act like it," Jericho told him. "Talk to Walter. He's got it down to a science."

Walter looked past the Box and Gulliver to address the gunslinger. "I take offense at that, Mister Laramie. Imagine how far behind we would be if not for my timely admonitions."

"Such as?" Jericho asked.

"How about my rather vociferous request for a *Port-a-Potty*? Think how much time we waste walking into the woods to do our business, to say nothing of the dangers involved. The last time I went I almost stepped in Remington's doo."

"How'd you know it was mine?" Rem asked.

"Because I saw you walking out of the woods no more than a minute or two before I had to go in. The pile was still steaming. I couldn't help but look, coming as close as I did."

"Given your gastronomic aberrations," Rem said, "I'm surprised you didn't mistake it for poo poo platter."

"I must say, Rem, you should consider radical dietary changes."

"Could have been those roasted peppers," Rem conceded. "I love those marinated red devils. But they don't sit well in my system, I'll admit."

"It reeked something terrible," Walter said.

"Whoa," said Weepy. "I think I've heard about as much as I care to on this subject."

"Walter's right," Fritz said. "They should get a *Port-a-Potty* in here for us. In the meantime, we need shit markers."

"It's a time management issue," Walter said.

"I don't give a shit how much time it saves," Fritz said. "I'm just sick and tired of having to walk out in the woods to take a dump."

"I'm surprised to hear you say that," Jericho said, "given that we all know you jerk off while you're out there."

"No I don't," Fritz said, not particularly offended by the allegation."

"It doesn't matter," Gulliver intervened. "Fritz can beat his meat in a *Port-a-Potty* for all I care. I'm with Walter on this."

Walter made a mental note to request a vote on the matter, thereby forcing Pierre's hand.

The Frenchman and his boss walked toward the men when they entered the building site.

"Let me introduce you men to the company superintendent," Pierre said.

"Not so fast," said Jericho. "I'm the one who makes the decisions regarding introductions, *Moan Sewer* Toussenant. For Mister Welter's enjoyment, I think I'll call on Box Car do the honors."

Box stepped forward, extending a clubby hand toward the man. His voice was unusually gruff. "What's your name?"

The superintendent shook his hand, surprised by the strength of Box's grip. "Richard Welter. You can call me Richard."

"As in Dick?"

"As in Richard."

"Good. You look like a dick."

Box gave the man's hand a final squeeze, amused to know he was close to crushing some of its finer bones, refusing to release it until Welter's reddening face glowered from the pain.

"These boys you see on either side of me are proud to call themselves Jericho's dog soldiers," Box said, "myself included. They're good men; that is, until you get to know them. Which means it's wise you keep your distance. You with me, Dickie?"

"Actually, people don't call me Dickie."

The unexpected retort offended the Box, his voice deepening into a gravelly growl. "Are you getting sassy with me?"

Welter glanced at his foreman. At a loss for words, Pierre could only hunch his shoulders.

"I'd like to be treated with a little respect," Welter said to the Box.

"*Respect.* What the hell do you know about respect?"

Box splayed his hands on his square hips, waiting for an answer.

Weepy took the opportunity to begin singing just above a whisper, an imaginary guitar in his hands. Gulliver smiled when he heard it, offering a low thumping voice for accompaniment.

"I don't understand the question," Welter said, oblivious to the merriment starting up behind the Box.

"Let me put it to you this way," Box said. "I get into a fight with your Great Dane after you sic him on me for threatening your family. I win the fight by squeezing the dog's balls. He howls for mercy but I don't let go till he's effectively neutered. Would that not command your respect?"

Welter looked into Box Car's dark gleaming eyes, unable to come up with a response. Rem and Fritz picked up the tune; *just a little bit ... just a little bit.*

"Well then," Box went on, "let's say I agreed to change the starter in your truck but I had to take a break because I pulled a boner in the act of positioning the fly wheel; is that not something you could respect?"

Again, Welter was stymied. Behind the Box, Walter caught the rhythm, swiveling his scrawny torso in loops and lurches.

"Okay, consider this," Box said. "You fire an entire work crew and one of them burns your house down. Are you telling me the man responsible doesn't deserve your respect?"

"I was only talking about my name," Welter said.

"Fine," Box said. "Richard's Richie, Rickie's Dick. You take your prick; I'll take mine."

Welter raised an unbelieving eyebrow at Pierre. He looked back at the Box, trying his best to survive the absurd moment. "Fair enough. Are you going to introduce me to the men?"

Box wheeled around, growling at the gay troupe. "*Cut the fucking horse play.* Did I request a soul sister?"

The men abruptly ceased their folderol.

Box Car poked his stubby forefinger at each member of the crew in punctual clockwise fashion. “This here’s Fritz Swilling, a loose canon who made it back from Viet Nam just to piss us off. Standing next to him is his bother Remington. Besides having rapid eye movement and a dandy bandy that he keeps at my place because his wife hates his foul cock, he can drink anybody under the table and in the process tell you where Freud and Jung went wrong. Gulliver, over there, is the youngest of the Swilling boys. An accomplished photographer with an adventurous mind, he is, by nature, hopelessly inert. Despite his linebacker mentality, the man second guesses everybody and everything. What’s worse, he plays the bass guitar like it was the lead. The intellectual blockhead next to him, Weepy O’Toole, cries like a baby at the slightest provocation, makes the world stop for his afternoon tea, and, in case you’re interested, has a mallet as thick as a Bud can.”

“Excuse me?” Welter found no amusement in the introductions, taking particular offense at the crude description of a man’s phallus.

“You interrupted,” Box said, his own amusement suspended.

“I have a problem with that last comment,” Welter said.

“Oh, you don’t get it,” Box said. “Imagine holding a can of warm beer; that’s what it feels like for Weepy every time he takes a whiz.”

Welter looked at Pierre, who raised an eyebrow and shrugged.

“No more interruptions,” Box said. “I haven’t finished. Weepy is a manic depressive, a major abuser, and the best singer-guitar player Vermont’s ever produced. A man of multiple internal conflicts, he’s also a martial arts expert and a long distance runner who’d run from everything if he wasn’t so fucking lazy. The albino over there – by far the most infamous pink eye – is Walter Birdsong, a pathetically wordy man who eats *Zero* bars, thinks he’s Walter Winchell, and has already approached the far end of a short life span. Like me though, he’s a helluva dancer. The crusty old geezer with eyes that can look through you and around you at the same time, a man of constant vexation who lets everyone’s troubles trouble him, is my brother Grumpy. I’m Box Car Bork, the only nice guy in the group, even if I do have a few quirks. Finally, a man you may already know, our favorite bounty hunter, Jericho Laramie.”

Welter swallowed hard, trying to make sense of it all. “Mind if I say a few words?” he asked.

“Of course I do”, Box said. “But go ahead, just this once.”

Welter took a moment to collect his shattered thoughts. “First off, I’d like to say that the forewarning I received about this group doesn’t come anywhere close to describing just how incorrigible you really are. You seem to have no respect at all for authority. If I didn’t know any better, I’d think you were the skilled tradesmen and Pierre and I are the laborers, instead of the other way around. It’s obvious to me there a few things you need to know. I would even go so far as to say that your understanding and acceptance of how we operate as a company is a necessary condition for your continued employment.”

Welter stopped to study the expressions on the men’s faces. They looked, at best, unconvinced; at worst, defiant.

“If Rudy’s not around,” he continued, “I’m the man who signs your paychecks. In fact, I’m the one who convinced him to bid on this horse barn.”

Welter again let his words sink in, studying the group with discerning eyes, surprised that there was no rebuttal to this point. "I don't mind having a little fun once in a while, but I get the impression there's been a lot more fun than good honest work around here. This happens to be a very important project. Its timely completion means a lot to our company. If you don't already know, it's going to be the biggest horse barn ever built in the state of Vermont."

"Be big for me," Jericho bellowed.

Welter and Pierre looked at each other, their expressions addled.

The crew remained silent. Welter couldn't tell by their nonplussed lack of response if his message was getting through or not. He shuffled his feet, recollected his thoughts, and resumed his diatribe. "The owners happen to be highly placed officials in state government. If things don't go right, your paychecks aren't the only things threatened. Our reputation as a contractor hangs in the balance. There's a lot at stake. And there certainly isn't any room for disrespectful attitudes."

Fritz untied his nail pouch and let it drop to the ground. Welter saw him but didn't know what to make of it.

"If we do the job right," Welter continued, "and on schedule, good things can happen. If we screw up, either by having to redo an entire section because it wasn't level or plumb, or if we overshoot the deadline, it could take a long time for us to recover. Do I make myself clear?"

No one answered. Several of the men stood with their arms folded. A few others had their hands in their pockets. Box's blocky fingers rested on his hips. Gulliver tossed his nail bag next to Fritz's. Grumpy's landed on Gully's. Walter's bag fell with a muffled clang onto the others. Remington's pouch was next.

"Right now, we're behind schedule," Welter said, looking down at the pile of nail bags, trying to ascertain their significance. "*Way behind.* Rudy is at the unemployment office this morning trying to get more help down here. All of the vertical beams are supposed to be in place by the end of the week. At the present rate, we're looking at the middle of next week, which would put this whole project in serious jeopardy."

The crew was unmoved, each man staring at Welter with unmasked disdain. The superintendent, despite his bravado, was becoming unnerved. The tension in the air was as taut as chilled nipples in a burlap bra.

The gravity of Welter's speech emboldened Pierre. "Richard is a darned good carpenter," he said, his voice thinner than he had hoped. "He's a busy man, which we have to respect – *oops*, sorry about the choice of words – but anyway, I think it's good that he's here. He's decided to roll up his sleeves along with the rest of us to help get this project back on schedule."

There was a long uncomfortable silence. Remington broke it. "Do you like pork?" he asked Welter.

The superintendent was caught off guard by the incongruous question. It took a moment to register. "Sure," he finally said. "I eat pork."

"Good," Rem said. "In November we have a good old-fashioned pig roast at Grumpy's place in Underhill. Been doing it for years. That's not too far off already."

Rem paused, turning toward the crew with a mischievous wink.

"Okay," Welter said, curious where this might be going.

"You a family man?" Rem asked him.

"I'm married. My wife and I don't have any children yet."

"That's okay," Rem said. "We're not too big on kids anyway."

"Oh, please be big for me," Jericho moaned.

Remington gave the gunslinger an obligatory nod.

"We have a grand old time," Rem continued. "Lots of good eatin', live music, plenty of sexual exploitation. And, of course, some disturbingly serious drinking. Might be some fisticuffs, you never know; an acceptable risk when you consider that hard feelings are bound to occur once everybody gets feeling good. In any case, here's what I'd like to suggest. If you're going to be part of this horse barn crew, even if it's just for a few days, we ought to get to know each other better; let our hair down a little. It might help build morale, which I'd have to say is at a low point right now, what with the project having gotten behind schedule – a condition wholly unbeknownst to us until this very moment – and what with all that scorn you just heaped on us."

"I didn't mean to be scornful," Welter said, more perturbed than apologetic. "What I was trying to get across ..."

"Tut tut," Rem admonished, his finger wagging. "The damage is done, I'm afraid. Please realize, *Wicked Dick*, the men of this crew are not without their priorities. None of us really gives a shit if Rudy's company tanks and all his top dogs end up on relief, bleeding the government out of our hard-earned tax dollars. In fact, it may be instructive to point out that therein belies a major difference between us and you, as it pertains to dog style. You see, hot dogs like yourself are always dogging it, or engaging in the nasty habit of putting on the dog, as Fritz likes to put it; whereas whore dogs like us, who like it dog, make terrific dog soldiers. Nevertheless, despite our total disinterest in the fortunes of anyone but ourselves, it doesn't mean we're completely bereft of humanitarian sensibilities; in other words, we have no burning desire to see any of you starve to death. Therefore, we'd like to invite you and Rudy and our good friend the Frenchman – and especially your wives – to our annual pig roast, a truly celebratory event no matter how you slice it. Oh sure, things can get out of hand, but by and large it's a congenial affair; one very special day of the year when we can all get together to give thanks and enjoy a lively feast. The idea is to get it over with in early November so that none of us is compelled to feel guilty about spending Thanksgiving Day playing and watching football. Everybody comes casual, especially the Box, who never wears a shirt no matter how cold it might get. It's one of the few times – maybe the only time – when you can be totally relaxed and feel relatively unthreatened with our group. Whenever you get the urge, feel free to ask the chief pig roaster, the Box himself, to grab one of his gleaming knives and whack off a slab for you. This can be done with impunity, I assure you. In fact, that's what the roast is all about; you want fun, you have fun; no hassles. You get hungry, you simply muscle your way up to the spit and have Box dig into

that big-ass pig for you."

Jericho rolled his head.

Remington paused to smack his lips, turning to the dog soldiers, who smacked their lips too.

"It's a lot of fun," Rem added. "Besides, it's the least we can do to honor the relationship that exists between Rudy and Jericho. Mister Laramie, as you may or may not know, is the man who rounded up all us old whore dogs. Our deep sense of loyalty to him demands that we extend a heartfelt invitation to the presumed honchos of this suddenly moribund corporation."

With that, the men cheered with lustful approbation: "Well said." "*Ruff, ruff.*" "Way to go." "Best psychobabble in more than a week." "Quite the dog and pony, Rem."

Welter's thoughts were again in disarray. As the banter quelled, "I'll have to talk to Dee Dee about it."

Remington was not impressed. "I don't think you understand the nature of this invitation, *Wicked Dick*. What I mean to say, a bit more succinctly, is that we're not near as likely to leave our nail bags lying on the ground over there, to say nothing of leaving a handful of tight little assholes high and dry, should you decide to accept."

Welter offered a troubled look at Pierre, who swallowed hard and looked down at the pile of nail pouches.

"Now listen," Rem added, "I know how contentious this may sound to you. And make no mistake; it's meant to. We appreciate how difficult it is to get good help on a job like this, what with all the backbreaking labor involved and bad weather headed our way. And while none of us considers himself to be indispensable, least of all Walter, I'm here to tell you these boys figure they've got a handle on this thing by now. It took a while, but we've got it down. As we understand it, this horse barn needs to be up and standing a week or so before Christmas. Thing is, if the dinks Rudy's been recruiting over at the unemployment office are any indication, it'll take twice our number to bull and jam this job to completion. As we're all painfully aware, however, it's far too late for that, even if was possible for you to gather up a fistful of dinks, which it isn't. Do I make myself clear?"

Welter's face showed a mixture of surprise, fear, and bewilderment. "I'm not sure I fully understand. Are you saying you'll walk off the job if Dee Dee and I don't go to the cookout? Or is Box Car saying he'll burn my house down if I fire this crew?"

Rem stepped toward Welter, putting both hands on the man's shoulders. "It's perfectly clear to me how it is you climbed so quickly up the rungs of this company's ridiculously short ladder. Now then, what's say you get those sleeves rolled up and let's have a look at your beaters."

The crew picked up their pouches and went back to work, splitting into two groups. Welter and Pierre stayed put, nervously discussing matters while pouring over the blueprints.

Weepy's speakers and amp were under a canvas tarp. Walter, Weepy, and Remington repositioned a stack of boards on top to dissuade the superintendent from looking under it.

Walter, thrilled to be able to cover his rent and fill his cupboards with wholesome food and a formidable supply of micronutrients, was concerned that the crew's days at the horse barn might be numbered. "*Jeepers*, Rem, you were a little hard on him weren't you?"

"Not to be reduplicative, Walter, but I wouldn't waste a hard-on on that hard ass."

"Okay, but I did notice the man's signature on our paychecks a couple of weeks ago. It was too flamboyant to accurately decipher, but it must have been his because you can tell Rudy's no problem."

"Look, you meatless apparition, we report to one man and one man only. And that's Jericho."

"True."

"You ever notice how Rudy never comes around here?"

"His absence is remarkably apparent, yes."

"That's because he's scared shitless of Laramie; even more so than the rest of us. He knows our trigger-happy gunslinger packs iron every day. The main reason I stepped in for Box back there was because I saw the look on Jericho's face. I aim to tell you he was close to yanking out that gun of his and doing some serious damage. Not to double up on negatives, but I wouldn't be surprised if I didn't save Welter's life."

"I don't believe Jericho is as dangerous as you think, Rem. Sure he carries a gun; we all know that. But he hasn't used it has he?"

"He will. Mark my words my pallid friend, long before we're finished with this gangly erection, Jericho will have fired that heater a bunch of times. *Pop pop pop*. I can almost see it happening."

Weepy had a greater concern. "Does this mean I have to work?"

"Yes it does," Rem told him. "In fact, why don't you start right now and toss a board up here. It's not as difficult as you might imagine."

"What happens if I get a sliver in one of my fret fingers?"

"Not to play trite with words, my tremulous friend, but it's nothing to fret about. I get slivers all the time. I just borrow somebody's lighter, heat up a blade on my jack knife, and dig the sonuvabitch out. It's no big deal."

"It is to me," Weepy said, shivering at the thought of it.

Three members of the crew hoisted one end of a post and pushed it toward the sky. Box bullied his bulk against the base to keep it in place. Fritz, Grumpy, and Gulliver walked the post into a vertical position, grunting with exertion. Gulliver spoke in huffs and puffs while Jericho nailed a bracing board to the post, then to a stake. "Let me see if I've got this straight. Rudy sends *Wicked Dick* down here to give us the shaft but Box threatens to de-nut the man's dog or torch his house, then Rem tells him he'd better eat pig or this company can shove the horse barn up its ass."

"Fine summation," Fritz said.

"Think I should write the man up?" Grumpy asked.

"For what?" Jericho wanted to know.

Fritz intervened. "Insubordination. Insolence. Failure to control the Frenchman. I can think of all sorts of infractions the Grump can cite."

"Go ahead and write him up," Box growled at his brother, "if that'll make you happy."

"Nothing makes me happy," Grumpy said. "But at least that prick'll know he didn't get away with it."

"Rem made sure of that," Fritz said.

"Good thing Rem took care of business," Jericho said. "I was about to pull out my little persuader. I'd have had that cocksure bandy rooster teaching Walter a new dance."

The superintendent and the foreman were impressed to see two posts go up quickly; Walter, Rem, and Weepy having joined the effort.

"Are we going to help?" Pierre asked his boss.

"You're right about one thing," Welter said. "They can bull and jam."

"How long can we keep studying these prints?" Pierre asked.

"Okay. Let's pitch in."

At eleven o'clock, two more posts were set. The men looked as one toward the top of the hill, having heard a vehicle with a loud muffler approach.

A new hire got out of an old International pickup. He walked a few perpendicular feet to take a whiz, performed a couple of jerky knee bends shaking it, zipped up, raised his cap by the bill, ran his dink hand over his balding head, put his cap back on, adjusted it, and turned to walk down to the site.

"Do we have Walter do it dirty, given the circumstances?" Rem asked Fritz.

"Not blatantly," Fritz said.

Walter heard the instruction.

"The new guy needs to be initiated," Fritz said, "but we have to be clandestine about it."

The others listened intently to Fritz's plan of attack.

"Box, when you're out of *Wicked Dick's* earshot, ask the man if he's got a hairy ass; tell him you'd like a piece of it. Weepy, you start humming an up-tempo Cocker tune whenever you're near the guy; *Hitchcock Railway* maybe, or something else the albino can dance to. Walter, whenever the man looks in your direction, get those hips going. And I want crankshaft action godamnit, eighty miles an hour. Grumpy, cite this idiot for every imaginable violation. Gulliver, you torment the guy with your typical scalding observations."

"I'll fire a shot over his head," Jericho said.

Fritz gave Jericho an objectionable look. "Does that sound surreptitious to you?"

Jericho laughed. "I was thinking as long as we're fucking with the guy's head, let's do it righteous."

"We want to scare him off without Welter figuring it out," Fritz explained. "We have to be discreet."

"That doesn't work for me," Jericho said, scowling.

"Okay then, you work alongside *Wicked Dick*," Fritz said. "Keep him sidetracked so we can get rid of this guy without that asshole smelling anything."

"Meanwhile, I'll keep Pierre busy," Rem said.

"Look," said Gulliver, "the Frenchman's already walking over to greet the man."

"Pierre Toussenant," the foreman said to the new employee, offering his hand.

"Orby Leland," the man said, shaking Pierre's hand.

Pierre looked back over his shoulder, pleasantly surprised to see that the crew had not yet gathered for its usual welcoming rite.

"Where you from, Orby?"

"Tunbridge."

"Long drive from there."

"Yup. Had no choice though. They wouldn't give me any more checks down at the unemployment office. Said I'd gotten all they could give me. I never knew there was a limit on them things. Then they told me I should haul ass over here if I needed money. 'Course, them ain't their words, exactly."

"What's your line of work?" Pierre asked.

"Last job I had was fixing flats at Leo's Garage. You know Leo?"

"Never met the man."

"I got a trailer up in back of Leo's. Made gettin' to work real easy."

"Sounds like you must've gotten fired, if you were drawing benefits."

"Yup, that's right. Pretty smart of you to figure that out."

"What happened?"

"Ah, me and Leo's kid didn't get along."

"What'd you do, get in a fight with him?"

"Naw. Well, come to think of it, we fought all the time. But it's not what you're thinkin'. The kid ain't but eight years old. Thing of it is, he got to enjoy whackin' me on the shins with a tire iron. Leo'd see it but he wouldn't do nothin' about it. That damn kid of his gets away with holy murder. Anyways, after a while I got good and fed up with it. That's when I says to Leo, 'Leo, this kid of yours is gonna break my leg one of these days if he don't stop. Every night I can barely make it up to the trailer I'm so damn lame. I can't take it no more'."

"That made him fire you?"

"Not exactly. I could've quit, but that way I couldn't draw unemployment, accordin' to Leo. So it ended up where I had to have him fire me."

"I'm surprised he agreed to do it."

"Yeah, but the point of it is I'm married to his oldest daughter. Leo's a good man and all, but the dumb son'bitch got himself seven kids altogether;

four other sons and the youngest a daughter, plus the one I ended up with. The whole bunch of 'em is always up at my place raidin' the cupboards and gettin' into the ice box. Thing of it is, he don't want my wife going hungry. And believe me when I tell you that woman don't go hungry. Ain't no tellin' what she weighs; the scales don't go up high enough." Orby chuckled. "I hardly know which wrinkle's the right one, if you know what I'm sayin'."

Pierre looked down at the ground, then back up at the new hire.

"I meant that as a joke," Orby said.

"I got it," said Pierre.

"Most people get a laugh out of it."

"Sounds like you could get your job back if you wanted it."

"Not with that rascal kid of his runnin' around swingin' a tire iron at me half the time. No way I'm puttin' up with that anymore. Thing of it is – what'd you say your name is again?"

"Pierre."

"*Pierre?* Sounds French."

"It is."

"That don't bother you?"

"Should it?"

Orby didn't seem to have the answer. "Thing of it is," he repeated, "I hate workin' anyways."

All Pierre could think about was Rem's description of the men the unemployment office kept referring to the horse barn. Orby was a perfect fit. "Have you ever done any carpentry, Orby?"

"Yup. 'Course it was a long time ago. I helped my grandfather build a chicken coop. I ain't a educated man by today's standards, but I can get the hang of somethin' if somebody's got enough patience with me."

"Come with me, Orby. I want to introduce you to the superintendent.

Welter talked to the man for several minutes, then walked with him back up the hill. Moments later, Welter shook Orby's hand and the man from Tunbridge climbed back into his beat up truck and drove off, his muffler audible miles away.

Fifteen

Plants and people tend to have a love-hate relationship with Vermont. The laziest flowering bush on the planet, the lilac, loves Vermont because it only has to bloom for a week. If not for the heavenly scent of their short-lived lavender flowers, nobody would have them. Gardeners love or hate Vermont because tomatoes may or may not ripen on the vine before the first heavy frost. Sun worshippers hate Vermont because the sun shows up no more than once or twice a week, irrespective of the season, and the short-sleeve portion of summer is restricted to the month of July. Transplants from the *Bible belt* are shocked to discover that winters in the Green Mountain State last six months, God willing.

With colder weather upon them and darkness falling sooner every day, the crew called it quits fifteen minutes early on Friday. In the Buick, Gulliver complained that he'd had insufficient time to shoot enough rolls of fall foliage, which had already peaked. Walter complained about getting chilled to the bone after the mercury began plummeting around two o'clock, dipping down into the upper forties by five. Remington complained about not being able to cash his paycheck in time for a major cockfight on the reservation the following night. Box Car complained about being hungry. Fritz complained about Box Car. Grumpy complained about everybody complaining.

No new hires had shown up since Welter made quick business of Orby, thereafter referred to as the Tunbridge dunce. Despite the failure to bring in fresh muscle, astonishing progress had been made. Pierre and Richard worked shoulder-to-shoulder with the crew – Weepy and Walter carrying their respective weight – installing seventeen more posts in two days. During the first construction phase, which called for as much swearing and bickering as sawing, hammering, and lugging, no more than three or four posts went up in one day. Not all of the posts would be in place by the end of the following day, but at the much improved rate the entire one-hundred and forty would be perfectly vertical before quitting time on Monday. The project wouldn't quite be up to speed, but close enough to prompt the superintendent to give faint praise to Pierre regarding the crew's commitment and hustle.

When the men crammed back into the car after their customary stop for beer and goodies, Walter resumed his pestering of Fritz, hoping the flash-tempered Vietnam vet would let him conduct an interview. What began early in the week as a simple entreaty had progressed, or digressed, into a whining exhortation. Until now, Fritz didn't want to know the basic topic. But whether from physical weariness or caught in a brief emotional slump, the volatile jarhead finally relented to the albino's request to ply his nascent journalism skills in a candid give-and-take.

"Okay birdman, I'll do it, if it'll stop your incessant puling."

"Just a few questions, that's all I want to ask."

Already regretting his submission, Fritz instantly turned combative. "You mean questions like what goes through a man's head when he's being shot at? Or, does a man who's been in heavy firefights – I'm talking about the real shit – have nightmares about his buddies getting blown to bits? Did the notches on my weapon signify how many Viet Cong I killed or'd they denote how many times I got the clap? Do I experience flashbacks, emotional numbness, survivor's guilt? How many suicide patrols did I go on? How many *hooch ba* did I bang? Do I consider myself lucky to have made it out of there?" Fritz's voice was escalating in volume, intensity, and wrath. "Did I scramble my brains with Buddha stick? Did I draw a peace sign with a magic marker on my steel pot? Did I torch villages on search and destroy missions? Am I a baby killer? Did I appreciate coming back to derisive name-calling by a bunch of gutless hippies? Would I be a conscientious objector if I had it to do over again?" Fritz rammed his fist into the back of the front seat, catapulting Rem toward the dashboard. *"What are the questions, Walter?* Exactly what the hell is it you need to know?"

"The piece I want to do is called, *Soldiering: the Ultimate Indignity*. I thought we'd start by me asking how demeaning it was for you to have to wear a uniform."

"What the hell kind of question is that?"

"It's one among several that may strike at the heart of the indignation soldiers must feel as pawns in political power plays they're not allowed to question or, under threat of treason, refute in any way."

"That's yellow journalism, Q-tip. You're superimposing your own biased opinion. You're engaging in advocacy, justifying your particular slant by begging the question, wording it in such a way that the answers can do nothing other than support your corrupted thesis. What do you intend to do, write for some sensationalist tabloid?"

"My goal is to write for the Washington *Post*. Jack Anderson isn't getting any younger. Perhaps I could replace him one day."

"Yeah, right after you win a Pulitzer Prize for this interview," Fritz chided.

"May we proceed?"

"Go ahead."

"Yes, well then; you all had the same haircut and you were issued the same …"

"*Whoa.* I'm not answering any questions about uniformity, belittling regimentation, mindless systemization, or rank and file dehumanization. You got that?"

Walter scribbled furiously in his spiral-ringed stenographer's notebook. "Thank you, *Mister War Returnee*. Now then ..."

"I'm not sure I appreciate the title you've come up with either, Walter. But before we address that, let's get something straight; I was a goddamn Marine, not a soldier. How many times do I have to tell you people that? Jesus Christ, I'm surrounded by fucking fools."

"I believe most people think of Marines as soldiers."

"*Marines are marines.* Soldiers are army guys. Listen Walter, journalists are supposed to be concerned about accuracy. If you're going to be a reporter, you've got to understand the ground rules. You've got to be fair and objective and totally accurate; otherwise, you'll be hit with libel suits left and right. It's also important to write with brevity, which you couldn't do if the skill saw sliced off seven of your fingers."

"I hope you know you're not discouraging me, Fritz. I happen to have facility with language, a natural inquisitiveness, and an unbiased perspective. Furthermore, I'm developing a sense for tenacity."

"What the hell makes you think being a Marine, or even a soldier for that matter, is an indignity? War requires combatants – on both sides. We who make such an honor roll toe and heal to a higher calling, to a purpose written in blood and glorified in tears, to a rigid belief in ideals worth protecting and advancing as we adhere in the strictest sense to a code of conduct that requires the wholesale sacrifice of individualism to the will of government and the patriotic zeal of the masses. And throughout it all, throughout our impossible ordeal, during every unimaginable risk, always in harm's way, we must be ever prepared to make the greatest sacrifice of all."

Applause erupted.

"There you go, you beautiful leatherneck," Remington yelled, spinning around to reward the eldest Swilling with his best Lyndon Johnson smile.

"My country right or wrong," Weepy said, adding a couple of *rah-rahs*.

"Tie Old Faithful to the antenna on this rig," Gulliver shouted out the window.

"Bombs away," the Box growled.

"Okay then," Walter said, "I'll entitle it, *The Humiliation of Soldiering and the Ultimate Indignity of Being a Marine*. That way, I've at least covered the ground war."

Grumpy slammed the brakes. Beer spilled everywhere. A car behind the Buick swerved into the other lane, narrowly missing a VW bus coming the other way.

"I'm in no mood for this kind of shit tonight," Grumpy said, making no attempt to pull his car to the side of the road. Cars honked, swerving into the opposite lane to avoid the Invicta. Grumpy's fingers gripped the steering wheel. He was angry and disgusted, his nerves frayed. "Can't you boys let me drive down the goddamn road without all this rubbish being tossed around every time you ride with me? If it keeps up, the Buick stays home and we all ride with Walter."

"He drives a Datsun," Rem said.

"That's right," Grumpy said. "It won't be fun will it, all of us cramped up in that little yellow rust bucket? Here I let you men ride in style and this is the thanks I get?"

"Take it easy, Grump," his brother said. "When we get to *The Man's Bar*, your first two beers are on me."

"I'll buy the next two," Remington said.

Grump turned around to look at the back seat riders, his scarred face menacing, his Jack Elam eyes covering all occupants.

"I'm good for one," Gulliver said.

"I'll buy you a beer," Fritz said.

"Weepy? How about you?" Grumpy asked.

Weepy pulled out his wallet and looked inside. "Okay," he said. "You're good for one beer on my tab."

A Grumpy eye swiveled toward the albino. "As for you, Walter Cronkite, you're the one who started this fiasco. Your punishment is to buy me three beers."

"That's a lot of beer, Grumpy, not counting the six-pack you'll put away before we even get there."

"*Three beers out of you, Walter.* That's the price you pay for instigating. And I don't want any argument about it. I've had about enough discord for one day."

Jericho was sighting the scope on his 30-30 out in the garage when Deirdre yelled to him. *"The phone's for yoooou."*

"Tell whoever it is I'm busy."

"It's Rudy."

Jericho took off his boots, placed them on the mat inside the kitchen door, and walked into the parlor to take the call. "What the hell do you want?"

"This is Rudy."

"So I hear. I've got a project going. Make it quick."

"I've got a project going too, Jericho. And I'm goddamned worried about it."

"Why? Things are going great."

"Not according to my superintendent."

"What'd that asshole have to say about it?"

"The first thing he told me was that he's never met a nastier, a more brazen, or a more uncivilized group of men in his entire life. I've gotta make a decision about this crew sooner or later, Jericho. For the moment though, I'm between a rock and a hard place."

"I hate that saying."

"What saying?"

"Everybody uses *between a rock and a hard place* to describe a predicament. Why can't you be original? Why can't you say you got your dick caught in a vice grip with a nail jammed down your pee hole? Or make up some other adage."

"You can't just make up an adage."

"Of course you can. Let's say you want to introduce something new. You want the idea to be accepted but you know it won't be if you go whole hog right from the get-go. You have to introduce it real slow. At the first sign of reluctance, you say, real casual, *just let me put the head in.*"

Jericho roared his own approval. "Think about it, Rudy; in no time everybody'd be using it. *Just let me put the head in* would be an instant adage. You could even call it a dictum."

"Can we get back to the subject at hand?"

"All right, tell me about the squeeze you're in."

"I scheduled a site visit with the owners for late afternoon Tuesday."

"Fine. We'll be ready for them. With bells on."

"That's not what Welter tells me."

"He's a horse's ass, whereas I don't give a rat's ass what Welter says. We'll be caught up by the time they get there."

"That's not the main thing I'm worried about. These are some sharp folks, Jericho; three of Montpelier's movers and shakers."

"They'll find out what that really means when they feast their eyes on the albino."

"Yes, well, he is a sight for sore eyes. But that's beside the point. These officials have a lot of money at risk. The horse barn is a very important project for them as well as for me."

"We like the project, Rudy. It pays decent. And these dog soldiers I recruited are humping their butts. It's not our fault that dumb Frenchman of yours didn't keep us up to speed on the timing factor. The men I brought in would have been showing up an hour earlier every day if we had known we were behind. As it is, we're almost there; been making all kinds of progress since those two flunkies of yours got off their derrieres and started doing some bulling and jamming with us."

"Pierre isn't a dumb Frenchman, Jericho; he's actually quite intelligent. He's working on his master's degree."

"In what, lollygagging?"

"Something to do with language."

"How could that be? The man hardly ever says anything."

"He wants to be a teacher."

"Enough about Pierre. Something else is corn-holing you. What is it?"

"I'm nervous, Jericho. What kind of impression do you think this godforsaken crew is going to make on these state officials?"

"If you knew these guys, if you really understood what they're all about – like I do, since I'm one of them – you'd never ask such a stupid question."

"All I know is I'm worried sick about this. It's not too late for the owners to bring in a new contractor if they're not happy. Come Tuesday, I could be in for a major embarrassment. It's no secret your boys can be incredibly rude."

"You're right; rude, crude, heavily booed, and tattooed to boot. That's the beauty of it."

"What I'm trying to get you to under …"

"*I don't want to understand any more than I already do.* Relax, Rudy. Pay no attention to that sorry-ass superintendent of yours. We'll get our own super before you know it. What you don't understand is that the dog soldiers take a lot of pride in their work. You'll find that out come Tuesday."

"Welter wants to fire them."

"And then what, bring in twenty or thirty numb nuts like that Orby character?"

"He was the only man I could get."

"All right then, you figure it out."

"I see what you're saying."

"You're stuck with this crew, Rudy. The irony is you should be glad you are. And you will be, before it's over. Best thing you can do is get rid of Welter. He's dog shit. And I'll tell you what else. By the time we're done with him, he'll be dog *meat*."

"Welter's a good man, Jericho. Smart as a pistol."

"He gets smart with me, he'll get a pistol whipping."

"Go easy on the man. He's got personal problems."

"Like what?"

"It's personal."

"Who'm I going to tell, *Deirdre*?"

"What do you want?" Deirdre called out from the kitchen.

Jericho put his hand over the phone. "*Nothing sweetie.* I'm still talking to Rudy."

Rudy let out a long breath. "Welter's got a problem with his woman."

"Don't we all?"

"Yeah, but this is serious."

"She bouncing around on him?"

"He suspects she might be. She had a reputation before they met. He knew about it before they got married but it was too late by then; he was smitten. You know what that's all about."

"I do? You're right though; that's personal stuff. Just because he's got domestic troubles doesn't give him the right to come prancing down to the horse barn getting the crew all riled up with his nose-in-the-air attitude. These men he was addressing from his high and mighty soapbox, they're anti-authority types. They aren't about to knuckle under to some cocksure pantywaist like him."

"What the hell does that mean?"

"According to Fritz, a brow beatin' namby-pamby pussy who thinks he's the cats meow."

"That explains it."

"But you give these boys a job to do and get the hell out of the way, they'll do it dog; kick butt, hump rump, and bust ass. That's what I call righteous."

"If you say so, Jericho."

"Get a good night's sleep, Rudy. It sounds like you need it."

"Thanks. I'll say good night then."

"You take care. And here's a piece of advice for Welter. If he wants his feline's fidelity, he needs to be big for her." With that, Jericho howled and hung up the phone.

The Man's Bar, predictably, was crowded on a Friday night. The men took their usual positions; Box, Grumpy, and Walter at the bar, Fritz and Gulliver joining some friends at a table, and Remington swigging a *Bud* at the end of the bar while he waited for a pin ball machine to become available. Weepy stayed out in the car to smoke a joint.

Grumpy left early, having drank twice his usual number of beers in half the time. Remington, driving from Burlington to Essex each morning, always rendezvoused with the Grump in the parking area outside Box's apartment. Since his pickup was a short distance away, it didn't matter to him if Grumpy left. Except for Weepy and Walter, the others lived close enough to walk home.

Grumpy didn't notice that Weepy was asleep in the back seat. Once he heard snoring he felt obligated to drive the entertainer to his apartment in Winooski before playing slalom with the dashes in the road during his race to get to Mabel's.

Close to midnight, ready to go home, Walter slid off his bar stool and walked over to the pinball machine where Rem had racked up a dozen free games. Wynona was standing directly behind the pinball wizard, her arms wrapped around his waist, her mouth behind his ear. Walter stopped, pondered the ramifications, and returned to his stool. "Another bloody Mary," he said to the bartender. "A little more horseradish this time, if you don't mind."

Wynona was tooted. She seemed oblivious to Remington's demand that she watch him play from the side of the machine rather than from over his shoulder.

"You're inhibiting my game," he told her.

"Why don't I take your place and you get behind me, real close. I want to make it hard for you to be inhibited."

"People looking over here are thinking they're seeing one thing when what's really happening ... *Hey, what the hell are you doing?*"

Wynona had slid her right hand lower and was unzipping his pants, breathing hotly into his ear. "I want to make it hard for you."

The pinball took a lazy route toward the left shoot. Rem pulled Wynona's hand out of his pants, zipped up, and turned to face her. He grabbed her wrists and held them to her shoulders. "Look, Wynona, you're drunk. And I'm trying to get that way. Why don't you have one of your girlfriends take you home?"

"Beverly's driving tonight. We got into an argument an hour ago and she took off. I'd like to go home but I don't have a ride." She appeared to be on the verge of crying.

"Listen," Rem said, dropping her arms. "My pickup's down the street, in back of Box's. Go get in the truck and wait for me. I'll play a few more games, then I'll come out and take you home. But I don't want any funny business."

Tears had welled up in her eyes. A blink sent them rolling down her cheeks. Her expression failed to dim an amorous glow.

Three games later, a scuffle broke out at Fritz and Gulliver's table. Box leaped off his bar stool and plunged into the middle of it, pushing three guys away from Fritz, who continued to egg them on.

"What's the problem over here?" Box growled.

"Fritz accused us of being murderers," said one of the combatants.

"You did?" Box asked, turning to Fritz.

"That's right. Let me at 'em."

"Calm down, jarhead. I'm trying to get to the bottom of this."

Rem walked over, fully aware of the powder keg Fritz could become when he'd had enough to drink. "How could these guys have killed anybody? They're not Nam vets! What's this all about?"

"Fritz was getting on us about working the Men's Softball Booth at the fair," one of them said. "He says everything we serve, the French fries, the potato chips, the deep fried onion rings, the hot dogs and hamburgers; they're all soaked in lethal fats. He claims a man who ate at our booth walked over to the grandstand and had a heart attack; that we were the cause of it. Is that some crazy shit or what?"

"*The man died*," Fritz yelled, shaking his fist.

Rem looked at Gulliver and Box. "Better take him home boys."

Box and Gully muscled the ex-Marine toward the door, Fritz pointing an index finger at Remington. "Don't be fooled. They're part of the conspiracy. They're no different than the drivers of *Wise* potato chip trucks, godamnit. They're killing people in the most insidious way; with weapons of sugar and grease, dyes and syrups, flaccid fiber and poison pesticides. *Don't be bamboozled by the unwitting complicity of bourgeois ignorance.*"

Fritz safely out the door, Gulliver and Box Car dragging him backwards from under each armpit, Remington apologized to his crazed brother's victims, one of whom played on Rem's softball team. "Listen boys," he said, "I work the booth too. That fat fuck Fritz was talking about was headed for a heart attack no matter what he ate that day. It could have been a pig-in-the-blanket that triggered it. Or fried dough. Even Al's French Fries, although they do a decent job keeping the grease on the surface, not letting it sink in too much. Anyway, Fritz is rabidly patriotic. He has this thing lately about what he sees as America's deteriorating diet. Vietnam didn't do him any good, make no mistake. He was a hothead before he ever went to Paris Island to become proficient in the art of legalized murder, but there's little doubt the war put him over the edge. It's anybody's guess where this is headed, but I'll tell you this much; it gets worse by the day. Take that as fair warning. What you witnessed here tonight is child's play compared to what Fritz is capable of doing in the name of saving us from ourselves."

The explanation, strange as it was, seemed to mollify the men.

Rem turned toward the bar to settle up his tab, bumping into Walter, who was standing directly behind him.

"I need a ride home," said the sallow one.

Rem scratched his head. "Damn it, Walter, you could not have picked a worse time to ask me for a ride."

"I know you live in the opposite direction, Rem, but Grumpy cut out of here around ten o'clock. I don't know how I'm getting home."

"Hold on a minute."

Rem went over and paid his tab, talking at length with the bartender. He turned to take a step but bumped into Walter again.

"Damn it, Birdsong, you're like an alter-ego; there when you least expect it. The bartender can take you home. He lives not too far from your place."

"When?" Walter asked.

"I don't know. When he closes up. It won't be long. People are pouring out of here."

"Okay, Rem. Thanks."

Walter climbed back onto a bar stool.

"You got time for one more if you want it," said the bartender.

"Okay, why not," Walter said. "Only this time, don't be so skimpy with the horseradish, if you don't mind."

Almost an hour had passed since Rem sent Wynona out to his truck. Outside Box's apartment, he saw a light on upstairs and climbed the outside staircase. He did not go up with the intention of seeing Box or to check on Fritz if he happened to be there. He wanted to see his prized bandy rooster.

Remington opened the hall closet and dragged out a small cage, his alarmed gamecock flapping excitedly. He got down on his knees and put his nose up to the wire mesh. "Tomorrow night, *Jim Dandy*, it's you and me. We're going to make some real money. No food till then, you understand. I want you pissed-off hungry. Then you can dig into your opponent like it's a Thanksgiving turkey." Rem shoved the cage back into the closet and went into the living room to say goodnight to the *Missing Link.*

"Any chance Sibyl will let you bring your cock home?" Box asked. "It's stinking this place up to high heaven."

Rem turned to leave. "Being a Libra, I have a strong appreciation for balance. My bird carries an ungodly stench, I'll grant you that, but let's face it Box, it's formidable competition for those foul farts of yours." Rem tapped the closet door, pleased to hear a muffled squawk, then stumbled down the staircase.

Sure enough, Wynona was sprawled out, dead to the world. Her head rested on the edge of the seat, wedged under the steering wheel. Rem shook her shoulder but she didn't waken. Deciding it was best that she sleep, he walked around the truck, opened the passenger door, and pulled her along the seat. Her feet stuck out. He grabbed her gingerly by the hips, turned her body to face the dash, folded her legs at the knees, closed the door, and went around to the driver's side.

Part way down Pearl Street, Wynona, snoring lightly, raised her head, pushed her feet against the door, and scrunched forward. Rem's right thigh was now her pillow, the back of her head jostling against his groin.

Mister Man, Rem said to himself driving past Suzie Wilson Road toward Fort Ethan Allen; this could get hairy.

Wynona, unconscious and uncomfortable, flung an arm over the steering column. Remington took her wrist, raised the arm as one would carry out the garbage, and placed it over the edge of the seat. Seconds later, the arm flew over her head. Then it fell across Rem's leg. No harm done, he let it lay there.

The road in front of the fort was under construction. He slowed down to minimize the bumpiness. Wynona's right arm slid down his leg and fell to the floor. Unconsciously, it wandered back up on his leg, only to slide back down. She groaned and repositioned herself to face the other direction. Her left hand slipped under Rem's leg. The other reached around and cupped his pelvic bone like it was the edge of a pillow. Her head rested on his crotch, vibrating with the road's corrugated surface. Her cheek nestled against his restless appendage, swelling now with bull-headed thoughts.

Wynona could not get comfortable. Rounding the corner at St. Michael's College, her cheekbone sensing that the pillow had turned to brick, she flipped her head in the opposite direction. Her other cheekbone rode the rising swell. Coming into Winooski, she turned her head back the other way. Again, comfort was denied by the rubbing of bone against bone. Suddenly, her hand slid from his hip to find a better handle. Her fingers curling, she pushed it away, as if shifting from second to third. She held it in third all the way to the traffic signal at Main Street, pulling back on the stick when the truck slowed down.

Rem caught the light green and hung a left toward Burlington. The signal at the bridge spanning the Winooski River was red. He applied the brakes. Wynona groaned. She removed her hand from the animate shifter, turned her face toward Rem's midsection, and snuggled into his navel.

He drove across the bridge, moving into the right-hand lane for Riverside Avenue. His judgment impaired by a boozy brain and a circumstantial conundrum, the truck was traveling too fast. He tapped the brakes a second or two before the light flashed a green arrow. The sudden jerk, though slight, disturbed Wynona. She turned her head back toward the steering wheel, her hand groping – *Good god* – until it clutched the stick again.

The muscles in Rem's thighs flexed and loosened, stiffened and relaxed against the press of Wynona's cheek. He feathered the accelerator and tapped the brakes in an effort to gauge each traffic signal and prevent a sudden stop. Less than a half mile after the bridge she rolled her head again. Approaching the next signal, her head turned back in the other direction. It stayed there less than twenty seconds before it was the other cheek's turn. Her right hand, all the while, maintained a loose but certain grip on the throbbing shifter.

Rem wondered if Wynona tossed and turned like this in bed. She was a conflicted person, to be sure; a woman whose sexual appetite was hardly in doubt, though her relationship with her husband might be.

Over the next mile, her grip tightening whenever he tapped the brakes, Rem recalled Wynona's jealousy of Sibyl during high school. Wynona, who had flirted with him at every opportunity, was incensed when he and Sibyl started dating. During a notoriously licentious drinking party at Brown's River one Friday night, Wynona made a vain attempt to win him over. Cornering him between two parked cars safely away from the crowd, she pressed him against one of the vehicles and grabbed his crotch, telling him in no uncertain terms that she'd gladly give him anything he wanted; everything her best friend refused to provide. Rem rebuked her advance. But that wasn't the end of it. At the reception following his marriage to Sibyl, Wynona was three sheets to the wind and hot to trot. Exhibiting everything except a sense of guilt, Sibyl's bridesmaid stole a fast moment with Rem, again letting him know she was his anytime – any way he wanted her.

Now, given the circumstances, Rem wondered if tonight's episode wasn't a ploy. Taking a shortcut to North Avenue through a small neighborhood, he shook her shoulder to wake her up. She did not awaken. He decided to let her sleep, since they weren't far from her home.

Braking for a stop sign, Wynona abruptly maneuvered the stick back and forth, like it was stuck in neutral. A fresh surge of hot blood rushed to the scene. She raised her head and turned it to the left, then to the right, as if looking in both directions before deciding whether to downshift. Then, with somnambulant indecision, her head dropped face down in his lap, her chin precariously perched, wobbling and grinding, on his pulsating projectile. When he pressed the accelerator, her chin slipped down and he could feel the warmth of her deep breathing seep through his jeans. Her mouth parted, positioned midway along his full extension.

Oh no, he heard his mind saying, she's chomping at the bit. She's nibbling. She's gnawing. She's masticating. She's gnashing. *Good god*, she's … she's *cribbing*. How can I allow this?

Wynona's breathing quickened. She raised her head and groaned from deep inside her throat. Her hand climbed upwards and squeezed the knob, then slid slowly down the shifter, squeezing at the base. Her mouth opened to take in the knob. Her breath was hot, her teeth playfully ruminating. She removed her hand and reached for his zipper.

"No," he said, "no don't. We can't …"

There was a stop sign. North Avenue. Rem hit the brakes. Wynona raised her head, moaned, then lowered her head and consumed the knob, reaching again for the zipper. Gripping the steering wheel with all his might, he turned right onto the Avenue. He reached down. *Too late.* In quick succession, the zipper was down, he was out, and then he was in. Out. In … deeper. Nearly out. Further in. Out. In. He gasped. His hand grasped hers where it held him tight. Sudsy sounds filled the cab; sloshing, slurping, gulping, sucking.

Rem caught his breath, lost it, took a shallow breath, coughed it out, breathed in, held it, and breathed out again with soughing hesitations. The truck swerved. He brought it under control. He slowed down. Wynona speeded up. He reached down again, closing his hand over hers. He pulled his hand away to grab the steering wheel, trying to concentrate on keeping the truck in the right hand lane. He glanced at the speedometer. Not too fast, not too fast, he told himself. The Avenue's street lights illuminated the cab with intermittent flashes. He looked down. Faster, Wynona, his other mind said. *Faster*.

His mind went back and forth between speeds, Wynona's head bobbing; slowly, faster, slow again, then fast. This can't be happening, one voice said. *Good god*, she's fabulous, the other one told him. I have to stop her, said one. Don't let her stop, said the other. I can't be doing this! Yes, don't stop.

"Now, Rem," he heard her say, her mouth plucking, rimming, popping. "Now. Give it to me now."

He saw the sign for her street flash by on the left. Does she know it's me? Of course she does; she said my name.

Wynona squeezed and stroked, squeezed and stroked, plunging and withdrawing, diving and coming off, panting and gorging, squeezing and feasting; sucking, sucking, sucking.

He turned onto a street he'd never been down before. "Oh no! I'm going to …"

"Yes," she said, squeezing and jerking harder and faster, her mouth an inch away. "Tell me when baby."

His legs flexed. "Now," he groaned.

Her mouth closed over him.

"Good god, Wynona. *Now.*"

The street dead-ended in a cul de sac. There was no mess. She had guzzled the nozzle sapless. He steered the truck around the tight circle. Wynona sat up, complaining that her pants were wicked wet, asking if he enjoyed it.

"It was the best," he said, crawling back up the street. "The best ever. But …"

"But?"

"I just ... I wish it hadn't happened."

"*Are you nuts?* I give you the best head ever and you tell me you wish I hadn't? Why you goddamn ingrate. I've never been so insulted in all my life."

Rem swallowed hard. "I'm sorry, Wynona."

She looked away, huffing, looked back, slid closer, and reached down to fondle him. "*What the hell?* You're still hard."

Rem brought the truck to a stop, pulled her hand away, tucked himself inside, and zipped up. "I know."

"That's the weirdest thing ever. When will it go down?"

"When I fall asleep. Or after I wake up Sibyl and we have a good roll."

"You will not," she said, slapping his arm.

"You're right. I won't. Not after this."

"What's that supposed to mean? I don't like the sound of it."

"It means I'm feeling guilty; ashamed. I meant what I said Wynona; I wish this had never happened. You caught me at a weak moment."

"Oh bullshit, Remington Swilling. You've always wanted a piece of me and you know it."

"No I haven't."

"Yes you have."

"Have not."

"Have too."

"You're the one who wanted a piece of me."

"And I damn sure got it, didn't I?"

Rem couldn't help but chuckle. "Yes. Yes you did."

"Not just a piece, either." Wynona smiled. "All of it."

Rem nosed the truck back onto the Avenue toward Wynona's street. "What will you say to Bud, after he sees my truck?"

"Bud's sound asleep. Nine, nine-thirty, he nods out in his chair, even during a good movie. By ten he's stumbling into the bedroom. Thirty seconds later, he's out; too tired to brush his teeth or take a piss. Doesn't move for eight solid hours. Exciting, huh?"

"You'll tell him your friend Beverly brought you home?"

"He won't even ask."

"It doesn't bother him, you going out so much?"

"He never says anything. I know what you're driving at. You don't want Sibyl to know you took me home. It's nothing to worry about, Rem. I don't either."

A moment passed. He turned onto her street.

"I know what else you're thinking."

He stopped the truck a half dozen houses before hers and turned off the headlights. "What?"

She was leaning against the door, ready to get out. "You're wondering how a girl's best friend can go after her husband like I did." Wynona put her head in her hands and wept.

"That wasn't the first thing that came to mind," he said.

"What was then?" she asked, collecting herself, sniffling and rubbing her nose with the back of her hand.

"I can't figure out what you see in me, besides the fact that I'm married to your best friend. You know as well as I do I've never done anything to encourage you."

Wynona unlatched the door. "I'll walk from here."

Rem said nothing while she stepped out of the truck. Before closing the door, she leaned in. "I'm glad it happened. For your information, I was awake the whole time."

"You were not."

"Okay, believe what you want. You don't have to feel guilty, Rem. It's not your fault. It's not something you can do anything about." She closed the door, stared at him through the glass for several seconds, then turned to walk home.

Sixteen

The crew showed up at eight am, the dog soldiers dog-tired. And hung over.

Grumpy claimed he never got to sleep the night before, but refused to elaborate.

Gulliver had stayed with Fritz till the wee hours, trying to keep him under control. During the drive to work, after less than two hours of sleep, Fritz professed to remember nothing about the previous night's event. But he was not unhappy to hear about it. "Serves 'em right," he said, his ire rekindled. "They might think they're serving food at the Men's Softball Booth, but they're not; they're dishing out fucking poison."

Rem had lain awake in guilt-ridden turmoil till he didn't know when, half in the bag and half hard.

Walter complained about the myriad things the bartender had to do after he'd locked up *The Man's Bar*, not getting him to his apartment until almost three o'clock.

Weepy had gotten a great night's sleep, which meant his energy level, for once, was up to speed with the others.

When the men were piling out of the Buick, a gunshot fired.

"Damn," said Weepy. "That's more disconcerting than the alarm clock I bought a few days after I started this gig."

The crew, curious but not so alarmed as Weepy, sauntered down the makeshift road to the construction site less than fully alert. The tall toothy posts with their network of braces protruding at odd angles had a grotesquely sinister appearance, like some gigantic nest a pterodactyl still trying to procreate after twenty million years of faulty evolution might have instinctively crafted to trap an unsuspecting mate. Half way down the road, another shot was fired.

Jericho, his pistol gleaming in the morning sun, waved it in a wide arc over his head.

"You weren't shooting at us were you?" Rem asked him when the crew entered the cagey structure.

"I was firing in the air, celebrating," Jericho said. "But I might lower my aim a little if you ask any more stupid questions."

"What's the cause for celebration?" Gulliver asked.

Fritz responded first. "That piss ant Welter and his lackey Frenchman aren't here. I'd say that calls for a celebration."

"That ain't it," Jericho said, blowing across the end of his gun and slipping it into his pants.

"What is then?" Grumpy grumbled. "We happen to like a good celebration, but we might get a little more enthusiastic about it if we had an idea what the hell we're supposed to be celebrating."

"Pierre called me just before I left the house," Jericho said. "Welter didn't want to spend the money for it, but Rudy okayed it. So it's a go."

"What's a go?" Rem asked.

"*The Port-a-Potty.* Walter called for a vote and the only man who was against it was the superintendent."

"*Wicked Dick's* a prick," Gully said.

"Doesn't matter," said Jericho. "He lost the vote. I expect Pierre to be getting here any minute with our own portable toilet. Walter, you've been elected to dump the bucket when we finish up each night. We figure the contrast should be interesting."

The albino was horrified. "I can't do that. I'll get sick to my stomach."

"All you do is burn the shit," Fritz said. "Like we did in Nam."

"How'd that go?" Jericho asked.

"You dig a hole ten or twelve feet behind the shitter. You drag the honey bucket over to the hole and dump it in. You pour diesel fuel over it and toss a match in. After it burns down for a few hours, you toss dirt in the hole to cover it up. Next day, you do the same thing all over again about six feet away from the previous hole. It's called shit detail."

"Since you know so much about it, why don't you do it?" Walter suggested.

"I've burned all the shit I'm going to burn," Fritz said, spitting his rebuff in Walter face.

"Good point," Jericho said. "Walter, you've been chosen for shit detail, fair and square."

"I never heard a vote on that," Walter said.

"Look at it this way," Fritz said. "Shit detail is a unique experience that requires guts to deal with unsavory subject matter, determination to handle repugnant issues and shit-stained tissues, the will power to overcome all kinds of nasty emanations, and, of course, the intestinal fortitude to deal with exposure to putrefaction in all its distinctive guises; in other words, it takes damn near heroic tenacity. You want to be a journalist? Here's a story loaded with potential."

"At least a dozen stories every day," Jericho said. "Shit; it's a reporter's dream."

"I'll play some Doors for you," Weepy said. His guttural laugh ripped out of him like explosive defecation. "How about I do *Light My Fire*?"

Work went slowly throughout the morning, the men at less than full strength. Pierre must have had a problem finding a *Port-a-Potty*. At eleven o'clock, he still hadn't shown up. After watching the first post of the day being erected, plumbed, and braced, Weepy tossed boards from the tarp covering his equipment, unfolded his metal chair, rolled a joint, and began tuning his guitar with his usual admonition that he would not be taking requests. The men had no intention of making any, experiencing enough futility as it was with the heavy lifting and the constant bickering about who was bulling and jamming and who wasn't. Weepy toyed with a couple of blues numbers.

"I don't want to hear any blues songs," Box Car shouted at him. "They're depressing."

Weepy opted for folk, launching into *Bob Dylan's Dream*:

"While riding on a train going west
I fell asleep for to take my rest.
I dreamed a dream that made me sad
Concerning myself and the first few friends I had.

With half damp eyes I stared to the moon.
Where my friends and I'd spent many an afternoon.
Where we together weathered many a storm
Laughin' and a-singin' till the wee hours of the morn.

Weepy stopped when he spotted Gulliver pointing with alarm to the top of the hill.

"Call me a horse's ass," Gully said, "but I could swear the Buick is dancing. That song's impossible to dance to."

The others looked as one toward the bluff. To their amazement, the Invicta was indeed bouncing up and down.

Grumpy threw his hammer to the ground in anger.

"How'd you teach your car to do that?" Rem asked him.

"It ain't the car doing that," Grumpy said, staring at the Buick with a far away look, his hands pressed against his hips.

"No?"

"No."

"All right then, what the hell's making it do that? Your answer better be good, Grump, or I'm never riding in that fucking thing again."

"It's Mabel."

"Who?" the men asked, nearly in unison.

"Mabel Broome. Any of you know her?"

The men shook their heads.

"She's a nurse; lives in South Burlington where she rooms with three other nurses. I was scoping out sluts when I met her at a barn dance the weekend before this job got started."

"Is she the one you were with that night I jumped in the front seat?" Rem asked.

"That's right. You were supposed to go out for sloppy seconds."

Rem's gaze dropped to the ground. "I couldn't. I'm a married man."

"I don't remember her riding here with us," Gulliver said. "Where the hell is she, in the trunk?"

"You guessed it," Grumpy said. "I banged on her window last night till she finally woke up and came out to the car. We sat in the driveway and drank half a fifth of tequila, then we took off to Griswold's gravel pit. She ain't much of a drinker, but that's about the only thing she can't do. I was horny as all get-out when I drove over to her place from *The Man's Bar*, but by the time we got to parking I was too drunk to get it up. She got madder'n a hornet and started pounding on me. I don't put up with that kind of shit for only so long. 'Course, when it comes to sex Mabel doesn't like being disappointed. It ended up where I got out and opened up the trunk, dragged her drunken ass out of the car and crammed her into the trunk, along with the rest of the fifth. Then I drove home. Once I made it to Underhill, I forgot she was in the trunk. In fact, I never gave it another thought until I looked up there like the rest of you and saw the car shaking."

"Think it might make sense to get her out of the trunk after all this time?" Gulliver asked.

"I suppose," Grumpy said. "I'd be surprised if she doesn't have to take a piss by now."

The men had just finished putting up the second post of the day, although they should have had at least four in place by then. Grumpy trudged up the hill to rescue Mabel. Fritz suggested they get one more post up before breaking for lunch.

"Why isn't Pierre here yet with the *Port-a-Potty*?" Walter wondered aloud. "I gotta go pretty badly."

"Do your business out in the woods," Fritz said.

"I don't like going in the woods," Walter said. "It gives me the creeps."

"It's just woods, for crissakes," Fritz said. "What're you afraid of, wild animals?"

"That's one thing," Walter said. "I'm not the outdoorsy type. Don't forget, I'm probably the only Vermonter who doesn't hunt. I tried to get over my fear of the woods back when I built the tree house, but it didn't work."

"You mean the tree house Jericho and I built," Fritz corrected. "Just to jog your memory, the tree you picked wasn't even in the woods; it was on the edge."

"It was a very daring thing for me to attempt," Walter said.

"Go take a shit in the woods," Fritz told him. "You've done it plenty of times since we've been working out here."

"Looks like I'll have to. I've been squeezing it in half the morning. But I'm telling you, I'm fearful of something every time I go in those woods; like I'll fall into some quicksand if I'm not careful."

"The only thing you have to be careful about is stepping into one of Remington's messes," Fritz said. "I almost stepped into one the other day myself. If we hadn't declared squatting zones and put up those markers, I'd have been knee deep in it." He looked at Remington with discerning eyes. "You've got a serious problem with your bowels, little brother."

"I don't know what the story is," Rem said. "I have normal bowel movements everywhere except here. For some reason, whenever I have to take a dump over in those woods, I make an awful mess. I can't explain it, unless it has something to do with sitting next to Box Car on the ride out here every day."

The banter stopped when Box and Jericho, staring up at the bluff, howled with laughter. They were watching Grumpy being worked over behind the Buick, Mabel slapping at his chest and kicking at his legs, her plenteous tresses whipping around like the tail of a horse swishing a swarm of flies.

The furious altercation ended in a stand-off. The adversaries, exhausted, seemed to have arranged a truce, the details of which involved climbing into the back seat. A moment later, Grumpy emerged with Mabel's clothes. He laid her blouse and jeans across the hood, draped her bra over the outside review mirror, tossed her panties onto the top of the antenna, and walked back down to the barn.

"She'd already pissed," he said, rejoining the group. "A bunch of times. She'd been lying there in a puddle for who knows how long. Didn't know it till she woke up. During our little scuffle she told me she'd had a nightmare about being buried alive in a septic tank, her eyes stinging from all that piss. She was desperate to figure a way out. Thrashing around and pounding on the trunk lid; that's what got the car bouncing."

"And now she's sitting in the Buick bare-assed, stinking to high heaven," Fritz said.

"I keep some clean rags up behind the back seat in case my defroster goes on the blink and I have to swab the windshield to see. She's using those to get dry. She keeps all kinds of perfume in her pocketbook; I imagine she's dousing herself by now."

"Her clothes won't be dried out by the time we go up for lunch," Box grumbled.

"We got it worked out where she jumps in Jericho's truck when we take our break," Grumpy explained. "*Hey Jericho*, would you mind eating in the Buick today?"

"Matter of fact I would," Jericho said.

"Do me this one favor," Grumpy said.

"Forget it. Throw her ass back in the trunk. I'm eating lunch in my truck, like I always do."

"There's no way she's getting back in that trunk. C'mon, Jericho; be a gentleman."

The image of Jericho as a gentleman was too much for the crew to accept and they broke out in derisive laughter.

"I may not be as suave as Fritz. And I am a married man, like Rem. But hey, if I'm told to have lunch with a naked woman, who am I to argue? Like they say, it's okay to look as long as you don't touch. Besides, she looked pretty stacked from down here."

"She is," Grumpy said. "She may not be much to look at from the neck up, but from there down she's a real thoroughbred."

"Now that you mention it, I did notice rather horse-like features,"

Gulliver said. "Aggressive stance, spirited temperament, superb confirmation; quite the filly."

"And a thrill to ride," Grumpy added.

"That settles it," Jericho said. "She can get in my truck and watch me eat. If she behaves, I might even give her a bite of my meatloaf sandwich."

"Be careful," Grumpy warned with a raspy chuckle. "That may not be the only meat she'll want."

Jericho chomped down on his meatloaf sandwich while Mabel sat on the other side of the seat staring through the windshield, her cerulean eyes soaring through the interminable distance, her arms folded over her chest, partly obscuring her bounty. "Want some?" he asked.

She looked over but did not reach out for the sandwich as he had hoped.

"You must be hungry as a horse," he said, trying to entice her.

"What's that supposed to mean?" she asked with an air of insolence.

Unable to pull back on the reins of his imagination, he set the sandwich on his lap and brought his hands up under his chin with his fingers down, waving them like a couple of frantic hooves. For enhanced effect, he whinnied.

Mabel guffawed. "What was that supposed to be, a kangaroo with pleurisy?"

Jericho laughed. "Close enough," he said. "Listen, I could feed it to you if that's what you want."

"I can put it into my own mouth," she said with curt impudence.

"I was just trying to make it easy for you to have something to eat without exposing your breasts."

"That doesn't bother me," she said, dropping her arms to her sides with enough emphasis to set her gigantic jugs jouncing. "I didn't have my arms folded because I was embarrassed; I'm just cold." With that, she wrapped her arms back around herself.

Jericho cranked the engine. "No problem. I'll have it good and warm in here in no time."

"Hand me that," Rem said to Gulliver.

"It's Mabel's pocketbook," Gulliver said.

"You're incredibly observant," Rem said. "Hand it up here."

Gully obliged. Rem rifled through it. "*What's this?* Perfect. Fucking perfect," he said, pealing the wrapper from a cylindrical tube.

"Is that what I think it is?" Box asked.

Remington looked at Grumpy. "You got any tape in the glove box?"

"Might be some electrician's tape in there. Why?"

Rem showed Box the italicized writing on the package – *for heavy flow* – and shoved the container back into Mabel's purse. He reached into the glove compartment, grabbed a roll of black tape, put his hard hat on his lap, yanked the string out of the tampon, had Box hold the string in place, wound the tape around the hat three times, put it back on his head, and turned to the back seat occupants gloating with vainglorious gumption, the tampon dangling over his ear. "Well boys, it looks like I'm the new *super* around here."

Applause broke out.

"Stick it to 'em," Fritz cheered.

"Go with the flow," Box roared.

"*Let it Bleed*," Weepy seeped, stone-faced.

"Way to take discharge" Gulliver exhorted.

"We know who pulls the strings on this job," the albino enthused.

"*Wicked Dick's* been demoted," Rem shouted.

"He's dead meat," Fritz said.

"A wet noodle," said the Box.

"A lame duck," Gulliver said.

"A limp biscuit," said Walter.

"A shriveled weenie, Weepy said.

"Rem's dead meat too if Mabel finds out he took one of those," said the Grump.

The former superintendent drove up behind Jericho's pickup with Pierre following in his VW.

"I forgot Welter had to come too," Fritz said. "They needed his truck to bring the *Port-a-Potty*."

"Get down," a frantic Jericho instructed Mabel.

"But I hardly know you."

"Two of the bosses just showed up. We can't let them know you're here."

Mabel turned parallel with the seat and hoisted her legs onto it, her knees raised together, her feet pushed against Jericho's thigh.

"Your knees are too high. They'll see them."

"I can't stretch out my legs with you sitting there."

"You need to get your knees down somehow," Jericho said, wolfing down the last of his sandwich.

The only way Mabel could lower her knees was by letting them drop to each side. Jericho was in the middle of a big swallow when her legs parted. Bread and meatloaf bound in a ball of saliva lodged in his throat. His breathing stopped. His eyes watered. He tilted his head back against the seat to stretch his neck. He tapped his Adam's apple with the back of his hand. The large lump refused to go down. His head turned again toward Mabel. A fuzzy image, moist and dark, appeared in his nebulous vision. He could see a shag carpet, ripped down the middle. A moment later it was a one-eyed bear. Soon the furry creature morphed into an octopus winking at him through a shroud of ink. Next, he saw a deep cave with one gleaming stalactite. That image transmogrified into an ovoid pearl glistening in the tangled thicket of an eagle's nest. Then he was staring at a delectable triangular whoopee pie. He tried to speak but could only manage a gagging hack. He grabbed the top of his throat and massaged it downward. In the rearview mirror, he could make out the crew admiring the *Port-a-Potty* in the cargo bed of Welter's truck. He rubbed his eyes, still unable to swallow.

Mabel's eyes closed. He thought sure her hands were caressing her inner thighs. Suddenly, he felt a bulge moving. But there was no swallow. It was a different bulge. Mabel stretched a leg, her toes squeezing. Not one to panic under almost any circumstances, Jericho sensed that his marriage, if not his life, was threatened. He was, in a breathless word, panicking.

He unlatched his door, pushed it open with his shoulder, and dropped to the ground gripping his throat. He climbed to his knees, then rose awkwardly to his feet. He staggered around his truck toward the group. Box Car was the first to see him. The gunslinger's face was as red and glossy as a beefsteak tomato. His tongue hung out, purple as an eggplant. His eyes were hard boiled eggs. If he'd had cauliflower ear, he might have been mistaken for a chef's salad.

Box ran over and hugged him from behind, administering a quick decisive jerk to the solar plexus. Bread and meatloaf surged out of Jericho's mouth on whips of saliva. There was no time for anyone to react. The closest observers, Pierre, Weepy, and Gulliver, were splattered.

Jericho dropped to his knees clutching his throat, coughing and spitting. He looked up at the *Missing Link* with blood-shot eyes, a fleshy color returning to his face, his voice hoarse but audible. "I owe you one, Box."

"The least I could do," Box said.

Jericho climbed to his feet, huffing oxygen into his brain.

Grumpy ran to his car, grabbed three rags from the back seat, and tossed one each to the victims of his brother's life-saving maneuver.

"This thing smells like piss," Gulliver said.

"Keep your ungrateful mouth shut," Grumpy snapped.

"Where's this rag been?" Pierre wanted to know.

"I got a part-time job cleaning toilets," Grumpy chuckled. "I don't advise you to wipe your mouth with it."

Pierre wiped his cheeks, forehead, and neck with the rag. He cleaned off his mouth with the back of his hand.

"Is that what I think it is hanging from your hard hat?" Welter asked Remington.

Rem gave him and the others his best Lyndon Johnson smile. "May as well get used to it *my fellow Americans* – especially you, *Wicked Dick* – I'm the new super on this job." With that, he gave the tampon a playful cuff, touting his newfound authority.

Nothing about this crew surprised Welter at this point. He smiled back as if accepting a good joke, saying nothing but telling himself this was one more strike against them.

He and Pierre got into the truck to take the *Port-a-Potty* down to the horse barn. They drove around the Buick with more than cursory glances at the assortment of clothes draped on the Invicta.

Fritz and Rem walked down to help unload the plastic outhouse.

Jericho got back in his truck and shut off the engine, leaving the keys in the ignition. "You get cold, go ahead and start her up," he told Mabel, who was lying on the seat curled up in a fetal position, her arms around her knees. "But stay low, especially if you see either of those guys in the truck down there looking back up here."

"I can't drive," she said.

"You don't have to drive anywhere. Just turn the motor on. The heater's set to blow warm air. The cab warms up in no time."

"How long do you think it'll be before my clothes are dry?"

"How wet were they?"

"Soaking wet. I slept in my own pee for hours."

"Grumpy's a horse's ass for letting that happen." Jericho had the urge to whinny, but he held back. "Are you saying you don't know how to start an engine?"

"I've never done it before."

"All you do is turn the key forward. When you hear the motor start, take your hand off the key. You don't have to step on the gas pedal; she'll turn over all by herself. Whatever you do, don't touch that shifter or the truck'll take off and you'll be in a world of hurt."

"It sounds complicated. Will you come back up in a while and do it for me?"

"You're telling me you can't turn the goddamn engine on?"

"I'm afraid of what might happen."

Jericho slapped his hard hat onto his head. "If I can't, I'll send someone up." He closed the door and walked down to the site.

As soon as the *Port-a-Potty* was in place Welter left, telling Pierre he had to check on the company's other projects. On the way out he paused at the Buick, got out of his truck, looked inside the car, got back in the truck, and continued on his way.

Their hangovers worn off, rejuvenated by the events of the day, the men hustled. They were committed to setting the remaining eight posts before dark.

At two o'clock, Jericho was up for some shock value. *"Oh Pee-ehhhr."*

"What do you want?"

"Can I ask you to do me a tiny favor, my *leetle wee wee*?"

"I don't like the sound of it," Pierre said, the men looking on.

"I got something in my truck that can't be allowed to get cold. Would you go up and start the engine for me; let the cab warm up for five or ten minutes?"

"That's all?"

"Simple enough, even for a Frenchman."

The men resumed work sporting mischievous grins. Pierre trudged up the hill. The Frenchman opened the driver's door and immediately closed it. He took two steps toward the barn and held his arms out in questioning fashion.

Jericho flashed him a thumbs up.

Pierre went back to the truck, opened the door again, and climbed inside.

Twenty minutes later, he sauntered down to the barn, a shit-eating grin smeared across his pudgy face.

"How'd that go?" Jericho asked him, the men looking on.

"Best pair of boobies I ever saw."

"Mister Toussenant, *you're all right*," Remington said, slapping him on the shoulder. "A few more weeks around this band of misfits and you'll be one of us."

Weepy tuned his guitar and turned up his amp.

"Anything else catch your attention?" Jericho wanted to know.

"What do you think?" Pierre asked.

"I think he got demonstrably excited," Weepy said, revising a Credence Clearwater song.

"I see the nail bag a-risin'.
I see trouble on the way.
I see earthquakes and lightning.
I see good times today."

And the crew sang,

"Don't let Mabel get wise
To the French man's surprise –
There's a nail bag on the rise."

The rest of the day it was bulling and jamming at its finest. The crew had developed a system that speeded up the process, the pace assisted by a virtuoso performance from Weepy O'Toole featuring songs by The Animals, Mountain, the Stones, and, in honor of Mabel, a little ditty by Captain Beefheart and The Magic Band – *Her Eyes Are a Blue Million Miles*.

The last post went up at five-thirty. Throughout the afternoon, Box Car, Walter, and Gulliver took turns warming up Jericho's truck. As the last light of day lingered on the western horizon, the men put away their tools. They were dog tired again. The day had been long but fruitful, what with the arrival of the *Port-a-Potty*, being treated to a lascivious lollapalooza lounging in her birthday suit, getting a new self-proclaimed *super* on the job, witnessing the saving of a man's life, being treated to an outdoor rock concert, and finally completing the shell of the horse barn. They were proud of themselves, and rightly so. More importantly, they had worked up a powerful thirst.

Mabel's clothes were still moist at the end of the workday. She spread them out under the window behind the back seat and climbed into the front, squeezing between Grumpy and Rem – in the buff. Her perfume, though a light fragrance, permeated the car. Except for the Grump, the men liked the scent. The Buick headed for a bar. After Remington expressed displeasure about the prospect of missing his cock fight in New York, Gulliver asked the horse woman to identify her perfume.

Mabel turned and winked at the youngest Swilling. *"Eau de toilette."*

Grumpy pulled into a parking lot in downtown Montpelier.

"Are you going to sit out here freezing your ass off or are you coming into the bar with the rest of us?" he asked Mabel. "There's a chance they won't let you in without any clothes on."

"The stores are still open, Slumpy. You *could* go buy me something to wear."

"She's got a point," Rem said. "We're right in the middle of the capital city's central business district and it's still early on a Saturday evening. There must be a clothing store nearby. Let's all chip in and buy a dress for the Lady Broome."

"I want to see her go in naked," Box growled.

"I can't go in there nude. And I'm not putting those stinky clothes back on. If you won't go buy something for me to wear, Grouchy ..."

"Grumpy."

" ... then I guess I have no choice but to sit out here and freeze to death while the rest of you drink yourselves into a stupor and have loads of fun."

Mabel's head dropped, her long slinky curls concealing the golden brier between her legs.

Rem leaned forward and looked at the Grump. "Have a heart!"

"Oh all right," Grumpy said. "Rem and I'll go see what we can find. But don't expect nothing too damn fancy."

The men were not familiar with Montpelier's bars. The restaurant-bar they unwittingly chose, *Capital Idea*, catered to legislators and bureaucrats, businessmen and professionals. Soft white recessed lights glowed overhead. Accent lighting similar to the blue lights on airport runways ran along the baseboards and around the bottom of the bar, imbuing the cavernous digs with the transcendental black light luminescence that had been popular with the hippie set years earlier.

"This place has all the ambience of a psychedelic crypt," Gulliver quipped.

More than sixty patrons clustered around white-clothed tables or huddled along the muted glitz of the S-shaped bar.

"How can this many people in one room be so fucking quiet?" Fritz wanted to know.

Indeed, the subdued buzzing, like bees in a hive, affected a droning murmur similar, probably, to the ceaseless dribble the queen puts up with.

Box Car Bork, two of the Swilling brothers, Walter Birdsong, and Wilmer O'Toole, stood just inside the entrance wondering what to make of the dulcified atmosphere when the nattily attired *maître d'* approached them with a dark red cloth draped over his forearm. "Welcome, gentlemen. May I show you to a table?"

"Got one near the piano? Gulliver asked.

"Surely. Right this way."

The men were seated. Flickering flames from a candelabrum bedeviled their faces. They were politely informed that their server would be along momentarily to take their drink order.

Box looked across the table at Walter. "Make yourself useful and douse those things. Looking at an albino in candle light is enough to make me reconsider the concept of life after death. I don't want to have to think about that right now."

Fritz, Gully, and Weepy, having glanced at Walter, rose as one to blow out the flames.

Rem held a garment at arm's length in front of him, then yelled to the Grump, four aisles away. "How does this look?"

Grumpy cocked an eyebrow. "What the hell is it?"

"I don't know. Let's ask the lady at the counter."

Rem walked up to the clerk. "Can I bother you for some assistance?"

"Yes, of course. How may I help you?"

"I'm assuming this is some kind of dress."

"It's a type of dress, yes. It's called a muumuu."

"Wrong animal," Grumpy said.

"Yeah, but I like the price," Rem said.

"I'm surprised we even have that." the clerk said. "They were popular once upon a time, but not anymore." She peaked at the tag. "I'm sure that's why the price is so low."

"I didn't see any others on the rack," Rem said. "This one was stuffed in the middle of a ton of other dresses. Besides being the color of hen's eggs, or better yet, the tender skin of a Polynesian nubile, I like the luscious little strawberries strewn all over it, especially the rather intriguing convergence of them right there."

The woman leaned over the counter for a look at the section of the outdated dress Rem was pointing to. She quickly straightened up, her cheeks flushed. Clearing her throat, "Yes, well, perhaps that's one reason this particular garment hasn't sold."

"Yeah but, for 35-cents, how can you go wrong?"

She had to think about it. "This, of course, is none of my business, but may I ask whether you intend to buy this for a woman to actually wear?"

Rem flashed Grumpy a presidential smile. "She thinks we're a couple of transvestites."

"No! Oh my heavens, no," the clerk countered. "What I meant was … a *girlfriend*. Or a wife, perhaps."

"What difference does that make?" Grumpy asked.

"I suppose it … oh my goodness, I really am sorry to pry so; it's just that, a dress like this may not be suitable for all occasions."

Neither man could come up with a response.

"That is to say," she added, "perhaps there are other choices you might wish to consider. This … this *muumuu*, although it is gaily colored and quite cheery – I believe those are cherries by the way – is not only out of style, I'm afraid it is also very much out of season."

"I can understand that," Rem said. "This thing can't weight three ounces, what with no sleeves or collar. The material's so thin you could fold it eight times and wind it around your head six times before it would make an effective blindfold."

The clerk reached over the counter and pinched the fabric. "Yes, I'm afraid you're right; in certain light ... my heavens!"

"We just need it for tonight," Grumpy said. "Like my friend said, the price is too good pass up."

Grumpy reached into his pocket for some change but the clerk waived her hand summarily. "I'm quite happy not to have that thing in the store. Please take it. There's no charge."

"Thanks," Rem said, tossing the muumuu over his shoulder.

"Would you like me to put it in a bag for you?"

"Nope," Grumpy said. "We're only taking it a couple of blocks."

"Hey Weepy, go tell that lazy-ass piano player to play some upbeat music," Box growled. "I'm tired of all this gloomy shit."

"It's blues," Weepy said. "I like it."

Gulliver noticed that the buzzing discourse of the demure clientele abruptly dropped by several decibels. He sat up and craned his neck, looking in the same direction everyone else's attention seemed to be focused.

Standing at the first swerve of the bar, Remington, Grumpy, and Mabel were listening to the *maître d'*.

Box saw a middle-aged man take a seat by himself at the nearest table, realizing his friends needed a place to sit. He walked over and grabbed the opposite end of the table with both of his blocky paws. "We got guests coming. Mind if I ask you to go sit someplace else?" With that, he dragged the man's table away.

The customer, dumbfounded, continued sitting in a chair that suddenly had no table. He looked in various directions as if expecting someone to come over and reverse what had just happened. He toyed with the burgundy dinner cloth on his lap. A minute passed. The man looked around the room, absently fondling the corners of his cloth. Box got up and walked back over to him. In his most polite growl, "Are you capable of getting up by yourself or am I going to have to drag your chair, with you in it, to some other fucking table?"

With that, the man stood, picked up his chair, looked around the room again, put the chair back down, tossed his dinner cloth onto it, and walked away.

Fritz quaffed his second beer and wiped his mouth, then chortled loudly when he saw the *maître d'* escorting the trio to the double table. Speaking with Satanic mirth, "It looks like you got your wish, Box. Mabel may as well have walked in here butt naked; in this lighting, you can see clear through that flimsy dress."

The sight held no mysteries for the horse barn crew but it was a shocking spectacle for regular patrons. Some pointed discreetly. Others pretended not to notice. Still others gawked transparently. The bawdy display of a posh tush, berries in a bush, and the poised protuberance of ruby-tipped boobies pushing against the diaphanous muumuu put a muzzle on the mealy-mouthed assembly.

Several times, the waiter tried to hand out menus when answering the crew's frequent beckons for another round of drinks. Each time, he was rebuffed.

"How many times do we have to tell you," Fritz said, "if you eat when you're drinking, you'll fuck up your drunk. Take those things away."

"It occurred to me that perhaps, by now, you might have worked up an appetite," the server said.

"All day long we worked hard to work up a thirst," Box growled. "We're here to drink, not eat."

By ten o'clock, the crowd had swelled to nearly a hundred. Weepy, during the piano player's last break, convinced the background entertainer to let him sit in. As Weepy was setting up and plugging in, the unlikely duo discovered a number of songs they both knew.

Box flashed thumbs up when the next set began with a lively rendition of Canned Heat's *Goin' Up Country*, the pianist applauded by the suddenly enthusiastic crowd for merely attempting Alan Wilson's peculiar vocals. When the lines,

Well I'm going where the water tastes like wine
You can jump in the water and stay drunk all the time

were sung, the crew stood as one and cheered.

When they sat, Box Car remained on his feet. Overcome with frightful excitement, he took his frenzied dance technique – more menacing than the final stages of a ravaging autoimmune disease – to the small area of parquet flooring in front of the piano.

Realizing an earthquake was about to shake Montpelier's *Capital Idea* to its foundation, Remington and Gulliver got up and motioned frantically for the patrons sitting nearest the piano to slide their tables and chairs back in deference to the impending tremor.

Seeing the short stocky bearded beast dangerously close to them, sensing a disruption of seismographic proportions when they saw the blocky barrels of Box's head and torso convulse, his arms and legs and hands and feet quivering violently from some intrinsic force, the diners, appalled and distressed, dutifully obeyed.

The floor trembled. Tables shook. Beer, water, wine, and spirits sloshed in their mugs and glasses. The ambience itself seemed to vibrate out of its palliative calm, precipitously rumbling toward a cataclysmic eruption.

Box Car was dancing.

Mabel, three sheets to the wind after five black Russians, contorted and cavorted in her seat while the impromptu duo, the pianist donning a hands-free harmonica and Weepy encrusting his voice, honky-tonked *On the Road Again.*

"C'mon, Dumpy," Mabel shouted into Grumpy's ear. "Let's dance."

"I don't dance," he hollered back. "I thought you didn't either."

"This dress makes me feel like dancing."

"What about the black Russians?"

"I'm not bashful. I'll dance with anybody."

"Walter's a dancer," Grumpy said. "Ask him."

Walter overheard the conversation and was on his feet before Mabel could find him in the blue-white light. She jumped to her feet and yelled across the table, "Let's boogie, Casper."

The turbulent Lady Broome, the tremulous Box, and the ghostly albino swept around the tight confines of the dance floor like whisks in cake batter. Box shuddered and spasmed. Walter swished and swiveled his skinny hips in salacious gyrations. Mabel clutched the hem of her muumuu, raising it high on her alluring legs, skipping and kicking, swooping and swooning.

"*Hey Casper*, give those hips a couple of spins for the boys," Fritz yelled.

Walter threw his arms in the air and twirled with tumultuous fury, evoking the effervescent distress of a hooked whitefish.

"Whip it off," Box Car shouted across the floor to Mabel, sounding more like Canned Heat's Bob Hite than Weepy.

The besotted tart high-kicked along a row of tables, whooshing her muumuu to and fro across her smooth muscular thighs, bending forward and arching back, lowering the dress to her ankles, then lifting it to within a hair of the dusky delta barely concealed beneath the gauzy gown. Then she steered herself precariously back to her maniacal partners, bounding and romping, leaping and lunging.

People behind the nearest tables left their seats to gather round the reckless dancers.

The crew joined the aroused audience, clapping, goading, exhorting, and inciting.

Revelry and debauchery reigned. Walter frolicked and whirled, rollicked and twirled. Box Car shook and shivered, shuddered and quivered. Mabel taunted and teased, jiggled and jostled, tempted and pleased.

The swarming crowd hooted and cheered. Waiters scurried about in a panic. Chefs doffed their aprons, hurrying out of the kitchen to see what was cooking. The bartender poured a highball for the disconsolate *maître d'*.

Weepy and the pianist went from one song to another without pause as Walter flitted and flouted, Box Car twittered and twitched, and Mabel, not to be outdone, can-canned, fanned her skirt, and flaunted her fantastic fanny.

Box yelled again for Mabel to *whip it off.*

Boisterous businessmen and licentious lawmakers, forsaking the bar for a closer look, pushed to the front, clapping and chanting, "take it off … take it off … take it off."

"Take it off?" a dizzied Mabel yelled to Casper.

"Yes," the crazed ghost shouted, *"Whip it off"*.

Mabel whirled in an uncertain circle, roused the crowd with a shimmy and a swim, then twirled anew, inching her muumuu higher. The clapping and chanting grew louder. The lustrous lady, glistening with sweat, gathered her dress in bunchy folds and drew it to her navel to uproarious applause. Higher and higher the muumuu climbed till it graced the titillating rounds of her oscillating bosoms. Up and over the twin nectarous nips went the dress. The audience shouted, *"take it off ... take it off ... take it off"*. Mabel squeezed the folded dress and slid it from shoulder to shoulder, her breasts stirring, her hips swaying, her lush red mouth orbicular and racy, her lubricious eyes a blue million miles.

The clapping was clamorous, the chanting lustful. The pooped out ghost swiveled away, disappearing into the crowd. The rumbling Box Car derailed between the piano and Weepy's amp. Center stage, the impetuous tempest reeled and wriggled, teetered and jiggled, her apricot body aglitter, burnished by the hyaline light.

Up and over her head went the flimsy muumuu to the throng's raucous delight. Around and around the titian Mabel danced, waving the wispy garment high in the air till she tossed it with naughty hauteur into the applauding crowd.

In dizzying circles the disrobed temptress gamboled and trundled, skidded and stumbled. With a half-spin back on her heels, she pitched and rolled along a row of lechers who groped her globes, pinched her bottom, and shoved her back onto the dance floor.

The limpsy Lady was hopelessly imbalanced. Her steps faltered in widening circles. She wobbled like a top falling out of precession.

Deranged, delirious, dizzy, and drunk, Mabel lurched one way and then another, corrected, lurched again, caromed off the side of the piano, fell into and out of someone's arms, bumped into and away from someone else, tilted, teetered, and dipped on rubbery knees. She listed, righted herself, canted, and veered again.

Suddenly, miraculously, she found her balance. Her clammy amber body went inexplicably erect, shoulders back, legs together, hands loose at her sides. The dilated pupils of her vacant eyes rolled up and away. Her eyelids dropped. Her elegant lashes fell softly onto her rosaceous cheekbones. Listlessly, with the grace of a popsicle melting from its stick, she slipped from her rigid stance. Her slack body compiled in a twisted heap on the parquet floor. She uncoiled, face up, in an awkward decumbency, indelicately gnarled, bared to the crowd's unceasing approbation.

Mabel Broome, drenched in the spongy afterglow of an impassioned performance, felled by the burden of booze and the weight of exhaustion, lay sprawled on the floor stark naked and lathered with sweat, her flaxen hair a tumble, her arms and legs akimbo, her glossy orbs eddying and settling.

Management was in a conniption. The *maître d'* tugged at Remington's shirtsleeve. "This behavior is utterly deplorable. All of you must leave; at once

I say. We shall not hesitate to call the police to put an end to these shenanigans."

Remington looked into the irate man's eyes, pretending to be oblivious to his protestation and threat. Leaning into his face, "Was that the best fucking striptease you ever saw or what?"

"Oh my," the man said, befuddled and angry, desperate to bring an orderly end to the debauchery. "You must leave this instant. Your entire group, I say. And bring your shameless trollop with you."

Fritz and Box were having a difficult time keeping the gangly Mabel, heavy with unconsciousness, upright. They slung each of her arms over their shoulders to drag her away.

Remington tapped the *maître d's* chest with a stiff index finger. "Incidentally, foreskin face, you need to learn to speak to me proper." With that, Rem staggered off to help his buddies carry the wilted stripper to the Buick.

Grumpy and Walter helped Weepy carry his equipment, the first of the crew to leave the *Capital Idea*. Fritz, Rem, and Box followed, with Mabel in tow.

Gulliver was at the door, three steps behind the troupe, when the pesky waiter grabbed his arm. Gully turned and planted his feet, girding for physical or verbal battle. "What the fuck do you want?"

The nervous waiter handed over the check. "I'm sorry sir but you can't leave without paying for your drinks."

Gulliver took the slip of paper and looked it over with testy deliberation. The tab for the rowdy buttinskies came to the unconscionable total of one-hundred and eighteen dollars, a handsome tip slyly included.

Gully looked at the waiter with furrowed brow, vexation in his eyes. He looked again at the bill, his impatience mounting. He looked again at the waiter for a long discomfited moment. Seething, his hands palsied by angst, his mind perilously close to ripping its psychic seams, Gulliver spoke with understated vehemence, shaking the check inches from the waiter's face. "Let me see if I've got this right. We come into this somber joint – an infinitely more boring venue than even the most tedious and wearisome legislative session – with the wherewithal to roust your limp-dick piano player out of his fucking coma, we give you the most talented singer-guitar player this state has ever produced, we proudly display the down-and-dirty albino, we unleash the widely respected horror of the one-man earthquake … and then, *and then* … we treat your stultifying guests to *Muumuu Mabel* – burlesque queen extraordinaire – who bobs her boobs, rounds her rump, romps and stomps, and flaunts the best goddamn tits and ass ever bared in this one-horse town – and you want *us* to pay?"

With that, Gulliver crumpled the check, tossed it to the floor, and strutted proudly out the door.

Seventeen

Something heavy pressed against her. It was large and warm and it was making a whispering sound. Was she dreaming? Colorful butterflies had been flitting around lollipop trees before she felt the huge presence. Was it breathing? Out of fear, she kept her eyes closed. She sensed it was morning. Light was on the other side of her eyelids. Something heavy was resting on the top of her head. The trees had melted away and the butterflies were gone. Did she dare to turn over and see what was there?

Beatrice opened her eyes with a flutter of blinks. Five stuffed animals and her Raggedy Ann doll sat on her toy chest looking back at her. That's where they liked to sit after she and her mommy tidied up her room.

She blinked a few more times, then let her eyes stay open, getting accustomed to the light. The weight against her shifted. Her eyes went wide. She tensed, afraid that if she turned over she might find a monster in her bed.

Listening to the long breaths and the way they hissed, another thought came to her. She turned slowly, hoping … *yes, yes, it was her daddy.*

Bea smiled and reached up to touch his arm, which was plopped over the fat part of her pillow above her head. She touched his nose, careful not to wake him. He had a big nose that was round and puffy and a little bit pink. She put her hand on it, then on his forehead. When his breathing got interrupted, she took her hand away, sliding it under the blanket.

She stayed still and stared at his face. His eyes were closed but they were twitching underneath. Were they jiggling under there? She stifled a giggle, thinking about it. She loved it when her daddy made his eyes dance. Could he do it in his sleep? They were moving in awkward little jumps, darting and bouncing around. Then they stopped. Then they moved again. There was no way to tell when they would stop or when they would move. Maybe her daddy didn't know it was happening. He was sound asleep.

Why was he in her bed? Had he read a story last night? No, she couldn't remember that happening. A second later she understood; it was because her daddy loved her. That's what he always said to her, millions of times. He loves mommy too, she knew, but he didn't sleep in his own bed because he got home late last night and he came in to kiss her goodnight and then he decided to sleep in her bed to make sure she was having sweet dreams. Bea felt warm and safe under the covers with her daddy next to her. Better not wake him up. Maybe he only has a little while to sleep.

She knew he came home late all the time because that's what mommy said when she talked to Wynona, her very best friend. He didn't want to wake up mommy so he kissed me and then he crawled into my bed even though there isn't much room for both of us. He fell asleep even if he didn't mean to because he was too tired.

Beatrice let her eyes close. Her daddy made a lot of heat, which made her feel cozy and happy. She kept thinking about why her daddy was sleeping in her bed when a butterfly went by real fast followed by another one. They must be looking for their friends, she thought, who were over there near the lollipop trees. Everything was colorful and there was nothing to be afraid of because … because …

When Bea opened her eyes again she was alone in her bed. She was disappointed. Where did daddy go? A minute ago he was right there next to her, fast asleep with his eyes dancing underneath his eyelids. Had she been dreaming about him sleeping in her bed? Of course not. She had been wide awake. Maybe she fell asleep again and that's when her daddy woke up and went to tell mommy that she shouldn't be worried about him because he had been sleeping in her room all along.

Bea threw the covers off and sat up, swinging her legs around so she could push herself off the bed and onto the floor. She wanted to know where her daddy was so she could tell him that she knew he slept in her bed. And besides, she had to pee.

The bathroom was across the hallway. When she opened her door she could hear her mother talking to daddy in their bedroom. She walked quietly down the hallway. Their door wasn't all the way closed. Mommy was mad. She couldn't hear the words but her mommy's voice had a jabbing sound, quick and sharp.

Bea retraced her steps and went into the bathroom. Sitting on the toilet seat the sound of her pee in the water drowned out her mommy's voice. She was glad because she didn't like it when her mommy was mad at her daddy. She loved them both the same and it made her sad when this happened because she wanted them to love each other as much as she loved them.

Nine-thirty. They would be late for church if Bea didn't hurry up and finish her breakfast; corn flakes and toast with raspberry jelly. Bea was careful not to let anything spill on her Sunday dress, especially because it was the pink one; her favorite.

She and her mother always went to the ten o'clock mass. It took a while to drive there so Bea was quick to brush her teeth and hunt for her shiny black shoes in her closet. Her mommy was waiting near the door holding Bea's coat and the frilly hat that she didn't like to wear.

They left just in time to make it to the church with the organ still playing. The priest hadn't come in yet. Most people had already taken their seats. Bea looked around to see if any of her friends were there so she could wave to them without the grownups noticing, which was like sharing a secret.

Remington was upstairs taking a whiz when the phone rang. After a couple of poorly aimed shakes, he sauntered down the hallway in no particular hurry. At the foot of the stairs, rubbing the sting from his eyes with one hand and snatching the receiver with the other, he continued into the kitchen, the cord just long enough for him to reach the refrigerator.

"Who is it?"

"Fritz."

"What's up?"

"The game."

"What game?"

"Giants-Cowboys."

"Shit, it's Sunday. Two late drunks in a row; I forgot what day it is."

"New York's gonna get creamed. I can't wait to see the look on the faces of Giants fans when Dallas rolls up the score in the second half. For that reason, I invited everybody over to your place to watch it."

"I've gotta take Bea to the park."

"You can't be back for kickoff?"

"The timing isn't good."

"Doesn't matter; I know how to work your TV."

"Listen, I'm not exactly on Sibyl's good side right now."

"You haven't been on her good side since you started taking your cock across the lake."

"The point is you might want to consider watching it someplace else."

"The game's at your place, Rem. It's all set. Enjoy the day with your daughter. But make sure you're back before the game's over so you can hear me gloat."

"I have to listen to you gloat all the time as it is."

"That's right. But I had a talk with coach Landry this morning. I told him to run up the score so I can rub yours and Gully's nose in it."

"Nice of you."

"Thanks."

"Sibyl and Bea get back from church about eleven. After a few beers, I'll put the coffee right to me and be ready to head over to Ethan Allen Park as soon as Bea changes. With any luck I'll be back here by halftime. Besides Gulliver and Box, who else you got coming?"

"I know they're not football fans, but I invited Walter and Weepy. I called the Grump and told him he can come over too, as long as he brings his wild-ass lady with him."

"Did she put on a show last night or what?"

"Best striptease I ever saw. And I've seen a few. One time we had a chopper full of Korean strippers set down at a club near our hooch. The band sucked but they had four strippers with them. They weren't supposed to go all the way but a couple of us threatened to shoot the band if they didn't. It was one helluva show but it didn't hold a candle to Mabel's performance last night."

"Breathtaking."

"She may have a horse face but she's got the body of a goddess."

"Damn near mythological."

"That's exactly what she is, Rem; a female reverse centaur. She's the creature Homer and the boys forgot to tell us about."

Returning from church, Sibyl was surprised to see Rem dressed and ready to go.

"I've been looking forward to some quality time with my little honey bee," he told her.

"Make sure she keeps her coat on. Last time you two went to the park it was chilly and you let Bea take her jacket off. I'm surprised she didn't catch cold."

"What were you doing, spying on us?"

"The park's on North Avenue, Rem. A friend of mine happened to be driving by and mentioned it to me later. Make sure she wears her coat, that's all I'm asking."

"Fine. Oh, and listen; Fritz and the boys are coming over to watch the game today. Oughta be a good one."

"What?"

"Don't get mad at me about it; I didn't invite them, Fritz did. Nothing I could do about it."

"What time does the game start?"

"One o'clock."

"Okay then, make your visit to the park a short one. Be back here with Bea by quarter till one. She and I will go over to Wynona and Bud's for the afternoon. Bea loves their little dog. I don't want to come back to a living room full of beer bottles. I'm sure Box will be here. Is Walter coming over too?"

"Yeah. Why?"

"He and Box eat all kinds of weird stuff; pork rinds, blood pudding, tripe. They'll stink up the whole house. Make sure this place gets aired out. I don't want to come home to a big stinky mess."

"I think I can handle that."

"You'd better."

Rem and Bea had a wonderful time at the park. They teeter-tottered, played in the sand box, took a hike up to the lookout tower, and Bea started to get the hang of swinging. They talked about her school chums, Wynona's cocker spaniel, and why he had climbed into her bed in the middle of the night. Rem told her it was because, when he kissed her, he realized that he loved her so much he preferred to be there rather than in his own bed.

At Bea's insistence, just before the walk home, he made his eyes dance for her. He made them jiggle until she was clutching her tummy and laughing so hard he was afraid she'd get sick.

Sibyl answered the door. Box Car, Gulliver, and Fritz walked in.

"Rem here?" Box asked.

"He and Bea just got back from the park. They're upstairs. When they come down, Bea and I are going over to my friend's house. I don't want to be here for your little hootenanny."

"That's a good idea," Gulliver whispered to his brother when Sibyl went into the kitchen. "Grumpy might bring his slut. She has trouble keeping her clothes on."

"She's not a slut," Fritz protested. "She's a *goddess*."

Gulliver looked at his oldest brother, curling an eyebrow. "I can partially accept that. Only a goddess has a body like hers. Then again, if she's not a slut how is it that Grumpy hooked up with her?"

"Good point."

"I think a compromise description is required. It's my take that Mabel is a *slut goddess*."

"I believe there's a better description for her," Fritz said. "One with mythological proportions." He popped a can of beer and sat cross-legged on the floor directly in front of the TV, which was off. "She's an *equine sex goddess*."

Gulliver curled his other eyebrow. "Why that's precisely what she is."

Another car pulled against the curb in front of the house. Bea and Rem came down the stairs. A third car pulled in. Walter and Weepy came to the door. They said hello-goodbye to Sibyl and Bea as mother and daughter were leaving. Grumpy and Mabel walked in. Gulliver and Box finished loading the refrigerator with beer. Weepy sat on the floor and rolled a joint. Walter squatted next to Fritz and opened a bag of pork skins. Remington turned on the TV, tuned in to the local CBS affiliate, cranked the volume, and plopped in his easy chair to enjoy the game.

"Hold on a minute," Fritz said, standing. "I say we take a moment before kickoff to bow to the Lady Broome."

With that, Gulliver, Fritz, and Weepy got to their knees in front of the couch where Mabel had settled in, bent low with their hands outstretched and their palms down, as if facing Mecca, and sang her praises.

"Glory be to gargantuan globes," said Gully.

"May the dance of the seven veils forever take a back stage to the mysteries of the muumuu minx," said Fritz.

From Weepy, "Oh virtuous vestal virgins, give it up for the vertiginous voluptuary."

Mabel was stumped. "What was that all about?" she asked the Grump.

"They like your body," Grumpy informed her. "Remember? You danced naked for half of Montpelier last night."

"Oh," she said, reaching over to snatch a pork rind from the bag on

Walter's lap. "The only thing I remember is Casper peeing on me."

"I keep telling you, that never happened," Grumpy said.

"Are you sure?"

"Yes I am; no it didn't."

"But what about that horrible nightmare? Something white was splashing all over me.

"What have you got against white?" Walter asked her.

"I prefer purple," Mabel said.

"Purple's okay," Walter said.

"Shut up and watch the game," Fritz yelled. "Dallas ran the kickoff to the forty-seven. I've seen the playbook. Watch what happens. The halfback's gonna take one up the middle for at least fifteen."

As Fritz would have it, the Cowboys led by two touchdowns at the half. Walter and Box Car hit the kitchen to cook up half of the tripe, the other half to be eaten raw. Beer bottles littered the coffee table and both end tables. Mabel, a vodka bottle resting between her legs, her eyes lost in the distance, laid her head on the back of the couch and toyed with the buttons on her blouse.

Weepy, sitting to the right of the television, was working on a pastel drawing of irises, auto-suggestively blending purples when Fritz asked him what he thought of the game.

"The football game?"

"That's right, the goddamn football game. What'd you think of those blitzes Dallas came with in the second quarter?"

"Oh yes," Weepy said. "Very convincing."

"And that button hook to the wide-out. Did he fake the corner or what?"

"Never saw anything quite like it," Weepy said.

"You watch what happens in the second half. The Cowboys will smother New York's quarterback with red dogs. They'll stuff the run, snuff out the screen, and force the long ball. That oughta cause a turnover, don't you think?"

"I think I'd rather see Mabel turn over after she finishes unbuttoning."

"Forget about the goddess," Fritz said. "Enjoy watching the Giants get creamed."

New York was making a game of it in the fourth quarter, giving Fritz fits. His eyes darted between the gridiron and the plate on Box's lap, where a raw piece of pickled tripe quivered every time the *Missing Link* got excited.

First and goal at the eight for the Giants and Fritz couldn't take it anymore. "Hey Box," he yelled at the hairy one. "Get that cow's stomach out of my sight. I can't look at that slimy slug another minute."

Box grabbed the slippery slice of stomach lining and handed it to Walter. "You can have it. I've got one more fried piece left."

"I've had enough," Walter said, tossing it back onto the plate.

"Get it out of here," Fritz yelled.

Walter picked up the tripe and offered it to Mabel.

"What am I supposed to do with it?" she asked, taking the honeycombed mass in her hands.

"Some people use it to massage with," Walter said, "like a loofah sponge."

"They do?"

"Yeah. The waffled side. It works great."

Mabel held the opalescent jelly-like tissue gingerly with both hands. She brought it to her nose and sniffed. "Smells like vinegar."

"It's pickled," said Walter. "Vinegar is great for the skin; opens the pores so its healing properties can be absorbed."

"Really?"

"Absolutely. Give it a try."

Mabel applied the salty tripe to her neck. "Ooooh," she exclaimed. "It's cool and soft. Ticklish too."

"Stop 'em ... stop 'em," Fritz yelled, his attention back on the game.

"Rub it around," Walter said. "It's very soothing."

Mabel undid two more buttons and slid the wet tripe under her blouse, closing her eyes and caressing a shoulder.

Fritz pounded his fist on the carpet. "No. No. No."

The Giants scored. The extra point was good. New York led by four at the two minute warning.

Walter, like Weepy, had no interest in the game. But he tried to console Fritz, leaning forward on the couch and offering the wretched Swilling the last few pork skins in the bag.

Fritz slapped at it with the back of his hand. "Get that disgusting hog back away from me, Birdsong."

Fritz pounded the floor. "Score, Dallas. There's plenty of time. Take it down the field."

"The Cowboys are rattled," Gulliver said. "They haven't had anybody open since midway in the third. A field goal won't do it. They've only got one time out left. The Giants' secondary has been covering like glue. And the front four's been coming with wicked pressure. What'd you think, Weepy?"

"I think I'd like to be glued to Mabel, putting wicked pressure on her."

The muumuu marvel, her head laid back on the top of the couch, had lifted her blouse out of her jeans, unbuttoning all the way down and opening it. Weepy turned his back to the television, Mabel being a far more intriguing show hoisting a breast with one hand while the other ran the soggy tripe over and around the mammoth mammary.

"You like it don't you?" Walter asked her.

"Mmmmmm," she said. "It's like a thousand little wet feathers, smooth and slushy and sensuous."

"It's sensuous, all right," said Weepy.

"No!" Rem yelled. "You can't give 'em the short ones. They've still got thirty-five seconds and they haven't had to burn their last time out. Come with pressure, goddamn it. *Bring the fucking heat.*"

Dallas had marched down the field with a no-huddle offense, dink passes to the tight end over the middle, quick sideline connections to the wide-outs, and one wily quarterback scramble. The *'Boys* were on the Giants' thirty yard line, confident and determined.

Fritz rocked on his tailbone in a frothy frenzy, four bottles into his third six-pack of the day, guzzling them down as if the outcome of the game depended on how much beer he drank. Box and Grumpy had all but polished off the case and a half they'd brought. Rem and Gulliver were no less conspicuously consumed, lathered to the laces and imploring New York's defense to pancake the tackles, steamroll the center, and put a bone-jarring lick on the QB.

Reaching over an ashtray full of spent *Old Golds*, butted *Lucky Strikes*, and wasted roaches, Weepy was passing a freshly rolled joint to Walter when the sex goddess, her jeans unzipped, the shaggy tripe sliding down her navel, let out a terrifying squeal.

The frightful screech could barely be heard over the hoots and shouts of delirious Giants fans watching a desperate Hail Mary pass get intercepted.

Fritz pounded the floor with both fists, his head between his knees, when a slab of shorn tripe landed with a splat on his back.

Box, Gulliver, Rem, and the Grump jumped around the living room clapping and cheering. Mabel was on her feet too, bounding about and shouting, "It's a nightmare … it's a nightmare … look at all these squirmy white things on my skin?"

Fritz snatched the tripe and flung it in the air.

Walter and Weepy rolled on the floor in hysterics.

Sibyl, with Beatrice behind her, opened the door to a din of devastation and delight. She froze; shocked by a scene of unbridled vulgarity; horrified by the malodorous combination of cigarettes, pickled tripe, marijuana, and fried blood sausage; outraged by the litter of crumpled snack bags, scattered candy wrappers, and a hundred empties in pell-mell array. She turned to shield Bea from the lurid animation. "Go back out to the car, sweetie. I'll be along in a minute."

To Sibyl, the spectacle was pure orgiastic lunacy; a repulsive exhibit of unsheathed libido. Grown men, lechers all, were whooping it up, reckless with drunkenness and wild with arousal while a half-naked woman paraded soapy beach ball boobies that bounced and jiggled to her piggish squeals.

Attracting no one's attention – an intruder in her own home – Sibyl backed slowly away from the door. Outside, she grabbed Bea's hand and marched like a storm trooper down the driveway to her car. She would return later to confront Rem.

Eighteen

An emotionally sapped, physically weary Remington Swilling parked his truck in the parking lot at Box's apartment. The crew had been sitting in the Buick waiting for him for almost an hour.

"You're late," Box griped in his top-of-the-morning sandpaper voice.

"I know," Rem said. "Sorry, boys. I had a tough night. My daughter and I switched beds to prevent a crime scene from unfolding. I wouldn't be surprised if our little party cost me my marriage."

"I take it Sibyl was pissed," said Gulliver.

Rem looked at his brother through road map eyes. "If you consider World War Two a skirmish, yeah, I'd say she was a might upset."

"We helped you clean the place up," Fritz said with uncommon concern.

"It wasn't so much the mess that had her screaming at me from the top of her lungs for about three hours; it was the slut goddess."

"She's the equine *sex* goddess," Fritz corrected.

"Forgive me," Rem said.

"Did Mabel have her tits out when Sibyl walked in?" Grumpy asked.

"That she did. But it doesn't end there."

"Her pants were still on, I'll vouch for that," Weepy said.

"Wouldn't have mattered," said Rem.

"What's the big deal, then?" Fritz asked.

"The tripe was good and wet, wouldn't you say?"

"I'll vouch for that," Fritz said. "Mabel hit me on the neck with it."

"She rubbed it all over her half-naked body during the entire fourth quarter," Rem said.

"Yes. Yes she did," Weepy concurred, his voice breathy with the image.

"After using it like a loofah sponge, at Walter's insane suggestion, the tripe started fraying," Rem explained. "By the time Sibyl walked in, that blubbery membrane was hanging in tatters half out of the ash tray. I don't know how it ended up there but when I got rid of the cigarette butts, that's where I found it. Sibyl never saw the tripe. All she saw was this blonde bombshell flitting around the room half in the raw glistening with tripe jism. Sibyl thought Mabel's ear-splitting squeals were from sensual pleasure. The goddess's colossal titties were completely saturated; thousands of squirmy little tripe squiggles were plastered to them. You can just imagine what that conjured up in Sibyl's mind."

The inside of the Buick erupted like a tree full of howler monkeys.

"Jeepers," Walter said, the laughter diminishing to cackles and coughs, "I can see where no other explanation would suffice, the way Sibyl saw it."

"I might add," said Rem, "that the remarkably tangible evidence of O'Toole's excitement hardly escaped her attention."

"I reconciled that dilemma thirty seconds after I got home," Weepy said.

"Not the picture I was looking for," Rem said.

The men managed another laugh, their energy sapped from the previous outburst.

"Are you telling me Sibyl didn't buy the real tripe story?" Gully inquired.

"That's exactly what I'm saying," Rem said. "My marriage was already on thin ice. This was the last thing I needed."

Grumpy tried to come to Remington's rescue. "Maybe I could do you a favor and tell her about that time up at the barn dance in Westford when you had a chance to take over for me and you declined."

"That won't do any good," Rem said.

"But it proves you're faithful to her," Grumpy said.

Remington did not respond, gazing out the window at a scene of corrupted fidelity.

Despite traveling at dangerous speeds, the crew arrived at the horse barn forty-five minutes late.

They expected to hear about it, quickly lashing nail pouches around their waists. But Welter was in a surprisingly jovial mood, a smiling Pierre at his side while Jericho sat smugly on a pile of two-by-fours.

"How'd you guys get these last posts up so fast?" Welter asked no one in particular.

"We can bull and jam when the time comes," Fritz said in curt response.

"Darned impressive," Welter said.

Pierre was beaming with pride. "I told him you boys came up with a system that really speeded up the process. The new method could shave a good week off the next barn we build."

"There's only going to be one horse barn," Fritz said. "When it's done, we'll be doing some serious drinking. A crew like this comes together once and once only. Otherwise the course of history would be altered in irretrievably disastrous ways, not that the present course is any picnic."

The dog soldiers nodded in sober acquiescence.

"I'm needed elsewhere," Welter said, handing his hard hat to the Frenchman.

Rem donned his own hard hat, the mud-stained tampon dangling. "You're not welcome here anyway, *Wicked Dick*. I'm the super at the horse barn now."

Welter's demeanor returned to its normal state; contempt. "Pierre will instruct you guys regarding the strapping. The posts will be secure after the third horizontal row goes up. Then you can knock off the braces and pull the stakes. Every board must be carefully measured all the way to the top. When that's done, we'll lay the cap and bring a crane in to swing the trusses into place. Over the next few weeks, there'll be a lot of sawing and hammering to do. Your arms will get so tired you won't be able to lift a can of beer."

The men stared at Pierre's boss with equal contempt.

"Was that an attempt at a joke?" Gulliver asked.

Welter smiled. "I thought it was kind of funny, given how much you guys like to drink."

"We're not exactly keeling over with laughter," Gulliver said. "Even if we were all quadriplegics we'd figure out a way to get a beer to our mouths."

Fritz chuckled at his brother's comment. "Hear the news, *Wicked Dick*; you don't make jokes like that when you're pissing with the big dogs."

Welter turned to his foreman, brushing off the comment. "Pierre, they're all yours," he said, and walked away. Part way up the bluff, he turned around with some news of his own. "We're expecting another laborer to show up in an hour or so. Besides him, one or two more will be hired."

The superintendent grimaced, standing just inside the toothy structure. "I'd like you to know how distressing it is to Rudy and me that not a single new employee has lasted so much as a full day on this job. We've never encountered a situation like this. I've had some serious discussions with Mister Appling about it. For your information, every one of these workers has filed a formal complaint about this crew. Not just to us; to the Better Business Bureau, the Chamber of Commerce, and who knows where else. I don't know what goes on down here when a new guy comes on board, but it's pretty obvious these people aren't being treated with a shred of common decency. I know you don't care about this, but the company's reputation is being undermined by your behavior toward new hires. Whatever it is you're doing to alienate them, it has to stop."

The crew stared back at Welter, offering no sign of acknowledgement.

"Oh, and there's one last thing," Welter said. "The owners will be making a site visit tomorrow. For God's sake, please don't do anything to jeopardize our contract, which your jobs depend on. As you know, these are highly placed senior managers in state government. Their personal capital is at risk here. Unfortunately, Rudy and I will be at a builder's convention down in Brattleboro. We're both speakers, so we can't miss it. Pierre knows what to do. Let him handle everything."

With that, Rudy's first lieutenant walked up the hill and drove away.

Compared to the bull and jam work required to erect the posts, nailing two-by-fours was easy. Welter was right, though; a lot of hammering was required. To give their arms a rest, the men rotated on the skill saw. Since the boards were rough cut, each one needed to be cut to length.

Walter was pleased to find out that a saw line was made by placing a tape measure along a board, drawing perpendicular Vs at the correct measurement on both sides, laying the edge of a rule through the apex of both Vs, then drawing a straight line across the board. For this reason, and because his arms grew weary from hammering far sooner than anyone else, he took two turns with the skill saw through each rotation.

Pierre had no argument about Weepy's guitar playing and singing. The men seemed to work more efficiently to music. The entertainer's guitar and amp shared the generator with the electric saw. As usual, Weepy refused to honor any requests, although Grumpy continued to plead for *Hello Dolly*.

"You need a horn to do Satchmo," Weepy would say.

"I've got your horn right here," Grumpy would yell back to him, clutching his crotch.

When he finally tired of the Grump's exhortations, Weepy grabbed his pastels and went out to his favorite rock in the pasture and drew pictures.

At ten o'clock, a new worker drove up, parked, and walked down to the site. As usual, Pierre greeted the man. Just as usual, the crew halted their activities and gathered in front of a stack of texture 111 where Walter climbed up to do his down-and-dirty fandango.

Unlike the other new hires, Gray Popple enjoyed the albino's performance. When it was over, "That scrawny roll of toilet paper can unwind like there's no tomorrow; best damn show I ever saw." Then he tried to mimic the zealous dance, to the consummate delight of the applauding dog soldiers.

Gray was the first of the temps from the unemployment office to be nearly accepted by the crew. He was good with a hammer, could take a sick joke, and – complaining he'd never learn – was on his fourth marriage.

At eleven-thirty another new employee showed up. Roger Framingham's jeans were new enough to still have creases in them. His brand new work boots squeaked with his long strides. A tall man in his middle thirties, Roger wore wire-rimmed glasses and kept his hair closely cropped. His nose was unusually large and ungainly proportioned. Reddish purple with a bewildering network of crushed blood vessels from years of self-conscious rubbing, the man's snout was elephantine in both its size and shape.

As usual, Pierre greeted the new man, introducing him to the others while the crew gathered to watch Walter climb up and do it dirty.

Roger, an exceptionally well-spoken man, folded his arms across his chest and watched the frightening performance straight-faced. When Walter climbed down, the latest hire asked, "and your name again was?"

"My name *is*, not was," said the pooped albino.

"Yes, but I'm afraid I never got it," Roger said.

"Birdsong. Walter."

"Sounds backwards."

"It is."

"Why?"

"Because you blew the tense."

"Why don't you switch it around?"

"Why don't you?"

"I want it to be correct."

"It will be."

"Which way?"

"Switched around."

"Walter Birdsong?"

"That's my name."

Roger took off his glasses, breathed on the lenses, studied the evaporating mist, then placed them back on the massive bridge of his nose. "It didn't have to be that confusing."

"You made it confusing," Walter said.

"I didn't come here to argue," Roger said. "I came to work."

"Start working then," Walter said. "And the next time I dance, I'd like a show of appreciation. I put everything I've got into it."

"I could see that."

"But you didn't seem to appreciate it."

"I didn't. It was offensive."

"It was meant to be," Jericho interrupted. "That's the beauty of it."

"And you are?"

"Jericho Laramie. 'Have gun, won't travel'."

"You have a gun?"

"None of your fucking business."

"If you're carrying a gun, I'd like to know about it."

"You'll know about it a hair trigger before I blow your brains out."

Pierre stepped between the two men. "Hold on here, gentlemen."

"Do I look like a gentleman to you?" Jericho asked, frustration scrawled across his face.

"I didn't mean to call you that," Pierre said. "Here Roger, come with me."

With that, Pierre escorted the latest hire twenty feet away, where he gave the man a more detailed description of the dog soldiers.

"Just as I thought," Roger said, half to himself.

"What's that?" Pierre asked.

Roger looked around the construction site. "Nothing. What would you like me to do?"

Pierre teamed Roger with Remington and Grumpy. Jericho, Fritz, and Gulliver formed another team. Walter went back to the skill saw, Box Car holding the boards steady for him across the saw horses. Pierre and Gray repositioned a stack of two-by-fours closer to the hammer teams. Weepy toyed with a couple of Three Dog Night numbers.

"The honey pot can't go too many days before you'll have to dig a hole, yank it out, and burn all the piss and shit that's in it," Fritz said to Walter on the drive to work Tuesday morning.

"I already told you, my stomach can't handle that."

"That's too bad," said Grumpy. "You're the one we elected for shit detail."

Walter got faint at the thought of it. "I don't remember any vote being taken."

"Secret ballots," Box growled.

"Who tallied the results?" Walter asked.

"That's a secret too."

"But that smacks of skullduggery. It defeats the democratic process. The act of voting is secret but the actual votes are supposed to be tabulated out in the open."

"Screw democracy," Fritz snapped in his top-of-the-morning causticity. "Representative government is counterintuitive."

"What the hell does that mean?" Walter asked.

"It's a hoax, a manipulative contrivance, a preposterous lie on a national scale, counterfeit political dogma, a scandalous corruption of balanced opinion."

"Sounds abstract," Walter said.

"There's nothing abstract about it, bird brain. When 51 percent of the people can tell the other 49 percent to go piss up a rope, it's not representative government; it's dictatorship by the majority, oppression in populist attire. It's a Catch-22 for disenfranchisement."

"Could one identify this condition," Walter inquired, "as the snake of dualism rattling the poison tail of pluralism?"

"No, one could not say that," Fritz said, disdain wrenching his face. He turned his head and stared out the window.

"Down with democracy?" Walter asked. "Is that what you're saying?"

"Doesn't work for me," Fritz said, turning back to his interrogator. "Speaking for the minority, it's an abysmal failure."

A possible story at hand, Walter took out his spiral notebook. Fritz, he was thinking, may have flinted a philosophical spark capable of reigniting the counterrevolution that had, by then, all but died out. With proper goading, his friend's heated bluster might boil down to a need for society's ills to be reexamined. Lacking sufficient clarification, he pressed forward. "What you also seem to be saying, *schizo-Fritzo*, is that the system of government crafted by a representative group of exceptional visionaries in Philadelphia, which many believe protects our freedoms and liberties in every possible way, has failed utterly."

"My quarrel is not so much with the Founding Fathers. The separation of powers is a noble concept. The Constitution and the Bill of Rights are practical documents, versus, say, the canonical Gospels. It's the representative government malarkey that disenfranchises me."

"Malarkey?"

"For people like me, who are always in the minority, absolutely; it's hogwash, pure purple-headed poppycock."

"Those are nebulous terms, Fritz. Can you give me a substantive example of what you mean by *people like me*, since I don't know of any?"

"Take that idiot the voters of this state sent to the House. He doesn't represent my views. He's a hopeless conservative."

"As opposed to being a hopeful liberal, I suppose."

"You suppose wrong. I don't like soft-headed bleeding hearts any more than I like creativity-deprived right wingers."

"What you're saying is that you're neither a liberal nor a conservative."

"I'm a beleaguered iconoclast. I barely believe in government at all, even in a radically stripped down version. The very existence of government is evidence of social failure. What kind of person is it who actually *wants* to be governed?"

Walter finished scribbling and put away his notebook. "Fine and dandy, yankee doodle."

"You agree?"

"Reporters are like ghosts, Fritz. They have no voice. They do not agree or disagree, at least on the record. They merely record events and conduct interviews, thereby enlightening the populace as phantom guardians of the First Amendment."

"But there's more."

Walter opened his notebook again. "I'm not surprised. The reporter's job never ends."

"Until such time that we do away with the House of Representatives government cannot represent the people."

"*Jeepers*, Fritz; I do believe I'm at odds with you there. The concept seems contradictory."

"Apparent contradiction is a key ingredient of irony."

"Explain, please, how the absence of representatives translates to true representation. How do you pull that off?"

"You eliminate representation entirely by allowing for *direct vote*, that's how. You do away with the fucking middle man."

"But that's not possible. And even if it was, every major issue requiring a legislative decision would be tantamount to a national referendum."

"Voters could make decisions on issues of national importance right from the comfort of their homes, in the workplace, or at some designated location in their respective neighborhood."

"But there's no infrastructure in place to permit direct voter input."

"True. Technology isn't advanced enough. Look, I don't know how this comes about, only that it must. I'm not a visionary. I'm a Jeffersonian."

"Jeffersonian?"

"I have great respect for him. Besides putting Grumpy to shame as a renowned slut chaser, the man was obviously a closet anarchist. *That which governs least governs best.* Take that concept to its lowest common denominator and you end up with no government at all."

"Just the opposite has happened."

"The concept lost out to political egomania. Two hundred years later the fastest growing force in this country is the federal government. It's a menace. It's eating us up, pecking away at our liberties like a vulture on road kill. We're likely to live long enough to see the Bill of Rights decompose before our very eyes. Everyone, that is, except you."

"What? How can I accept that thought?"

"You have no choice. It would take a despot like me pulling off a daring coup to change course."

"I was going in a different direction."

"Then again, this voracious predator could be declawed. But that would require the counterbalancing force of disinterest to take charge. I wouldn't count on it, but it's an idea worth campaigning for."

"To elect what?"

"*Voter apathy*. It's gaining in popularity." Fritz chuckled. "Come to think of it, my candidate always wins."

"Apathy is an insidious sedative. We could be hoodwinked by a dictator."

"What the hell's the difference?"

"I'm looking for it."

"You said reporters don't get to express their opinion."

"Let's go back to the notion of me not living to see it."

"I'm trying to be optimistic, from your standpoint. You should be happy your chances are excellent you won't be around to witness the impending disaster."

"But I want to live a long time."

"You'd have to change your diet, bird man. It's killing you."

Box leaned forward to look past the snoring Remington at his grouchy brother. "I can't believe you haven't slammed on the brakes by now."

"Me either," Grumpy said. "I'm in no mood for political talk, religious arguments, or any of Fritz's *everybody eats garbage* garbage. The only reason I haven't slammed this rig into a tree by now is because I'm thinking about the visitors we've got coming today. What I'm trying to figure out is how we put the muzzle on the Frenchman."

Rem snapped to. "Don't worry about it, Grump. I'm the super on this job. I'll determine who does the talking when the bigwigs get there."

"I don't trust that Framingharp guy," Box said.

"I think it's Farmington," Rem said.

"That ain't it," said Walter. "It's Framingham. Roger."

"Sounds backward," Grumpy said.

"That's not the point," Fritz said. "Box says he doesn't trust him. I don't either. Something's up. I don't know what the hell it is, but this guy spells trouble."

"So what's the plan?" Rem asked.

"Does anybody know if he's married?" Fritz asked.

"Who'd marry a guy with an elephant's trunk for a nose?" Gulliver asked.

"Maybe his wife likes it," Weepy said. "Speaking of wives, is this Popple guy some kind of masochist?"

"He can't seem to get enough of them," Gulliver said.

"Popple is his own problem, not ours," Fritz said. "It's that Hammingframe guy we've got to be concerned about."

"So what's the plan?" Rem repeated. "The nose man handled the gyroscopic Q-tip like it was a Sunday sermon. I doubt he'd be fazed by my rapid eye movement."

"I have an idea that we may want to explore sometime later," Fritz said. "But for now, do you remember how we were going to have the Box get after that dunce from Tunbridge?"

Everyone remembered.

"I say we try that tact. If Box Car had the hots for me, I'd be on the next train out of town. What'd you say, Box? You up for it?"

"I've been wanting to yank out the 'ol crows nest for weeks now," Box said.

That settled, Walter asked Fritz whether or not the eldest Swilling thought the Immaculate Conception was a popular misconception.

Grumpy tapped the brakes before Fritz could answer.

At ten o'clock three cars pulled up to the brow of the bluff. Three persons got out; two men and a woman. The men wore gray suits and neutral colored ties. The woman wore dark blue business attire and a white blouse.

The owners walked down to the site. Pierre went to greet them. Rem, lifting his hard hat and shoving the soiled tampon inside, motioned to Gulliver to join him at the foreman's side.

A balding heavy set man extended a hand to whoever would take it. Gulliver stepped forward with a decisive grasp.

"Peter James," the man said.

"Must be nice to have two first names," Gully said. "Had you said James Peters I might have reversed them and gotten it right. I'm Gulliver Swilling."

"Actually, I hear that quite often," Peter said. "It's not infrequent that people get them backwards. In any case, let me introduce you to my associates. This is my friend, Jill Fornical, a director of special services in Montpelier. Jill, Swilling. Swilling, Jill."

"Gulliver," said Gulliver."

"And this is Ed Warwick. He's also a department head, like Jill and me. Ed, Gulliver. Gulliver, Ed."

"Pleased to meet you," Gulliver said. "And may I take a moment to introduce you to the crew? I'll do my best not to repeat redundancies."

"Why yes, of course, most certainly, by all means," Peter said. "I'm sure we would like that."

"To my left here is Pierre Toussenant. He's the foremost man on the job in terms of requisite expertise in the building trade; a man quite taken by words who seldom speaks."

"Pleased to meet you, Pierre," Peter said.

The Frenchman shook hands with each owner, nodding wordlessly.

"The gentleman to my right," Gulliver continued, "is Remington Swilling, a brother of mine who was intrigued enough with this project to take a sabbatical from his engagements in the field of phenomenology to enjoy the great outdoors, to participate in some wholesome exercise and, as you might imagine, to analyze our efforts from a subliminally exploratory perspective."

"My goodness, that does sound interesting," Peter allowed. "I've not heard of that particular discipline. May I ask what it entails?"

"By all means," said Gulliver. "Phenomenology is the philosophical study of perceptual experience in its purely subjective aspect. Contextually, as you may imagine, reality is incredibly abstract."

The owners, not expecting an exalted level of discourse with a rather uncommon laborer at their project, glanced at each other with befuddled expressions. "I see," said Peter, extending his hand. "We're all quite delighted to meet you, Remington."

Rem shook hands with the three owners, unable to prevent his Lyndon Johnson smile from appearing.

"Now then," Gulliver went on, "since the men are eager to continue their work – we're dealing with a challenging schedule, as I'm sure you're aware – allow me to introduce the rest of them from afar."

With that, Gulliver described the other dog soldiers in flattering terms, embellishing strong points such as Jericho's ability to spin a hammer and drop it smartly into the hook on his nail pouch, the hardy though dissimilar physiques of Box and Fritz, the formidable countenance of the Grump, the esoteric demeanor of the lamentably discolored one, and the winsome attributes of Mister O'Toole. Gully also waved cursorily at the temps, saying, "They're here too."

Duly impressed, the owners watched and listened intently as Gulliver spread out the blueprints on the saw horses, this being the first time he'd seen them up close. He explained how the footings were poured and the posts erected in lock-step with phased deadlines, how the strapping underway now would permit the bracing of the posts to be removed, how the capping would allow for the trusses to be craned into place even while four-by-eight sheets of vertically grooved siding would be nailed to the network of two-by-fours simultaneous to the precarious work necessary to secure the trusses. By the first of December, Gulliver noted, work would begin on the stalls, where precise positioning of hinges and handles, clasps and bolts, and only the highest quality hardware would be entrusted to the most capable hands.

The owners were all smiles, having made the acquaintance of such an outstanding group of workers and having been treated to a circumspective narrative of the project's critical time-sensitive phases.

Gulliver escorted the small entourage back to their identical vehicles. It was obvious that a deep sense of confidence had been instilled in the group, given their gratuitous comments regarding the remarkable progress being forged on their barn.

When their cars were out of site, the crew peppered the youngest, most eloquent, Swilling with hearty congratulations on his exemplary sales effort.

"Way to bamboozle a bunch of big-shot bimbos," Rem cheered.

"A blizzard of a snow job if I've ever seen one," said Weepy.

"Had me wondering if we were building a horse barn or re-creating the Taj Mahal," Fritz gloried.

"Flim-flam artist, snake-oil salesman, showboat charlatan; a great future awaits you, Gully," said the Box.

"Gave me goose bumps," Grumpy said.

"Gave me an erection," Jericho said.

Gulliver doffed his hard hat, taking a bow with each accolade. When the shower of praise had subsided, "What about you, Walter? What'd you think about my little act?"

"I wasn't really listening," he said, placing three aspirins on his tongue. "Fritz has me worried about my longevity."

"What'd you bring for lunch today?"

"Pickled beets, Vienna sausages marinated in a cayenne mustard sauce, cream of carrot soup, and a slice of brie."

"And you question Fritz's concern?"

Gulliver turned to the Frenchman. *"Oh Pee-ehhhr, my leetle leetle wee wee.* What was your impression?"

Pierre looked relieved. "I was just happy I didn't have to say anything."

By mid afternoon, Box had convinced Walter to let Roger have a turn with the skill saw. Roger protested, not wanting to get sawdust on his pants.

"Get your ass down here," Box said. "I want those nicely framed hams as close to me as you can get 'em."

Not sensing a serious threat, Roger untied his nail bag, placed it on a stack of boards, and walked over to the saw horses.

Box Car swiveled his hips in albino fashion and groaned in a low voice. "There's something about an unsociable fellow who wears glasses like those that gets me all hot and bothered."

"I don't seem to have that affect on most people," Roger said.

"I'm not like most people."

"I can see that."

For the next hour, Roger held to an unexpected stoicism in the face of Box Car's fruitless intimidations.

Frustrated and disappointed, Box grumbled. "Nothing I do fazes you, does it?"

"That's not entirely true," Roger said. "Some of it I find reprehensible. Some of it borders on being noteworthy. And I'd say some of it may even contain an element of humor. Your behavior toward me is interesting in that it demonstrates a certain reckless sincerity. But if you're surmising that it doesn't shock me, then I would say your assessment is essentially accurate."

"What if I reached in here and hauled out the ol' crow's nest?" Box asked, shoving his clubby hand down his furry navel into his dungarees. "Would that get you going?"

"I'm afraid I'm not familiar with the term *crow's nest*."

Rem yelled to Roger. "He's got a big hairy bag."

"And how is that supposed to interest me?" Roger wanted to know.

Rem stepped down from the first row of strapping and walked toward the two men. "What the hell *does* interest you, Farmingharm?"

"Framingham."

"That's not the answer."

"This project interests me. As do each of you."

"What interests you about us?"

"During my brief time with this crew I believe I have picked up on a compelling dichotomy that I find intriguing."

"Sounds plausible. Please continue."

"There's a vile and roguish aspect to your collective disposition, a depraved bravado common to miscreants who revel in debauchery."

"Well said, especially for a common laborer. But where's the dichotomy?"

"I've overheard the philosophical banter between the inquisitive albino and the depressed musician. Their discussions are not the stuff of unrefined hooligans. And I listened with great curiosity to the eloquent speech of your younger brother; a surprisingly effective spoof. There's an obvious division of opposing forces; crude treatment, mocking parodies, and blatant disrespect of others in all outward appearances; contentious intellectualism behind the scenes cerebral enough for you to consider yourselves a self-contained intelligentsia."

"Truth be known, our behavior toward each other couldn't be more contentious if we were engaged in a prison riot," Rem responded.

Roger pondered the image. "Yes, well, I suppose I'm not privy to that."

"Now that you have us pegged, Haminframe, kindly tell us something about your regular line of work."

"And why would that be of interest to you?"

"What's interesting to us, if not downright suspect, is that you're as much of a misfit on this job as any of us."

"Let's just say I'm a person whose typical day involves a lot of paperwork, which I find boring at best and, at worst, detestable. When I was given the opportunity to do something physical for a change, I jumped at it."

"You're none too good with a hammer and saw."

"True enough. But certainly I'm no worse than that odd pink-eyed fellow with the white hair or the entertainer with the fine physique who hangs his head most of the time hoping for nothing to do. Furthermore, I'm a man of noteworthy physical strength who learns quickly and is not deterred by the prospect of honest work."

"Walter and Weepy, although worthless in terms of work ethic, bring special values to this job," Rem said. "What I'm trying to figure out is what value you bring, if it isn't expertise with tools of the trade."

"I would ask, simply, that you give me a chance," Roger said. "I *am* trying, despite formidable impediments."

"Were you sent here by the state unemployment agency or do you have an in with the general contractor?" Rem pressed.

"Yes and no. No, I have never met the general contractor, although I understand he has a solid reputation as one of the area's finest builders. And yes, the state sent me to the horse barn. Is that not okay? Can I not be one of the boys, so to speak?"

"The jury's still out," said Rem, walking away.

"I'm as hungry as a horse," Box said. He looked at Roger. "And I'm tired of working with you. After we eat, switch places with Walter again. At least that flimsy Q-tip doesn't take two or three minutes brushing off his pants every time he saws a board."

Roger was giving his cuffs a final swipe when Rem came back. "One more question, Farmington."

"Framingham."

"Are you married?"

"No. Why would that be of interest to you?"

"Since you're not a member of the intelligentsia, you don't get to know."

The brilliant show of candent scarlet, glowing gold, and bleeding burgundy had closed its curtain completely by the first week of November. The falling leaves of late autumn, starched stiff by death, had turned to dog shit brown.

Sharp winds plunging down from Canada knifed through Vermont with a cutting chill, foretelling winter. The laconic Laramie, the sultans of Swilling, and the boisterous Bork brothers enjoyed the cold. They found it stimulating, invigorating, challenging. Walter and Weepy hated the cold. To them, it was a time to stay indoors, hunker down with epic novels, fidget with the thermostat to adjust the coziness of a room, and complain, like many a Vermonter, about the weather.

In addition to his distress about plummeting temperatures, Walter had been having tummy aches. It seemed that no amount of the fortified version of his grandmother's legendary tomato soup and no amount of *Pepto Bismol*, milk of magnesium, and aspirin could alleviate the pain. As the vigorous work sawing and nailing 1,482 two-by-fours horizontally to 180 vertical posts continued at a steady pace – the foreman ever mindful but never vocal about the project's demanding schedule – Walter took a moment to mention his condition to Remington when the two teamed up on the saw horses.

"Have you ever seen blood in your stool?" Walter asked.

"No. You?"

"Once. Last week. Scared the shit out of me."

"Sounds like hemorrhoids."

"Think so?"

"You'd know it if you had 'em."

"How? I can't tell for sure."

"You reach back to wipe your ass and if you have to shove a bunch of grapes out of the way, you've got 'roids."

"You've had them?"

"Nope. But that's what I picture."

"That ain't it."

"You bled once. That was a week ago. It hasn't happened since?"

"That's right. But it's alarming, Rem, to see your own blood on toilet paper, even if it's only once."

"Was your asshole burning when it happened?"

"No, but I had wicked stomach cramps. I've been getting them from time to time."

"You're a hypochondriac, don't forget. You're bound to make something more serious than it really is. But let's face it, Walter; your diet leaves a lot to be desired."

"You may not think so, Rem, but I do eat healthy, most of the time. Just because my victual pleasures may not be appetizing to you doesn't mean they aren't healthy."

"*Zero* bars? Pork rinds? Pickled tripe?"

"Granted, I should stay away from those crispy pig skins. But chocolate, even white chocolate, is a mood enhancer. I get despondent this time of year. Chocolate is a flavorful antidote. Furthermore, anything pickled improves gastric secretions, enhancing digestion. And how about oranges and grapefruit, to say nothing of pumpkin seeds and sunflower seeds? I eat tons of tomatoes; raw, stewed, juiced, or cooked a variety of ways. And I eat the sharpest Vermont cheddar, usually with an apple."

"I've seen you eat an apple. You salt the piss out of it."

"I could cut back on the salt."

"I'll bet it's all those aspirins you wolf down, Walter. They're the culprit. Lay off the fucking aspirin for a while; see if that makes a difference."

"But nothing else works for my aches and pains. This is very demanding work. I'm quite certain this physical strain is hastening the approach of rheumatoid arthritis. It may also be true that bursitis has attacked my shoulders. Nothing assuages these horrific pains like aspirin, Rem. Besides, I think I'm addicted to those little white pills. Most people swallow them with a glass of water but I let them dissolve on my tongue. I relish their bitter taste."

"Suit yourself, Walter. But if I was bleeding out my ass, I'd switch to *Bufferin*."

Nineteen

Two more employees came on board simultaneously in the middle of the week.

As usual, all activity came to an abrupt halt when the fresh hires – jovial as they introduced themselves to each other on the walk down from the bluff – approached the work site.

Grumpy greeted the men in his usual gruff manner. Without further adieux, he escorted them to a stack of boards Walter had climbed onto. Weepy placed his pastel crayons back in their box, stuck a half smoked *Old Gold* under the strings on the fret of his guitar, and tuned up for a beguiling paradox featuring Santana's *Black Magic Woman* and the albino.

If there is safety in numbers, two isn't enough when in the presence of dog soldiers. Scandalized by the albino's perverse frolic, a wave of terror went through them when they turned to discover a beastly creature, his pants at his ankles, proudly hoisting his genitalia for their inspection. The *Missing Link* groused and grunted, grinned and groaned while Jericho's recruits barked and howled in fiendish applause.

Heavy rain soaking northern Vermont the previous day gave way to a dreary drizzle, ensuring mucky mud in the construction area.

Climbing to the third tier of strapping, hammers slung in their freshly filled nail pouches, the new men were met by a clamorous ex-Marine who demanded they *mock the cock* before pounding any nails.

Too frightened to respond, the pair looked blankly at Fritz when he pointed to the ground in the center of the barn. "Like that," he told them.

Gulliver and Remington were on their knees, chest-to-chest, thigh high in mud, arms bent at the elbows, flapping hysterically to their own blood-curdling shrieks. The demented Swilling brothers groveled and clashed, ramming each other with terrific force. Pierre, Popple, and Roger watched the violence from a safe distance. The new hires scrambled down from the strapping, untied their nail bags on a dead run, and were never seen again.

When they were driving away, Jericho whooped and hollered. He emptied his pistol – *pop, pop, pop* – reloaded, and emptied it again.

"This is Jericho."

"Rudy."

"What the fuck do you want? The horse barn is going great guns, so I know that ain't it."

"Actually, Jericho, it is and it isn't."

"Explain yourself."

"It isn't because I'm being investigated."

"What makes you think?"

"I got a strange phone call. The person wouldn't identify himself, other than to say he's with an investigative agency. He said if I didn't cooperate by answering all his questions he'd have my business license suspended until I did. Shit, Jericho, I'm full tilt on four projects. I can't afford to be shut down."

"What were his questions?"

"They had to do with people the unemployment agency sent to the horse barn."

"Is that the agency doing the investigating?"

"Probably. He wouldn't say."

"Go back to his questions."

"Apparently, all six of the new guys – that's his count; I thought there were seven – lodged multiple complaints with the chamber and the business bureau."

"Those groups don't have any clout; they're non-government."

"I don't think they're the only ones, for that very reason. It would take an official agency of the state to pull my license, not a special interest group."

"Tell me specifically what the man asked. I got things to do."

"Goshdarnit, Jericho, show a little empathy. My back's up against it here."

"Just get to the meat of it. I'm tired of sucking on all this fat. You haven't said a thing yet that's the slightest bit incriminating. Who cares if a wheelbarrow full of tweedledees and tweedledums got carted off with boils on their asses?"

"Hard to visualize, but you might be right. Keep in mind I haven't actually seen any of the complaints, assuming they've been formally written up. If you were in my shoes, you'd be upset about it. I've never had my license threatened like this."

"I'm going to ask you one more time to tell me what that asshole asked. If I don't get a direct answer, I'm hanging up."

"Okay. I've been holding back on this, but one thing he wanted to know is whether or not I've got an employee at the horse barn who carries a gun."

"I'm sure you told him, '*yessir*, one of my trusted dog soldiers has a Colt .45 tucked in his pants and if you go anywhere near the horse barn he's more than likely to whistle a few rounds past your ears'."

"Be serious, Jericho. Of course that's not what I told him."

"I've got a constitutional right to carry a gun. Speaking of licenses, I've got one for that very purpose. Just the other day I had to apologize to Deirdre for failing to see a hare before it ducked into the woods; otherwise, we'd have chowed down on some good old fashioned rabbit stew. Man's got a right to bag his own supper, Rudy."

"A worker who has a gun on him can be intimidating to some of the other workers, Jericho."

"Some sonuvabitch wants to tell me he's intimidated by it and I'll tell him to go suck a ball."

"That oughta help."

"What else was this investigator curious about?"

"The albino. A number of complaints make the claim that your pasty friend conducts himself in lewd and lascivious ways. I didn't have the foggiest notion what he was talking about. Do you?"

"Walter likes to treat the new guys to a little dance, Rudy. It's nothing more than an initiation rite. There's no harm in it. In fact, one of the men the unemployment agency sent over recently told us it was the best performance he'd ever seen. Case dismissed. What else?"

"Let's see here. Outlandish behavior, harassment – I'm looking over my notes – degrading criticism, crude language, threatening comments; oh yes, more than one said they felt like they might be attacked, sexually. What else here. Oh yeah, cruel mocking, insulting jokes about family members – even *mothers*, for goodness sakes. I got tired of writing at that point."

"All legal in my book. What else?"

"I don't know what else. But I didn't get the sense one phone call is all I'm going to hear about this."

"That may be, Rudy. All I know is we're right on schedule, nobody's gotten hurt, your dumb Frenchman is learning a thing or two, and that suck-ass superintendent of yours knows where he ain't wanted. Seems to me you've got a lot to be thankful for."

"I am thankful for one thing."

"Really?"

"The job's going well from one standpoint. I got a call from James Peters, one of the owners."

"You sure that ain't Peter James?"

"To tell you the truth, I don't know which it is."

"What'd he say?"

"I about fell out of my chair, Jericho. This man's high up the food chain in state government. He couldn't say enough about what an outstanding crew I have on this project. The man went on and on. Apparently, one of your guys impressed the heck out of all three of these state officials. That was great to hear. These people've put up their own capital for this horse barn."

"That was Gulliver. You don't want to lock linguistic horns with Gully; he'll tear your ass up."

"Richard was worried as all get-out about this site visit. So was I. But from Peter James' – or James Peter's – account, it couldn't have gone better."

"That's the beauty of it, Rudy. If you'll recall, I said as much. Get some sleep. It sounds like you need it."

"Thanks. Sorry to bother you, Jericho."

"I'll let you off, this time."

"Good night then."

Click.

Horse Barn

Marsha Leeks sat in the waiting room at the Attorney General's office, ten minutes early for her weekly interview with Vermont's lead legal beagle. Twice, she had dug behind the scenes for information leading to exclusive reports that had come out of these otherwise spoon-fed sessions. The local daily, Barre's *Times-Argus*, hated to be scooped by a weekly. The stories weren't earth shattering but they constituted her only shining moments at the *Chronicle*, a couple of gems she could put on her resume.

The door to the conference room on her left was ajar. Inside, several individuals were engaged in a lively discussion. She left her seat to stand near the door for a better listen.

"Any chance of a civil suit or criminal charges being filed?" one person asked.

"Difficult to assess, since the actual complaints didn't come to us directly."

"We put a man on it. Has he filed a report yet?"

"Indeed he has. It contains disturbing descriptions of strange and possibly dangerous individuals. Their behavior is shocking to say the least; insensitive, perverse, bordering on inhumane. Furthermore, there seems to be no rational basis for it other than creating conditions leading to humiliation for humiliation's sake, thereby achieving a good laugh at the expense of others, including themselves. That said, I haven't necessarily seen anything that smacks of civil rights violations. Close, but nothing so far that would allow us to swoop in. Criminal proceedings, of course, would require formal charges lodged by an alleged victim."

"Our agent is undercover, as I understand it," said another.

"That's right. He's unskilled in carpentry, but then too, none of these men – save the foreman, an educated man with remarkable tolerance – know any more about the building trade than our guy. That's a saving grace, in terms of allaying suspicion."

"Hardwick area, according to my notes. Some rough characters in that neck of the woods."

"Strangely enough, these men drive out to the work site every day from Chittenden County. Roger's trying to get a handle on that. Lord knows the unemployment situation here in Washington County has reached distressing levels while Chittenden County enjoys a vibrant economy, what with IBM and General Electric, the University and Saint Michaels College, a large hospital and ..."

"Never mind all that," said one of the agents."

"But hey, I've seen lines a half mile long outside Beansie's French fry bus at Battery Park over in Burlington's north ..."

"*Whoa.* Let me remind you that we work for the entire state; all fourteen counties. Economic disparities between counties are not our concern. Let's get back to this horse barn investigation if you don't mind."

"But I live in Washington County. I'd like to know why in holy hell a local contractor has to go outside the county for workers."

"That has nothing to do with whether or not we'll be able to bring charges against these derelicts. We're here to discuss Roger's report. The complaints he requested from the chamber and the business bureau; what do they allege, specifically?"

"The allegations are scurrilous, make no mistake. Unfortunately, they fall short of being blatantly illegal in my estimation. The complaints were made by common laborers sent to this horse barn project by the unemployment agency. In every case, these men were driven off the job the very first day by cruel and unusual treatment. Essentially, they were victims of derogatory appellatives; crude epithets."

"You mean name calling."

"In layman's terms, yes."

"That's all?"

"There's more, most of it sexual in nature."

"That's our hook. Sexual harassment on the job is getting more and more play these days. What do you have?"

"There isn't much. These temporary workers – all males, as you may have surmised – claim they were the object of another man's desire."

"But were they threatened? Physically threatened?"

"Unfortunately, the complaints aren't very specific in this regard. The alleged assailant is apparently more of a beast than a person. He has the build of a freight … no, that's not it. Here it is, a *box car*. He's covered with hair and has a distinctly guttural voice. Very frightening."

"Sounds like the elusive simian connection."

"Indeed it does."

"Let's have Roger get close to this, ah, *person*, to see if he becomes a victim. What else do we have?"

"I'd be surprised if that hasn't happened already. Anyway, three of the complainants allege that one of the workers packs heat."

"He carries a gun?"

"In layman's terms, yes."

"But there's nothing illegal about that, assuming he's licensed."

"If he uses it though, let's say in some way that in no way can be deemed to be hunting, per se, we'll most certainly have a violation worthy of assailment."

"You mean we can swoop in."

"Yes."

"In one respect, we'd be too late."

"That's true."

Marsha took copious notes. There was nothing immediately newsworthy here, but by the sound of it, a story was brewing. A scoop to boot.

Apparently, at the construction site of some horse barn, a backwoods coterie of uncommonly uncouth laborers were intimidating, *Deliverance*-style, every unemployed person who had the ill fate of being sent there for temporary work. An investigation was underway to identify this group of uneducated ruffians and, at the appropriate time, to nail them with various civil rights violations or perhaps criminal indictments. Not a bad story. In fact, a rather good story, given the angle of bad people menacing good people. Quite well balanced, in fact. Listening to the give and take, the investigation appeared to be very much under wraps – and under the radar of her competition.

Hardwick wasn't far from her office. While a specific location wasn't given, she could take a map and drive around scouring the general area. With any luck she might happen onto the construction of a horse barn. She could, luck permitting, assume a deflective guise, *à la* an investigative reporter.

Closing her stenographer's notebook, she stuck her pen in the spiral binding along the top and went back to her chair to await the Attorney General's executive secretary.

The week went well for Pierre. For whatever reason, Jericho's recruits cooled their browbeating of him and two of the new guys, Gray and Roger; preferring, instead, to hector, abuse, and generally oppress each other.

That was an odd trait of these rough-edged crazies; not only did they take great delight in terrorizing complete strangers with spoofs and bullyragging, they impulsively inflicted their invective on one another with unrestrained jubilance.

It was as if this tight circle of social misfits held to a sacred boast; the ability to withstand derisive attacks was the test of a man's mettle, a viable valuation of self worth. The strategy for survival was to be stoic enough to withstand extreme forms of torment. Any hint of submission was a contemptible failing. Every human flaw or weakness was meant to be dramatically exposed for swift exploitation leading to insufferable ridicule. Curiously, these traits were not only considered honorable, they were mandatory. Only a person as deranged as them could ever hope to gain a foothold in their inner sanctum secure enough to be declared deserving of entry.

These unsavory jesters were hell-bent for agitation, tension, and disruption. The peace and harmony cherished by common people were completely foreign to them, and therefore suspect. Their constant jousting brought acrimony and pleasure together to create a fulcrum that balanced ball-busting brutality with enthusiastic camaraderie.

Pierre's take on this bizarre paradox was conflicting. On one hand, the tyranny of Jericho and his dog soldiers exceeded mere intimidation; it was downright scary. On the other hand, it held within it an unexplainable magnetism, a mysterious force-field that, if one could penetrate it, if one could be attracted as an equal, then some exalted form of brotherhood might be experienced in a spiritually satisfying way.

It should hardly matter to him, he thought, having been introduced to their game so late. All he could hope for was peripheral acceptance; to be allowed to participate on the boundary, placing a tenuous toe inside only when extraordinary circumstance permitted. Perhaps this was best for a man of his civility, especially if it happened that the group's comical wrangling and playful disparagement shrewdly hid, at the deepest level, a cynicism bound to permanent alienation; an enmity that could never be disarmed, a loathing of society-at-large well past the point of being tempered and rerouted toward assimilation, an estrangement and ire that would never be rectified or reconciled with even the most basic of social norms.

He didn't know. It was, to him, a fathomless enigma. He only knew that he was somehow taken by these wild eccentrics in the way that swimming in a cold stream hurt at first but soon became energizing, enlivening the senses and animating the soul.

The weekend was, by the standard of tumult long established by the original members of the horse barn crew, tame.

Rem, temporarily forgoing cockfights at the reservation, made it a point to get home at a relatively early hour, climb into Bea's bed, stay there until he was fairly certain Sibyl was asleep, then sneak into the bed he had once passionately shared with his wife.

On Sunday, he and his precious honey bee strolled hand-in-hand to Ethan Allen Park. They rode the whirligig till they were silly dizzy, daydreamed aloud on the swings – Bea now mastering the art of the pendulation – and teeter-tottered until the jerks and jolts caused Rem to feel the queasiness of an impending hangover and he finally begged off.

Beansie had closed up his French fry bus the previous week so they stopped at a small grocery store during the walk home to buy hot dogs, chips, a root beer, and three sixes of the King of Beers. Rem glanced at his watch, nervous about making it back to the house in time for the kickoff of the Giants-Eagles game. Then his mind replayed the previous weekend's fiasco and he was close to panicking about whether or not any of the boys would show up.

Gulliver and Fritz watched the game at Box Car's.

Again, Fritz heckled and berated the Box for his feedbag gluttony while the munching beast chowed down two jumbo bags of *Wise* potato chips, several slabs of beef jerky, pickled hard-boiled eggs that had taken on a sea-green hue, and popcorn lavishly adorned with salt and drenched in oleo-margarine.

Fritz explained to Box, patiently at first but with increasing vehemence, that the difference between them was that the eating habits of the eldest Swilling held to lofty standards of healthy choices such as fresh fruit and vegetables, yogurt and whole grains, and only those fish that were proven not to have ingested too much mercury; whereas the Box was a stooge of the food giants, an unwitting victim of exploitative marketing financed with unlimited budgets and driven by a powerful greed for outsized revenues and unconscionable profits that claimed, as its calamitous casualty, the otherwise good health of the hapless hypnotized masses who would ultimately be sacrificed to the profiteering drug cartel.

Drinking his beer from bottles – refusing, as always, to drink from aluminum cans – Fritz would rise from his squatting position on the floor in front of the television to stagger into the kitchen, toss each empty into the waste basket, and stand there for a moment scowling and hissing. The ex-Marine was consumed by malevolence toward the demonized food conglomerates. He was bitter about their products, frustrated about their tactics, and hostile over their collusion with the pharmaceutical industry. He hungered for reprisal.

Another reason for his misery was yet another Giants win.

At the end of the game, Box belched, hoisted his formidable bulk up from his easy chair, emitted a long rumbling fart, and groused to his friends, "Let's go eat."

"I'm going home," Gully said. "Fritz turns into *Mister Lovely* after a measly ten or twelve beers. I don't want to be anywhere near him."

"What about you, Fritz?" Box asked. "I was thinking about going over to the Lincoln Inn. I've got a hankering for some of their red bean salad."

"Just what you need," Fritz said, "a big bowl of beans. No thanks. I've inhaled enough of your stink bombs for one day. I'm going to pick up some more beer, head over to my place, and see if I can't devise some crafty way to foil the junk food scam."

With that, the men left the apartment and went their separate ways.

Saturday night with Mabel had taken a lot out of the Grump. He ached everywhere, especially in the testes, which had been wrung out time and again with unmerciful rapacity. Stretched out on his sofa, he moaned with agony having to get up to answer the phone.

"Grumpy," he grumbled.

"Yeah, I could tell," said Weepy.

"What'd you call here for? Either you're not coming to work tomorrow or you've had a change of heart and you'll sing *Hello Dolly*."

"I called to ask you about Mabel."

"What about her?"

"You and she pretty tight?"

"I'm tight as hell after she spent the night here. But there's nothing tight about her."

Weepy laughed. "But you are going out with her, right?"

"You don't go out with Mabel; you go in. Then you hope to God the time comes when you can get out. Why?"

"She may not be much to look at from the neck up, but she's got a wicked body."

"Tell me about it."

"I'd rather you tell me about it."

"Find out for yourself."

"How?"

"You've got a car. Drive over to her place."

"We hardly know each other. You think she'll let me in?"

"Oh she'll let you in all right."

"And you don't mind if I try my luck?"

"I could give a shit less. Mabel's high spirited, always chomping at the bit for a new experience, rearing to go. She's more than this cowboy can handle."

"Think she'd have a problem with me?"

"I doubt it. She's indiscriminate. That's what makes her a goddess."

"Right. Goddesses are all about giving. The goddess of rain provides the occasional deluge. The goddess of enlightenment shows the way. The fertility goddess makes sure eggs ovulate and spermatozoa are tenacious seekers. The equine sex goddess gives a wild ride."

Grumpy gave him directions to Mabel's, hung up, and struggled back to the couch to rest his weary body parts.

Weepy put the phone down and hunted frantically for his car keys.

Walter yanked a piece of paper out of his typewriter and scanned it for typos. He wasn't writing a story – not yet – but he had drafted a formal outline of an idea that he believed had considerable merit. Pretending to be the editor of everything he wrote, it irked him to see misused words, shaky grammar, or sloppy syntax. This particular outline, he said to himself, would please any editor's eyes, to say nothing of satisfying the media's insatiable appetite for creative material.

He would title his article, *Lack of Money is the Root of All Evil.*

The first paragraph would explain why the worn but trusted adage about money and evil was backwards, entirely missing the real truth; that crime and poverty were consequences of not having enough money.

With this revelation revealed at the top of the story, in customary pyramid form, the reader couldn't help but want to know more.

Paying court to another popular aphorism, that there are things money can't buy, he would cite a Beatles song, pointing out that the group had been correct to state that money could not, per se, buy you love. Then he would note that honesty and friendship also did not hold pecuniary value.

But not happiness! Money, without question, could purchase a great deal of happiness.

Conversely, misery, despair, and emotional lassitude of various descriptions were often the result of inadequate financial resources. Walter knew from personal experience that it felt good to have a few extra bucks in his pocket, or in the bank, but it felt lousy when there were no such funds available. He was, as a prime example, considerably happier when he wasn't poor.

To be destitute, wherein gut-wrenching hunger was a daily condition, is to be the victim of an unrelenting, unforgiving evil. To be penniless, unable to feed oneself – or, in the case of bread-winners, unable to put food on the family table – robbed a person of their dignity and sense of self-worth. And what was the root of this evil? *Lack of money.*

Walter had hoped to avoid religious connotations in this particular piece. But it was exceedingly difficult. True, spirituality, whether or not it was related to any specific god dogma, was not something that could be purchased outright. True too, people who died wealthy were ultimately bankrupted by death (Walter liked this play on monetary concepts and took a moment to underline the phrase); they could not, as the saying aptly went, take it with them.

However, wasn't it curious that the *Bible belt* looped through the country's poorest states? And wasn't Jesus himself short-changing his followers by upending tables in the temple's marketplace while voicing his strongly held opinion that a place of worship was no place for business transactions? After all, what's the one thing you always saw in places of worship? *Money plates*. Long-handled baskets to reach the most reluctant soul. A smiling preacher's hand avariciously grabbing tithings. And what about the saying that it's easier for a camel to fit through the eye of a needle than it is for a wealthy person to be admitted to the kingdom of heaven? What the hell sense did that make?

Walter took out his red pen and put large question marks in the right and left margins. Maybe these points were too sensitive, especially for Christians, to be dealt with in such a forthright manner. A real editor might take out his paring knife.

Then there was Robin Hood. Okay, he was a thief given to sudden acts of violence. But the man was sick and tired of a feudal system that kept the peasants down on the farm eating mutton and dark bread while wealthy dukes and lords feasted on brazed duck and white bread slathered with delectable jams. Certainly Robin understood the evils of poverty, taking by sword from the haves to redistribute to the have-nots. It may not have pleased the haves, but there were a lot more have-nots back then and they were no doubt happy as all get-out for an unexpected handout. Heck, entire governments had been founded on this very principle. Hence, taxation, by itself, wasn't evil; it was the necessity of feeding the unfortunates by extracting from those more fortunate that was the real evil. Taxes merely exemplified evil.

People with nice homes and nice cars who went on fabulous vacations were, for the most part, happy – notwithstanding cranky kids. People who lived in squalor, rode the bus, and never traveled to interesting places were unhappy. What was the root cause of the difference? Happy people had money; unhappy people didn't. Ergo, lack of money was the root of inequity, the root of discontent and envy, the root of pain and suffering, the root of all-encompassing evil.

Walter grabbed his red pen again and put an exclamation point in the left margin. This last observation was notably pithy, very close to profound.

And what about medicine and health care? Pity the panhandler with a toothache. He had to steal a pair of pliers from a careless mechanic's toolbox to put an end to his agony. Contrast that with those who could afford a dentist. With the proper dose of Novocain in just the right place, extraction of the offending tooth was virtually painless. How else to describe the panhandler's plight as anything other than a circumstance that could have been mitigated if not for the evil of lacking the money to step into a dentist's office?

The same would, of course, be true for every imaginable illness. Some people had health insurance or could afford treatment out of pocket. Those who lacked money faced utter humiliation, having to go into a hospital and be identified as indigent.

Contrary to popular opinion, money was the root of happiness. It was the lack of money that caused an enormous amount of unhappiness, desperation and fear, anxiety and dread, anguish and sorrow; it was, by default, the root of all evil.

Walter placed the sheets of paper in a manila folder labeled, *Ideas and Thoughts Regarding Possible News Stories and Articles Potentially Worthy of Publication*, pushed his chair back from the kitchen table, stood and yawned – the hour getting late – and walked into the bathroom for more of the tasty pink syrup that seemed to work better than anything else on the rather crippling stomach cramps he'd been having lately.

Twenty

The weather in early November was unusually warm. Since the crew had not heard otherwise from Pierre, it was safe to assume that construction of the horse barn was progressing on schedule. But on days like this, when the weather cooperated, it made sense not to let excessive banter interfere with a brisk work pace. Ribbing, reproval, and rebukes could be well enough accomplished while the men pounded away astraddle two-by-fours laddering toward the two-by-six capping boards that would form the base for a long row of trusses. The men hoped to get ahead of schedule, knowing that their work would be slowed when temperatures dropped and cold rains, biting winds, driving sleet, or an early snowfall came across New York from Lake Erie or pushed down from Quebec.

Gray Popple, a wiry man who never complained about hard work, harsh elements, or the incessant criticism of his southern accent, his restricted vocabulary, scruffy looks, and Appalachian upbringing, was a good fit. A jack of several trades and master of matrimony – *Pop Pop Popple* – as Jericho dubbed him, Gray could go with the flow of abuse far better than anyone else sent to the horse barn by the unemployment agency.

Gray had noteworthy attributes; muscled arms adorned with tattoos penned by amateur practitioners, a solid work ethic, a desire to get away from his hen-pecking wife, and sufficient restraint to accept the fact that Weepy refused to play any country music. Further, Gray was unfazed by the albino's frightfully perishable appearance.

While not to be counted among the true dog soldiers, Popple was worthy of the crew's cruel treatment, dishing out almost as well as he received. The men liked that his sense of humor was without boundary. And they appreciated that he carried more than his end of a rigorous work load.

The dog soldiers, however, were not so amicable toward Roger Framingham. The imperturbable man with the studious gaze, gifted tongue, and monstrous snout who had his work clothes pressed and wore safety goggles when using the skill saw remained aloof, distant, and only guardedly approachable.

Remington had become the incognito agent's primary tormenter. "Hey Hammerham, you coming to the pig roast?" he called down from four tiers up.

Roger, between cuts at the saw horses, straightened up and looked through his double eyewear to find Rem. "I hadn't heard about it."

"It's happening Saturday over at Grumpy's place in Underhill."

"Is this a formal invitation?" Roger asked, sliding the goggles onto his forehead.

"Consider yourself formally invited, Bone-in-hand."

"That's Hamminframe, if you don't mind. *Framingham. I mean, Farmington.* Goddamnit, you guys've got me forgetting my own name."

"You got a girlfriend?" Rem asked from his high perch.

"Not at the moment."

"No wife and no girlfriend? What are you, queer?"

"I beg your pardon."

"You don't get a pardon that easy my friend," Rem said. "I asked if your preference is boys or girls. Not that I personally give a shit; the boys here are curious."

"I'm heterosexual, if that's what you're asking."

"It is indeed. Nothing to be ashamed of. I happen to get pretty sexed up over heteros myself."

"Why would my sexual preference be of interest to you?"

"Let's go back to your former occupation. I'd like to know more about that."

"What's to know?"

"You tell me."

"I went from white collar to blue collar. What's the big deal?"

"I don't care about your collar color. I want to know what it is you used to do, or what it is you still do except for an apparent hiatus here at the horse barn."

"And why would that be of interest?"

"Because we don't trust you, that's why."

"To do – or not do – what?"

"That's what we're trying to figure out."

"Am I not carrying my weight around here? Is that your concern?"

"You're not anymore cut out for this kind of work than the rest of us; but no, that's not my concern. We get the sense you're spying on us; a ringer for Rudy, or, more'n likely, for *Wicked Dick*."

"I don't know either of them."

"You've mentioned that you haven't met Rudyard Appling. You're saying you don't know *Wicked Dick* either?"

"I can't imagine who you're talking about."

"You drawing two paychecks, Roger?"

"I cash one paycheck, just like everybody else. And I'm none too pleased about the numbers on it, I might add."

Rem secured a two-by-four with his shoulder, drove a nail into one end, then pointed the hammer at Roger. "We're going to find you out, Rammaham. You can fool all of the people some of the time. And you can fool some of the people all of the time. Abe Lincoln said something like that. But you can't fool a dog soldier any of the time. I said that. On Friday, assuming you're still on the job by then, Grumpy'll give you directions to his place."

"Thanks," said Roger. "I wouldn't miss it."

When it was time to break for lunch, Fritz climbed down and walked over to Walter, who was unlashing his nail pouch to place it on a saw horse.

"Right after we eat, bird man, I'd say it's high time you dug a hole behind the *Port-a-Potty* and dragged the honey pot out to burn some shit."

The albino took off his hard hart and drove a rake of bony fingers through his fleecy hair. "I keep telling you, Fritz, that's not something I have the constitution to contend with. Especially after eating."

"I think you'll find there's very little difference between what you eat and what you'll find in the honey bucket. No sense digging into that shiny red lunch pail for any of your foul ruminants when you can reach down for a few of those fat dogs floating around in the shitter."

"You're making me sick."

"You've got shit detail, Walter. We're all agreed. It's a critical part of your job here."

Walter unplugged the skill saw and placed it on the ground, then wound up the power cord and hooked it over the end of a saw horse. "I demand a recount."

Fritz snarled. "There won't be any recount, tweety bird. The ballot box was locked up a long time ago."

"Assuming I work up the courage, and I'm not saying I can, shit detail will have to wait until the last hour or so in the day. I can't go into that putrid outhouse while I'm still digesting."

"Don't try and get out of it," Fritz said. "An hour before quitting time, we'd better see a shovel in your hands. That *Port-a-Potty's* been filling up for a couple of weeks. When I went in there to take a crap this morning I had to rise up so I wouldn't be dipping."

"You're a thoroughly disgusting individual," Walter said, brushing sawdust from his shirtsleeves while walking up to the bluff.

Alone in his truck, Jericho wolfed a meatloaf sandwich and a large slice of apple pie, pausing a few times to buff up the barrel of his sidearm with a red paisley neckerchief. The men in the Buick ate heartily, chided Rem about being on the outs with Sibyl – Rem saying it was far more serious than that – needled Fritz with continuous offers of cheese puffs and ring dings, wheedled a sheepish Weepy about his weekend exploits, and flung shit-duty jokes at a dubious albino who barely touched his smoked oysters, crumbles of gorgonzola, box of raisins, and cellophane-wrapped bowl of black olives.

Box gurgled through a mouthful of potato chips, "Look what the hell we got here." The grizzly one rolled his window down and pointed at Pierre. The Frenchman, lunching in his VW bug next to the blue sedan, was about to peel a banana that he was holding to his mouth.

Box leaned his head out of the window and groaned a strip-tease tune while Pierre peeled the phallic fruit. Instantly, the dog soldiers picked up the notes. Fritz rolled down his window to cat call.

Pierre smiled but refused to look over at the men, closing his mouth over the top of the pulpy fruit. Trying to maintain his composure sitting next to a pack of barking dogs in the four-door kennel a few feet away was a difficult task. Unfortunately, the size of his banana was unusually large. It would take a lot of bites to eat it all.

As the stripper tune grew in volume, punctuated by barks and howls, Pierre decided that the best way to deal with his dilemma was to emphasize it. Thus, before biting off another piece of banana, he slid the fruit into and out of his mouth with a smile and a wink for his audience. The crew roared its approval. At the end of the exhibition, the men scrambled out of the Buick to give the Frenchman a resounding round of applause. Pierre had, by joining in the gibes rather than defending himself against them, dramatically improved his standing in the hearts and minds of the wild eccentrics. It was, he said to himself, his just dessert.

Around three o'clock, a car pulled up near Jericho's truck. Weepy and Walter, on one of their frequent smoke breaks, were the first to notice. Weepy called out, "*We've got female company. Everybody on their worst behavior.*"

Pierre thought the guitar player's comment was understated humor. He turned to Gulliver. "Did he mean you guys have *not* been on your worst behavior?"

Gully sneered. No, *Pee-ehhhr*. Up to this point, we've been on our best behavior. Let's face it, we've pretty much had to create opportunities to behave badly, and even then, they've been barely frequent enough to stave off mind-numbing boredom." Watching the woman walk toward to the construction site, Gulliver added, "But it looks like that could change rather quickly."

When Marsha Leeks reached the apparent entrance to the barn, Rem motioned for her to join the crew gathering in front of a stack of texture 111. Roger, not surprisingly, continued working at the other end of the structure. Marsha stepped inside the structure. Walter climbed the stack, tossed his hard hat into the crowd, and stretched and limbered in preparation for his ritual dance.

All eyes were on the albino when Remington said to her, "Welcome to the horse barn." With that, he turned on the heels of his work boots, raised both arms with heightened drama, and pointed to Weepy with a maestro's flair. Weepy launched into the mid-sixties' Dave Clark Five song, *Glad All Over*. Jericho slapped a drumbeat on Walter's hard hat and sang along, *so glad you're my-yi-yi-yi-yine.*

Marsha was the bewildered recipient of a maniacal performance by the spindly creature whose shock of white downy hair puffed and poofed about his head while he danced down-and-dirty, flailing and thrashing his wispy arms, jerking his bony pelvis with lewd abandon.

Weepy gave a final strum on his guitar, the exhausted albino bowed, and the crew erupted in bellows and bawls of delirious gratification.

Fritz eyed the visitor, then went to her, grabbed one of her hands and led her back up the road with polite determination, as if to steer her clear of anticipated calamity.

Marsha wrested her hand from his. "What are you doing? And what in God's name was the purpose of that insane act?"

"Listen," Fritz said in a hushed voice. "It's very dangerous for you to be here. You should leave immediately."

"But I'm fairly certain this is the place I was looking for."

"I'm sure it is. But your safety is threatened. Believe me, this is the last place you want to be." Fritz reached for her hand. "I feel the need to rescue you before something ugly happens."

Marsha refused his hand. "In case you missed it, something ugly already happened. That was grotesque and deplorable, a scene right out of *Mad* magazine."

"Madness reigns at the horse barn," Fritz said, his arms out to his sides, palms up, pleading with the woman. "*No one can rein it in.* That's why I'm trying to lead you away from here. This is no place for a person like you. Incidentally, I'd like you to take me with you."

"But I'm a horse woman," she said, surprising herself with the impromptu rationale for being there.

"Can't be," said Fritz. "Mabel is the horse woman."

"Who's Mabel?" the reporter asked. "I don't see any other female here."

"Our equine sex goddess, the horse woman. One helluva ride, from what I'm told."

"*Equine sex goddess?* That's preposterous."

"Yes. Yes it is. You're obviously very astute, in addition to being magnetically attractive. But the point is you can't be a horse woman when we've already got one. A place like this doesn't deserve two."

"I don't understand. You are building a horse barn, aren't you?"

"That's what they tell us."

"How many stalls will there be?"

"I have no idea. Hundreds, maybe. I haven't studied the blueprints."

"I was thinking I might want to board my horse here."

"You can't. It isn't finished."

"I realize that. I'm just scoping it out."

"Don't use that word."

"What word?"

"Scope."

"Why not?"

"Because I suddenly realize it's the one thing I forgot."

"I don't understand that either."

"You don't have to. All you need to understand is that it's incredibly dangerous for you to stay here. You need to leave at once. And I really would appreciate it if you took me with you."

"Are you trying to escape or something?"

"I wasn't. But it strikes me as a wonderful idea."

"You can't go anywhere with me. I want to know why it's so dangerous for me to be here. Are some of these workers lunatics?"

"Again, that's absurdly perceptive of you. With one, maybe two exceptions, they're all lunatics."

"What do you think they'll do to me if I stay?"

"Hard to say. But it's not them I'd be worried about if I were you."

"Who should I be worried about?"

Fritz put his hands on Marsha's shoulders with a chivalrous smile. *"Me."*

Marsha shook free, taking a quick step back. "Don't try anything, mister. I'll make sure you're front page news if anything happens to me."

"Great," Fritz said. "I'd like that."

Marsha took another step back. "You're a crazy man."

"Again you astonish me with your discerning cognizance. But if I am, indeed, nuts, I'm nuts about you."

Marsha backed away one more step. "What the hell is that supposed to mean?"

"Lust at first sight. Bitten with smitten. Head over tea kettles in love." Fritz felt an urge to demonstrate his desire. He dropped to his knees like his brothers did whenever they engaged in the game, *mock the cock*. He pinned the backs of his wrists to his sides, threw his head back, flapped his elbows, and cackled hoarsely, *"Er-er-er-er-ooooooo; I'm your rooster, baby, when not any cock'll do."*

Marsha took two more steps back. "You can't come on to me like that."

"I can't?"

"No!"

"Oh," Fritz said, his head dropping. He stood up, heartbroken. He turned, repositioned his nail bag, and shuffled back to the barn without another word.

Marsha, her knees shaking, tried to collect herself. My goodness, she was thinking, the AG's office is really on to something. This place is bananas. First an emaciated freak is the featured attraction of a one-song outdoor rock concert, then an obvious sex fiend goes on the attack. Should she stay? *No way.* This place really is dangerous. There's no telling what could happen next. Sensing imminent peril, the Washington County *Chronicle's* daring sleuth retraced her footsteps up to her car, walking backwards the entire time to keep an eye on a work crew that acted as if she had already gone, not one of them looking her way.

Her hand fumbled to insert the key in the ignition. She started her car, let out a long breath, jammed the shifter into reverse, backed up, turned the steering wheel with nervous hands, and stepped on the gas. Pebbles flew up from her tires, splattering the tail gate of Jericho's truck. And she was gone.

Gulliver was impressed. "What the hell did you say to that woman to make her tear out of here so fast?" he asked the eldest Swilling.

"I told her she'd entered a loony bin. I had to inform her that she was one horse woman too many. I have to admit though; I was so aroused by that woman it felt like my heart was in the middle of a stampede."

"Something scared her."

"She's never met a man like me. Whether she knows it or not, she's terrified I might be *Mister Right*."

At four-thirty, a truck with an enormous white tank inched its way down to the site. Walter was looking around for a shovel when the truck appeared. The vehicle turned to drive along the side of the barn where the stakes and bracing had been removed. Walter noticed that the letter *S*, large and bold, was painted three times in bright red on the side of the tank. He squinted at each *S* trying to discern the words that went with them. When he could make them out, he lifted the bill of his hard hat and wiped his forehead with his shirtsleeve. Phew! *Sam's Septic Service* had arrived.

The driver got out and dragged a long hose toward the plastic outhouse. The relieved albino, all smiles, looked up at Fritz, whose legs were wrapped around a two-by-four twenty feet off the ground.

Fritz looked down at him, returning the smile. "Looks like you're shit out of luck, Walter."

Twenty-One

Tuesday morning a cold rain rode in on the harsh squalls of a north wind, lashing window panes, rattling tin roofs, waving road signs, licking windshields, and pricking faces with sprays of tiny needles. Pierre, mute for fear of dampening the crew's spirits or dousing their determination, knew that the forecast called for heavy rain mixed with sleet for the next four days.

Only two men, the foreman and Roger Framingham, had brought rain gear. By ten o'clock, the others were soaked to the bone and thoroughly miserable.

Grumpy tried to keep his mind on other matters. "Mabel's got the day off," he said when the men gathered under Weepy's equipment tarp for a brief respite. "I should have brought her. We could have taken turns going up to the car for an occasional warm up."

"Go get her," Gulliver said, shivering. "We'll cover for you."

"Driving all the way to South Burlington and back in these conditions, there'd only be an hour or so left in the day by the time we returned. I should have thought of it earlier. Don't worry though; I'll write myself up for it."

"Peachy," said Gully. "That makes me feel a lot better."

The work pace slowed appreciably. Two days of this, Pierre knew, and they'd fall behind schedule.

During lunch, forced to keep the windows rolled up, the dog soldiers yipped and sniped at Walter when he opened a can of anchovy paste to smear on his roasted pepper sandwich, the stench powerful enough by the end of the break for the crew to exit the Buick and brave the brutal weather.

By mid afternoon, the unrelenting rain had crystallized into knife-edged pellets pelting the men's hard hats. Fritz, trimming two-by-fours with a chainsaw four tiers up, threw the heavy implement into the mud and climbed down. "I've had enough. You guys can keep at it if you want, but my hands are numb. Throw me the keys, Grump. I'm going up to the car to warm up. And I'm not coming back down here the rest of the day."

Box went behind Walter and unplugged the skill saw. "I've had it too," he said. "If I get electrocuted but escape death, I might end up looking like Walter. I ain't taking that chance."

Remington and Gulliver climbed down after Fritz.

Pierre had a mutiny on his hands. But he couldn't blame the men. Even with his raincoat and waterproof pants, he was cold, his neck was stiff, his gloves were sopping wet, and he could barely feel the ends of his fingers. Continuing to work in these conditions would only risk injury. Not much was getting accomplished in any event.

He hollered up to Roger and Gray, who had started on the fifth tier. "Come on down, boys. We're calling it a day."

Cranking up the Buick, Grumpy could hear Pierre tapping the window on his brother's side of the car. Box cracked the window a smidgen. "What do you want?"

"I want to suggest you bring some rain gear tomorrow. Who knows how long this will last."

"Good advice," Box said. "I guess that's why you're the foreman. None of us uncommon laborers would have thought of that."

Pierre couldn't blame the Box for his sarcasm. The real surprise was that the men lasted until this late in the day. He'd worked plenty of outdoor jobs over the years in some terrible weather, but he doubted that any other crew could have persevered under these conditions for more than an hour or two. If the dog soldiers' attitude toward him had improved lately, his opinion of them was also much enhanced, despite their near criminal lunacy.

There was no letup in the gusty winds and icy rain all day Wednesday. Yet the men kept up a steady pace, staying right on schedule, in Pierre's estimation.

Thursday was more of the same. The crew stayed at it. The mud inside the perimeter was, by now, nearly a half foot deep.

Pierre felt sorry for the albino. Walter was not nearly as strong as the others. His thin legs were visibly weary as he trudged with newly sawn boards through the quagmire, sometimes having to climb several tiers with ponderous mud-caked boots to hand them up to the men.

Fritz was on edge during the drive to work Friday morning. The rain and sleet and whipping winds were without cessation for the fourth successive day. The merciless weather made the crew members cranky and short tempered; but no one more so than Fritz. Having to keep the windows rolled up meant that the smell of Walter's coffee inside the Buick was pervasive. This annoyance, the thought of having forgotten to get the phone number of the new horse woman, and the sight of Box Car, Rem, and Weepy chomping on powdered donuts were enough to send the senior Swilling into a freefall of vitriolic verbiage.

He went on a twenty minute tirade. Donuts, he said, were uniquely symbolic of the country's dietary masochism; a contrived delectation more treacherous than snow cones imbedded with bits of razor blades that Viet Cong children sold to G.I.s, and more sinister than a pedophile posing as Santa Claus in a department store. These inflated wheels of naked calories, as he described them, were concocted of nutrient-stripped white flour submerged in boiling fats, bobbing up when sufficiently greased to be injected with jellies and creams and laced with syrups, sprinkled with sugar, then served with saucy smiles to the flabby-minded masses at the countertops and drive-up windows of self-destruction all across the country.

Vowing to call dramatic attention to the atrocities of junk food merchants and to the accursed marketing methods of the packaged goods industry – the *enemies within*, as he called them – Fritz spat and railed, condemned and foredoomed, and pounded the back of the front seat until Box, tired of the beating, let out a ferocious growl and Grumpy slammed on the brakes, the Buick sliding sideways down a slick Montpelier street and coming to rest at the edge of the parking lot of a dimly lit diner.

"I'm going inside for a coffee and donut," Grumpy announced, righting the car and parking it in acceptable fashion. "I ain't listening to any more of Fritz's ranting and raving."

The men piled out of the car and sloshed through the slush to find a seat inside. Except, that is, for Fritz, who sat in the Buick fuming and scheming.

Grumpy grabbed a stool at one end of the service counter, telling the others they'd be wise to sit as far away from him as possible. What he needed most was quiet.

Gulliver and the Box sat on swiveling chrome seats near a trucker who was hunched over a plate of over-easy eggs, rashers of bacon, and hash browns. Rem sat between Weepy and Walter at the end of the counter.

The guitar player lit an *Old Gold* straight, the albino a *Lucky Strike*. Rem asked the roly-poly counter man wearing a white paper hat the shape of an envelope to serve up three black coffees and three plain donuts.

"Make mine glazed," Weepy said.

"You'd have one with extra sugar after hearing Fritz's condemnation of donuts?" Walter asked.

"I could ask you the opposite," Weepy said. "How could you possibly order a plain after Fritz made such an appetizing case for the dazzling donut?"

"Never mind Fritz," Rem said. "Take a look at Grumpy down there, sipping his coffee, trying to get things straight in his head after listening to yet another confusing diatribe. Shit like that rattles the hell out of him."

"You'd think he'd get used to it," Weepy said.

"He can't get used to it," Rem said. "He's a left-brainer, just like my wife."

"As opposed to being a right-brainer," Walter said.

"Yes, Walter, that would be the other side."

"Separated by the corpus callosum," Weepy interjected.

"Correct," said Rem; "the bundle of transverse fibers connecting the cerebral hemispheres."

"I'm a helpless right-brainer," Weepy said.

"Like no other," Rem said. "I believe it's safe to say that Grumpy is the only left-brainer among us, including Jericho. Which is too bad for the Grump since it's basically a left-brain world out there and he got caught up with the likes of us. He's the perfect example of a person running with the wrong crowd."

"Clue me in on the difference," Walter said. "I smell a possible story."

"It's not news," Rem said. "It's a subject of ongoing study. There's no scoop for you."

"Let me be the judge of that, if you don't mind," Walter said, realizing the mistake he'd made showing his ignorance on the subject.

"Look at the Grump," Rem said, waving the dense smoke away from his face and taking a sip of his coffee. "He's utterly baffled, irate, consumed by confusion. It could take three cups and half a dozen plain donuts before he's back on track."

"He hates it that we're going to be late for work," Weepy said.

"Precisely," Rem said. "Left-brainers are incredibly time conscious. Come to think of it, Grumpy is the only one among us who wears a watch."

"It has to do with his need to be organized," Walter said, pleased that his comment might put him back in the know.

"That's it exactly," Rem said. "Grumpy needs organized movement, punctuality, logical processes, regimentation, schedules, and controls. The fact that we're completely out of control at all times is unbearable for him."

"You said Sibyl is a left-brainer?" Walter asked.

"She's an accountant, for chrissakes. Her life is all about filling up columns with numbers, staying inside the lines, adding and subtracting until everything balances out. How much more organized and calculating can you get? The woman isn't happy unless the teeter totter of life is perfectly flat; no disruptive influence at either end."

"Wonder what attracted her to you?" Walter asked. "You're as imbalanced as anybody I know."

"Thanks, Walter. I happen to believe that stupid saying about opposites attracting is a crock of shit. It must be. We're as opposite as two people can be and our marriage is in the toilet."

"Okay boys," Grumpy shouted, standing and opening his wallet. "Time to ride out to the horse barn. Since it was my idea to stop in here, I'll pick up the tab."

No one argued. On the way out, Rem asked the Grump if he'd left a tip.

"Couldn't," Grumpy said. "The check came to exactly five dollars. I wasn't about to break another bill just to leave a tip."

Walter dashed back inside and placed two quarters on the table, fully aware that Grumpy's logic made perfect sense.

"How we doing for time?" Rem asked Pierre when the crew broke for lunch.

"You get a half hour, like always," said the Frenchman.

"That's not what I meant. Are we on schedule or behind?"

"I'd say we'll have some catching up to do when the weather clears."

"We're in Vermont," Rem said. "The weather might never clear."

The foreman thought about that. "If it doesn't, we're in trouble."

"Good," Rem said. "That's the way we like it."

At noon, the rain abruptly stopped. Twenty minutes later, the sun peaked through. The men were so elated they grabbed their lunches and ate outside, despite a chill wind.

"Any idea what the forecast is?" Rem asked no one in particular.

"Clear skies right through the weekend with warming temperatures," Pierre was happy to say.

"Just in time for the pig roast," Box grunted.

"You haven't forgotten about the pig roast have you Farmingman?" Rem called over to Roger.

"I've got the directions," said the sleuth. "Rain or shine, I'll be there."

Rem turned to the Frenchman. "You intend to bring the Misses?"

"You said I could."

"Absolutely. She's got a right to know you haven't been lying about the crew you're working with."

"She still won't believe it, especially after she's met everybody."

"That's the beauty of it," Jericho said.

Ten minutes after the crew was back on the strapping, a car pulled up. The men could hardly believe their eyes, especially Fritz. It was the surrogate horse woman.

The eldest Swilling slipped his hammer smartly into the loop on his nail pouch, climbed down from twenty feet up, grabbed a handful of ten pennies to drop in for extra weight, and trudged through the mud toward the entrance to greet his distressed damsel.

Marsha Leeks was nervous about her second visit but had summoned the courage to come back to the horse barn in hopes of gathering enough background information to write a detailed story in the event the AG's investigation led to formal charges. As Fritz approached, she held up a hand. "Don't try anything."

"I don't blame you for being afraid of me," Fritz said. "Common sense dictates you should be. But I'd also like you to be aware that I will always respect your wishes, even if you decide not to go to bed with me."

"I can't believe how bold you are."

"I'm being honest."

"Honesty like that can get you in a lot of trouble."

"It always has."

"I'd like to ask a few questions," she said, unraveling the wrapper on a granola bar in the hopes that a snack would ease her tensions.

"By all means," Fritz said. "What is that, a candy bar?"

"No. Candy bars aren't good for you. This is a granola bar. It's got whole grains and raisins and lots of other healthy ingredients."

"Somehow, I knew you weren't one to be hoodwinked by the sugar conspiracy."

"I don't know what that means. Can I ask a question now?"

"Go ahead."

"Who's in charge here?"

"Everybody except that Frenchman over there," Fritz said, pointing toward the crew. "He's the one who's about forty pounds overweight, isn't much with words, and puts Linda Lovelace to shame going down on a banana."

Marsha tried to erase the image that flashed in her mind. "There's no single person in charge?"

"I'm single."

"What I meant was, is there no one who's the boss?"

"An adroit change of tenses; *was, is*," Fritz said with a delighted wink. "I like that. Such cleverness of the tongue bespeaks an acrobatic wit, perhaps qualifying you for a contest of linguistic gymnastics on the balance beam of philosophical positions."

Marsha, clueless, squinted into the gray abyss of Fritz's eyes. How could this crude lout befuddle a professional word-worker? His proffered challenge made little sense to her. "Come again."

"That would be premature."

"Do I detect a *double entendre*?"

"I wouldn't know. Ask Pierre. He's a Frenchman."

"I'm merely trying to find out if anyone here holds a position of authority."

"We do have a super on the job, if that's what you meant to mean. You want to talk to him?"

"Yes, please," Marsha said, relieved to have finally gotten somewhere. "I only have a few questions."

Fritz hollered to Remington. "Come down here and have a word with this lady. She's got some questions and she doesn't trust me."

"I never said that," Marsha said. "I actually remarked upon your honesty."

"Your remark was negatively charged," Fritz said.

"Can you blame me?"

"There's no one else to blame."

"You're impossible."

"To the contrary. Anything's possible with me."

Rem walked up with a congenial extension of his hand. "Remington Swilling, ma'am."

"My name is Marsha Leeks," she said, her eyes quickly diverting to the rain-swollen tampon. "Is that what I think it is dangling from your helmet?"

"Thanks for noticing, Ms. Reeks. I'm the super on the job. And incidentally, this is a hard hat. Helmets are for football. Steel pots are for war. Envelopes, I believe, are for donut heads."

"Apparently you're an expert on hats," Marsha said, trying to joke.

"That I am."

"Incidentally, it's Leeks, not Reeks."

"Won't make that mistake again, ma'am," Rem said.

Fritz stood next to his brother, his arms folded, staring with unabashed rapture at the covert reporter. Fritz's fixation was unnerving but Marsha held her ground.

"This building is going to be a horse barn," she said to the super.

"That's what they tell us."

"And if I wanted to board a horse, I suppose this would be a good place to do it."

"Not yet. We haven't finished building it."

"I can see that. And who might the owners be?"

"State officials."

"Really?"

"Yup. High up, we're told. They've inspected our work, of course. Rest assured they were thoroughly impressed. And why wouldn't they be? We're right on schedule. Every post and board is plumb and level. The crew is always on its best behavior, since we're non-union. And we never complain about the weather, about the blueprints getting all smudged with mud, or about the lame brains the unemployment office keeps sending over here."

Marsha could hardly believe what she was hearing. *State officials?* Happy about the work crew, their constructive attitude, the progress being made? The comments were completely contrary to the discussion she'd overhead at the Attorney General's office. And yet, this had to be the horse barn the agents said was under investigation. She had driven every primary road, secondary road, and dirt road in three counties to be sure. There was no other horse barn under construction. Still, that last comment was troubling.

"Lame brains?" she ventured.

"Right."

"What about them?"

"You tell me."

"I asked you."

"They're lame brains."

"Did they last long on the job?"

"Of course not, or they wouldn't be lame brains."

"That sounds like a double negative."

"She's into doubles," Fritz said. "Kinky."

Marsha ignored the insinuation.

"They were all negative," Rem said. "Must have been at least half a dozen of them."

"But if they didn't stay, maybe it was because they were …"

Rem waved off the line of questioning with a dismissive sweep of his arm. "Forget about lame brains, left brains, right brains, or brain drains," he said. "You want to come to a party?"

"Excuse me?"

"I'm inviting you to a party."

"What kind of party?"

"It's a family picnic. We have one every year at this time. At one of the dog soldier's houses."

"Dog soldiers?"

"That's what Jericho calls us."

"I don't know what that means."

"Neither do we; something about dog and soldiers. Oh yeah, seems like he mentioned an elite band of native warriors; a tortured analogy that only a twisted mind like his might entertain. So how about it?"

Marsha hadn't made many friends in Vermont. The *Chronicle* was, for her, a lonely place. Still, she didn't know any of these people. "Will other women be there?"

"Sure. Lots of them. Wives, mostly. And, of course, the horse woman; our equine sex goddess."

There was that troubling term again. Marsha stifled her curiosity about the reference to an apparent mythological figure. "Will there be a lot of drinking at this party?"

"You betcha! Live music too. Horseshoes. Badminton. And all the food you can eat. It's a pig roast."

Marsha had heard about pig roasts but she'd never been to one. Vermont probably had a lot of them, given all the farmers. "When does this party take place?"

"Tomorrow."

"Oooh! That's short notice."

"If you've got other plans, that's okay. You'll miss out on some real fun though."

"And where will this party be?"

"Underhill. You know where that is?"

"Not really. I've heard of it, but I've never been there."

"You got a pen and some paper? I'll give you directions. It's easy to find."

"Yes. Yes I do. There's a notebook in my car."

"I'll walk up with you," Rem said.

Fritz went with them, but did not press his perceived good fortune.

Sitting in her car watching the two Swillings walk back down to the construction site, Marsha looked over the directions, taking a few minutes to add to her notes from her earlier visit. She took a bite of her granola bar, questioning what she had gotten herself into. Hearing about this work crew, she was thinking, you'd swear they were illiterate rednecks, sexual deviates, uncivilized backwoods ingrates with a violent bent. Certainly her first impression, up close and personal, exceeded the worst of her expectations. But that impression all but vanished when she engaged a couple of them in a rather baffling conversation. These two, at least, were anything but illiterate. Indeed, their comments seemed to employ riddles. There were overtones of parody and a disarming candor cleverly mixed with elusive innuendo. Were these men actually dangerous or were they simply spoofing? She found herself wrestling with a beguiling paradox; a taffy pull between curiosity and fear, between clear repugnance and vague attraction.

Her trepidation soon surrendered to the reporter's instincts as she considered the unexpected opportunity to dig deeper. Despite the pull of an undercurrent of anxiety, she drove away with her confidence rising. Hey, you don't look a gift horse in the mouth.

Welter showed up just before quitting time. He was surprised to see that the strapping was about eighty percent completed, having imagined that the bad weather would have knocked the crew off schedule.

Grumpy walked over to the superintendent and handed him a perfectly hand-drawn map to his place in Underhill. "You haven't forgotten about the pig roast have you?"

"Dee Dee is looking forward to it," Welter said.

"Things'll get cranking around ten o'clock."

Welter walked past the Grump to have a word with Pierre.

Weepy had covered his equipment when he saw Welter's truck and was stacking lumber on top of the tarp. The men untied their nail bags and dropped them, along with their hammers and measures, into the tool box. When they walked up to the bluff, Pierre was right behind them. Strangely, Welter and Roger were still at the barn, engaged in a serious conversation.

When Grumpy cranked up the Buick, Box growled. "What'd you make of that? Looks like Roger and *Wicked Dick* know each other after all. Hold up a minute, Grump."

Box rolled down his window and motioned to Pierre to roll his down.

"Are Welter and Arminham friends?" Box asked.

"I doubt it," Pierre said. "I just introduced them to each other ten minutes ago."

"Seems like they hit it off pretty good."

Pierre looked down at the barn and nodded. "They do seem to be having quite the *têtê-á-têtê*."

"Makes sense they'd get tight," Fritz said. "One's a prick and the other's an ass."

"If we keep staring at them we'll all turn into pillars of salt," said Weepy, "putting the horse barn somewhere between Sodom and Gomorrah."

"Weepy's right," Rem said. "Let's get out of here. Salty language makes me thirsty."

The crew waved to Jericho and Pierre and headed for the nearest store to load up with beer and snacks. On the way to *The Man's Bar* their mood was jovial. They were happy to be getting their first Saturday off since the horse barn enterprise began in mid September. Despite the ineptness of the unemployment office finding quality help, some nasty weather, distractions caused by the owners' visit, *Wicked Dick's* impotent upbraiding, and two visits by the would-be horse woman, the project was actually a day or two ahead of schedule. No doubt having their own super on the job had a lot to do with it.

For once, Fritz didn't fuss about Walter's *Zero* bar or Rem's favorite beer. Perchance the mysterious woman with the notebook had temporarily mollified his umbrageous temper. More importantly, Grumpy was given no reason to hit the brakes or steer his Invicta toward a tree.

Horse Barn

The crowd at *The Man's Bar*, though a Friday, was sparse because of the early hour. There was room at the bar for the entire crew, although Weepy decided to remain in the car to stoke up some ganja and pick his acoustic.

When Walter ordered a soda water, Fritz went into his ill-temper mode. "You niveous pussy willow, why can't you order a real drink like the rest of us?"

"Leave the snow cone alone," Rem said. "He's had stomach problems. Horseradish and Tabasco aren't the best substances for him right now."

"Why can't he have a different mixed drink? Why does it always have to be a bloody Mary? I'm sick of his fastidious blending and mixing of this and that ingredient. *Hey bartender.* Give this man some good old fashioned rot gut." Fritz chuckled and clinked his beer mug against Walter's glass. "Just kidding, Birdie. I know you're a sick man. Drink whatever you think might buy you one more day."

"There you go again, Fritz, talking like I'm a goner. I intend to be around for a long time; if for no other reason than to see how you land that reporter in the sack."

"*Reporter.* Who the hell are you talking about?"

"That lady who visits the horse barn."

"What makes you think she's a reporter?"

"I saw the notebook she was using when Rem gave her directions to Grumpy's. Only a reporter uses that kind of notebook. I should know."

"You don't say?"

"Yes I do. What's more, I don't believe she knows diddly about horses."

"And what makes you say that, you tenacious little bird shit you?"

"I could hear the conversation from the saw horses. Horse people, especially when they're near a horse place, only talk about horses. That's all they care about. Marsha only mentioned a horse once. And she never pursued it. If she was a true horse person she would have asked all kinds of questions about the barn; how much it's going to cost to board a horse there, whether or not riding lessons will be offered. She would have requested the name and maybe a phone number of one of the owners so she could inquire with the right people. But no, the main thing she was concerned about was what happened to the workers the unemployment agency sent to us; until, that is, Rem invited her to our party."

Fritz and Rem were impressed. "That's incredibly observant of you," Rem said. "But why would a reporter be interested in the horse barn?"

"I think she was simply looking for *Mister Right*," Fritz said. "And she found him."

"That ain't it," Rem said. "Walter's on to something. What else did you notice?"

"It took very little persuading for her to accept your invitation to the pig roast," Walter said. "Think about it. She doesn't know any of us. She's obviously scared to death of Fritz, for good reason. And since she probably lives somewhere around Hardwick, getting to a small town in Chittenden County means almost two hours of driving over unfamiliar roads. She could have declined the offer, which was the response I would have expected. She could have said she'd think about it, not wanting to hurt anybody's feelings but clearly intending not to go. Or, after a serious amount of coaxing and convincing, she might have reluctantly agreed to show up; hoping one or more of the owners will be there so she can negotiate a low stable fee for being one of their first customers."

Rem stared at the albino in disbelief. Walter wasn't finished. "Furthermore, during her first visit, she threatened to make Fritz front page news. Who could do that except a journalist?"

"Shit, Walter, you may end up a reporter yet," Rem said. "All those things went right by me. I was thinking the reason she readily agreed to come to the party is because she's so enamored by the suave swain over here, the gallant musketeer, our own swashbuckling bucko, my brother the swaggering dandy …"

"Enough's enough," Fritz shouted, slamming a fist on the bar.

"See that, Walter?" Rem said. "Fritz can even evoke one of her favorite scenarios, the double-do. You watch; tomorrow, he'll offer her a stick of double mint gum and tell her he's a Gemini."

"It's true, though," Fritz said. "Marsha is taken with me. She's coming to the pig roast because she knows I'll be there. Woman's intuition is whispering to her that I'm *Mister Right*. Sooner or later, it'll be loud and clear."

"She'll be there because she's looking for a story," Walter said.

"I agree with the Q-tip," Rem said. "If he's right, it proves one thing."

"Not that Walter can make it as a journalist," Fritz said.

"No," said Rem. "It'll prove you can't fool a dog soldier."

The men made a short night of it at their favorite bar; saving up a modicum of brain cells for the party in Underhill. Rem maxed out all three pinball machines despite constantly looking over his shoulder for Wynona to show up, which she did not. Fritz, with the exception of a snide remark about Box's weakness for sausages pickling in a huge jar next to the cash register, was remarkably docile. Gulliver placed a wager that he and Rem would once again win the horseshoe tournament; the Grump only too happy to snap up the bet. Box angered the bartender by ordering pizza delivered from the shop across the road directly to his bar stool. Walter succumbed to pressure and drank two bloody Mary's, sending him into the men's room six times. And Weepy was doing pastel drawings in the darkness of the Buick after seven bowls of Panama Red.

By midnight, every dog soldier was in bed.

Beatrice woke up when the hall light came on at four am. Her mom was mad because her daddy had to pay a man a lot of money for his hobby. She smiled on her way back to sleep, knowing her daddy would be climbing in next to her.

Twenty-Two

Taking a radical turn, the weather Saturday was gorgeous for a mid November day. The temperature an hour after the sun came up was pushing fifty degrees. The forecast called for the mercury to rise well into the sixties by early afternoon. Unusual conditions, indeed.

Rem pulled around to the backyard and parked his pickup alongside the house, the tailgate a few feet from the back door. Grumpy came out of the kitchen to help unroll a canvas tarp. Under it stood four half-kegs of draft beer surrounded by a ton of ice. Bea's plastic swimming pool covered the bottom and the sides of the cargo bed, helping to contain water when the ice melted.

They folded up the tarp and took it to the garage, returning with two cases of beer each. After two more trips, they ripped open the cardboard containers and placed 288 cans of beer all around the kegs.

It was a site to behold; enough beer to satisfy a battalion of desperate tosspots back from maneuvers in the Mojave Desert, and enough ice to keep the kegs cold throughout the day and well into the night.

Grumpy checked his watch. "You got here late, Rem."

Remington grabbed Grumpy's wrist to have a look. "Shit, you're right. I was ten minutes late. What a catastrophe. The others will start showing up in about an hour; only enough time for me to drink three beers. Had I gotten here at the appointed hour, right on the dot, I might have gotten four beers in me before the others arrive."

"I had it planned where we could be all set up before anybody gets here."

"What's to set up? The horse shoe pit's been in the same place for ten years. The band doesn't play till the afternoon and we don't set up till an hour before. What the fuck's your problem?"

"I was talking about the badminton set."

"Gee, you're right. That could take all of five minutes. Where is it?"

"In the hallway closet. Hold on, I'll go get it."

Grumpy went into the house and Rem walked around to the side of the garage where twenty jumbo size bags of charcoal, already torched, had been dumped into an oval pit. Two sturdy iron prongs were driven deep into the ground at each end of the pit and an eighty-pound pig, cleaned to the hide with a bell scraper and smiling like a happy Buddha, was stretched out along a spit that had to be turned every half hour.

"Where'd you go?" Grumpy called.

Rem stepped from around the corner of the garage. "Pig smells great.

When'd you fire up the pit?"

"Box did, at six o'clock. He's crashed out on the couch. He said once you got here you could take a few turns turning the spit. Give it half a spin and we'll get this badminton set set up."

"If I wasn't so goddamn sober, I'd swear you were stuttering."

Rem turned the spit and followed Grumpy to the back of his spacious lawn, which bordered a hay field that needed mowing.

"Right here's good," said the Grump. "I figured Sibyl and Bea'd be with you."

"There you go again."

"They coming later?"

"Nope."

"Is that stick-in-the-mud wife of yours still pissed off at you because of the tripe dance?"

"She's pissed at me for all kinds of things. Says I gamble away my paychecks, which is a true statement, to this point. Not that my own cock doesn't stand up to a good thrashing. The problem comes when I bet on the other birds. Sibyl hates it that I drink only with the boys; never with her. And she claims I don't show her any affection unless I'm boned up for some serious belly slapping; which, by the way, hasn't happened in at least a month. That's tough on an old whore dog like me."

"I'd make the suggestion that you give Mabel a try but I know how you are about that fidelity shit."

"I took a vow. It's always been my intention to keep it."

"I'm sure she holds up her end."

"I wish to hell," Rem said, finding a reason to chuckle while stretching a string from the top of a flimsy post and tying it around a plastic stake. Shoving the stake into the ground, he gave the Grump a painful look. "Sibyl's true blue all the way. So am I, for the most part."

"Do I detect a slip there, ol' Rapid Eye Movement?"

"Yes and no. Wynona's been laying it on me pretty heavy these days."

"I've seen her. So has everybody else, except Sibyl."

"I don't want anything to do with Wynona. But she's obsessed with me. Has been ever since high school."

"You got any kind of history with her?"

"Not really. I had a chance once, before I was married. I'd been partying pretty hard when she made her move. But I was more interested in Jack Black than I was getting laid. She started necking with me, which made it difficult to take swigs from the bottle. So I told her she had halitosis. Seems like ever since then she's been breathing down my neck. And not because she wants to prove she doesn't have bad breath."

"This could be a long day for you. I imagine she'll show up for the party; always has."

"With any luck, her husband will be with her. I'm hoping that'll cool her jets."

"Bea had a great time last year," Grumpy said. "Too bad Sibyl didn't let her come with you. There'd be plenty of people to watch out for her while you're playing."

"Bea cried buckets about it. She remembers last year's picnic, especially dancing up a storm with Walter. She drank so much soda pop she got sick to her stomach. But that didn't slow her down. She and that skinny package of *Good & Plenty* dancing together were the center of attention."

"That should do it," Grumpy said, standing up and tossing four rackets and six birdies under the net. "Time for you to take another turn turning that pig."

Families and friends, friends of families, and families of friends arrived in droves between ten and one o'clock. By two o'clock, when members of the band began testing their mikes, more than seventy people were milling around.

Nine and a half two-person teams – Walter unable to find a partner – began the first round of the horseshoe tournament. Kids and grownups played badminton while others played croquet with a set someone had brought. A long line of people stood at the back of Rem's pickup to draw beer. Another line had already formed outside the only bathroom in Grumpy's ranch style house.

The shirtless Box Car stood in front of the roasting pig wearing an apron and a chef's hat. He wielded a long fork and a gleaming knife, using the implements to wave people away whenever someone came by to sniff the pig's sizzling flesh.

A large folding table at one end of the pit held several tall stacks of plastic plates along with a couple hundred plastic forks and knives and a dozen or more packages of paper napkins.

Near the back hooves of the pig, Box had hung an iron cauldron. Every once in while he'd carve a piece of fat from the pig and toss it into the pot of steaming beans.

Tucked away in the refrigerator, to be brought out to the table at three-thirty, were two bowls of tossed salad, a potato salad, three different kinds of pasta salad, trays of sliced cheese, and a variety of hors d' oeuvres and relishes courtesy of many of the party's participants. On the kitchen counter were dozens of packages of bread and rolls.

A barbecue grill had been placed ten feet from the pit for those who preferred hamburgers to pork.

On the kitchen table were pies and cakes, cookies and brownies.

Grumpy's pre-Thanksgiving pig roast had never run out of food during its seven-year run and it wasn't likely to happen this year either.

Among the notables, Jericho and Deirdre showed up around noon, followed ten minutes later by Pierre and his wife, Lorraine. Richard and Dee Dee Welter pulled in at one o'clock, just ahead of Roger Framingham.

The general contractor and his wife would not be coming. Rudy was boycotting the event because employees were partying instead of working. Jericho had informed the company owner that the dog soldiers had to watch football on Sunday, therefore the roast had to be on held on Saturday or the crew would be unable to attend its own party; a point that Rudy failed to understand, much less accept.

At quarter after two, the band launching into the third number of its first set, Marsha Leeks took the last turn shown on the hand-drawn map unfolded on the seat beside her. She could hear music in the distance. Around the turn, she saw dozens of cars and trucks lined up along both sides of the road. She considered turning around. There was obviously a very large crowd at this picnic and she didn't know a soul. But she waived off her anxiety and pulled over to park.

She folded the map and put it in her purse. Still uncomfortable, she lingered in the car mulling over many thoughts, first among them the dire warnings of her would-be suitor. If she wasn't safe at the horse barn, would she be in any less danger here? But then, didn't this Fritz guy tell her it was he who was the real threat? No doubt Fritz would be at the party. Did she fear this man? At first, maybe. But for one so bold, there seemed to be a self-limiting factor to his advances. And didn't he say he would always respect her wishes? Even if – *oh my*.

Prior to her second visit to the horse barn, she had done some digging. From what she had gleaned while eavesdropping on the discussion at the AG's office, the complaints being hashed about had not come directly to the state's most powerful investigative agency. What route they took to end up there was a mystery.

An interview with an official of the Washington County unemployment office revealed that five or six men had made serious allegations about being harassed and humiliated by a crew of uncivilized desperados who were building a horse barn near Hardwick. A review of recent complaints made to the Chamber of Commerce mirrored those at the unemployment agency; the same construction company – the owner identified as Rudyard Appling – the same complainants, the same allegations, and identical descriptions of the alleged offenders. A third check, this time at the Better Business Bureau, produced the same results. Each of these groups had allowed Marsha to make copies of the complaints, which she had taken back to the newspaper for a thorough read. To this point, she had not made phone calls to any of the injured parties.

Injured? How? Not physically, according to what she had read. The one thing every allegation boiled down to was an injured ego. So what? Do attacks against the ego constitute a violation of civil rights? Her mind screamed *yes*, of course they are. And yet, common sense suggested that attacks against one's pride were commonplace. A motorist might get angry at another driver and shout something contemptible. Employers upset at lackluster performance or chronic tardiness often resorted to verbal attack. Preachers consumed by wrath when a member of their flock succumbed to temptation hardly kept their ire a secret; hells bells, this very thing was the focus of many a damning sermon. A notable percentage of those in the teaching profession were legendary for causing psychological problems with ego-damaging castigations. Jealous friends were capable of vicious verbal assaults. The list went on and on; everyday conditions of life in a world that could sometimes be harsh.

But wait! Sexual harassment is a serious matter, a frequent occurrence in the workplace that was gaining greater attention these days. No fewer than three of the complainants, while not physically violated, were victimized by threats that were, without question, loaded with sexual innuendo. Their statements, all quite similar, alleged that one particular member of the horse barn crew, a man with a nickname having something to do with trains, had squeezed their buttocks when they least expected it, rubbed up against them when their backs were turned – presumably using his genitalia – constantly grunted and groaned like an animal, and occasionally grabbed his "crows nest" in a manner that was nasty, provocative, and terrifying. *Crows nest.* What the hell is that?

Then too, every complainant stated that the grotesque and offensive dance of the emaciated albino was a mandatory introduction to the project. One particular official who recorded this information likened it to a barbaric ritual on the order of an aboriginal celebration prior to some sordid, perhaps cannibalistic feast. Marsha had witnessed this galling display with her own eyes. It was unnerving, to be sure. But could it not also be said that it was all in jest? She recalled that the live music was, in fact, quite good. And except for the assault on one's basic sensibilities, was any real harm caused by it? Was there an implied threat, beyond its obvious shock value, that foretold a specific doom, irreparable injury, or lasting emotional disability? She thought not.

And yet, the intimidation hardly stopped there, according to the initiates. The man known as Fritz – her personal tormenter – was, in the words of one, warlike. Certainly the man was contentious, judging from her personal experience, but she would not go so far as to describe him as overtly bellicose. Fritz had undoubtedly seen plenty of combat. One of the laborers, having been subjected to harrowing stories with gruesome outcomes, gave this issue serious weight in his complaint.

Could it be that Fritz was one of many Vietnam veterans who brought the war back with them? Marsha's journalistic mind drifted. Was this not a potential story in its own right? She made a mental note to explore this very topic with the intense man whose sleet gray eyes told of so much while revealing so little.

Fritz seemed, in her mind, to be more enigmatic than anything else. Perhaps he was a person with a double personality. Was he crude or courtly, savage or suave? Does the man's heart beat cold or does it flutter with the inarticulate speech of yearning, an inaudible plea for intimacy? He did, of course, come on to her like gangbusters. But then, as quickly, he receded like a wounded animal in the face of her rebuke. His offensiveness yesterday was at least tempered by refreshing honesty.

Suddenly, she no longer felt threatened by this Fritz person. Rather, she was intrigued by him. Maybe he was ... *No*, for goodness sake, banish the thought. There were lots of men around. And she was, by no means, unattractive. Indeed, if her own ego had its say, she was one heck of a catch for the right man.

And what about Fritz's brother, the so-called *super* on the job. Remington Swilling was identified as a prime instigator of significant folderol. Personally, she saw him as having a ready smile and a disarming wit. It seemed to her that he was not the same person who was described as rowdy and intimidating by those who couldn't survive a full day at the horse barn. She could be wrong, but he also did not strike her as the kind of person who might be pained by internal conflict. To the contrary, he was funny, articulate, and polite; a really super guy.

Marsha's mind was having its own picnic, feasting on a smorgasbord of thoughts and images that mixed the good with the bad, the negatives with the positives, the pros with the cons.

That's it, she said to herself. By combining evidence in the complaints with reflections sparked by personal discovery, the stark reality of the horse barn crew was gaining a puzzling clarity. These so-called dog soldiers were nothing more or less than *self-styled con artists*. Not in a criminal sense; rather, in a manner fabricated to produce self-indulgent entertainment. Their behavior – provocative and insulting, to be sure – underscored a need to overtly mock social convention; a condition informed by an arrogant self-esteem that resulted in scornful but, if only for them, hilarious humor. Could it be that in their self-imposed, cloistered environment, this handful of derelicts engendered a world view filled with outlandish perspectives on the human condition that offered surprisingly novel methods for coping with, with – *with what?* Marsha took out her notebook, snapped off the cover of her pen with her teeth, and scribbled: *for coping with the burden of what they know.*

She decided it was warm enough to leave her jacket in the car, got out, locked the doors, and walked briskly up the gravel road, excited to be going to her first pig roast.

Roger reluctantly accepted the idea of teaming up with Walter in the horseshoe tournament, as long as Walter agreed not to do it down-and-dirty until after they were eliminated so that Roger could busy himself with other options rather than be forced to endure yet another of the albino's risqué performances.

Grumpy wanted Rem to make sure the band stayed on his predetermined schedule of sets and breaks.

"I can't do that," Rem told him. "The band breaks when Gully and I need to hit the horseshoe pit, you know that."

"It'll be easy," said the Grump. "You started at two o'clock and played for forty-five minutes. Everything's perfect so far. If you break for half an hour, go back on for another forty-five minutes just like I planned it out, the second set will end when it's time for you to make the announcement that the pig is ready."

It was difficult to find fault with his line of reasoning but Rem had no control over tournament play, which took precedence.

"Besides," Grumpy said, "the crowd is more interested in hearing you guys play than whether or not it's yours and Gulliver's turn to throw the shoes."

"We don't care what the crowd wants, Grump. We play music because we like to play music. If there happens to be a crowd around when we're playing, that's fine. For the most part though, we play for each other, just like we do everything else. If we don't happen to be on stage when the pig's done, you can grab a microphone and make the announcement yourself."

"I'm not much for public speaking, Rem. I get all nerved up and the words don't come out right. I need somebody else to make the announcement."

"So pick someone to do it for you, for chrissakes. You're annoying the hell out of me."

Grumpy looked around fretfully, scratching his head.

"It's all the people, isn't it Grump? They're everywhere. Kids are running around making all kinds of racket. People are going in and out of the house, letting the screen door slam. You've got lines for the bathroom, lines for the beer, lines at the horseshoe pit; lines and more lines, everywhere you look."

"If they were really lines, it wouldn't bother me so much, Rem. But people don't line up and stay in position. They mill around. Somebody cuts in front of somebody else and there's a dispute. If that ain't bad enough, instead of being straight, the lines curve like a damn snake. It's an awful sight, Rem. Gets worse every year."

"I know it does. Look at it this way; late tonight they'll all be gone and you can think about the clean-up in store for you tomorrow, getting the place all neat and orderly like you had it. Now isn't that a nice thought?"

Grumpy scratched his head. "I guess so. Maybe I shouldn't get so uptight."

"That's it. Calm down. Draw yourself another beer and go with the flow. The party just got started. There'll be plenty of frustration for you later. It's better not to come all unraveled this early or you and your brother will end up getting into it like you did last year. Nobody wants to see that again, especially since Box refuses to put the knife down."

Rem gave the Grump a friendly pat on the back, then waved an acknowledgement to Gulliver who was calling him over to the horseshoe pit.

When Rem got there, his younger brother couldn't be happier.

"We drew Walter and Roger," Gulliver said.

"Good," said Rem. "That means we can find Weepy and start the second set on Grumpy's schedule."

"We don't play on any schedule," Gulliver said.

"I know that. But Grumpy's acting like he's our road manager; got everything all laid out. Scared to death he'll have to take the mike when the pig's ready."

"I'll make the announcement," Gulliver said, "even if we're in the middle of a game. I did it last year; I can do it this year."

"Yeah, but you caused a fist fight between Box and Grumpy."

"That fucking Grumpy can scrap, can't he?"

"He had to, what with the Box swinging that sword around. All the kids got pretty scared over it, if you remember."

"Bea too?"

"No. She thinks Box is a swashbuckling pirate."

"I'll figure out something else to focus on this year instead of which Bork can growl the loudest," Gulliver promised. "Something that keeps Jericho from entering the fray."

"Hand me those shoes," Rem said. "I'm ready to kick the albino's pink ass."

"You ready, bird man?" Rem called down to the other end of the pit.

Walter, who had been waiting patiently for the game to begin, nodded and stepped back, getting into position for his first throw. Little did anyone know, but he had secretly practiced horseshoes during the four months leading up to the horse barn job in hopes of avoiding a repeat of last year's embarrassment when not one of his shoes landed in the pit. Three times during the previous tournament one of his shoes bounced at a sharp angle and hit someone on the shin. By the end of his team's second match, which was a skunk, everyone knew enough to clear the area to prevent getting injured by his errant tosses.

Besides all the practicing in a neighbor's back yard, Walter had bought a book on positive thinking. The words *psycho cybernetics* caught his attention at the bookstore and he had to know what it was about. The book explained how one could condition the mind to expect success in all endeavors by using the mind's eye to visualize and constantly rehearse winning situations. Thousands of times, as it pertained to horseshoes, Walter closed his eyes and pictured himself throwing ringers. It had no effect initially, but during his second month of practice he finally threw a ringer. He got so excited about it that he was unable to continue the game, his arm quivering with eagerness, his mind unwilling to settle down. By the middle of the fourth month he was throwing ringers routinely; seven in a row on one occasion. Now, in this moment of real consequence, his mind was again afflux with nervous anticipation. His arm tensed and trembled.

"Come on you anemic miscreation," Gulliver yelled to him.

Walter steadied himself, took a tenuous first step, found his balance on the next step, his rhythm on the final step, and heaved himself into the throw. The horseshoe sailed in a high trajectory, flipped twice end-over-end, and landed eight feet shy of the pit.

"Nice try you weak-armed aberration," Gulliver shouted with a taunting chuckle. "Go again."

Walter shook his head, wondering what went wrong. He had measured his neighbor's pit before beginning his arduous practices. It was regulation distance, same as Grumpy's. Okay, no big deal. He would compensate for the discrepancy on his next throw.

Again the shoe tumbled twice in a perfect arc, this time scattering Rem and Gulliver and landing eight feet over the pit.

"Didn't know you had it in you, Birdie," Rem called out. "That was a good looking throw, even though you way overcompensated. You got me worried down here."

Rem took his turn, the first shoe close enough to the pin to garner a point, the other a leaner for two.

Roger, a tall athletic man with strong arms, had always enjoyed horseshoes. And he was good at it, though his method was to spin the shoe rather than flip it. His first toss clanged against the iron pin and bounced too far away to register a point. His second throw hooked the pin and settled around it for three, much to his partner's delight.

"I'll get better," Walter said, his spirits buoyed. "Watch and see."

"Sure thing, pinky," Roger muttered.

Gulliver's first throw hit the pin, knocking Rem's leaner a foot and a half away although his shoe fell close enough for a point. "Sorry," Gully said to his teammate.

His second toss skidded into the sand at the front of the pit and landed a foot short. Roger and Walter three. Remington and Gulliver two.

To everyone's astonishment, Walter's next toss landed straight on the pin, an inch short of qualifying for a ringer but getting a point. "I'll move that in," Walter confidently stated to his partner, backing up for his second throw. Sure enough, this shoe landed on the first, nudging it into ringer position, skipping slightly and clanging hard onto the pin.

Gully and Rem ran up for a closer look. Both shoes were undeniable ringers.

"How the fuck did you do that?" Gulliver hollered to the albino.

Walter was smug, nodding to his foes but saying nothing.

Roger put both of his shoes close to the pin. Eight points in all.

Rem threw his shoes for a point each. Gulliver followed with one wayward toss and then a ringer. Five points. Roger and Walter eleven. Rem and Gully seven.

The final score, with Walter throwing one more ringer and a leaner and Roger connecting with a ringer and two other points, was Walter and Roger twenty-one, Gulliver and Remington fourteen.

At the end of their first round, Rem walked smartly up to Walter and poked him in the chest with an index finger, knocking the albino backward. "You've been practicing, you sick sonuvabitch; admit it."

"What makes you say that?"

"Don't give me any shit. No way you got that good without practicing.

And I mean one helluva lot of practicing. *Mister Man*, you couldn't even land a shoe in the sand last year."

Walter smiled and gave his friend a feeble return poke. "Must be luck. Let's go get some beer."

Mabel's circadian rhythms were always awry. In a typical week at Fanny Allen she worked two or three first shifts, once or twice on the second shift, and the third shift once or twice. Grumpy had picked her up at the hospital the night before, a few hours into the third shift, and brought her to Underhill. Wide awake at two o'clock in the morning when the Grump went limp and fell asleep under her thrashing convulsions, she slipped off him and skipped downstairs to watch TV. As daylight peeked through the windows, she drifted into a deep sleep, remembering nothing of Grumpy carting her back upstairs and depositing her on his bed.

At two-thirty in the afternoon, well rested, Mabel took a long shower, shaved her legs, and got into the cream colored bikini she had put in her overnight bag. Grumpy was at the back of the truck drawing a beer when she came out the back door shucking and jiving to the live music.

"What the hell are doing wearing a bathing suit?" Grumpy asked her.

"You said Remington was bringing a swimming pool."

"For one thing, the pool is in this truck. We're using it so the ice won't drip all over the place when it melts. For another thing, *it's fucking November*. Who goes swimming this time of year?"

"But it's warm out today, Stumpy. Don't get mad at me. I just want to have fun. Do you want me to change out of this suit?"

"You can run around in your birthday suit for all I care," Grumpy said, drawing a beer for her. "The color of your bathing suit makes you look naked anyway. *Here.* Go have fun."

Wynona's sense of rhythm was better in bed than on the dance floor, but over the years she'd taught herself to be loosey-goosey, clapping as well as anyone to a simple drum beat. In high school, Rem and Sibyl appeared together three times on *Dance Date*, a half-hour show on Channel 3 that played pop music and featured students from a different school each week. Consumed by jealousy, Wynona could hardly watch when they were on. She vowed to get good enough to someday woo Rem to her cause, but since he only went to dances when his band was playing she had to be content glancing up at the stage occasionally to see if he was watching her slinky technique.

Peering between his cymbals and seeing Wynona slither seductively to a Kinks number, Rem felt a pang of anxiety when he couldn't find Bud in the crowd. Despite staring at Rem a few times during the second set, she wandered off with her friends at the end of it, making no attempt to engage him.

Gulliver placed his bass guitar on its stand and walked back to his microphone to make an announcement. Box stood behind him providing information.

Ladies and gentlemen, may I have your attention please.

Box tapped Gully on the shoulder to tell him something. "Really?" Gulliver asked.

Box said something else. Gully balked, then turned back to the mike. "The head chef informs me with a note of frustration that his helper failed to turn the pig at the proper times. One side has finished cooking but the other has not. It will be another forty-five minutes before he can carve the meat."

Gulliver leaned back. "What's that? You're shitting me?"

"However, folks, I do have some news that's sure to please someone, although I can't imagine who. I'm told that the Box himself took great pains when he butchered the pig outside his apartment around midnight last night, carefully draining its blood into sauce pans that were immediately stirred over a fire to prevent quick coagulation. Hold on a minute."

Gulliver leaned back again. "You don't say?"

Stepping again to the microphone, "Chopped onions and various spices were then sprinkled into the simmering blood which, when fully cooked, was encased in the pig's intestines. Give me another sec, folks."

Gulliver leaned back a third time to hear what Box was saying.

Turning back to the mike, "The head chef was up half the night preparing this blood sausage, blood pudding, or *boudin* as the French call it – *eh*? It's now the Box's supreme pleasure to invite each and every one of you to mosey over to the chef's table and enjoy his specially prepared boudin while you wait for the pig to finish roasting."

With that, Gulliver turned off his mike and walked as far away from Box as he could get.

Ten minutes later, three large bowls of boudin on the table in front of him, Box motioned Remington over. "Nobody's come by for my blood pudding. I worked half the night making it."

Rem bent over one of the bowls. "Who can blame them? This stuff looks like it came out of the *Port-a-Potty*."

Box reared back and thumped his chest with a gorilla's roar, his butcher knife glinting in the afternoon sun. "They'd better eat it, goddamnit, or they ain't getting any fucking pig. Go grab a mike and tell 'em."

"You want me to announce that you won't start carving the pig until all this blood pudding has been eaten?"

"That's right."

Pierre walked up to the table with his wife. "Did I hear Gulliver say you made *boudin*?"

Box regained his composure. "Got tons of it right here in these bowls."

"Lorraine and I are French. We love boudin. Mind if we have some?"

"Of course not. Have all you want. Meanwhile, I'm going to walk around with one of these bowls and see who else wants some. Must be most people didn't hear the announcement."

Twenty minutes later, frantic, Box walked up to Jericho. "Listen

Laramie, I need your help."

"What kind of help?"

"Nobody's eating any of this blood pudding I worked on half the goddamn night. I've offered it to just about everybody. The only one's who've had any so far are Pierre and his wife. And Walter, of course."

"What do you want me to do about it?"

"You got your gun in the truck?"

"No. It's tucked in my pants. Why?"

"I need you to walk around with me. I'll offer people the blood sausage I got in this bowl; anybody who says they don't want any, you put a gun to their head and get ready to shoot the bastard."

"Sounds good to me," Jericho said. "Who's first?"

Box and Jericho walked over to the horseshoe pit, stopping play. Edgar and Frank politely declined Box's offer, whereupon Jericho yanked out his pistol, trained the barrel on Frank's temple, and cocked the trigger. "Eat this pig's blood or you're dead meat."

Frank was friends with Jericho but he'd always questioned Laramie's sanity. "Do I need a fork?"

"Just grab one with your hands," Box groused. "The intestines are every bit as edible as the blood; a little crunchy 'cause I overcooked 'em a little, but they're still scrumptious."

Frank eagerly reached into the bowl and grabbed a shiny four-inch length of blood sausage, brought it to his mouth without looking, and chewed it like there was no tomorrow. *"Mmmm,"* he said. "This actually tastes pretty good. I never would have thought."

Jericho, wild eyes sparkling, pointed his gun at Edgar with the hammer still back. "What about it, Edgar? Think you'd like some blood pudding too?"

Edgar snapped up a greasy black sausage, studied it with wrinkled apprehension, then nibbled at one end of it.

"Take a goddamn bite," Jericho yelled at him.

Edgar chomped on the boudin, chewed it with the expression of a man struggling with constipation, then swallowed. "*Not bad.* Not bad at all."

Frank reached in for another piece. "I can't believe how good these are."

"That's you're last one," Box said. "I want to make sure there's enough to go around."

Jericho and Box walked to the other end of the pit and offered boudin to Bart and Sylvester, both of whom snatched sausages out of the bowl without hesitation.

Other teams came forward to enjoy Box's unusual delicacy. When the bowl was empty, Jericho aimed the gun over the hayfield and fired six quick shots. "Just wanted you boys to know it was loaded," he said. "Come on, Box. I'll go out to my truck to reload; you go get another bowl of that pig shit."

The boudin finally gone, Box went back to his carving table and Jericho went to the microphone where he yodeled for three excruciating minutes before announcing that people could start lining up for some roasted pig.

Roger got in line about fifteen persons back, directly behind Mabel whose backside he studied with rapt scrutiny. He moved closer and sniffed her hair, which smelled heavenly. As the line inched forward, Roger distanced himself by a few feet, squinting through his thick wire-rimmed glasses for a more discerning look. With Mabel's bikini approximating the tone of her skin, he blinked through the sun's reflection in his glasses trying to distinguish between fabric and flesh. The task was marvelously difficult.

Roger's next ploy was to get as close to her as possible. Tall for a woman, she was nevertheless several inches shorter. With a pronounced shake of her rather ponderous head, Mabel's hair shifted and tumbled over her right shoulder. Roger leaned to sneak a sniff of her bare shoulder. Mabel turned toward him. "Oh! *Hi there*. Are you trying to smell me?"

Roger was shoved back by her ebullient bounty, keen to the depth of cleavage, tongue-tied by the bluntness of her question.

"I showered with *Ivory* soap. It doesn't sting your eyes. I can lather up from head to toe and watch the bubbles slip and drop and drip and pop. Smells heavenly, don't you think?"

"It does indeed," said Roger, holding onto his composure by a flimsy strand.

"Here," Mabel said, standing on her tiptoes and rounding her shoulder toward his face. "Have a *good* smell."

Roger slid the sucking nostrils of his prominent nose along her clavicle. "Yes. Heavenly."

"You've got quite a nose there," Mabel said with a giggle.

"Oh that," Roger said, slightly embarrassed. "It is rather large, I suppose."

Mabel batted her eyelashes provocatively, smiled, rose up on her tiptoes again, and whispered with huffing breath into his ear, "You know what they say about men with big noses."

Roger crinkled his brow. "No," he said. "I don't believe I do."

"You're joking with me."

"Actually, no. I'm not entirely sure I want to know, but I suppose I am curious. What do they say?"

"I don't know for sure if it's true or not," said Mabel. "It's just what I've heard."

Mabel was next up at the table and Box shouted to her. "Hey! Horse woman. You want some pig or not?"

The equine sex goddess spun around. "Oh! I'm sorry, Boxy. Yes. And some potato salad, please."

"Get your own potato salad," Box said. "All I do is cut the meat."

Roger heaped his plate with pork and beans. Mabel was standing at the end of the charcoal pit sinking her sparkling enamels into a hunk of roast rump. "Want to go somewhere and eat together?" he asked.

"Okay."

They walked toward the badminton set where families and a few lonely hearts were scattered around the lawn sitting cross-legged, eating and chatting, enjoying the picnic.

The sun winking its goodbye, the band – well lit by now – fired up the third set with the Doors' *Love Me Two Times*. A rush of dancers, like gnats to a porch light, swarmed in front of the band to jitter and jump with bumps and kicks, flutter and flit with dips and skips.

Dancers burst into clamorous applause at the sight of a frenzied maniac-in-masquerade buzzing into the thick of the thrashing throng. The band knew instantly from the disjointed grinding that the gussied grig was none other than the spindly albino, egregiously garbed in a skeleton costume.

Love me two times, girl
One for tomorrow
One just for today
Love me two times
I'm going away

Wynona joined the juggling bones, others following suit.

The third half-keg tapped, the Bork pig roast went into a higher gear. Deirdre corralled Jericho, telling him to put a muzzle on his irritating yodels and get his sorry ass onto the dance floor. The horseshoe tournament went into its last leg with the final four teams. Roger and Mabel, under cover of creeping dusk, cunningly ducked into the hayfield's high grass. And Marsha, incognito to this point, was discovered by the marauding Marine.

"I didn't know you'd made it," Fritz said.

"I've been here for hours," Marsha said. "The skeleton; isn't that the lewd dancer from the horse barn?"

"Birdsong," Fritz said, having to shout over the music. "He's long gone."

Fritz noticed that Marsha's plastic cup was empty. Reaching for it, "Let me get you another beer."

"I shouldn't have too many. I've got a long drive home."

"Drive drunk," Fritz said, heading for the truck. "It takes the boredom out of it."

Marsha watched the band and the frolicking dancers while she waited for her refill. She had succeeded at being invisible by huddling in small crowds, never straying off by herself, and by limiting her conversations. Now though, after four beers and another on the way, she felt like getting out of the observation mode and enjoying the party. She wondered if Fritz liked to dance.

He returned with her beer. "Here. Nice and cold."

Marsha took a long sip. "Great band."

"They're better when I'm playing."

"You're a musician?"

"I'm a lyricist who happens to play a mean guitar. But I only play music that I've written. The band likes popular shit because that's what gets Walter going. He's *their* entertainment."

"You can't work out your differences?"

"Not a chance. Except for Weepy, the dog soldiers are hopeless optimists, which I detest."

"Hopeless optimists? Isn't that a contradiction in terms?"

"Not if you're describing Giants fans."

"Do you like to dance?"

"I hate to dance. But I will, if it means I can watch you."

"You can be frightfully honest."

"Gets me into a lot of trouble. Then again, as Jericho would say, *that's the beauty of it.*"

"You up for a dance now?"

"With you, I'm up for anything."

When the band went on another break a long line formed behind the tailgate of Rem's truck. Grumpy went around to the front of the house to say his goodbyes – *thanks for coming* – to couples with kids who had to leave early. Box was in the kitchen washing his forks and knives in the sink. Walter got out of his costume, tossed it in the back seat of his Datsun, and went looking for Roger so they could throw the shoes against Gulliver and Rem to determine the winner of the tournament. Pierre and Lorraine, with Welter and Dee Dee, stood in a group at one end of the horseshoe pit while Deirdre and Jericho, with Marsha and Fritz, blended into a crowd at the other end.

Finally, Walter showed up with Roger. Mabel, hair disheveled, could be seen walking with ginger steps across the lawn toward the house to take another shower and change into something warmer.

The game was a thriller, all tied up at ten when Dee Dee excused herself, ostensibly to use the bathroom. What she really needed was a closer look at the Box, who had intrigued her from the moment she laid eyes on him.

"Hey there," Dee Dee said, walking into the kitchen. "I hear they call you Box."

Box Car wiped a knife with a checkered dish cloth and placed it in a drawer. "That's right. Who are you?"

"My name's Dee Dee. I'm Richard's wife."

"Wicked Dick?"

Dee Dee laughed. "People call him Richard."

"We don't. To us he's a wicked dick."

"As in prick?"

"That's right."

"He might be a prick, but a wicked dick? No way. I should know."

"We're splitting hairs," Box grumbled, sliding another knife and a large fork into the drawer.

"Speaking of hair, you sure do have a lot of it."

"Thanks."

"I'm fascinated by hairy men. I really like your beard. You look like one of those guys in ZZ Top."

"I've been growing it since I was twelve."

"Can I ask you a personal question?"

"There's no such thing as a personal question with me."

"Oh wow. That's great. Do you have a hairy chest?"

"Yeah. I'm covered with hair. What's it to you?"

"*I love hairy chests.* Richard doesn't have a solitary hair on his. Even the hair on his head is thinning. He'll probably go bald just like his dad. Richard can't even grow a mustache."

"That's too bad," said Box.

Dee Dee's eyes gleamed with anticipation. "Can I see your how hairy your chest is?"

"Sure," Box said, doffing his apron, "as long as you reciprocate."

"Oh wow! I've never seen so much hair." Dee Dee was ecstatic. "As long as I what?"

"Reciprocate. Never mind. I was only joking. I don't expect you to show me your chest."

But that's precisely what Dee Dee did. Barely five feet tall, not a lot shorter than Box but weighing about a third as much, her breasts, previously concealed under an oversized loose-fitting sweatshirt, were disproportionately large.

Box grinned and growled. "*Urrrrrrr.* Small frame, big tits."

"Do you like them?" she asked, holding the sweatshirt to her chin.

"Are you shitting me? Not counting the sound of a Harley engine, that's just what you want."

Dee Dee walked up to the Box with a devilish smile. "I want to rub my boobies against that big hairy chest."

"Rub all you want," Box said, puffing his chest.

Dee Dee pressed against him, slithering and moaning and tugging with both hands on a mass of gnarled hair behind his neck.

Box throated a low groan and reached around to cup her tight cheeks in his massive hands.

Dee Dee whispered into his ear. "What else would you like to compare?"

Box thought about it. "Crows nests."

Dee Dee stepped back. *"Crows nests?"*

"Right here," said the Box, clutching his crotch. "Mine's got a couple of huge eggs in it."

Dee Dee laughed. "Okay, you hairy Box. I'll show you my crows nest if you show me yours."

"Right here in the kitchen?"

"Wherever you want."

"Come with me," Box said.

Dee Dee followed him up the stairs, giggling and pulling at tufts of hair on the back of his thighs.

Box shushed her inside Grumpy's bedroom. "Stop giggling. The sex goddess is taking a shower."

"The what?"

Box grabbed her by the hand and led her down the hallway. "There's another bedroom next to this one."

A minute later – the score at the horseshoe pit locked at eighteen – *Wicked Dick's* wife was amassed with hair.

Twenty-Three

Fritz took some ribbing on the way to work Monday morning for his swainish dalliance with the horse barn's mysterious visitor.

Walter sipped his coffee, Fritz sneering when his skeletal friend offered the jarhead a taste. "So tell us, Fritzie, is she a journalist or not?"

"I don't know. I was trying to get to know her as a person."

"Who the hell are you shitting," Box groused. "You were trying to get in her pants."

"No, really," Fritz said. "I don't care what Marsha does for a living. That's not important to me. I'm interested in her concerns about life. I want to know what bugs her, what tickles her fancy, what plagues her thoughts or raises her spirits, what pisses her off or gives her pause for some remote glimmer of hope. I want to know if she likes kids or if she can't stand the bastards. I want to know if she's been duped into cola addiction, if she undermines her metabolism with junk food or if, as I suspect, she's hip to the chemical conspiracy and yearns to be nutritionally enlightened. I want to know if she's pro or anti-government. I want … I want to know *who* she is first and *what* she is later. Frankly, Walter, I could care less if she's a reporter or if she mops floors at some loathsome elementary school in the Northeast Kingdom."

"Let me see if I've got this right," Gulliver said. "Here we have this sure ruse user usurping Mabel by showing up out of nowhere at the horse barn – *twice*, mind you – saying she wants to board a horse when she knows darn well the barn's nowhere near finished and asking questions about people who are *not* working on the barn. Then she shows up again, this time at the pig roast, trying to appear invisible – as if we're not going to notice – and the guy who pony's up to her puts the blinders on and falls in love. What a bunch of horse shit."

"I'd say it's none of your business," Fritz said.

"I'd say you're a horse's ass," Gully said.

"Yeah, nice intelligence work, Fritz," the albino chimed in.

"Shut the fuck up, Walter, or you'll be a skeleton *without* a costume."

"I did some intelligence work for us," Box said.

"That's an oxymoron," Fritz snarled.

"You're the goddamn moron," Box said. "You had an assignment and you blew it. Own up to it and we'll get off your back."

"Just tell us what you know, you hairy cockatrice." Fritz countered.

Box didn't know whether to be offended or not. "What the hell does that mean?"

"Crocodile kin. Legendary poisonous horned serpent-dragon hatched from a cock's egg. Genetic fluke incubated by a toad. Royal basilisk with a lethal breath that kills by its looks. Hence the term, *evil eye*."

"There it is," Box said, not appreciably appeased.

"And how were the mystical people protected against this mythological creature?" Weepy wanted to know.

"I didn't say the cockatrice was mythological; I said it was legendary."

"You're splitting hairs," Weepy said. "How was the cockatrice thwarted, denied, restrained, nullified, emasculated, contained?"

"*Read the Bible*, Weepy. Look for cockatrice eggs in the Vulgate. Isaiah couldn't stop talking about it. Check out Milton's description of Satan. Or go all the way back to Pliny, the Roman historian."

"I don't happen to have a Bible with me, nor did I bring Milton's works or Pliny's volumes. Just answer the goddamn question."

"If I remember correctly," Fritz conjectured, "the cockatrice had to be wrapped in the furry skins of some detestable animal and trapped inside a thick metal box."

"Let's stick with cock," Box said, oblivious to the analogy. "And hair. Those are the things my intelligence work comes from."

"Now you're making sense," Fritz said.

Grumpy's patience was severely tested. "What the hell'd you find out, Box?"

"Roger Hamminframe is an undercover investigator for the state of Vermont."

"What?" six voices shouted in unison.

"You heard me."

Remington looked in horror at the cockatrice, *aka* the *Missing Link*. "How the hell did you find that out?"

"When you guys were playing the final game of horseshoes did you happen to notice that *Wicked Dick's* wife split?"

"I didn't," Rem said. "I was too busy wiping my ass with this miserable Q-tip."

"Hold it right there, Rem," said Walter. "We had to go all the way to thirty before you and Gully finally pulled it out."

"Come to think of it," Gulliver said, "I saw Welter standing next to the Frenchman and his wife. Fee Fee, or whatever her name is, was nowhere in sight."

"Dee Dee," Box said. "She's got a thing about hair. Came into the kitchen and damn near tore the clothes right off me. Hers too."

"Go on," Rem said, still aghast.

"We were upstairs throwing our nests together when all of a sudden she starts crowing about Roger's nose; how she'd like to know if the saying is true or not."

"What saying?" Rem asked.

"Can't imagine. All I know is Roger went to Welter's house a couple of times after he started at the horse barn. Dee Dee didn't say his name. Kept calling him the undercover guy with a giant nose. When she was getting dressed and I was sprawled out on the bed trying to catch my breath, I asked her if the nose-guy's name is Roger. She says *Hey, that's it* and then she told me – not making any connection to the horse barn – that Roger works for the state."

"How'd she come to know that?" Rem asked.

"She heard him mention the Attorney General's office a bunch of times."

Rem turned toward the back seat. "Well boys, looks like the real investigative reporter isn't Walter *or* Marsha. It's Box, the cocky cockatrice."

During the final twenty miles to the barn the conversation focused on Welter, Roger, and Marsha; whether two of the three or all three were in cahoots – and why.

No one could recall having seen Roger and Marsha making verbal contact during the picnic. Neither could anyone remember seeing either of them making eye contact during Marsha's visits to the construction site. But then, that could be yet another ruse, integral to whatever undercover operation had been set in motion.

And what, exactly, sparked an investigation in the first place? Could it really be about the crew's treatment of the lazy dog-asses sent to the barn by the unemployment agency? They decided to discuss that possibility.

The albino, they noted, was a fright to anyone seeing him for the first time. No doubt watching the waxen wraith wriggle and writhe as a rite of passage was burdensome for anyone's sensibilities. But since when did a good humored travesty, offensive as it may be, warrant the attention of the state's top legal beagle?

"Come on", said the albino, miffed.

The crew freely admitted to having subjected the one-day wonders to emotional abuse. And yes, they had questioned the men's sexual orientation, often citing bestiality if some physical defect suggested aberrant genetics. But then, who wouldn't? Furthermore, what better way to assess a person's ability to defend their heritage? In their minds, behavior such as this was not only acceptable, it was commendable.

Sure, Box Car could be hard on some people, owing to his unusual physical characteristics and his unique style of harassment and intimidation. But did it qualify as molestation? The crew was undecided on this matter, although Box was firm in the precarious stance that indeed his advances were best interpreted as oppressive in nature; his subjects true victims in every sense of the word.

Then there was Jericho. The gunslinger was dangerous; no argument there. Certainly the flunkies sent to the barn couldn't help noticing the polished handle of Laramie's pistol whenever his shirt was raised in the act of handing up a board or reaching with both hands for someone's throat. Did the prospect of assault with a deadly weapon cause them to lodge their complaints? Did Jericho ever directly threaten to shoot any of these men? *Probably*, the crew decided, though they couldn't recall a specific instance. Either way, seeing a fellow worker brandishing a gun had, for a lot of people – including Weepy and Remington – a chilling effect. Jericho, they reasoned, had to be the primary subject of the investigation.

Or maybe it was Rudy. Had the contractor stretched himself too thin and wasn't bonded for all the work he had simultaneously undertaken? If so, was this serious enough to involve the Attorney General? Not likely. Or, had Rudy fallen behind on his payment of employee withholding taxes? Couldn't be. If so, this would be a matter for federal and state revenue agencies to look into, not the A.G.'s office. Was Rudy engaging in discriminatory hiring practices? This seemed plausible. After all, no female workers had ever shown up at the horse barn. Perhaps the unemployment agency had referred a few and Rudy had blocked their employment.

It was a long twenty miles, over which the crew considered many possibilities. Having determined it was highly unlikely that any of them had ever done anything so outrageous, scandalous, flagrant, or notorious as to prompt a state investigation into their activities, practices, deeds, or general conduct, the men turned their attention back to their antagonists and the need to take appropriate measures to expose and rectify any and all maliciousness against the righteous dog soldiers.

After Walter revealed that he'd caught Roger coming out of the hayfield with Mabel – the goddess lathered, giddy, and, judging by her gait, positively sore – the dog soldiers worked up a plan to uncover the nosy snoop.

They had difficulty trying to figure out the extent of Welter's culpability. It was possible that Roger's house visits had been made in the due course of his investigation, which may or may not have lent greater credence to, or deeper suspicion of, the remarkably lively encounter the two had had at the horse barn. While the specifics of the plan failed to fully develop, the crew nevertheless decided that *Wicked Dick* had something coming to him; they just didn't know what – yet. They would trust their instincts to instruct them as to the right time and place to hang his sorry ass.

As for Marsha, the crew deferred to Fritz, although their instincts told them Walter was the better man to objectively pursue the purpose of her pursuits.

Plywood, pressed board, corkboard, and texture 111 all serve the same purpose. Nailed to studs, all are effective enclosing a building. Texture 111, however, doesn't require any other surface, such as clapboards or wood shingles, to be installed over it. Its rigidity and countrified appearance serve double duty as an effective barrier against the elements and as a rustic facing. A cheap way to go, some might say, but worthy enough for a horse barn, which should not be so tight as to prevent air flow from cooling hot-blooded steeds.

Texture 111 sheets measure eight-feet tall and four-feet wide. Given the barn's enormous dimensions, 14,400 square feet of surface area – not counting the triangular areas of the gable ends – would require nearly 500 sheets of siding. With thirty nails needed for each panel the dog soldiers could look forward to a lot more bulling and jamming.

There was only one pneumatic nail gun. Most of the men would be hammering by hand, taking turns using the powerful tool.

The crew hauled sheets to the far end of the barn, leaning them against the frame in preparation for the new phase of construction to begin. Nails for the pneumatic gun came in foot-long clips. The large clips used to nail two-by-fours to the posts were carefully segregated from the clips to be used for the siding.

The work would be tedious but the men were happy about sealing off the barn from the chill of November's winds sweeping across the valley. Two-thirds of the crew assigned themselves to the texture 111 while the other third was designated to finish up the strapping before capping the walls with rough cut two-by-sixes.

During the pig roast on Saturday, Rudy taking advantage of the crew's absence to inspect the project, the trusses were delivered. Once the cap was on, a crane would be brought in to hoist the trusses into place. Two three-man teams, one atop each length-wise wall, would position the trusses along the cap, nail them in, and install the braces. Rudy was pleased. Despite the loss of an entire workday and the fact that only two new hires had actually stayed on the job, the horse barn was not only taking shape, its construction was slightly ahead of schedule.

Tuesday evening, Rudy called Jericho.

"How was your picnic?"

"Dandy."

"That's all you want to tell me about it?"

"If you were interested in the picnic, you'd have gone to it."

"I was curious what Melanie and I may have missed."

"Did you go?"

"You know we didn't."

"Then I'd have to say it's pretty likely you missed all of it."

"Why are you always so unsociable to me?"

"I'm unsociable to everybody. Why would I treat you any different?"

"Because I'm your employer?"

"Nice try."

"There's something I can't figure out, Jericho."

"That why you called?"

"Yes."

"Shoot the works, shit a brick, or shut the fuck up, Rudy. I got things to do."

"It's about the complaints."

"I know a way to end the complaints once and for all."

"Really? How's that?"

"Stop sending numb nuts to us. We don't need them. Let me and the dog soldiers take it from here on in."

"That might be a good way to prevent any future complaints, but it doesn't make the existing complaints go away. Those are the ones I want to discuss."

"Talk to somebody else. I'm tired of hearing about it."

"I have to talk to somebody and you're the one with the best insight. You know these roughnecks better than anyone else."

"That's because I'm one of them. But hey, you knew about the friends I keep right from the get-go."

"That may be true, but I never imagined how primitive these guys would turn out to be."

"That's where you're wrong, Rudy. A couple of these guys got IQs that are right off the charts. Why don't you come around sometime and shoot the shit with them? You'll think you walked into a philosophy class over at Goddard College."

"If that's the case, why in hell do they act the way they do?"

"You ever met a genius that wasn't a social misfit, an oddity that no one can understand or even wants to? Geniuses do strange things, Rudy. More than one of these guys walks that fine line between sanity and insanity, and all the while the others are yelling *jump*."

"Their sense of humor is sick, Jericho."

"That's the beauty of it. But listen to me. The main problem with these guys is the prospect of boredom. They'll do anything to prevent it. That means they take everything and nothing seriously, depending on the subject, their mood, and who they're spoofing, including themselves. Their humor is not only derived from shocking others, but each other. If happiness is the opposite of sadness, humor is the opposite of boredom. Think about it. It's impossible to be laughing and bored at the same time.

"Same could be said of anger. The one who fears boredom the most is Fritz. The mere thought of being bored makes him angry as all get-out. He's able to avoid boredom with anger. We help by tormenting the man. It's a lot of laughs annoying a leatherneck, but nobody's better at it than Walter; his antagonizing can produce electrifying shock value.

"Of course, Fritz can stay angry enough without a lot of help. He hates tradition, normalcy, convention, triviality, the commonplace. Whoever said 'moderation in all things' is Fritz's mortal enemy. He deplores what he calls the intellectual bankruptcy of the masses. Virtually anything that's popular, in his mind, is cause for distrust – and for distress. Fritz is a radical. He lives in extremes. He's capable of a good laugh once in a while, but usually he's pissed at something. There's no middle ground for him. He goes from one extreme to another, from laughter to hatred. And it works. The man is never bored."

"Is he dangerous?"

"Of course he's dangerous. We all are. That's the beauty of it."

"Thanks for raising my comfort level. Can we get back to the complaints?"

"You don't believe me do you?"

"About what?"

"The genius thing."

"No, I don't. I'm not convinced these guys are intellectuals; but if they are, they're intellectual thugs."

"Excellent description, Rudy. I'll have to remember that."

"For someone with important things to do, you sure are talkative tonight."

"My apologies. The complaints. What about them?"

"My business license is in jeopardy because of your dog soldiers, Jericho. I need to get to the bottom of this. That's why I took the trouble to call every one of the men who filed complaints against the horse barn crew. If it sounds like I'm down on your boys more than usual it's because some of the things I heard defy the imagination."

"I know all about it. I'm there everyday, don't forget. And by the way, as far as I'm concerned it took a lot of imagination to come up with more than a few of the abuses those sick puppies from the unemployment office complained about."

"I realize you understand the gist of these complaints. But listen, it's not the complaints themselves that baffle me."

"No?"

"No."

"I'm listening."

"I finally identified the state agency that's conducting the investigation into activities at the horse barn."

"How'd you find that out?"

"The investigator I told you about called me again. This time I asked him who he's working for. I figured I had a right to know."

"And he said he works for the Attorney General."

"How'd you know?"

"It goes like this: you can fool some of the people some of the time, and sometimes you can feel pretty foolish if you get fooled by some people; but don't ever be foolish enough to try and fool a dog soldier if you don't want to end up the greater fool."

"I'm not going to ask you to repeat that."

"Good. I couldn't anyway. The point is my guys know all about the Attorney General's investigation."

"How?"

"Geniuses don't always tell you how they know what they know, only that they know. What'd the agent say that's got you baffled?"

"Nothing."

"Now *I'm* baffled."

"What I don't understand is that none of the men I talked to – the guys who filed all of these complaints – has ever talked to the A.G.'s office."

"So what? That just means the unemployment office or the Chamber of Commerce or maybe the Better Business Bureau referred the complaints to the Attorney General's office."

"I talked with each of those agencies. The complaints filed with them stayed right there. Nothing got referred to the Attorney General."

"If that's the case, how'd the A.G. get involved?"

"That's what baffles me."

"The dog soldiers will find out, if they don't know already."

"How can they find out?"

"I told you, Rudy, more than a few of them are fucking geniuses."

"Something doesn't add up, Jericho."

"I know. But it's nothing to lose sleep over."

"It isn't?"

"No. Get yourself a good night's rest, Rudy. You're going to need it."

"Sounds like sound advice."

"Good. Good night then."

"Good night."

The siding was going up fast. Weepy, tired of listening to Grumpy's requests for *Hello Dolly* and perhaps aching for something more than tangential credit for the progress being made, left his guitar in the Buick on Wednesday to help out with the barn.

That was a mistake.

Around three o'clock, Remington opened a new box of nail clips. He failed to see they were the spikes used to nail two-by-fours to the posts. Rem was on the outside of the framing getting into a secure position to zip nails into a sheet of texture 111. Weepy, on the inside, held the sheet in place. Standing on the lowest board with one hand holding an edge of the siding and the other gripping the top, Weepy turned his head to lean his neck against the middle two-by-four for better balance. Rem decided he'd nail the sheet in place by shooting nails left to right along the middle board. The fourth nail fired clean through the two-by-four into Weepy's neck.

At first, Weepy didn't know what had happened. Rem continued popping nails. Suddenly, there was searing pain. He yelled for Rem to stop nailing. Remington peered over the texture 111. Blood was streaming out of Weepy's neck. Rem could see from the neat row of nail points extending more than an inch through the two-by-four that the nails he was using were the wrong ones.

Weepy jerked his neck from the board with a pop, a swoosh, and a gurgle. He dropped from the strapping in an awkward lurch, slumping to his knees with one hand pressed against his neck. Frightened and helpless, blood poured through his fingers. He took his hand away from the wound and held it up to his face. It was completely drenched. He put his hand to his neck again, a river of blood flowing down his wrist and onto his forearm. Large red globules dripped from his elbow and splattered on the ground. The gory site of his life force pooling in gloppy plops made him light-headed. A second later he collapsed in a gelatinous heap, his eyes a blue million miles.

Dog soldiers came running and yelping, leaping and yipping from all directions when Rem barked out the distressing report that he had nailed his friend to the barn by inadvertently slapping the wrong clip in the nail gun.

Pierre ran up to his car with the doddering urgency of an overweight man severely challenged by a steep hill. He snatched a first-aid kit from the glove compartment and skittered back down as fast as his squat legs could manage the tricky gravel descent.

The crew hovered over him. Weepy's breathing was labored. Box moved the victim's hand and pressed his own against the deep puncture wound, blood instantly seeping through his fingers.

Weepy gurgled something.

"What was that?" Fritz asked. "He's trying to tell us something."

Gulliver put his ear to Weepy's mouth, the entertainer's mortified eyes floating through the atmosphere in a soaring search for death's door.

"I can't make it out," Gully said. "*Wait.* I think … I think it might be a song."

"What song?" Rem asked, his voice quaking.

"Hold on," Gulliver said. "I can almost make it out."

No safety or surprise ...

Gulliver repeated the words.

"What's that supposed to mean?" Grumpy wanted to know.

Pierre arrived and asked the Box to move. Box Car obliged, seeing the Frenchman open the first-aid kit.

"There's more," Gulliver said.

Pierre pressed a square patch against the wound and had Box hold it there while he unwound a spool of gauze.

I'll never look into your eyes, again ...

Gulliver repeated the words in a low voice, trying to mimic Weepy's gargle.

Pierre wrapped the gauze around and around Weepy's neck.

"There's more," Gulliver said, his ear to the victim's mouth. "I think I'm picking up the song. It sounds like the Doors. Hold on. Let me see if I can put the words to the right melody."

Can you picture what will be
So limitless and free
Desperately in need...
of some ... stranger's hand
In a desperate land.

"I know that song," Walter said.

"We all do," Fritz said.

Pierre asked Box to press tightly while he ripped the last of the gauze down the middle and began tying it off.

"Let's sing it with him," Gulliver suggested.

Pierre was satisfied with the dressing but puzzled by Weepy's faint warble through trembling lips. He was shocked to see the crew stand as one and scream …

Kill kill kill kill kill kill

… mystified to hear them sing along,

This is the end
Beautiful friend
This is the end
My only friend, the end.

Twenty-Four

That night, Rudy called Jericho in a panic.

"Tell me about the accident!"

"What're you worried about? The man didn't die did he?"

"He took a ten penny in the neck. I heard that you raced him over to the clinic."

"Yes. Yes I did."

"Did he get a tetanus shot? Did the doctor say anything about lock jaw?"

"The man's fine, Rudy. Calm down. Accidents happen."

"I knew I was taking too big a risk with so many unskilled laborers."

"*Uncommon* laborers. Let's get the term right."

"This could be serious trouble."

"Sounds like you're more worried about a lawsuit than the man's condition."

"I'm just as concerned about an insurance claim. Personal injury on the job, especially life-threatening, can put an owner out of business. Whenever an insurance company has to pay a claim they drop you like a hot tamale."

"Potato."

"Whatever."

"Piece of coal."

"*Let it go.*"

"Phew!"

"After that, you're lucky if you can find another carrier. And if you do, you can't afford the hike in premiums. This could be real trouble, Jericho."

"Weepy won't file a claim. He won't sue either. Relax."

"What makes you think?"

"Getting a lawyer is the last thing any of these guys would do. That's not what they're about."

"How can you be so sure? This guy came close to biting the bullet, according to Pierre."

"True. But everybody's having a good laugh over it by now. If you stop and think about it, Rudy, it is pretty funny."

"Not to me."

"The lingering problem, in my mind, is that nobody'll ever trust Remington again; not with a gun in his hands."

"The man's dangerous as hell."

"Only to himself, you get right down to it."

"What makes you ...?"

Calm down.

"I'm trying to. But I don't know these crazies like you do. Are you sure there won't be a lawsuit or a claim over this?"

"Weepy'll be back on the job, watch and see. Oh sure, he'll take tomorrow off, cry baby that he is. But the dog soldiers'll be barking at his door first thing Friday."

"Now that you mention it, it is rather amazing those boys of yours never take sick, not counting that human chalk stick. Unruly as they are, they show up on time every day no matter what the weather. Between you, me, and the lamppost, they do all kinds of shit work – and for shit pay, if I must say. On top of that, notwithstanding all the trouble they cause, you're saying they won't cause trouble over this."

"They've got plenty of troubling causes as it is."

"If that's the case, I should do something special for them. Not in their paychecks, mind you, although it's a thought; but a good deed, some unexpected perk, a token of my appreciation for their surprising work ethic and non-litigious perspective."

"It's about time you showed a little gratitude."

"As for that weepy guy, I'll pay him for any days he needs to take off, Jericho. Make sure he knows that."

"He takes enough time off as it is."

"What?"

"Forget I said that; it doesn't matter. What matters is that your state of mind is improving. My advice to you is to knock back a handful of heavy-duty downers. Quaaludes oughta do it. They're a terrific sedative. Wash 'em down with a couple belts of Black Velvet. When you wake up in the morning, assuming you do, you can shake it all off and go about your business."

"I'll take a shot or two, but I'll probably skip the pills."

"Count your goddamn blessings, Rudy. Consider yourself lucky I was able to recruit such a high caliber of men to build this horse barn. Accidents are bound to happen. I'd venture a guess this won't be the only one. Sure, a man took a nail in the neck deep enough to cause a serious loss of blood. But look at the bright side. It missed the jugular. The man's alive to tell about it. And don't think he won't. Shit, we'll be talking about this nail-gun incident for years. In fact, when all's said and done, this particular tragedy, avoidable as it was, will just be one more sordid little episode in a painfully ludicrous drama."

"You're not saying the horse barn is a farce."

"Not entirely."

"That makes me feel better."

"Get some sleep."

"Thanks. I'll try."

"Good night, Rudy."

"Good night, Jericho."

The crew was in a jovial mood following Weepy's crucifixion, despite Rem coming unglued by the accident. Predictably, Fritz and Box Car took full advantage of Remington's precarious emotional state.

On the ride to work Thursday morning, Weepy laying low in his apartment, Fritz yelled at Rem from the back seat. "How could anybody be so fucking stupid? The clips for the framing are twice the size as the clips for the siding. But since I find it impossible to believe you're quite that stupid, I'm of the opinion you did it on purpose."

"Fritz is right," Box said. "You've had it in for Weepy for a long time. I talked with him on the phone last night and urged him to file attempted murder charges against you. *And soon*, since I'm not sure about the statute of limitations."

"You did like hell," Rem said. "Weepy knows I didn't mean it."

"Nobody will ever believe that," Fritz said. "I get the sense you've been itching to do somebody in for years. Those gory cockfights are nothing more than a warm up."

"Oh sure," Rem said. "I'm one dangerous sonuvabitch, I am. Better get the word out. Nobody's safe around me."

Gulliver chimed in. "Face it Rem, you've always been touchy with a gun in your hands. I've seen the look of trepidation on your face every time we go deer hunting. I don't happen to share Fritz's opinion that you were actually out to kill Weepy. I, for one, accept your guilt-ridden excuse that it was simply a grievous and truly unforgivable accident. I really do. But I'm also acutely aware that accidents tend to occur when a person is nerved out, when the mind wanders – which yours does constantly – or if some deep-seeded fear unconsciously coerces a phobia-ridden individual into irrational action."

"Look who's the phenomenologist now," Rem said, unconvinced.

"Listen, it can happen behind the wheel of a car, walking through the woods with a hunting rifle, or loading a fresh clip into a nail gun. When a man gets nerve bombs, he doesn't think straight. No doubt holding that nail gun in your hands made you nervous, which proved to be the unwitting emotional precursor to a tragic incident."

"Nothing nerved me out when I was wielding that nail gun," Rem said. "But look, I'll be honest with you; I'm not comfortable around guns. That has more to do with all the close calls I've had hunting with Jericho, that fucking crazy horse. It's happened with Fritz, too. I remember popping up from behind some bushes one time and there was Fritz, less than fifty yards away, aiming his 30-30 right at me. That'll unnerve anybody."

"Good thing it happened before I went to Nam," Fritz said. "Instead of mistaking you for a deer, I might have mistaken you for Charlie. You'd be a dead man right now."

"You knew it was me. You were just trying to scare the bejesus out of me."

"Sounds like I did."

Trapped in a conciliatory moment, Rem was dangerously forthcoming. "I'll let you in on something else. I don't dream a helluva lot, but I do have one recurring nightmare that wakes me up in a cold sweat every time."

"What's it about?" Walter asked. "Sounds like one of mine."

"Can't say, other than being wretchedly miserable. The worst thing is I don't know how it ends."

"What happens before it almost ends?" Walter wanted to know.

"I'd liken it to an out-of-body experience. I see myself walking around in an endless circle with a loaded gun in my hands, waving it around in a state of incoherent lunacy. Imagine that? I'm no more dangerous than that cry-ass guitar player or this withering wimp in the back seat."

"Could be you're waving a nail gun around," Gulliver said. "Did you ever see Weepy in your nightmare?"

"Not Weepy. Some short guy. He's ridiculously short. What's weird is that I'm the same height. He's coming at me, but before he gets there ... shit, I don't know. The only thing I know for sure is that my misery is so irreconcilable I'm stark raving gonzo."

"You were stark raving *stupid* with that nail gun," Fritz said. "You're not allowed to use it anymore."

"That's all right by me," Rem said. "Even though I was getting pretty good with it, looking back, I could sense something bad was about to happen."

"You almost killed a man," Box said. "That's relatively bad."

"Get off it!" Grumpy shouted. "It's over. Weepy might be sore as hell, but he's alive. From now on, we joke about it. And the sooner *you* can laugh about it, Rem, the sooner your nightmare ends."

"Thanks Grump. I needed to hear that."

"There's something else I want to zero in on," Fritz said.

"A change of subject suits me fine," Rem said.

"I know we've been tossing around the idea of taking Frame-a-ham to the cleaners to get the goods on him. It has merit. But I believe I've come up with a better way to nail him, one that get's *him* in trouble, not us."

"Let's hear it," Gulliver said, rubbing his hands together.

"We catch him riding Mabel."

"Where? How? When?" Gully asked.

"I figure Roger figures we figure he's in pretty good with us by now."

"That's a lot of figuring," Walter noted.

"Hear me out, goddamnit," Fritz snapped. "We can't argue that the man's turned into a decent laborer. He even put his hands over Weepy's eyes to close them when he figured Weepy'd cashed it in. On top of that, he came all the way out to the picnic, played some hellacious horseshoes, and got tight with Mabel."

Gulliver tapped Grumpy on the shoulder. "Is that possible?"

"Is what possible?"

"Getting tight with Mabel. From what I hear, that's a contradiction in terms."

"For me, yes. For Roger, who knows? When I dropped Mabel off at her place the other night she was in a Dizzy Miss Lizzy tizzy about him, going off the deep end about what a great nose he has. She couldn't stop talking about it, giggling and rubbing the goose bumps that came out on her arms. As far as I can see, it's just huge. I can't imagine what she finds so thrilling about it."

"Perhaps his prominent proboscis portends a prodigious prick," Gulliver suggested.

"What the hell does that mean?" Grumpy asked.

"Whoa," Fritz yelled. "Don't let smarty-pants here go on a tangent about dragon dicks, walrus wangs, bison boners, wizards' wands, or dinosaur dongs. We'll never hear the end of it."

"What Gully's saying," the albino asserted, "is that maybe Mabel looks at a man's nose the way some women look at a man's feet, making a comparative judgment about incomparable anatomy."

Grumpy whipped around to put an eye on Gulliver sitting directly behind him. "Is that what you're saying?"

"How could it be otherwise?"

"Forget about noses for a minute," Grumpy said. "I want to know what the hell women care about men's feet?"

"It has to do with the rule of seventy-two," Fritz said.

"What's that?"

"Girth notwithstanding, length is typically seventy-two percent of shoe size. What size shoe do you wear?"

"Six," Grumpy said.

"Okay, figure it out, you idiot."

"That's a lot of figuring."

"Put it this way," Fritz said, "if you're ever hospitalized, don't walk around the hallways with your johnny on backwards. Anyway, recognizing Gulliver's expertise with a camera, this developing plan of mine could work. Roger not only has it in for us but, in a different way, for Mabel too. And she's openly taken by him. If we can catch this snoop in a compromising position with the equine goddess, it'll compromise his investigation."

Gulliver considered the scenario. "I like it. Roger believes he's worked his way up to dog soldier status. Engineering diabolical circumstances should not be difficult."

Grumpy shook his head in dismay. "Come again?"

Fritz sneered. "Gully's saying the idea is brilliant, you dinky-dicked dullard."

Turning off paved road for thirteen miles of dirt road, the subject changed again.

"Whatever happened with those charges filed against you?" Rem asked the albino.

"They came under the other rule of seventy-two."

"What could that be?"

"I have to put in seventy-two hours of public service."

"Doing what?"

"They gave me a list of choices. Picking up trash at City Hall Park. Filling out a log for the radio dispatcher at one of the ambulance services. Riding around with the dog catcher looking for stray mutts. Posting bulletins at the grocery stores about properties being auctioned off for taxes. All sorts of good stuff."

"So the judge found you guilty."

"Nope."

"I don't get it."

"My neighbor, who convinced the police to file charges against me, came to my defense."

"And that didn't get you off?"

"I was found innocent on all charges except failing to reveal the identity of the real offender."

"The gunslinger."

"Bull's-eye. My neighbor was the key witness against me on that one."

"Sounds duplicitous."

"She felt sorry for me but couldn't bring herself to forgive me for pretending not to know it was a friend of mine who offended her, even though she described him perfectly – right down to the first rule of seventy-two."

"So you perjured yourself."

"I pleaded *nolo condendere*. Hey Fritz, that reminds me; don't you think it would be a good idea for me to do an investigative piece about how lawyers pull the wool over our eyes by using Latin?"

"Who cares?" Fritz retorted.

"Everybody *should* care," Walter said.

"Why?" Fritz asked.

"Because it's a dead language. Almost. It lives only in the halls of purported justice. How can ignorance of the law not be an excuse if understanding the law requires one to know Latin? Why can't they just say *no contention*? Why does it have to be *nolo contendere*? For that matter, why does it have to be *pro bono* or *in abstentia* or *dominus* goddamn *vobiscum*."

"I think that last one has to do with the Catholic mass," Fritz opined.

"It has to do with *insertus dictum*," Walter said. "Lawyers use Latin to fuck us."

"I have no objection to your argument," Fritz said. "But it would take an act of Congress to change how the law is written."

"Maybe you're right," Walter submitted. "But it seemed like a worthwhile story to me; *The Spurious Impudence of Juris Prudence*."

"Catchy," Fritz said. "Usually I think your ideas are cockamamie. This one almost has merit."

"Thanks."

"I'm surprised one of the networks hasn't called you by now. They love it when somebody can take a simple subject and make it complex."

"That's why I rewrite my resume at least once a month."

Fritz's chuckle withered into hissing disgust. He turned his head to stare out the window and let the blur of passing trees clear his mind.

When Grumpy hit the brakes on the Buick at the top of the bluff all eyes were on the huge machine in the middle of the horse barn. The crane had arrived.

Box Car was the first to notice the inscription painted in black cursive on both sides of the crane's bulbous yellow body: *"B.F." Beauchamp Frontenac's Crane Service*. "Look who we got here," Box said to the crew in a low rolling chuckle; *Butt Fuck's* Crane Service."

Pierre introduced the crew to the owner-operator, a rotund man dressed in a dark green construction outfit sporting a three-day stubble on his treble chin and a crescent grin that stretched from ear to ear. B.F.'s smile, his eyes squinting in sympathy with his rubber-band lips, was immediately plastered onto Rem's face. The men roared their approval when Rem turned to show them his perfect imitation, complete with a mirthful echo – *hee-hee-hee*. The laughter escalated when Remington put his hands on his hips exactly like B.F., pursed his imploded lips into a wider smile, and squeaked out a derisive, *"My name is* Butt Fuck. *My name is* Butt Fuck*"*.

"Gentlemen, let me introduce you to Beauchamp Frontenac," Pierre said. "He's the best crane operator in the entire vicinity."

"From here to where?" Jericho, fresh on the scene, wanted to know.

"Anywhere 'round these parts," B.F. said in his own defense, his voice remarkably similar to Rem's portrayal.

Jericho motioned for Fritz to step forward and do the honors.

Fritz shook hands with the crane man, a dead ringer for Pvt. Doberman on *The Phil Silvers Show*. "It falls to me to introduce you to the crew, *blow champ*."

"Call me B.F.," said B.F. "I use that because some people have a problem with French."

"That's good," Fritz said. "French is a problem for all of us. I'll name each man as I point to him. Ready? Here we go: Box Car Bork, Grumpy Bork, Jericho Laramie, Walter Birdsong, Remington Swilling, Gulliver Swilling, and me, Fritz Swilling. Let's go back through to make sure you have the names down. I'll randomly point to a man; you repeat his name to me."

"I can't do that."

"Why not?"

"Because I don't remember everybody's name."

"That can't possibly be true. Who's that guy?" Fritz asked, randomly pointing.

"I don't know."

"What's this guy's name?"

"I can't remember."

"How about him?"

"Nope."

"Or him?"

"Him either."

"This man's name is …"

"I don't know his name."

"Or his?"

"I forgot already."

"How about mine?"

"I must've forgot yours too."

"In other words, *born chimp*, you not only can't remember the names of these men; you can't even recall one of their names. Am I right?"

"You went kind of fast."

"I'm getting a little exasperated, but I'll slow the fucking routine down for you. First, the first names; last, the last names. Ready? Here we go: Box, Grumpy, Jericho, Walter, Remington, Gulliver, Fritz. Now then, Bork, Bork – sorry if it sounds like I'm barfing – Laramie, Birdsong, Swilling, Swilling, Swilling. That's seven first names to match up with only four last names, for chrissakes. You should be happy Weepy O'Toole isn't here. I know I am. So come on, *bone chomp*, put 'em together and give 'em back to me. Start with the hairy one."

"Now I'm really confused."

"You are?"

"I don't think I've ever been so damned confused."

"And yet you know how to operate this heavy equipment?"

"I'm the best there is at it."

"What makes you think?"

"I've been doing it for over thirty years."

"No, no. I want to know what makes you think. From what I can tell, nothing does."

"Whoa," Pierre said. "Rudy contracted with B.F. because he's the best crane man there is around here. We've had him raise trusses for us on three or four different jobs. He's precise and he's fast, the first being important for safety reasons, the second because we pay him by the hour. He doesn't have to remember everyone's name."

"Not even one?" Fritz asked.

"The important thing is B.F.'s the best crane operator around."

B.F.'s smile reached from one ear lobe to the other in response to Pierre's flattery. *Hee-hee-hee.*

Fritz threw up his hands and walked away, hissing with disgust.

"Let's get to work, men," Pierre said.

"Hold your horses," Jericho protested. "Rem's gotta show him the eyes."

With that, Remington walked over to stand face to face with the crane man. "Watch closely," he said, his eyes beginning a frenzied dance.

A minute into the show, B.F.'s hands planted firmly on his hips, the crane man *tee-heed* almost out of control. "Damnedest thing I ever did see," he said when Rem's pupils jiggled to a halt. "I had an uncle once who could do that. Gave me laughing fits. I'd stand in front of a mirror for hours trying to figure out how to do it but I never could get the hang of it. I just made myself dizzy. *Hee-hee-hee.* He died when I was in the eighth grade. When they were closing his casket I could'a swore he opened his eyes at me and made 'em jiggle one last time. Nobody else saw it, but I sure did."

"Anybody who can perform the Rapid Eye Movement gets to do it one more time after they're dead," Rem said.

"That's what I always figured," B.F. said, pleased that the experience with his dead uncle was no illusion.

"Can we get to work now?" Pierre asked.

"Where's Roger?" Grumpy wanted to know.

"He called the house last night," Pierre answered. "Said he had to attend a meeting this morning."

"Where?"

"I have no idea."

Grumpy covered the crew with his Jack Elam eyes, raising a wistful eyebrow. "We better act fast boys," he told them.

"What's that?" Pierre asked.

"You're not in on it," Grumpy said. "Go about your business."

Twenty-Five

Friday morning, less than a week before Thanksgiving, Vermont was hit with its first major snow storm of the season.

Weepy's neck was heavily bandaged. He was still moaning for sympathy when the Buick pulled into the parking lot at Walter's apartment.

"Am I going to have to listen to this shit all day?" Fritz asked.

"Yes you are," Weepy said, his voice weak and tremulous.

"Are you able to sing?" Gulliver asked the guitar player.

"No. I wouldn't set up in a snow storm even if I could."

"You'll have to work with the rest of us then," Fritz said.

"I'm not working around any nail guns."

"We're putting up trusses," Rem said. "It took half the morning to get the first gable end up. The next seven went pretty quick. We got a three-man team up on the capping on one side but only two of us are on the other side because Popple quit; said he was tied up in divorce proceedings. It would go a lot faster if we had another man to help with the bracing. Are you afraid of heights?"

"No. But Walter is. Have him do it."

Rem liked the suggestion. "You know, you're right. We could have had some fun with that. Hey Box, where in hell was Walter yesterday? I don't remember seeing him."

"We could have used him to help finish the siding," Box said. "I thought he was up on one of the caps."

"No way in hell," Rem said. "He's deathly afraid of heights."

"Walter was with the Frenchman part of the time," Grumpy said, "re-stacking two-by-sixes for the stalls. But I know he spent some of the day in the Buick. I caught him there when I went up to clear snow off the windshield. He was curled up in the back seat; told me he was sick to his stomach."

"If you're not going to work on the trusses, Weepy, you'll have to work with Roger and Box Car on the texture 111," Fritz said.

"Maybe I'll throw the tarp over my head and play instrumentals," Weepy said.

"The only one who'll be able to hear you is you," Rem said.

"This may sound selfish, but I'm the only one I care about hearing me."

Walter opened Fritz's door. The leatherneck stepped out into the snow squalls to let the albino get in.

"*Phew*, this is one heckuva a snow storm," Walter said. He settled into the seat, opened his thermos, and poured himself some coffee. Leaning his head into the steaming vapors, Walter paused to savor the aroma, then offered a sniff to Fritz.

Fritz turned his head toward the window and cranked it down a smidge. "Get that sludge away from me. You should be happy about this heavy snowfall. If it keeps up you can slack off the entire day; nobody'll be able to find you."

Rem swiveled to face the back seat, focusing on Walter. "How's your stomach been lately?"

"To tell you the truth I came within a breath of dying yesterday afternoon, although I started to feel better on the way home. I was fine when I got in bed last night, but I woke up around midnight in excruciating pain. Have you ever hurt so much you wished you were dead, Rem?"

"Emotionally, yes. Physically, no?"

"It took damn near lethal quantities of aspirin and milk of magnesia for me to fall back asleep."

"I'm glad you gave up on that pink stuff," Rem said. "Your skin's starting to resemble it. I never know if I'm looking at you or watching a sunset."

"I still take *Pepto Bismol*," Walter said. "If one's not working I assume the other will. I alternate between them."

"That explains it," Rem said. "One's white. The other's pink. You're both."

"How much of that shit do you take?" Box Car growled in his heavy-grit top of the morning sandpaper voice.

"An economy-sized bottle of each."

"Every week?"

"Of course not. One of each every other day."

"You're killing yourself," Fritz scowled at his pallid friend.

Walter reached into his cow-barn lunch box for something to nibble.

"It's a vicious cycle," Rem said. "All those aspirins are tearing your insides out and that causes you to overdose on tummy elixirs. Too much of those make you nauseous so you to take more aspirin. Aspirin gives you stomach cramps so you swig down more pink syrup or that milky paste and you end up getting sick all over again, which causes you to …"

"I hear you Rem. *Jeepers.*"

"Fritz is right for a change," Box said. "And so's Rem. All that shit'll kill you."

Walter extracted a baggie filled with dried prunes and offered one to Fritz.

The jarhead scoffed. "Those things are saturated with sugar, you sorry sack of sow snot."

"True, but I've become concerned about the prospect of diabetes," Walter countered. "It's quite possible these stomach cramps are brought on by low blood sugar. If so, perhaps I can ameliorate the condition with an assortment of refined treats. I also brought a bag of dates. And a stack of *Fig Newtons*. Would you prefer one of those, Fritzer?"

"You've fallen right into the trap," Fritz said, pushing the cookies away.

"What trap?"

"The sugar trap. You're not diabetic, Walter. You've simply created another psychosomatic affliction. But you will be if you keep dumping raw sugar into your system." Fritz's angst was climbing. "Half the stupid country will be diabetic before you know it. Why? Because there's a ton of sugar in everything these days, from ketchup to breakfast cereal. Canned pork and beans are loaded with it."

"There's sugar in beans?" Rem was curious.

"Read the label. I'm telling you it's pervasive, insidious, ubiquitous. The sugar lobby is one of the strongest in Washington." Fritz slammed his hand into the back of the front seat, jolting the Box. "*Fucking food industry.* Something's gotta be done about it."

"I don't understand what the hell you've got against sugar," Rem said. "It's the next best thing to alcohol. And donuts, by the way, are a close third."

"You're killing yourself, Rem, just like Walter."

"Suicide by sugar?"

"Unwittingly, yes; unless you heed my warnings. Sugar is evil. It's the work of the devil."

"Sugar is heavenly," Rem argued. "Granted, there's hell to pay the morning after a good drunk. I'd even go so far as to say that too many donuts can create a kind of purgatory in the gut. But all that other confectionary conjecture is a suckers' debate for dweebs hung up in limbo."

"Take Halloween," Fritz said, dismissing Remington's comment. "What was otherwise a marvelous pagan holiday full of wondrous witchcraft and other forms of nature worship has been turned into a bonanza for the sugar cartel. Nowadays, Halloween is all about satanic costumes meant to intimidate people into handing over caramelized popcorn balls, candied apples, chocolate bars, lollipops, bubble gum; all sorts of sugar-laden treats."

"I don't understand what you've got against kids, either," Rem said.

"They're brats," Fritz said.

"What about *Zagnuts*?" Walter asked.

Fritz ignored the wan one's query, continuing his assault. "A joyous holy day to celebrate perfectly innocent gods has turned into a fiendish farce, a travesty rooted in the sweet tooth craze, a nocturnal grotesquery of avaricious juveniles, a deplorable greed-driven exploitation of the mindless masses perpetrated by masked ghouls marauding through neighborhoods threatening dire consequences for anyone who fails to come across with the goods: *Trick or Treat ... Trick or Treat ... Trick or Treat.*" Fritz pounded the top of the front seat with his fist. "It's enough to make me want to destroy every candy counter I see."

"What about Easter?" Box asked. "What's so evil about celebrating somebody coming back from the dead; you know, a holiday with baskets full of painted eggs and foraging for chocolate eggs filled with marshmallow or cream?"

"Some have air inside," Weepy noted, his quivering voice unable to hide disappointment and a sense of betrayal. "Chocolate on the outside; nothing on the inside. What an evil thing to do to a child."

"Christ didn't come back from the dead with baskets full of chocolate Easter eggs," Fritz exclaimed. Then, with startling suddenness, his anger transformed into amusement. He slapped the front seat with joyful exuberance, glorying in a sinister revelation. "That's it. That's it. *The Easter bunny is a false prophet.*"

Except for Grumpy, the crew regaled in blasphemous laughter.

Gulliver scratched his head. "Let me see if I'm right about this. Ostensibly, Christ's body was taken down from the cross and placed in a cave. Three days later one or more persons looked inside and, according to conflicting reports divined in the canonical Gospels about who, exactly, participated in the failed discovery, the body was apparently gone, either having been removed or leaving of its own accord. A number of people went in search of the Messiah's missing body under the assumption that finding it would give rise to the ascension theory. Irrespective of two-thousand years of debate regarding the outcome, it was the exultant joy of the search itself that, today, finds its echo in the annual event we know and worship as the hallowed Easter egg hunt."

Rem was ecstatic to learn that Easter's historical evolution went from one hunt to another, chocolate enjoying equal status as a symbol of salvation. "Jesus, Gulliver, you're a fucking genius. I've been a true believer of that ever since the first time you got down on your knees in a pile of our neighbor's bird shit and begged me to *mock the cock* with you."

Grumpy slammed the brakes. The Buick fishtailed down Route 2 in four inches of snow, narrowly missing the guard rail and finally coming to a rest sideways in the middle of the road, effectively blocking both lanes.

"I'm out of here," Grumpy grumbled, flinging his door open and kicking up snow as he beat a path down the obscured center stripe.

The crew scrambled to get out of the car before another came from one direction or the other. Walter, getting out on Gulliver's side, stepped on the car keys Grumpy had flung down. He reached down and picked them up, then climbed into the driver's seat. He started the car, feathered the gas pedal, and steered the blue beast over to the right shoulder, facing it toward Washington County.

The crew got back in. Walter kept the car in low gear, crawling along the highway until Grumpy was alongside. He cranked the window down half way to talk to the disgruntled pedestrian. "Get back in, Grump. We'll be serious the rest of the way there."

Grumpy hunched his shoulders, as much to weather the snow and the wind as to block Walter's view with the collar of his coat.

"Come on, Grump," Walter pleaded. "We'll quiet down. I promise."

Grumpy peaked over his collar. "I want to hear that promise coming from Fritz."

Fritz slid toward the middle of the back seat and yelled through the driver's window. "I promise, Grump. But *you* have to promise not to stop for donuts in Montpelier."

"I promise if you promise," Grump shouted into the car.

"Deal," Fritz said.

Walter stopped the car. Grumpy, to the surprise and chagrin of all, climbed into the back seat next to Gulliver. "You keep driving," he said to the albino. "I'm too nerved out by all that ridiculous chatter."

Over everyone's protest, Walter picked up speed.

The final thirty miles to the horse barn was uneventful, save the slew of warnings from Fritz and Box for Walter to slow down here or speed up there, and to watch out for this or that intersection, stop sign, or tight corner.

At the top of the bluff, the dog soldiers breathing a collective sigh of relief that they'd made it all the way with the sickly wraith at the wheel, Walter tapped the brakes. He had misjudged the distance required to come to a complete stop in the powdery snow. The Buick nudged over the brow of the hill. Walter, panicking, pressed the brake pedal with every muscle of his twitching leg. The tires locked up. In full skid, the weight of the car propelled it forward with increasing velocity.

Pierre, Roger, and Beauchamp Frontenac, seeing the Invicta picking up speed slithering down the hill directly toward them, turned and ran toward the outhouse.

Walter turned the steering wheel hard to the right, then to the left, then back to the right, his foot planted firmly against the brake pedal. The car went opposite his frantic steering, miraculously sailing through the opening of the barn past three stacks of lumber blanketed with snow. Inside the barn, the Buick slid another twenty feet before finally half spinning to a stop in an explosive cloud of fluffy snow inches from the saw horses.

Uproarious applause erupted inside the car.

Walter turned toward the back seat. "Hand me my lunch box, Fritz. I need a cup of coffee to calm me down."

The men piled out of the car and the audience of three approached from behind the shitter. "You'll never get that thing back up the hill," Roger said.

"Who cares?" said Weepy. "If Walter's driving, I'm walking home."

"I can yank that car up the hill with my crane," B.F. said.

Grumpy, his arms folded on his chest, aimed one eye glowering with contempt at the nerve-shattered albino while the other watched Beauchamp wrap a chain around the back of the Buick's frame and fasten the other end to the hook on his crane.

Soon, the machine's tracks scraped along the ground with B.F. maneuvering up the hill and depositing Grumpy's prized possession next to Jericho's truck, which had just pulled in.

"What the hell happened here?" Laramie asked the crane man.

"That skinny fella with the pink eyes tried to kill three of us."

"Which three?"

"The tall guy with the elephant's nose, me, and the other Frenchman. We got out of the way just in time."

B.F. unhooked the chain, dragged it up into his machine, and snaked it into a pile behind the seat. "This'll cost some money, but of course, that's what we're here for."

"You're gonna charge for doing that?"

"You betcha. This crane don't come cheap."

"I don't think that'll go over too big with the dog soldiers."

"Fifty bucks ain't so bad," B.F. said, swiveling his rig around to chug back down the hill.

The crew was milling around recounting the horror of Walter's inept driving when Jericho, walking alongside the slow moving crane, called out to the sallow one. "If someone was to give me a choice between handing you the keys to my truck and drinking a bucket of buzzard puke, I'd be buzzard hunting about now."

"The brakes on Grumpy's car are very touchy," Walter countered.

"You don't slam on the fucking brakes in four inches of snow," Grumpy said. "You tap the brakes with a cautious foot. And you do it way before you need to stop."

"I'm real sorry about the slip up – or down, rather," Walter said.

Grumpy blinked his Walter eye, the other wandering up the hill to his car. "The important thing is you didn't wreck it."

"To say nothing about the injuries we could have sustained if that fading phantasm had rammed into a corner post on this barn," Weepy said.

Grumpy turned his Buick eye on the guitar player. "If I said it once, I've said it a hundred times; I don't give a fuck for your life or mine either. That priceless Invicta up there didn't get a scratch on it; that's all that matters."

B.F. climbed down from the crane and ambled over to the Grump. "That'll be fifty dollars."

Grumpy's eyes fought each other to zero in on the man. "I ain't paying you one plug nickel, Butt Fuck. I could've done the same thing blindfolded."

"That crane costs a hundred bucks an hour no matter what the job is," B.F. said. "It took a good half hour for me and my machine to get your car back up that hill. You gotta pay up or I'm hauling my equipment out of here."

One of Grumpy's eyes found Jericho. "Go back up to your truck, grab your gun, make sure it's fully loaded, then get your ass back down here and put four or five bullets into this man's head. Save at least one for Birdsong."

"I don't want to hear about no threats," said B.F., more angered than worried. "Whenever me and that crane are working, we get paid."

"Jericho, go get your gun," Grumpy said.

The thought of the gunslinger having a reasonable excuse to shoot a man made Remington nervous. "Hold on a minute, Butt Fuck; I've got a question for you."

"What is it?"

"Are you a betting man?"

"I might go with a wager once in a blue moon, providing I like the odds."

"How about if whether you get paid or you get shot comes down to whether or not you can guess this ornery cuss's age? I'll give you ten years on either side, twenty years leeway altogether. What do you say?"

B.F. squinted his eyes at Grumpy and chirruped with such mirth his belly quaked. "What's the bet again?"

"First of all, let me be very clear that I don't think you've got a prayer of winning it, even though I'm giving you all those years to play with. But here's how it works in case you're up to the challenge. You guess the Grump's age inside of a decade – for instance, if you say he's twenty-five then he can't be under fifteen or over thirty-five – you get paid your fifty bucks and then, of course, you get shot. You miss his age by more than ten years, not only do you not get paid but you don't get shot either. Pretty fair odds, you think about it."

Beauchamp scratched his head. "You boys sure are a confusing bunch to talk to. But I might be a good one for a gamble if the moon's right. Let me take a gander at this fella."

"Take a good long look," Rem said. "And remember, it's either the money and your life or neither one, depending on how accurate your guess is. Take all the time you need, Butt Fuck."

"I wish you wouldn't call me that."

"Sorry, but that's what your initials mean to us. There's no changing it now."

"I get ten years, you say, on either side of this man's actual age?"

"That's right."

The crew gathered round. Pierre and Roger looked on from a distance.

"He's either a helluva lot younger than he looks or he's more like the age you'd take him to be," B.F. surmised aloud.

"You need more than ten years to play with?" Rem asked with a note of drama in his voice. "Maybe I can get with the crew here and see if we can't make it a might easier for you."

"Would that Jericho fella really up and shoot me?" Beauchamp asked.

"No question about it," Rem answered. "He's a gunslinger with a hair trigger. Give him the least little excuse and he's only too happy to blow a man's head clean off."

B.F. grinned and chirped. "Can't be he'd shoot a fella over fifty dollars."

"It's not about money with him. It's about opportunity. He's had more than a few chances to shoot my young ass. The only reason he didn't is because I won bets with him each and every time, just like you've got a chance to do."

"But you and him are friends. I'm sure that counted for something."

"Not on your life."

"I'm forgettin' how the bet goes. Let me run it back by you to make sure I understand it."

"Go ahead."

"If I guess the man's age to within ten years that means I get my fifty bucks and I either don't get shot or I do, that's the part I'm forgettin'. Or, if I miss my guess outside of ten years, I lose my money and I either don't get shot or I still do. Which is it?"

"Both."

"Both?"

"Yup."

"And you're saying this Jericho fella is a gunslinger?"

"You betcha."

Jericho walked through the barn's entrance and fired a round into the air, then stared into B.F.'s squinting eyes. "Guess that man's age, blow champ, or the next round burrows into your skull."

Beauchamp shuffled his feet. "I get ten years on either side don't forget."

"You don't get shit," Jericho said. "You either guess the man's age right to the month or you can start naming your pall bearers."

B.F. turned to Remington. "How come the rules are different coming from him?"

"Hold on a sec," Rem said, taking Jericho by the gun-toting hand and escorting him outside the barn's entrance.

When they came back, Remington looked relieved.

"I explained the rules to him," Rem said. "Let's go over them again to make sure we're all in agreement. Guess Grumpy's age within a decade and you get to live another day but without the fifty dollars you're trying to charge for doing a good deed. Miss his age by more than ten years and the money's yours even though your life isn't."

Jericho twirled his pistol.

B.F. did not appear to be nervous. "Let me ask about the wagering conditions one more time."

"There's no mystery to it," Rem said.

"Maybe so, but if your life depended on it, you'd want to be sure you understood the rules wouldn't you?"

"My life doesn't depend on rules," Rem said. "But go ahead, repeat the wager conditions if it'll make you more comfortable."

"If I figure out this man's age inside of ten years, I get my fifty bucks and this fella here'll shoot me. If I'm off by more than ten years, I don't get shot and I don't get paid either. Am I right?"

"Fair enough," Rem said.

B.F. scratched the stubble on his chin for a long moment, his eyes squinting first at Grumpy, then at Remington, then at Jericho, then back to the Grump.

Jericho stepped closer, cocked the trigger, and aimed his gun at B.F.'s head.

The crane man stopped rubbing his whiskers, put both hands on his hips, and gave Rem a long look. *No bet.*

The crew broke out in laughter listening to the crane man chirp. Jericho, laughing the loudest, fired the rest of his bullets into the air. *Pop, pop, pop.*

"*Hee-hee-hee.* You can keep your fifty bucks," B.F. told the Grump. "Truth of it is I don't give a pickled turd what your age is."

"You don't?" Rem asked.

"Sure don't. I was stringing you boys along the whole time. I ain't never made a bet my whole life; I ain't about to start now."

"I thought you said you'd gamble once in a while."

"I said I might, *once in a blue moon.* When's the last time you seen one that color?"

"In a way then, you won the bet without even making one," Rem said.

"That's the way I see it," B.F. said, climbing into his crane and grinning from lobe to lobe. Cranking up his rig, "Let's get a few of these trusses up before the whole morning's shot."

"Just out of curiosity," Rem shouted up to him, "how old do you think this ornery cuss is?"

Beauchamp gave his chins a few scrapes with the back of his hand. "That fella ain't a day over fifty."

Twenty-Six

Work went slow during the ten days the chirping Beauchamp Frontenac hoisted trusses into place with his canary colored crane. Bad weather and Thanksgiving contributed to the diminished pace.

Walter and Weepy helped Pierre and Box Car build stalls, a laborious effort involving endless measuring and sawing, the monotony of repetitious nailing, and the tedious screwing into place of numberless hinges and hasps.

Gulliver, Jericho, and Fritz scooted their frost-numb butts two feet further along the cap each time they finished setting braces at their end of a truss while Remington, Roger, and Grumpy froze their asses on the other cap.

Box Car emitted deep corrugated grunts to Walter's incessant bellyaching about his intestinal maladies. Weepy, not to be out-bellyached, griped constantly about his fingers being too cold to play his guitar. And while the Frenchman endured the whining without comment, Box found relief fastening the chain onto trusses for the crane to hoist.

The gable end above the barn's front entrance was secured the first Wednesday in December. The crane man grinned and chirped saying his goodbyes, the dog soldiers barking their delight while Rem mimicked.

B.F. and his bulbous machine chugged to the top of the bluff where he shut it down, climbed off, yelled to Pierre that he'd send someone over sooner or later with a flatbed to haul it away, got into his pickup, and was gone.

During lunch the mood was uplifted by the sight of a horse barn that, at long last, actually looked like one. Remarkably, the trusses were all in place nearly two full days ahead of schedule.

Pierre was hoping to be able to trust Box Car, Remington, and Walter to continue constructing horse stalls while he and Roger built the swing-open doors and Fritz, Grumpy, and Gulliver laid slats for the metal roof.

Jericho, a master electrician, pulled wire for overhead lights, outlets, and mercury vapor lamps to be installed above the doors.

Other projects included the construction of box frames for the iron-barred windows, finishing off the plumbing to the lavatory and the clean-up area, and building a cupola. The final statement would come with the installation of the weathervane.

Weepy, in accordance with the crew's plans, set up his equipment in a stall that was first to benefit from a roof.

The dessert portion of lunch proved to be a delicious prelude to a special cultural lesson provided by the quiet Frenchman.

Pierre's wife had made the mistake of packing in his lunch a large banana in the unforgiving shape of a crescent moon. Sitting low in his VW beetle to *moan-sewer* cat calls and *bone-sure* taunts, *Ohhh Pee-errrh* pleased his hungry audience with a daring unsheathing of his phallic fruit and a tantalizing mastication of its succulent pulp. When the show was over, he rolled down his window and waited for the pandemonic applause to abate.

Fritz reached his hands out his window and slapped the side of the Buick with congratulatory fervor, shouting "Splendid performance, Frenchman. Splendid."

"Best burlesque this side of Bellows Falls," Rem bellowed.

"I finally understand the meaning of passion fruit," said Walter.

"A plate of come please is a *fait accompli*" Gulliver feted.

"Way to blow lunch," said Weepy.

"The French really know how to get down," Box growled with guttural gusto.

Pierre smacked his lips and smiled. "Did anyone ever tell you boys that the best things in life are French?"

"You're going to have to explain that one," Fritz said.

"Be happy to," Pierre said. "Take culinary pleasures. Which would you prefer, a drink before dinner or an aperitif? A cube steak for your entrée or a filet mignon? Scrambled eggs or a soufflé? Would you have your cook slap a pat of butter on your asparagus, or would you rather a gourmet chef caress it with hollandaise?"

"I get it," Rem said. "A meal is a meal unless it's a banquet. A restaurant is finer than a diner. Fritz, who hates the very thought of a donut, could order a croissant or maybe a *crêpe suzette*, eh?"

"Or, as a connoisseur of palette pleasing pastry" said the Frenchman, "he might enjoy his crêpe infused with chocolate."

"He might munch his brochette, nibble his *pate de foie gras*, and sip a sweet liqueur," Weepy suggested.

"Would you give your lady a bunch of flowers?" asked Pierre. "Or would you offer her a beautiful bouquet? Would you ride in a car or a limousine? Request a driver or a chauffeur?"

"You might be onto something," said Walter.

"What I'm onto, in this instance," Pierre assured his audience, "is that the best things in life are French."

"We want more," Fritz said, pounding the side of the Buick.

"Some of you might order a room in a hotel," Pierre continued, "but the debonair among you would request a suite. And if, once there, you wished to celebrate, surely you would call for champagne."

"And if I had my lady up there with me?" Rem wanted to know.

"You would embrace her," said Pierre, pausing for the denouement, "and you would bestow upon her the sensual magic of the best of kisses; the *French* kiss."

With that, the crew burst into tumultuous applause, showering the Frenchman with a deluge of *Ohhh Pee-errrhs*.

"Toussenant, the renaissance man," Gulliver declared.

"A veritable *cout d'etat*," Weepy cried.

Grumpy got out and slammed his door. "Banquet's over, gentlemen. Get your sorry *derrières* back to work."

Twice a week, like clockwork, Roger left the construction site during lunch break, returning an hour or so after the crew had gone back to work. His excuses had to do with unexpectedly long meetings with his lawyer regarding his insurance company's refusal to provide benefits for plastic surgery to truncate his imposing snout. Rudy docked his pay for the lost time but the nosy snoop never complained about it.

In actuality, Roger left to brief his cohorts at the Attorney General's office about his investigation into possible human rights violations perpetrated by members of the horse barn's work crew against temporary co-workers and, possibly, one subcontractor.

Roger missed Pierre's French lesson due to a regularly scheduled briefing in downtown Montpelier.

Although she had seen him at the construction site – and they had, as well, spotted each other at the pig roast – Marsha Leeks and Roger Framingham had never been formally introduced. Neither did either know the other's professional status. This would change momentarily.

Marsha sat in the waiting area going over her notes from the previous week's session when she overheard a discussion in the adjoining conference room that seemed to involve the same subject matter she had brought to the attention of her editor several weeks earlier. She'd brought her horse barn notes for today's session, intending to tell the Attorney General that she was aware of the undercover operation *vis-à-vis* the horse barn.

From her seat in the lobby she was able to overhear an argument about whether to bring civil or criminal action. When the argument subsided, she left her chair to eavesdrop by leaning against the door.

Questions concerning emotional injury were raised and debated. There were comments pertaining to curious occupational hazards, a possible conspiracy to keep unemployment in Washington County artificially inflated, plea bargaining, liability insurance, the danger of publicity, and the special challenge – if brought to trial – of finding enough people to be able to select a jury of so-called peers.

She scribbled furiously in her notebook, pausing when the word *deviant* was used to describe *Box Car* and, what was that? *Butt Fuck?*

Moments later her face flushed when that disgusting term for anal intercourse was used again. Strangely, there was a moment of laughter followed by a line of questioning about whether or not it would be possible to convince, what? *Some dumb Frenchman* with a huge crane to file charges relating to, what? *Abnormal* sexual aggression.

At the sound of chairs sliding on the floor, Marsha returned to her seat. Oh my goodness, she thought, conditions at the horse barn have taken a turn for the worse. Or for the better, in terms of the possibilities for a terrific scoop.

The conference room door opened. Marsha glanced up. Roger Framingham hesitated, turned around to say something to his associates, then came through the door alone and closed it behind him.

"I think we may know each other," he said.

Marsha stifled her astonishment. "You work at the horse barn."

"Ah, well, yes, that's true."

"But you also work here,"

"Well, ah, yes, that's true."

"That can only mean you're an undercover agent conducting an investigation into activities at the horse barn."

"May I ask who you are and what you're doing in this office?" Roger questioned, taking a few steps toward her.

She stood and extended her hand. "My name is Marsha Leeks. I'm a reporter for the Washington County *Chronicle*. This office is on my beat. I come here every week for an interview with the Attorney General.

"Are you planning to do a story about the horse barn? It was my understanding that you showed up there to inquire about boarding a horse."

"I can go undercover too, Mister …"

"Framingham. Roger Framingham," Roger said, shaking her hand.

"You tell me," Marsha said.

"About what?"

"Whether or not I'm onto a story."

"I'm afraid a story, at this time, would be premature, Ms. Leeks."

"Because it would blow your cover?"

Roger pondered the question, stroking his nose. "If I were to take you into my confidence, would it be possible to …"

"You mean, as a confidential source?"

"Yes."

"You'll tell me about your investigation as long as I agree not to write a story until the time is right. Is that correct?"

"I'm not saying there is a story. Or ever will be."

"What are you saying?"

"Are you aware that complaints have been lodged against the company contracted to build the horse barn?"

"Yes. I have copies of all of them."

"From how many groups or agencies?"

"Three."

"I see. And how close are you to writing a piece about the horse barn?"

"My editor and I have it under discussion now. We reviewed my notes and decided that it's quite likely there is, in fact, a story here."

"But not unless this office files civil or criminal charges against the construction company or one or more individuals among the work crew. Is that correct?"

"Not necessarily. The fact that the Attorney General's office is looking into possible human rights violations, either as a direct or indirect result of complaints lodged against the construction crew by workers sent to the horse barn by the unemployment office, is newsworthy enough for us to publish a story at any time."

"And yet, such a story would have considerably more impact if it should break coincident with legal action taken by the Attorney General's office, would it not?"

"Agreed."

"And isn't it safe to say that you're the only reporter who knows about our investigation?"

"I have no way of knowing that. Our business is highly competitive. We're all trying to be first with a major story. I'm not the only reporter who talks to the A.G. I might be the only one who's onto this investigation at this point in time, but that could change. I don't want to sit on it too long."

"And you believe this could be a major story?"

"Don't you?"

"I'm not sure. It depends on whether or not allegations of human rights violations have sufficient veracity. As of now, confidentially, these are merely complaints. They would have to be lodged in a more formal, legally binding, manner."

"Have any of the complainants agreed to do that?"

"That's not my area of responsibility in this investigation."

"But you attend these briefings. Surely you know how that end of it is progressing."

"Actually, we haven't pursued that aspect of it as yet. For now, my personal observations represent the crux of the investigation. Depending upon my findings, we may or may not speak to the complainants directly."

"But isn't it true that you learned about possible violations from the men who made the allegations?"

"I'm not at liberty to reveal our sources."

"What you're telling me is that the ultimate news value of this story will be largely determined by your findings."

"Suffice to say that any story regarding our investigation would be, at this time, premature. I would even suggest that the actual timing of a story could determine if it's front page news or whether it belongs in one of those ridiculous gossip columns your editor writes."

"I see. May I ask, Mr. Armaham, how close you are to filing a final report?"

"That's *Framingham*, if accuracy means anything. Quite close, in fact. The horse barn is within a few weeks of being completed. It makes sense for my report to dovetail with the finalization of construction. Whether you know this or not, the owners happen to hold high-level posts in state government. They've got their personal capital at risk on this project. There's no reason why our efforts should ruin theirs. Again, it's a timing issue."

"Marsha?"

The A.G.'s secretary had stepped into the lobby.

"Yes?"

"He can see you now."

"Thanks. I'll be right in."

Roger and Marsha shook hands again, a fragile relationship established, and exited the waiting area through different doors.

A week later, the roof two-thirds completed, the stalls three-quarters finished, most of the electrical wiring pigtailed, half the windows installed, the rear doors hung and the front doors nearly built, Marsha Leeks appeared at the horse barn for the first time since the pig roast almost a month earlier.

It was mid-morning. When she got out of her car, a *Take-Twenty* van pulled up next to her. She told the driver she had no idea whether or not it was okay for him to drive down to the barn. He decided to take his chances. Marsha caught Fritz's attention, motioning for him to come up the hill.

Fritz had the presence of mind to load up his nail bag. He gave Marsha a return wave, sneering at the van driver on his way up to the top of the bluff.

"How'd you find your way to this place?" Remington asked the *Take-Twenty* vendor.

"I stopped at a store in Marshfield for something to eat. Some guy playing checkers with the storekeeper told me there was a horse barn being built out this way. Looks like I'm too late to do much regular business here; I'll be parking this baby for the winter pretty soon."

The man flipped open the side panel of his van, adroitly positioning rods at each end to hold it in place. "Here we go, boys. I got *Clara Bell* brownies, *Sara Lee* cakes, *Aunt Jessie's* cookies, ring-dings, spongy pink-capped or white-capped snowball cupcakes with coconut crumbs, *Tom Thumb* pies, cherry-filled swirls, macaroons, Danishes, cinnamon buns, and éclairs to go with the hot coffee you see steaming away like that guy who just walked past me. And if you're dog-ass hungry, I got hot dogs, dilly dogs, Michigans, foot-long frankfurters, and my top dog, the famous devil dog. Lots of dogs here, boys. Lots of dogs."

"Whad'ya have to drink besides coffee?" Gulliver asked.

The van man peered inside a separate compartment. "For soda, I got orange, ginger ale, *Mr. Pibb*, *Dr. Pepper*, *Royal Crown Cola*, and *Cott* root beer. For juices, I got orange, apple, and grapefruit. I also got milk in small cartons, either to drink alone or if you want it for your coffee instead of these little creamers here."

While the dog soldiers dug in their pockets for dollars and change to buy coffee and juices and all sorts of snacks, Marsha was attempting to lever her nascent relationship with Fritz, querying him about any subcontractors that may have been on the job site recently.

"Are you talking about the crane man?" Fritz asked.

"I think so."

"Are you worried the trusses we put up are faulty and the roof might cave in on your horse once it's boarded here?"

"That would be a valid concern."

"As far as I could tell, the trusses were all good; no fractures or splits in them. I know they're nailed in real solid because I worked on them myself."

"I assume that's the subcontractor's crane over there."

"It's supposed to be hauled away any day. Must be he didn't have another job for it right away."

"Did anything unusual happen when the crane man was working here?"

"The question itself is flawed. Everything that happens here is unusual." Fritz folded his arms across his chest and chuckled. "That's what happens when you get a bunch of 'ol whore dogs like us on the same job."

"Let me try and get to the crux of the issue another way."

"You can get to the issue of my crux anyway you want," Fritz said.

Marsha stepped back. "You're so forward!"

"I'm just being honest with you. You're not the only one who has a problem with my candor. But don't worry; I won't let it piss me off."

Marsha glanced down at the horse barn, then back at Fritz. "It appears you're almost finished."

"About a week-and-a-half more, we figure. What is it you'd like to know about Butt Fuck?"

Marsha took another step back, unable to prevent her facial expression from revealing embarrassment. "Excuse me?"

"B.F. Beauchamp Frontenac. The crane man. He was a barrel of laughs. On top of that, he's the best crane operator in this entire vicinity. I'd recommend him without the slightest hesitation."

"There were no problems while he was here, either for him with the crew or for the crew with him?"

"No. Why? Is there something about him we don't know about?"

Marsha stared at the iconoclast with the straggly beard and the stone gray eyes for a long moment, wondering how to respond.

"Where are you going with this?" Fritz asked.

Marsha didn't know. There had been no additional complaints filed with any group or agency by any subcontractor since her discussion with Roger, whom she noticed out of the corner of her eye was standing apart from the crew drinking a cup of coffee and eating what looked to be a croissant. She had relied on her investigative reporting skills and the relationship she had forged with one of the so-called dog soldiers to gain vital insight into anything untoward that may have occurred between the work crew and a certain subcontractor. At long last, "Is he the only subcontractor that's been on this job?"

"You're a reporter, aren't you?" Fritz's question was posed more as a declarative statement.

Marsha took yet another step back. "Excuse me?"

"You don't have a horse, do you?"

"I beg your pardon!"

"You're privy to a state investigation and you want the scoop, right?"

"Now look who's full of questions."

"Doesn't matter. What matters is that I like everything about you. You're pretty. You've got a great body. You have a certain spontaneity that I find refreshing. And you have an air of dignity about you; a gracious comportment that I think goes quite well with my own suave and chivalrous style."

"Thank you. I think."

"I'm even hoping you're wise to the unscrupulous tactics of the oppressive food cartel – a much bigger story than this nonevent here, incidentally – and that, with any luck, I'll be able to convince you to join me in a *seek-and-destroy* mission against the food giants. In fact, your prowess as a journalist could prove to be instrumental while we work together to expose a terrifying plot designed to turn every American into a fat unhealthy slob prone to disease. And premature death, if there is such a thing."

"Wow!" Marsha exclaimed. "I wasn't expecting that."

"What do you say? Will you work with me?" Fritz asked.

"That's not exactly my take, although I'm very much against junk food. I prefer a less aggressive means of combating the problem. I've been studying orthomolecular pharmacology over the past year or so. Micronutrients, as a means of achieving optimum health, are an exciting new frontier, in my opinion. It would almost seem as though your interests and mine are fairly compatible. I'll have to think about it."

"Great. That's all I ask, for now. Except for one other thing."

"What's that?"

Fritz took three steps forward and gave her a quick kiss on the lips; too quick for her to react in a defensive manner.

"I wasn't expecting that either," she heard herself saying.

"There's a lot you can't expect, coming from me," Fritz said. "And yet, coming from me, you can expect just about anything."

"I think I should leave now," Marsha said.

Fritz watched her drive away convinced they would be together again, perhaps the next time in more compelling circumstances.

Walking back to the barn, the gaga ex-grunt was aghast at the scene unfolding near the entrance. A flurry of pastry flakes was imbedded in Box Car's beard. A daub of lemon meringue clung to the corner of Remington's mouth. Weepy crammed an entire devil dog into his mouth and immediately unwrapped another. Jericho licked the sticky rim of a cinnamon bun. Grumpy stuffed his face with muffins. Gulliver swigged from a large carton of orange juice between bites of a foot-long frankfurter. Pierre glanced around furtively, chomping on his own dog. Roger leaned against a corner post sipping coffee, careful not to dunk his nose. And Walter sat straddling a saw horse clutching his stomach and moaning in agony. Except for the sight of Walter doing penance, the phony-food fest was Fritz's worst nightmare.

The flash-tempered jarhead, trying to stay calm, splayed his hands on his hips and shook his head. "You men disgust me."

"Why's that?" Rem asked.

"Look at you, cramming confectionary concoctions. Poisoning your metabolisms. Gorging your guts with naked calories. Demanding the impossible from your insulin pumps. Flooding your brains with excess glucose."

Fritz's composure evaporated faster than the steam from Roger's coffee. He walked over to the van and slammed his fist down on the metal awning. One of the holding rods somersaulted into the air and clanged on the ground. The left corner of the panel tilted out of kilter.

"Hey, you can't do that," the van man shouted at the Marine.

Fritz snatched the other rod and threw it to the ground, the metal awning slamming down. He stepped toward the vendor, glaring and shaking with anger. "Listen up you slime-dog sugar charlatan. You've got thirty seconds to high-tail it out of here or I'm going to wipe out your entire inventory."

The vexed vendor knew trouble when he saw it. With Jericho pounding out a ferocious drum beat on the back of the van and Remington verbalizing an organ accompaniment – *Na-ner-ner-ner-ner-ner-ner-ner-ner-ner-ner-ner-ner-ner-ner-ner ... Na-ner-ner-ner-ner-ner-ner-ner-ner-ner-ner-ner-ner-ner-ner ... Wipe Out* – the van man picked up his rods and tossed them inside the food compartment. He snapped the latches, hustled around to the driver's side, jumped in, turned the engine over, slammed it in gear, and peeled out.

"Your lady friend was a decoy," Gulliver said to the eldest Swilling. "We had her come out here at the same time as the *Take-Twenty* van to keep you busy while we wolfed down all these goodies."

Fritz stared at his brother for a moment, ran his eyes around the group, then walked over to Roger. "Your time is coming, Haminhand."

"Whoa," said Roger. "What the hell did I do to deserve that?"

Remington stepped between them. "What did any of us do to deserve anything this crazy Marine does? Think nothing of it, Damningfart. Sugar does this to him."

"But he didn't have any," Roger said.

"I'm talking about the sugar conspiracy that's flambéed his head like the crust on a *crème brulee*. Something about a secret anti-American plot he claims the food industry's wrapped up in. Fast food joints, the cookies and chips section in your favorite grocery store, junk food of every description; all those things send this war-torn derelict right over the edge. Pay no attention."

Roger shook his head and walked away.

Fritz walked over to Walter and bent down to find his pink eyes. "Serves you right, you gutless ghost."

Walter peered into the sleet-gray eyes of his demon-ridden friend. "I wish to hell I was gutless. The one I've got is killing me."

"All right then," Gulliver announced to the crew, "what do you say we take advantage of our serendipitous sugar spike and do this job righteous?"

"Suits me fine," Box growled. "I got my next meal stored in my beard."

Twenty-Seven

Grumpy showed up at Fanny Allen Hospital Saturday morning an hour before daybreak to corral Mabel and take her to the horse barn with the crew.

"I don't like leaving my shift three hours early," Mabel said to the Grump.

"We need you with us today. After work, we intend to party pretty hard."

"That does sound like fun. Will the tall man with the great big nose be there?"

"That's the plan."

"Great."

"You've really got a thing for that jumbo schnoz of his don't you?"

Mabel giggled. "You've got such a way with words, Dumpy."

"I never would have guessed you can tell what a man's got in his pants by the size of his nose."

"If he's a man, he'd better not have the same thing I've got down there."

"I'm not talking about gender, I'm talking about size. Makes me self-conscious. My nose is tiny."

"What does the size of a man's nose have to do with what he's got in his pants?"

"You tell me."

"You're the one who's making the comparison. I never heard of such a thing. Shoe size, sure; but not nose size."

"The size of the nose has nothing to do with the size of the hose?"

"Not that I know of."

"Then what the hell excites you so much about the size of Roger's freakin' nose?"

"Oh my goodness, Bumpy. Do you really have to ask?"

Grumpy's imagination gave him the answer he wasn't looking for. He smiled inwardly, his sense of self-worth restored. He rubbed his nose and looked at Mabel. I guess this one doesn't do a whole lot for you."

Mabel glanced at Grumpy's nose and quickly looked away. "I'm sorry to have to say this, Stumpy, but it really is inadequate."

Despite the repetitive *faux pas* with his name, Mabel's comment did nothing to undermine his renewed confidence. "You got a change of clothes?"

"You wanted me to wear something sexy, right?"

"That's right. Whad'ya bring?"

"Remember that Hawaiian nightgown you bought me?"

"You mean the muumuu?"

"If that's what it is."

"That was Rem's idea, and a damned good one. But we don't need you to do a strip-tease."

Mabel giggled. "I still can't believe I did that."

"You were drunk."

"Will I get drunk at the party later?"

"If you need to."

"Okay, but I don't want to get too drunk; not enough to dance naked in front of a lot of people again. It's not like I ever got paid for doing that."

"That may be, but we didn't have to pay for our drinks because of your entertainment value. It all evened out."

Mabel doffed her uniform, rolled down her white panty hose, unhinged her breast harness, slipped out of her panties, and shimmied into the muumuu.

In Winooski, Grumpy pulled up to the curb and honked for Weepy, the first of the crew he picked up each morning.

Weepy was pleased to see the horse-woman in her flimsy dress. "You look sexy," he said to her.

Mabel smiled, staring at the singer-guitar player for a long moment. "Weepy's nose is small," she said to the Grump.

"So what?" Grumpy said.

"So you can't compare the two. His are way different."

Grumpy smiled outwardly. "Must be the reason for his name."

"Weepy?"

"No. His last name."

"What is it?" she asked.

"O'Toole," Weepy said, rising to the occasion.

Mabel giggled and winked at the entertainer. "I like names that fit."

Weepy winked back. "Then it should come as no surprise, Lady Broome, that you sweep me off my feet."

The equine goddess was sprawled out on the back seat of the Buick fast asleep at nine-thirty in the morning when Rudy made his first workday visit to the horse barn since September, wheeling his spanking new Chevy pickup past the Invicta and barreling down to the construction site.

The general contractor walked around inside the barn toting an eight-foot long level.

Jericho climbed down from the roof faster than a barn spider. "What the hell are you doing here? Nobody invited you."

"The owners are coming Tuesday for their final inspection. I want to make sure everything's hunky-dory."

Jericho was outraged that the G.C. would, at this late stage of the project, question the work of his dog soldiers. "Give me that thing," he said, yanking the level out of Rudy's hands.

The gunslinger walked over to a corner post. "Get over here," he yelled to Rudy. "You see this? Every single bubble down the whole length of this ridiculous level is lined up perfect; dead nuts."

Jericho walked part way down the side of the barn and slapped the level onto a stud. "Check this out. Dead nuts here too, goddamnit."

The incensed mountain man positioned an extension ladder, cradled the level in the crook of his elbows, and climbed all the way up to the cap where he placed the level against a two-by-six and yelled down. "Can you see these bubbles from there, you fucking hoot owl? Dead nuts again!"

Jericho climbed down, grabbed the ladder, dragged it to the other end of the barn, climbed up to the bottom of the gable truss and placed the level against it. "How about here, Mister Construction Company big-shot?" Jericho hollered. "Dead nuts. Dead nuts everywhere." Jericho repeated the statement with an earth-shaking bellow. *"Dead fucking nuts everywhere."*

With that, Jericho grabbed the middle of the level and held it like a javelin. He reached back and flung it at the contractor, one end sticking with a soft thud into the crusty mud not more than four inches from Rudy's left foot.

"Now get the hell out of here," the gunslinger yelled at him. "And I don't want to see your sorry ass at this horse barn again."

Rudy picked up his level, walked over to the Frenchman for a few quick words, strutted out of the barn to his truck, got in, and drove back up the hill. The crew flew into hysterical laughter. Rudy's truck paused next to the Buick, then drove away.

Walter hadn't eaten since Tuesday. It wasn't the partaking of pastries the day before that made him cramp up – he never partook – but the mere sight of pies and cakes, rolls and buns, hot dogs and devil dogs being wolfed down by everyone else that had turned his stomach into a cauldron of burning acids and boiling bile.

During lunch break with the rest of the crew, the withering albino opened his shiny red lunch box, searched around inside, brought out three bottles, and washed down six aspirins with loud gulps of pink syrup and milk of magnesia.

Fritz watched the apothecary demonstration with unbridled horror. "This is the fourth day in a row your lunch has consisted solely of counteracting medicines. What the hell have you been eating for breakfast and dinner these days?"

"Coffee for breakfast, of course. Then I have the same thing for dinner as I had for lunch, except I throw in a *Zero* bar for mood elevation and a half cup of soup for a modicum of nutrients."

"You'll waste away in no time if you don't get some real food in you."

"My stomach has become allergic to food."

"That's impossible."

"Everyone is allergic to one type of food or another. I'm that rare individual who's allergic to all foods."

"How long do you expect to live if you don't eat?" Box asked.

"Naturally, a person must eat to stay alive. But lately, I either upchuck within minutes of eating solid foods or they go right through me, exploding in a foul steamy effluence."

"Would you mind sparing us the details?" Weepy requested.

"I've been doing some research on Celiac disease, a chronic disorder that severely debilitates digestion, leading, as you might expect, to malnutrition. I think that's my problem right there."

"Maybe that greasy tomato soup is to blame; killing you from the inside out," Fritz suggested, "although it certainly looks the other way around from my point of view."

"*Jeepers*, if not for the palliative effects and revitalizing potential of grandmother's soup, enhanced, of course, by a healthy infusion of borage oil, there's no telling how stricken I'd be. No, what's got me in its deadly grasp now is either a rare disease that I can't put my finger on or some dastardly parasite that's gotten out of hand. Then too, given the newly touted concept of biochemical individuality, my system may lack a critical substance; some micronutrient my body craves but never gets despite my success crafting a healthy diet."

Remington seemed to find the albino's self-diagnosis distasteful, judging by the tortured groan he emitted.

"I wouldn't call the kettle black if I were you," Walter said.

Remington groaned again, his head rolling on the top of the seat.

Walter felt insulted. "Listen Remington, your emotional demons are every bit as threatening to your psyche as any pathogen might be to my digestive system."

Rem rubbed his eyes, spinning on his spinal axis to look at Walter. "What are you saying?"

"You're one to be so critical; that's what I'm saying."

"Critical of what?"

"The battle raging in my stomach versus the monsters warring in your head."

"How'd you know about the war in my head?"

"Maybe he didn't," Gulliver said. "Explain yourself, Rem."

"Okay, I'll give it a shot. Remember when we were kids?"

"No," said Gulliver. "I was too young."

"We played all sorts of games, most of them violent."

"Have they stopped?" Gully asked.

"Except for *mock the cock*, yes. I'm talking about cops and robbers, cowboys and Indians, the Huns against the Romans, the Nazis against …"

"Great fun," Fritz interrupted. "But what's all that got to do with a war going on inside your head?"

Rem shifted around for a better view of his audience in the back seat. "Remarkable as it may seem, Walter's remark was accurate. Seems like every time I close my eyes lately, a skirmish develops. It's seldom all-out war like we used to have, but there's always some crazy battle underway. And I'm always in the middle of it."

"Pitted against that battle-ax wife of yours, no doubt," Gulliver said.

"Strangely enough, she's usually on my side. But more often than not, she gets killed by friendly fire. Next thing you know I'm in court doing battle with her family for custody of Beatrice. The only thing I can think to do to prove that my daughter loves me is to make my eyes jitterbug in front of the jury, figuring they'll love the trick every bit as much as Bea does and reward me with custody."

"I don't want to know the verdict," Weepy said.

"Me either," Rem said.

"I want to know where the friendly fire came from," Fritz said.

"I knew you'd ask that, you bastard," Rem said.

"It's *you*, isn't it? You're either shooting from the hip or shooting off at the mouth – and Sibyl is always the casualty."

"Let's not get into that," Rem said. "When Walter disturbed the snooze I was having a moment ago I was dreaming about a horrendous firefight."

"You couldn't have been napping for any more than ten minutes," Box said.

"A lot can happen in that amount of time."

"A fucking war?"

"It wasn't so much a war as it was a skirmish, an isolated battle, a firefight."

"Was Charlie in it?" the Marine asked.

"No. The Viet Cong was noticeably absent, you demented jarhead."

"Was I in it?" Gully was eager to know.

"Yes. Yes you were."

"I want to know about the weapons," Fritz said.

"At first, it was a war of words."

"Surely I had to be in it," Fritz said.

"You were," said Rem. "We all were; Jericho, the Frenchman, even Mabel."

Grumpy looked at Jericho's truck. "Ever since I sent her over there to make room for us to eat, Jericho keeps looking over at me with a shit-eating grin."

"She's wearing a muumuu with nothing under it," Weepy said. "Why wouldn't he be grinning?"

"When I laid her out on the seat, I made sure her head was on the passenger side," Grumpy said, "to prevent any funny business."

"His fear of Deirdre is prevention enough," Box said. "My guess is Mabel gives him a sideways smile when he stares up her muumuu. Jericho's trying to return the favor."

"Forget about the gunslinger," said Fritz. "I want to hear about the firefight."

"It started as an argument," Rem said. "A vicious battle of words ensued. Fritz had an unfair advantage because he could breathe fire. Then Gulliver figured out how to do it and the two of them were singeing each other's hair and clothing. Box Car moved in, turned around and bent over. Next thing you know this thick purple cloud enveloped my brothers. The Frenchman came out of nowhere with a huge nail gun and slammed about thirty ten-pennies into the Box, the ones hitting his head bouncing harmlessly away. Suddenly, Gulliver came out of the cloud and attacked Rudy, who was rubbing his hands along the horse woman's flanks because she was all lathered up. Jericho had an even bigger nail gun. He was up on the roof of the horse barn firing at everybody. Not to be outgunned, Weepy's guitar was able to shoot nails the size of railroad spikes. He shattered Jericho's knee with one of them. The gunslinger slid off the roof, rolled twice on the ground, and came up firing. Grumpy walked up behind him and put a nail gun to his head. Then Walter showed up with a shiny red plastic squirt gun that shot poison darts. Everybody fired at the albino only to discover that he was a ghost. Nails went right through him with no effect. He was about to massacre the whole kitten caboodle of us when I heard him holler, *jeepers*, followed by a bunch of mumbo-jumbo. That's when I woke up."

"Where the hell were you during this ridiculous firefight?" Fritz asked. "I didn't hear you mention your name."

"I had Gulliver's camera. I was running around taking some great shots. It was incredibly realistic. Gully, I'd be surprised if the roll of film you've got in there right now doesn't chronicle the entire battle. I just hope I captured the look on Jericho's face when Grumpy had that nail gun trained to the back of his head."

"Did you use up the whole roll?" Gulliver asked.

"Yeah. I ran out of film about the time Walter said, *jeepers*."

"I'm happy to have been able to end your little skirmish," Walter said, "and to have emerged as a villainous hero. But the entire episode, it seems to me, is fraught with psychological messages, all disturbingly sexual in nature. Care to analyze them for us?"

"No time for dream analysis now," Grumpy said. "The Frenchman is back in the barn. Let's get to work."

Walking down to the site, Gulliver gave Remington a shove.

"What the hell was that for?" Rem asked.

"You used up all my film, you sonuvabitch. I needed it for tonight's caper, remember?"

Remington gave his brother a queer look. "You may the most articulate storm trooper around these parts, but you're hands down the most gullible person on the planet."

It took more persuasiveness than the crew anticipated, but the unsuspecting snoop dog, mindful of how close he was to concluding his investigation and cunningly circumspect about not sabotaging the fragile détente he'd forged with the menacing pack of horse barn hounds, reluctantly agreed to end the week by partying with them. Sensing that his incognito status might be undermined by a chance encounter with one or more of his cohorts in Montpelier, he suggested a bar in Barre that was usually empty.

Roger was pleasantly surprised to see Mabel getting out of the Buick in the parking lot on the south side of *The Ailing Ale House* shortly after six pm.

Mabel was slow to keep pace while the crew, seemingly oblivious to her presence, darted for the door. Roger locked up his spacious Lincoln Continental and caught up with the horse woman, who was shivering inside her flimsy muumuu.

"Oh hi," she said, her eyes lolling, her smile enamoring, her cork-tipped nipples provoked to perfect points by the chill air. "Imagine seeing you here."

Roger rubbed his hands together briskly, sidling up to her. "I was thinking the same thing. What brings you here?"

"I'm friends with all the guys. On special occasions, they like it if I come with them."

"What makes tonight so special?"

"I guess maybe I don't know. But your being here makes it special, to me."

"It's nice of you to say that. The fact that you're here makes it special for me too." Roger took off of his parka and draped if over Mabel's shoulders. "Do you happen to be going with any of these friends of yours?"

"Thank you," she said. "No. Not actually. I mean, not seriously, if you know what I mean."

Inside the *Ale House*, Mabel handed Roger's coat back to him.

"You look sexy," he said. "Just like I remember from the picnic."

Mabel reached her hand to his face and stroked his elephantine nose. "I was hoping you might bring that up."

Roger gently squeezed the wrist of her stroking hand and spoke discreetly. "If we get the chance, maybe we could enjoy some private time later this evening."

"Oh yes, the special occasion."

"What's that?"

"I mean, that's what would make it a special occasion."

"Great," Roger said, looking up to see the crew motioning for him and the goddess to join them at their tables.

The expanded crew, minus Jericho and Pierre, made their first round of beers a double order. Mabel asked for a black Russian. Remington, meanwhile, grabbed a long phantom level and reenacted the gunslinger's treatment of the general contractor to howls of laughter.

"We should force the Frenchman to be Master of Ceremonies when the owners inspect the job next week," Fritz said. "It's about time he earned his pay."

"He clams up in those situations," Box said.

"I don't mind doing the honors," Walter said.

"We do," Grumpy said. "If everything goes well and we finish the job ahead of schedule, we qualify for a bonus."

"How do you know that?" Walter asked.

"Rudy told Jericho he was looking for a way to recognize our good work. Jericho convinced him to cough up some extra cash. But if you're in charge of the tour, the owners'll think everything else is fucked up too. They'll complain to Rudy and our bonuses will go flying out the window. I say we go with Gulliver again."

"Thanks for the vote of confidence," Walter said.

"Face it," said the Grump, "you get stomach cramps in the middle of your presentation and puke all over them, they're bound to get upset. Besides that, they won't understand a word you're saying."

"But they don't understand a word Gulliver says either."

"Yeah, but they like to think they do. And that makes all the difference. Gulliver plays right to their egos. He's a terrific showboat. Not a half bad flimflam artist, either."

"Rein it in," Fritz said, slapping the table. "I want to hear some music. Loud, so I don't have to listen to any more of this horse shit."

"Nothing but honky-tonk in this joint; that's my bet," Rem said.

"Weepy, go get your guitar and amp out of the trunk," Fritz said. "You can set up here in the corner."

"I've been playing all day. I just want to relax and get drunk, like the rest of you."

After a long day – intrigue looming – the crew was quick to order another round. Grumpy waved off another drink for Mabel, worried that too many black Russians could thwart the game plan.

Loud music suddenly filled the bar. Remington danced his way back to the tables to *Hey, Hey, You, You, Get Offa My Cloud* ... "The juke box is all rock & roll," he shouted. "Who'da figured?"

The usual cantankerous banter abounded while round after round of frothy brew was delivered to the tables. Weepy leaned across one of them to ask Walter a confidential question. Speaking in a tempered voice, "What were you doing alone in the car with Mabel all that time?"

Walter looked violated by the intrusive query. "If you must know, an hour or so after lunch, I was feeling queasy. I had to go up to the car to lie down. I don't want to hear any more about it."

Weepy asked the Grump to trade places with him so he could sit next to the albino. "But I saw you get in the back seat. After we ate, Mabel fell asleep. Grumpy carried her back to the Buick and that's where he laid her."

Walter was flustered. "You did? I did? She did? He did?"

"You can't fool me, you lecherous creamsicle. You woke her up and did the dirty deed with her; come clean."

"Mabel and I ended up having a nice conversation, after which I felt much better and went back to work."

"You were up there for more than an hour. Conversations with Mabel don't last more than a few minutes." Weepy raised his voice. *"I want details, damn it."*

"*Jeepers*, Weepy, it really is none of your business."

"She's one helluva ride, isn't she?"

"As I said, we enjoyed a highly informative and thoroughly satisfying exploration of some rather sensitive areas."

Another round was delivered to the tables.

Weepy was frustrated. "About what, you wishy-washy prick?"

Walter sipped his beer. "It is, of course, a well known fact that, *in her secret heart, every woman wants an albino*. However, the thrust of my tryst with the equine sex goddess was to conduct an interview."

"An interview!"

"Correct. As a budding neophyte in the field of journalism, I must be resourceful, innovative, vigilant, and tenacious; always on the prowl for new material, unique situations, interesting personalities, special insights into the human condition."

"You expect me to believe that cock and bull story?"

"I believe, in fact, that I have in my notebook the makings of an emotionally telling exposé concerning unchecked libidinal development, parental frigidity on the paternal side, and the all-embracing paradoxical desires of promiscuous women."

"Paradoxical?"

"Did you happen to know that Mabel's father was particularly cruel in a nonverbal, nonphysical way?"

"That does seem paradoxical."

"He divorced her mother and moved to Utah when Mabel was thirteen. Up until that time, the man came home from work every day, had dinner with his wife and his daughter, watched television with them, even stayed home on the weekends. And yet, Mabel has no recollection whatsoever that he ever said a word to her."

"Maybe he was mute."

"I asked that question. But no, he spoke to everyone but her. Had conversations on the phone, talked to friends and neighbors, and argued with his wife in customary fashion. But he never spoke to his one and only daughter. He never celebrated her birthday. He never held her in his arms. He never showed any interest in her at all."

"Did she try to talk to him?"

"Yes, except for the last couple of years when she had finally given up."

"That's incredible."

"Can you imagine such detachment, such raw coldness, such brutal nonphysical and nonverbal abuse?"

"I really can't."

"The upshot is that she craves the affection of men, which she believes she gains through sex. But it's not about sex."

"It is when I'm alone with her."

"In that sense, I'm sure your coital conquests are quite curative."

"Thanks. So you figure your interview with Mabel is worthy of a story?"

"Absolutely. I intend to entitle it, *Nymphomania: the Stampeding Need for Compassionate Steeds*."

"Fabulous, Walter. I'm sure we'll see that one on the cover of *Time* in no time."

Fritz slapped the table, causing beer suds to foam up and slosh out of several mugs. "You're too damned quiet over there," he yelled to Roger, who was engrossed in Mabel's curiously elegant profile. "Would you rather be someplace else?"

"Not at the moment," Roger said. "I'm enjoying the company, thank you very much."

Delivering the sixth beer with the fifth round, Mabel's third black Russian included, the waitress asked if anyone wanted to order pizza from the adjacent parlor. "We got an arrangement between us," she said. "There's a new law says we have to provide food to our customers if we want to keep our liquor license. I was surprised to hear we did since the owner is forever telling us he's losing his shirt with this place. Anyway, we complied by putting a swinging door in the wall over there. It goes into a pizza joint. My boss's brother – he's got a shit load of money – owns it."

"Pizza would subvert our drinking," Fritz shouted, pounding the table again. "If we eat now we'll never get drunk. Ask again after another ten or twelve rounds."

The waitress shrugged her shoulders and left.

The black Russians loosened up the equine goddess. With a wink to the Grump, she reached a hand under the table and placed it on Roger's knee. The unsuspecting government sleuth, considerably more relaxed after many beers on an empty stomach, raised an eyebrow, shuffled in his chair, sniffed Mabel's hair, and smiled at his hayfield Aphrodite.

"I'm surprised you're drinking beer," Rem said to the albino. "A nutritious bloody Mary might do you good."

"I'm worried the horseradish would cauterize the lining of my stomach," Walter said.

Box barked across the table. "Hey Roger, you wouldn't happen to be friends with any of those horse barn owners would you?"

"Nope. What makes you ask?"

"They're state officials."

"That's what I hear. Is that supposed to mean something to me?"

Fritz threw a punch into Box's thigh under the table, causing certain damage to his wrist.

"Not necessarily," Box said. "I figured since you're from around here, maybe you'd know one of them."

"Can't say that I do," Roger said, reaching under the table to slide Mabel's hand part way up his leg.

"It might not have hurt our cause if you had," Box Car backtracked, "considering we've got a bonus coming if they're satisfied with our work."

Four more beers and another Black Russian later, Mabel's searching hand reached a solid object.

Roger grinned, his enormous nose twitching with excitement.

Mabel giggled when she closed her hand over the bold protrusion. Her eyes fell back into her head, lazily returning to focus on Roger's massive beak. "Oh my goodness," she said, *"It's true."*

Roger leaned toward her. "What's true?"

"That the nose knows the hose, I suppose."

Roger gave her a queer look, thinking the booze was making her giddy.

Mabel's hand climbed the distended appendage, which was generating extensive heat.

Fritz gave a knowing glance at Rem. "Hey Roger. If you and Mabel feel like going out to your car to cool off, we won't mind."

Mabel leaned her head onto Roger's shoulder and brought her hand out from under the table to touch his nose. She gave it a playful tug. "Please, Roger? I'm burning up inside this muumuu."

Roger whispered into her ear. "I'd be embarrassed to stand up right now. I've got an erection."

Mabel stared at him with pinwheel eyes. Nuzzling his ear, "I should hope so, you big stud. If you don't, I'm in serious trouble."

With that, Roger pulled his parka from the back of his chair and stood with the coat draped in front of him.

Mabel rose slowly from her chair and steadied herself by wrapping an arm around one of Roger's. The preoccupied pair staggered out of the bar.

"How long should we give them?" Gulliver asked.

"She comes on pretty fast," Grumpy said.

"It'll take a while for the car to heat up," Fritz said.

"Mabel knows she's supposed to give us plenty of head way," Weepy said. "The heads up will come when we look at the Lincoln and we can't see their heads."

"Is your camera ready to roll?" Rem asked Gulliver.

"Yes. Yes it is."

"We'll give 'em ten minutes," Fritz said. "Five minutes to warm up the car and five minutes for Mabel to prime the pump. Then it's show time."

"The show'll be over by then!" Walter protested.

Weepy gave the albino an elbow to the ribs. "You lecherous cadaver."

"Get your head out of your ass, Walter," the Marine yelled. "Without penetration, we've got nothing. Furthermore, when Gully takes his shots, we need to be in the pictures too, cramming our faces against the windows, smiling and pointing to the complicit creep. The reality is he can't possibly write an objective report about us if it looks like he owes us for pandering to his prurient predilections."

"Come again?" said the Grump.

"Catching Roger in the act isn't good enough," Fritz said. "We have to be in the act too; partisan participants, collusive consorts, parties to the party. We're all in it together."

"Let's get outside," Rem said. "The timing should be just about right."

There had been four cars in the parking lot; the Buick, the Continental, and presumably those belonging to the bartender and the waitress. No other customers had come into the bar. The crew stood outside the doorway staring at three cars. The Continental was gone.

They were dumbfounded. "What do we do now?" Box asked.

"We blew it," Rem said. "The sonuvabitch must've taken her home with him. We should'a figured. He's too old to be gettin' it on in a fucking car."

The outmaneuvered dog soldiers went back into the bar to order another round, their carefully laid plan foiled by the wily undercover man.

Fresh brews half drank, Weepy noticed that Walter wasn't among them. "Where do you suppose the albino went?" he asked the group.

"Fritz humiliated him to the point where he'd rather sit in the Buick than be with us," Rem suggested.

"Either that or he's sick to his stomach again," Box proffered.

"He can't be in the Buick," said the Grump. "It's locked. And I've got the keys."

Walter came through the swinging door.

"He's been eating pizza," Fritz said, pounding his fist on the table.

"Hey boys," Walter said, approaching the group almost out of breath. "We're in luck. Roger's car is in the parking lot of the pizza parlor. Furthermore, from a distance, it looked like their heads were down."

"Thanks for the heads up," Gulliver said, grabbing his camera and making a dash for the swinging door.

The rest of the crew was hot on his heels, creating a mild panic inside the pizza parlor when they scampered through it, dodging customers like halfbacks avoiding tacklers.

Box Car slowed his pace to savor the aroma of pepperoni and sausage, cheeses and spicy tomato sauce. However, recalling Fritz's sage words, he picked up speed and ran out the door into the parking area.

Unlike the *Ale House*, the pizza joint's parking lot on the north side of the two-tenant building was filled with cars. Nestled among them was a handsome ebony Lincoln Continental. The dog soldiers went into a crouch, approaching the vehicle slowly. Gulliver was the first one there, motioning for the crew to get low, stay quiet, and move to the opposite side of the car.

Gully squatted by the rear left door, then rose slowly to peer into the back seat. Roger and Mabel were nowhere in sight. He squatted again and scuttled to the driver's door. He rose up, his camera at the ready just below his cheekbone. He snapped off three shots of the front seat where, to his bafflement, there were no inhabitants. "What the fuck?"

Fritz slapped the front passenger door in frustration. "Are we sure this is Roger's car? It's just like Walter to lead us down the primrose path to a black hole."

"It's Roger's car all right," Rem said. "I noticed a long time ago that he has vanity license plates. I figured VTSAG13 must be his rank in the Vermont State Attorney General's office. Besides that, his car has modified hubcaps; same as these."

"So where the hell are they?" Fritz asked.

"Let's go back in the bar and strategize," Gulliver suggested.

Rather than be tempted by the smell of pizza, the men took the long way around the building and went inside *The Ailing Ale House* to order another round and discuss how the undercover agent outsmarted them.

Meanwhile, Roger opened the door of the men's room in the pizza parlor and walked out to his car, Mabel staggering along beside him. Inside the car, Roger cranked the engine, pulled out of the parking lot, drove thirty yards down the street, turned into an alley that led to a small parking area behind a drug store, turned up the heater fan now that the engine was warm, and asked Mabel to show him what she was wearing under her muumuu.

"Now where'd that sick little albino go", Fritz asked the group.

"There he is," Weepy said, pointing to Walter entering the bar from the pizza parlor.

"We're in luck," Walter said when he got to the table.

"Again?" Rem asked.

"When you guys took off, I had to pee so bad I went back into the pizza joint. The men's room door was locked. So was the lady's room. Then a lady walked out and I went in there instead of waiting for the men's room. When I came out, I decided to take the same route you took back to the bar – the smell of pizza was making me sick – and that's when I noticed Roger's car leaving the parking lot. He turned left and drove a little ways down the street. I saw him pull in behind a building. Let's go. I know right where he is."

"If that's the case, we've got time to drink another beer," Fritz said. "All this running around is beginning to sober me up. I hate that."

"Fritz is right," Gulliver said. "That big cruiser of his is just now warming up. Maybe he and Mabel decided to get some pizza before going parking. If they were standing in line, we wouldn't have noticed, running through the place like we did."

"Can't be," Box said. "I wanted a pizza so bad I almost got in line myself. But I didn't want to kill my drunk, so I caught up with you guys. I had time to look at the people in line, though. Roger and Mabel weren't in it."

"They were in the men's room," Rem said. "That sly dog knows we're up to something. He's trying to outfox us, pure and simple. As soon as he saw that the coast was clear, he trotted the horse woman out to his car and took off. I say we get our asses over there, pronto."

The waitress brought a tray of frothy mugs to their table.

"I'm having another beer," Fritz said. "We've got plenty of time."

"First you tell me you're not hungry," said the waitress, placing beer mugs around the tables, "next thing I know you're all running into the pizza parlor like you haven't eaten in a week. I'm usually the one who puts in the food order. But since you already did that, I don't mind checking next door in a few minutes to see how your pizzas are coming?"

"We didn't order any pizzas," Fritz said. "We intend to do plenty of drinking in here tonight. But we've gotta take off again, right after we down these babies. We'll be gone about fifteen minutes."

"You didn't order pizzas?"

"No."

"I get it," she said, balancing half a dozen empty mugs on her tray. "You boys like to go out and smoke the wacky weed. That's okay by me. If it happens to be Panama Red, how about slipping me a nickel bag. I'd rather score some pot than get a regular tip."

"We'll take care of you," Weepy said. "Just make sure nobody takes our table while we're gone."

"Yeah," said the waitress, scanning the empty tables. "Like it's standing room only in here."

"How far a walk is it from here?" Rem asked the albino.

"Only a couple of minutes. I went about half way and stood there for a while to make sure he didn't come back out. He's parked behind a drug store."

"We'd better drink these beers up quick," Grumpy warned. "Once Mabel gets after him, he won't last long."

"We've got at least fifteen minutes," Fritz said.

"I'm here to tell you," Grumpy said, "When it comes to Mabel, no man alive can stay in five."

"Is that true?" Weepy asked Walter.

Walter was taken aback. "Why are you asking me? You're the one who splits time with the Grump."

"If Grumpy's right, we need to haul ass now," Rem said.

"I'm right, all right," Grumpy said. "That's why she's a goddess."

"Drink up," Gulliver said. "I don't want to blow it again."

The crew quickly quaffed their brews and clamored to their feet. Moments later they were marching haphazardly down a narrow alley into a dark parking area behind the drug store, which was closed. Handicapped by pitch black conditions and befogged by encroaching inebriation, the men were moving past the Lincoln when Weepy walked into the back bumper in full stride. The entertainer grabbed his right knee and hopped around on one leg trying to stifle a dozen *oooh-ooohs* and half a dozen *Oh Shits*.

The dog soldiers surrounded the vehicle. Gulliver fired off a bevy of flashes, his camera aimed at the back seat, then the front seat, then back to the back.

Fritz's hand came down hard on the hood, a metallic reverberation echoing in the still night air. "Godamnit, they're not in there."

Their eyes more accustomed to the dark, each man pressed his face against a window and peered in to see that Fritz, to their astonishment, was correct.

"What the hell do we do now?" Box asked.

"Obviously they went for a walk," said Rem. "I say we split up. Two men should stay here in case they come back. Four of us will go back out to the street, two going one way, the others the other."

"What about me?" Walter asked.

"How'd you know you're the one I left out of the plan?" Rem asked.

"I had a hunch," Walter said.

"It was a good one. You never stick with the program. You're like some vanishing apparition, always fading away to some other place."

"But twice now my hunches have paid off."

"Not exactly," Gulliver said. "I'm almost out of film because your hunches have led us to an empty car."

"Because of my inquisitive instincts, we're hot on their trail."

"We're going to be gone from the bar longer than we said we would," Rem said. "Why don't you be the first to go back? If the waitress gets uptight you can take her outside and blow a joint with her."

"You got one rolled?" Walter asked Weepy.

While the entertainer rolled a reefer, it was decided that Gulliver would stay at the car with Weepy while Rem and the Box, Fritz and the Grump scoured the road in both directions.

"Let's torch this one," Weepy said to Gully. "I'll roll another for the waitress."

Walter, Gulliver, and Weepy leaned back against the car and smoked the first joint.

"Tell me again how we intended to blackmail Roger with X-rated photographs of him and the goddess," Weepy said. "Were we going to threaten to mail them to his employer or to his wife?"

"He's not married," Walter said.

"I wanted to blow up about a hundred of the best shots in my dark room," Gulliver said. "I don't necessarily agree with Fritz that Roger would be sufficiently threatened if we sent them to his employer. I wanted to threaten him with tacking them up on bulletin boards all over Washington County. I got that idea from one of Walter's civic duty jobs, the one about foreclosure notices."

"The point being that unless he agreed to write up a favorable report about us, the whole world would know his nose is no fluke." Weepy surmised.

"Precisely."

"Maybe he'd like that. All of a sudden he'd be in huge demand. He could quit his job to be one of those guys who gets gagging gigs out in Hollywood."

"Weepy's right," Walter said. "I have a hunch your plan could backfire."

"Have you got a better plan?" Gulliver asked the albino.

"Not really."

"Then I want to suggest you hustle that skinny white ass of yours back to the bar before our waitress starts freaking out about us being gone so long."

"Gulliver's right," said Weepy. "We've had it with all your damn hunches."

"I was just following up on *your* hunch," Walter said.

"Get out of here," both men shouted.

When Walter walked into the bar, he couldn't believe his bloodshot pink eyes. There, at one of their tables, sat Roger and Mabel.

Walter ordered a beer from the bartender and chitchatted with the waitress. He had no idea what he'd say to the necking couple without tipping his hand. One thing was certain; the pictorial opportunity, for whatever it might have been worth, was shot.

Gulliver and Weepy walked through the swinging doors. Seconds later, Rem and Box Car, Fritz and Grumpy came through the front door. The dog soldiers froze in their tracks, mystified to see their prey huddled together and giggling about something spread out on the table.

Walter reached the table ahead of the others, in time to see Roger scoop up what looked to be playing cards and stuff them into his shirt pocket.

"Where the hell have you been?" Remington asked. "After a while, we got worried and went looking all over the place for you."

Mabel smoothed down her muumuu and blushed.

Roger smiled at the men and explained. "We went out to my car, then decided to take a short drive. When we were driving away, we decided to stop in next door for a slice or two of pizza. But it was too crowded. After using the restroom, we took off again. We were only going a short distance and we could have walked, but Mabel was cold in this skimpy dress she's wearing, so we decided to get back in the car. My bother owns a drug store down the street. He got robbed a few months ago and gave me a key to the place to check on it after hours. We parked the car out back and went inside. In less than five minutes it went from warm to incredibly hot in there. We decided a nice walk back to the bar would cool us off."

The men guffawed.

"Did you have a good time?" Weepy asked.

"Fabulous," Roger said. "Mabel and I have decided to date."

"That's wonderful," Rem said.

"I want details," Fritz said, pounding the table.

"Details?" Roger asked.

"Fritz is surprised," said Remington, "that the two of you got so close this quickly. You hardly know each other."

"Show them how close," Mabel said to Roger. "I'm not bashful."

"What's she talking about?" Grumpy asked.

"These photographs," Roger said, tapping his shirt pocket with the back of his hand. "Just for kicks, I keep a Polaroid in my glove compartment. Mabel wanted me to capture a special feat that obviously gives her a deep sense of gratification." The undercover agent chuckled. "Before you know it, we were passing the camera back and forth blowing the whole roll."

"We want to see them!" Fritz shouted.

"Tut-tut," Roger said, flipping his hand over and pressing it tight against his shirt pocket. "Don't be so darned nosy."

Twenty-Eight

"Did you have to embarrass me like that?"

"I didn't intend to."

"What were the men supposed to think? You derided me. You chastised me. You took my expertise for granted and flaunted my leadership. You showed me up, goddamnit, and I'm calling to find out why. What in holy hell ever came over you, Rudy, to even think of doing such a thing?"

"A general contractor has a right to check the level of the structure he's building."

"We're the ones doing the damn building. We haven't seen hide or hair of you since before we sawed the first board or drove the first nail."

"That may be, but it's my project."

"But I made it clear right from the get-go that me and the dog soldiers would build this horse barn righteous, that we'd build it on time, and that we'd come in under budget. Did I not? *Well didn't I?* Or weren't you listening?"

"Lighten up, Jericho, for God's sake. I never thought the day would come that I'd be saying this, but your boys have done one helluva job. I'm happy, okay? *There.* Isn't that what you wanted to hear?"

"Yes. Yes it is. But I also want to hear an apology from you for showing up this morning acting like King Tut."

"I did not go there to embarrass you."

"But the fact is you did. Say you're sorry."

"For what?"

"For embarrassing me, goddamnit. I called you for an apology."

"Fine. *I'm sorry*, if that makes you feel any better."

"It does. Thank you. That's the last you'll hear of it."

"What else?"

"Nothing."

"I've got something."

"All right, but make it quick; I got shit to do."

"At ten o'clock at night?"

"That's right. What's on your mind?"

"Welter knows about the Attorney General's investigation."

"You don't say?"

"I never brought it up. He did."

"And you told him you already knew about it?"

"No. I played dumb. I wanted to find out how much he knows."

"How much *he* knows?"

"Right."

"You dumb shit, Rudy; the reason Welter knows about the investigation is because he's the one who called for it."

Dead air.

"Did you hear what I just said?"

"Forgive me," Rudy said with pinched vocal chords. "You hit me right between the eyes with that one. You're saying the A.G.'s office is conducting an investigation into the behavior of the horse barn crew because my own superintendent requested it?"

"That's not only what I'm saying; it's what I said. Past tense. Present tense. Present progressive. Your man created a very tense situation for me and the crew no matter how you say it."

"But he had to know the negative impact it would have on me. I'm the owner of the company. My reputation is at stake. It's not just your so-called dog soldiers who are under scrutiny here, Jericho; it's the man they're working for."

"Of course he knew. You think he gives a flying fuck about your reputation?"

"Welter's my right-hand man. I've always trusted him. I think the world of him."

"Yeah? Well guess what? He doesn't think shit about you. In fact, if you go down, it's no longer about him being your right-hand man; he becomes *the only man*."

Silence.

"Did you hear what I just told you?"

"Yes. I see. And you're sure about all this?"

"Sure as the nose on Hamminframe's face."

"I'll have to do something about it."

"Do whatever your heart desires. We got our own plans for *Wicked Dick*."

"Would you mind letting me in on them?"

"Yes I would. Let's just say ol' B.F. Beauchamp Frontenac did us a favor leaving his crane at the site a little longer than he may have planned."

"I don't think I'll be able to sleep tonight. This is a real shocker. You think you know a man …"

"It's nothing to lose sleep over, Rudy. Be happy you've got loyal crew members who were observant enough to pick out the punky wood in the wood pile."

"Thanks for putting it that way. As you know, I'm sensitive about those kinds of things."

"Seems like there's no end to the things I do for you."

"And I appreciate it, Jericho. I really do."

"Good. Get some sleep."

"I'll try. *Oh wait.*"

"For what?"

"There's something else."

"Looks like I won't get anything done tonight. What else do you want to talk about?"

"When I was leaving the horse barn I saw a woman stretched out on the back seat of that blue Buick, possibly sleeping. She wasn't wearing much, from what I could see."

"That was Mabel. She keeps the dog soldiers in line, you might say."

"What was she doing at the horse barn?"

"She's a horse woman."

"What the hell does that mean?"

"Voluptuous female centaur. She's mythological. Brings luck, in the sense that some of us get lucky. Weepy wrote a song about her; *The Fabulous Fable of the Horse Barn Fortuna*. It's all about how good luck is coming with a goddess. I love the chorus, Rudy: *Hi-dee, hi-dee, hi-dee ho ... Hi-dee, hi-dee, hi-dee hay. In the saddle here we go ... Giddy up and ride away.* Sing it with me, Rudy.

"Good night, Jericho."

"Hi-dee, hi-dee, hi-dee, ho ... Hi-dee, hi-dee ..."

Click.

The men tried everything they could think of to convince Roger to show them the scintillating pictures of his titillating minutes with the golden haired bangtail, but to no avail.

Fritz's wit was frazzled and frayed at the end. He banged his fist on the table and called upon the tormented dog soldiers to end their relentless, humiliating, and futile pursuit. The crew stood as one and said their goodbyes to the wily sleuth, paid the tab, slipped a nickel to the waitress as an extra tip, coaxed the good goddess out to the Buick, and headed for *The Man's Bar*.

Walter moaned during the entire drive, begging Grumpy to let him off at his apartment because he was out of pills and elixirs.

"Nope. This is your punishment for leading us on a wild goose chase. You're going to *The Man's Bar* and you're going to get drunk, just like the rest of us."

"But my stomach is cramping up like there's no tomorrow. I'm not used to drinking this much beer."

"We don't care!" Fritz shouted at the man bent over next to him clutching his guts and groaning louder than Mabel, who was sitting high on Weepy's lap, snoring.

When the men piled out of the car in Essex, Remington went over to Weepy's window and tapped on it. The entertainer peeked around a ponderous breast. "What do you want?"

"You coming in?"

"No."

"Why not?"

"Because I'm not coming out."

Rem noticed that the bottom half of Mabel's muumuu was rolled up rather neatly, resting high on the curve of her pelvis. "What're you up to, Weepy?"

"Don't talk so loud; you'll wake her up."

The Man's Bar, on this night, was no fun. Grumpy was faced with having to defend the size of his nose against Gulliver's pejorative evaluation. Box Car got into a heated argument with Fritz about the nutritional value of *Slim Jims.* Walter sat at the bar sipping a banana liqueur, moaning in agony. And Remington, at a pinball machine, recognized the arms that wrapped around his waist from behind.

"I've decided I want to be friends," Wynona said, Rem firing a ball into play.

"I was afraid of that," he said, agitated.

"*Oh c'mon.* You're treated to the best rim job on the planet and you've got the gall to complain about it?"

"You seduced me and you know it," Rem said.

Wynona took her arms from around his waist. "I haven't seduced you, Remington Swilling … *not yet*."

Moments later, the bartender yelled to Box. "Hey man, get this guy out of here; he's puking all over the bar."

Remington let his pinball bounce off a lower bumper and fall between two idle flippers. Walter was slouched over the bar, retching. Rem and the Box got to the albino at the same time, stared at the Indian red muck pooling on the counter, then stared at each other with painful analytic expressions.

"Looks like fried pig's blood to me," Rem said.

"He had at least one dark beer back in Barre," Box said. "You sure that's not it?"

"This steamy puke isn't just dark; it's dark maroon, with a dissipating sheen."

The bartender wiped up some of the fuliginous sludge with a towel. It was redder on the towel that it looked on the bar.

"You're right," Box said. "Walter's puking blood."

"Hey Grumpy," Rem shouted to a nearby table. "We gotta get Walter to a hospital. He's upchucking globs of blood that're either black or red, we can't decide."

Box slapped Walter on the back to help him with one last heave. He collected the spaghetti-boned albino in his massive arms, slung the kecking creature over a shoulder, and lugged him out to the Buick.

Weepy and Mabel were fast asleep in the back seat. Grumpy jumped into the driver's seat, flung the crumpled muumuu toward the back, started the car, waited impatiently until everyone else was inside, and laid rubber for an eighth of a mile heading for Pearl Street.

"Should we stop at Fanny Allen or try to make it all the way to Mary Fletcher?" Grumpy asked no one in particular.

"Mary Fletcher," Rem said. "If we go to Fanny Allen, Mabel's liable to wake up, think she's supposed to be going to work, and walk inside stark naked. We don't want to cause any problems for her."

Fritz was remarkably silent, seething to see his dire predictions being manifested in Walter's desperate condition; too distressed, even, to gloat. Every couple of miles, he punched the back of the front seat. Though mute and somewhat contained, the fire in his mind raged as hot as Walter's incendiary belly.

An emergency room intern came out from behind a curtained bed where two nurses took off the albino's clothes and replaced them with a johnny, snaked a long plastic tube down his throat, and administered an IV. They dabbed his forehead with a wet cloth, checked his pulse, shined a tiny flashlight into his wane unwilling eyes, and peppered him with questions.

"He's going to be here at least overnight, fellas," said the intern. "It's my advice that you go home and get some sleep. Visiting hours start at noon tomorrow."

"Can you tell us anything about what's happening to him?" Rem asked.

"I can tell you his stomach's bleeding. At this time, we don't know why. It could be an ulcer, but we can't be certain at this stage. We'll run some tests tonight. You did the right thing bringing him here. We don't know how much blood he's lost but he certainly looks anemic."

"He's an albino," Remington said. "He always looks that way."

"I see. Well, we'll know more tomorrow. We sedated him right after we inserted a tube into his stomach. I must say he has a perfectly functional gag reflex. In any event, he won't be able to talk with you tonight."

The men peeked behind the curtain at the thin transclucent hose running out of their friend's mouth, tiny strings of clotted blood inching their way through the tubing. Walter breathed with choked gasps. His face was even whiter than usual. His pink eyes peeked from under their lids, lost in a blue million miles.

The crew staggered out of the ER and piled into the Buick.

Grumpy dropped each man off and continued on to Underhill, the naked goddess sprawled languorously on the back seat; her snores, to him, the spirited snorts of a ruttish mare.

The only time during the past month that it was okay for Remington to sleep in his own bed was when Sibyl and Beatrice went to church on Sunday mornings.

Bea always made a lot of noise scampering back and forth more than a dozen times between her room and the bathroom getting ready, hoping she might accidentally wake up her dad so she wouldn't have to wake him up for real. Since that never worked, she had no choice but to shake his shoulder until he did wake up to see how nice she looked in her Sunday outfit, even though she didn't like the silly bonnet. He always told her she would be the most beautiful young lady in church; and if she thought of it, could she please say a prayer for her old dad. She always promised she would, even though she didn't know any prayers and her dad wasn't really old.

As soon as Rem heard the car pull out of the driveway, he got up and staggered into the bathroom to take a whiz. He shed his shorts and tossed them on the hamper, staggered down the hall, and climbed into the freshly made bed where he used to sleep with his wife.

He was dead to the world once again when the back door – left unlocked when mother and daughter went to church – opened at about the same time Sibyl and Bea were looking for space in a pew.

The intruder went into the kitchen and poured the last cup of coffee from the percolator, then paced the living room sipping and listening for any noise from upstairs.

Brazenly, when the coffee was finished and the cup rinsed, wiped, and put back into the cupboard, the clandestine day-prowler walked upstairs, went into the bathroom, and could be heard – had Remington been able to hear – running water in the sink for nearly ten minutes.

The door to Sibyl's bedroom was ajar, there being no need to turn the handle to enter. Rem was on the far side of the bed facing the wall. On Sibyl's side, the sheet was tucked neatly under the mattress. Stifling a titter, careful to pull down the blanket and sheet with as little disturbance as possible, Wynona – frisky but coy in a skimpy negligee – slipped under the covers, slid with lithesome prowess across the bed, and spooned Rem's moon into the soft hollow of her body.

She held to this position for several minutes, her eyes closed, her imagination swimming in a wishing well, her skin warming, her breath quickening, her heart galloping, her fluids secreting, her desire burning.

Remington's dreams, typically, were nightmares: somersaulting car accidents, deadly bar fights, hunting trips where he was the prey, going to prison for one heinous crime or another, being sober long enough to get trapped in a perpetual hangover; all sorts of delusional calamities. On this quiet Sunday morning, however, sleeping peacefully in his own bed, he lapsed into an engaging dream of lurid sensuality, of delightfully sinful scenarios, of salacious trysts with salty sylphs, of arching cravings for the tingling clutches of an inflamed woman's raw rakish lust.

Wynona breathed hotly into Rem's ear, pressing tighter against his buttocks and stroking his torso. "Take me," she whispered. *"Take me now."*

Blood rushed out of Remington's addlepated brain to prime his primordial pump. Groggy, inhaling deeply, he turned onto his back.

Wynona deftly maneuvered to the side, glancing at the peaking sheet, then peeking underneath for confirmation.

An orgy of pulsating shapes filled Rem's dreamy state. A gentle grasp guided him into the wet heat of an erotic passageway. Safe inside, his hands were drawn to malleable mounds of tender flesh.

In the dizzying distance, colors and shapes collided. Heavy breathing coincided with a lubricous rhythm. His eyelids flickered, the movement of his eyes rapid underneath. Then, in a wild impossible moment, they flew open. There, clear in his startled vision, a woman's head was tossed back, wavy hair dancing behind her. Her slender neck glistened with sweat. Her hands held his, by the wrists, to her breasts. Her hips moved against him. Sensing yet another presence, he turned his head. Sibyl stood in the doorway, her face emblazoned with horror.

The plan was to drink heavy while watching Sunday football in Walter's room at the Mary Fletcher. Grumpy would pick up his brother first, then Gulliver, then Fritz, and finally Weepy. Mabel wanted to be dropped off at her place for a change of clothes, though she admitted to having special feelings for her pasty pal and might catch a cab to the hospital later in the afternoon. Remington, his truck at Box's, would take Sibyl's car after church and drive over from his place on the north end.

The one hitch in the plan was exposed when the troupe's clumsy attempt to sneak past the security guard with paper bags containing eight six-packs of beer was foiled by the jostling of bottles and the clanging of cans.

Walter shared a room on Patrick 3 with Bernard Gerard, a farmer from the Fairfax area who had fallen into one of his silos three days earlier and nearly died from methane gas poisoning.

The farmer, almost fully recovered, was sitting up alert and in good humor visiting with family members gathered around his bed, most of whom were fixated on a religious show playing on the only television in the tiny room.

Walter, an IV in each arm, floated on the edge of consciousness, a tube still piped down his throat. His hair and complexion were indistinguishable from his pillow and the bed sheets. He didn't notice the dog soldiers marching in.

A teary-eyed Weepy, with Gulliver, Box Car, and the Grump, hovered over their stricken friend. They let him know they were there by whispering various greetings. Fritz stood at the foot of the albino's bed and addressed Bernard's visitors. "It's twelve-fifty," he told them.

"We know what time it is," said one.

"Then I'm sure you're aware that the game starts in ten minutes."

"Football?" asked another.

"Giants versus Minnesota. This one's got playoff implications written all over it."

"We always watch Billy Graham on Sundays," said a third. "Today's sermon is all about how the Prince of Peace taught his followers to turn the other cheek when oppressed in any way."

The short-tempered Vietnam veteran understood guerilla tactics, the object of which was to strike the enemy in unexpected ways; the element of surprise combining with daring creativity to preempt an effective counter. Fritz walked over to the small table between the beds and snatched the TV remote. "That's all well and good," he said. "But the Prince of Violence is about to turn the channel and watch the Vikings oppress the hell out of New York."

"But we want to witness the miracle of the Lord."

Fritz waved the remote above his head in mock defiance. "Okay then, watch the game. It'll be a miracle if the Giants win."

With that, the blasphemous apostate aimed the remote and switched to Channel 3 just as the Vikings were lining up to kick off to the home team. The men turned as one to face the set, the room immediately filling with jarring cheers and the jarhead's jeers; a form of jocular contentiousness reserved for sports enthusiasts.

"Should one of us get the head nurse?" Bernard's wife asked him.

"Sure, go talk to her, but only to find out what's holding up the paperwork. I'm supposed to be discharged any time now. Ain't no sense gettin' into it with these rapscallions. Go ahead on to the cafeteria. It's on the same floor. I'll have them wheel me over there on the way out."

When the farmer's family had traipsed out of the room, Bernard breathed a sigh of relief. "Hey boys, can you turn that thing up a little? My hearing ain't so good."

"You like football?" Weepy asked.

"Not too much. But I get tired of listening to preaching all day every Sunday. As soon as we get back from church, as if we ain't heard enough of it, the TV comes on and we get more damn preaching. Watching some honest violence is kind of nice for a change."

If Walter knew his friends were by his bed, he gave no indication. Two thin rows of white lashes were draped over his pink eyes. His breathing was labored. His body never moved, other than the twitch of a hand or a slight turning of his head.

At halftime, the scored knotted at fourteen, Grumpy slid off the stripped bed – Bernard having been wheeled out toward the end of the first quarter – and reached up to turn down the volume when a doctor walked into the room.

"You here to check on Walter?" he inquired.

The doctor glanced down at his clip board. "Mr. Birdsong. Yes. A curious case."

"Was it a stomach ulcer causing the problem?" asked the Grump.

"Not just one," said the doctor. "His stomach is riddled with them. He's also got diverticulosis, renal deficiency, an overtaxed pancreas, and we're more than a little concerned that we may discover other sources of internal bleeding. Further tests are necessary."

With a gentle prodding of his thumb and forefinger, the doctor pushed back Walter's eyelids and beamed a light at the bloodshot orbs, crimson irises rolling back into his head. The physician carefully placed the plastic tube to one side of Walter's mouth and shined the light inside. He checked his ears, peeked beneath the sheet to inspect the urinary catheter, placed his stethoscope on several spots under the johnny, and tenderly squeezed the albino's ankles.

"What's so curious about Walter's case," Weepy asked, "besides all those life threatening conditions you mentioned?"

"Actually, there are a number of curiosities. This man's been bleeding inside for a long time. It didn't start the night he presented. The pain must have been extremely difficult to endure. If he'd had any sense, he would have seen a doctor a lot sooner. His blood profile shows a dangerously low red blood cell count. He'll need plenty of cobalamin injections; that is, vitamin B12. You see, albinism easily masks anemia. Before we settled on an assortment of prescriptive medicines administered intravenously, your friend here had a remarkably lucid period of about twenty minutes early this morning. Baffling, to say the least. It seems he believes quite firmly that his diet is healthy."

"He does eat a lot of pork rinds," Weepy said.

The doctor jotted something down on his clip board before continuing. "Yes, well, Mr. Birdsong's biological system radically defies homeostasis. I would say, in fact, that his is the most acidic I've every encountered. I did not interview him personally, but the attending physician before I came on was able to list the most prevalent items in the patient's so-called diet. Most of them, I'm afraid, are terribly acidic. He drinks an enormous amount of coffee, much of it on an empty stomach. Tomatoes, which can be quite acidic depending on whether they're raw or cooked, juiced or stewed, etcetera – and which, by the way, he is probably allergic to – seem to make up the foundation of his food intake. He drinks copious amounts of orange juice and grapefruit juice which, in their commercial forms as opposed to whole fruit, can also be disruptive to the body's acid-alkaline balance. If that weren't trouble enough, he drinks lots of tea in the evenings, squirting liberal amounts of bottled lime juice into each cup. According to these notes, he's partial to raw meat, *Zero* bars, and anchovies. And when he finishes a jar of green olives he drinks the juice, which is mostly salt and vinegar. I could go on but I'm sure you get the picture. It isn't pretty."

"Nothing about Walter is pretty," Box said. "Will it take a long time for him to recover?"

"I would say so. Our immediate task was to control the bleeding. And we do believe we've done that, for the most part. When he comes off the IV in a day or two he'll be on a strict bland diet while he's an inpatient, which may be an entire week. It'll be up to him after that. Above all, he needs to stay away from tomatoes."

"Excuse me." Fritz had something to say to the doctor.

The doctor looked at the Marine's furrowed brow. "Yes."

"I'm going to have to ask you to leave now. The second half is starting."

On the way down the elevator to the main lobby, parched from having gone the entire game – a miraculous victory for the Giants – without a beer, Box had a question that must have been on everyone's mind. "How come Rem never showed up?"

The question was answered when the men walked out the front door. Remington, cradling a two-thirds empty bottle of Jack Daniels in his left arm, was about to go inside.

"You missed it," Gulliver said. "Giants pulled it out in the final seconds with a long bomb. Great game. Great game."

“The game sucked,” Fritz said.

Remington was drunk. Taking a moment to bring the men into focus, “What’s the deal with Walter?”

“Walter’s half dead,” Grumpy said.

“Still?”

“The doctor was very encouraging,” Weepy said, wiping a tear from his cheek.

“Walter’s been committing suicide,” Fritz said in a voice that was one part concern, one part anger, and one part didactic.

When they got to the parking lot, Rem reeling as he leaned against Sybil’s car to take a swig of Jack Black, Box Car snatched the keys the moment Rem took them from his pocket. “You’re too drunk to drive,” Box said. “Grumpy, follow me over to Rem’s.”

“Hold on. Hold on,” Rem said. “I can’t go home.”

“Why not?” Box asked. “Sibyl’s seen you like this plenty of times. Shit, she’s not above a good bender herself.”

“Sibyl yanked the house key off my chain and locked me out; said she’ll never let me back in. I want to see Walter.”

“Visiting hours are over.”

“Walter’ll let me stay at his place. I need his keys.”

Gulliver went back into the hospital to fetch the key to Walter’s apartment while the men plugged Remington about the circumstances surrounding Sibyl’s actions.

The albino’s personal belongings were in a plastic bag at the nurse’s station. Gulliver convinced a nurse that Walter had almost finished reading a very funny book when he took sick; retrieving it would do wonders to cheer him up.

Rem’s story seemed incredulous to Grumpy. “You mean to tell us you had no idea Wynona was even in the room?”

“All I know is, as soon as I found out my dream was real, it was a nightmare. My family life is over because of that wench.”

“Wynona or Sibyl?” Weepy asked.

“*Both of ‘em.* I need to get drunk. Take me to Walter’s.”

“Rem’s right,” Fritz said. “The best thing for him right now is to get dead drunk, preferably alone.”

Twenty-Nine

Jericho might have expected the dog soldiers to be licking their chops with satisfaction Monday morning. The last few stalls were almost completed. Pierre was up on the roof working on the cupola. The general contractor had been run off. The crew probably had the goods on Roger by now. The plan to expose Welter was finalized. There was no reason to expect any snafus during the owner's final inspection, thereby assuring their bonuses. Furthermore, the construction deadline of Friday would be eclipsed by two days, allowing the men some free time before the big celebration at his place Friday evening.

But the men were morose while giving the gunslinger the lowdown on the weekend's cataclysmic events with Roger, Walter, and Remington.

"Let me give you something else to chew on," Jericho said. "The Frenchman just told me Roger quit."

"With only a few days to go?" Grumpy asked.

"It's not what you're thinking. He quit his *state* job. Rudy called Pierre about it first thing this morning. Pierre was so stunned to find out Roger was sawing the board at both ends he could hardly make it up the ladder. I'm getting the story second hand, but according to the Frenchman, Roger told Rudy he'd rather work for him than the Attorney General; claims he's never had so much fun."

"Where's Roger now?" Gulliver asked.

"From the sound of it, he's probably handing in his resignation at this very moment. And here's something else. Rudy knows all about *Wicked Dick*; plans to give him the heave-ho at the end of the day."

"What about Roger's investigation?" Box asked. "These developments don't guarantee we're out of the woods."

"Can't say. But when he gets here, we'll get the story straight from the horse's mouth."

The morning came and went with no Roger. Despite Jericho's good news on two strategic fronts, Walter's absence was palpable, Weepy being the first to notice there were no foul smells during lunch.

The mood remained somber. Rem slurped spirits straight from the bottle while Grumpy, Box, and Gulliver debated the idea of stealing the weathervane. Gulliver wanted it as an artifact of his great adventure. Box wanted to present it to Pierre at Jericho's party. And Grumpy thought it might look good as a hood ornament.

Fritz, meanwhile, labored under the burden of what he knew until the accumulation of angst bubbled to the surface and he cranked his window down, yelling to the Frenchman.

Pierre rolled down his window with an obligatory smile. "Yes, I have no bananas."

"I don't give a shit about that," Fritz said. "I want you to get your superintendent over here."

"Welter?"

"Rem's our super, but you report to *Wicked Dick*."

"He's on another job."

"Go get him."

"Right now?"

"*Without further adieux*, goddamnit."

"What if he smells something and won't come."

"You're a persuasive man. Convince him."

"I'll try," Pierre said, starting up the VW and driving away.

"Grumpy," Fritz continued, "get up on that big-ass crane and drive it down to the barn."

Jericho overheard the command. *"Oh, be big for me,"* he bellowed.

Handing in his resignation turned out to be an affair that lasted most of the morning. Roger's cohorts had prepared what they believed to be an iron-clad criminal case and expected nothing less than a thoroughly incriminating report from the undercover agent. Sitting smugly around the conference room table, Roger's gray-suited associates were mystified reading his exculpatory findings.

The horse barn crew, the dossier stated, was incorrigible, monstrously disrespectful, incomparably critical in the most degrading and dehumanizing manner – though equally of themselves as of others – socially estranged and happily so, combative even in the absence of provocation, uncouth, vulgar, boisterous, truculent, as distempered as a pack of rabid dogs, sexually depraved if decidedly not deprived, inspirationally irreligious, vehemently anti-establishment, declaratively opposed to every cherished institution, despotically inclined, unruly and irreverent; but, nevertheless, not in any way criminal.

Paying court to the positives, the report went so far as to suggest that the average IQ of the crew was probably markedly higher than his own and unquestionably a damn sight higher than any of the individuals he had worked with during his tenured service in state government.

The agents were less than pleased with Roger's report; baffled the more to learn that he enjoyed carpentry and was, at that moment, changing careers in favor of the building trade.

During the initial stage of a ruthless interrogation, Roger explained that working on the A.G.'s staff had never been much fun, whereas every single day of work at the horse barn was entertaining beyond belief. Furthermore, he said, his experience was almost euphorically epiphanic, having taken him to a higher level of self-awareness, having given him an appreciation of amusement purely for amusement's sake, and having instilled in him an abiding respect for shock-value humor. All of this, he said, had culminated in a dramatic, astonishing, revelatory rise in self-esteem.

"Sounds like you got laid," one of the agents surmised.

Another agent, the chief investigator universally loathed for his fastidious elocution, shoved his chair back, stood up, and puffed his chest with the air of a prosecutor who believes his case is air tight. All eyes were on him while he paced in arrogant cogitation three times around the room. With theatrical timing, he paused across the table from the beleaguered turncoat, reached deep into a pocket inside his coat, and extracted a small stack of Polaroid pictures.

Roger's nose flushed and flared. "What'cha got there?" he asked, suddenly realizing the carelessness with which he had tossed his prized photos into the glove compartment of his Lincoln – an obvious repository for a curious operative to glom.

"We must confess," said the agent, "that we became suspicious of your work, Roger, when your interim reports began to turn positive, even as the behavior of the horse barn crew devolved into ever more deplorable acts of depravity. Indeed, when you were describing to us the undeniably grotesque hunching of the crane operator by the creature described as the *Missing Link*, we were struck by your apparent amusement of such offensive sexual aggression. Further, your emphasis was not attuned to the humiliation of the oblivious subcontractor; to the contrary, you seemed rather pleased that the hairy beast dogging the crane man was getting away with his despicably demeaning display of demented dogma."

"Those look like photographs."

The agent took his seat across the table, shuffled the pictures like a deck of cards, then flipped them one at a time to the other agents, excluding Roger. Throats cleared with crusty harrumphs, the agents inspecting the photos with the scrutiny of quality assurance experts.

"And what are we to make of these?" asked the chief. "Is this not the woman casually mentioned in one of your reports as the real work horse on this job, what with the lewd stories bandied about by the self-described dog soldiers? My goodness, Roger, we might have expected you to have considered this voracious tart to be every bit as crackbrained as her stable of odious studs. We certainly never anticipated that you would become one among them."

"I'm not one among them; I've replaced them."

The studious agents, their heads combining to analyze an especially vivid photo, were visibly intrigued by Mabel's assiduous tour de force.

"But you see, Roger, these rather sensational photographs expose multiple duplicity; a double agent double-timing while doing double duty. There can be little doubt that your work was compromised by unwitting entrapment. We can only conclude by this graphic revelation that you became favorably disposed to exonerate the horse barn crew. For that, I'm afraid it won't be possible to accept your resignation until after you've been cited for misconduct."

"You can't do it that way."

"Of course we can. The procedural step that will follow is the presentation of evidence directly to the Attorney General himself."

"But you're too late."

"What's that? Has he already left the office for one of his notorious six martini lunches?"

"I don't know if he has or not," said Roger. "What I'm trying to tell you is that I went into his office an hour before our scheduled meeting. I handed in my resignation and he accepted it. I even had him sign a statement to that effect, having given consideration to the possibility that this group might find fault with my findings and frame the facts in a farcical fabrication."

"Phooey," said the chief, rising abruptly to pace around the conference table.

Roger scooped up his photos, dropped them into a folder in his briefcase, snapped the attaché, shook hands with his former associates, and strode out of the room, his dignity restored.

As per prior arrangement, Roger would attend a brief meeting in Rudy's office, then drive to South Burlington to enjoy the rest of the day with his goddess.

The crew was working on the stalls when Pierre pulled up to the bluff at two o'clock. Welter parked his truck beside the bug.

The men dropped their tools and walked outside, the crane off to one side.

"Pierre says you want me to take one last look before the inspection tomorrow," Welter said to the group.

"Just in case there's any last minute problem," Gulliver said.

Welter studied the men. If he was surprised by their confidence in him, he didn't let on.

"Before I take a walk around I want to have another look at the blueprints," Welter said to Pierre. "You still have them?"

"Sure thing," Pierre said, walking into the barn.

A moment later the Frenchman handed the prints to his lame-duck boss.

Welter fished the hammer from Pierre's belt, reached into Gulliver's nail bag, then tacked the blueprints to the barn door.

Grumpy, meanwhile, climbed into the crane. When he started it, Welter turned around with a wary glance.

"Don't mind him," Fritz said. "They're coming to get this rig any time now. Grumpy's just driving it up the hill for the flatbed."

Welter turned back to the plans with the Frenchman peering over his shoulder. Fritz nodded for Grumpy to run the winch. At the most propitious moment, Gulliver and Box grabbed Welter's arms. Fritz slipped the hook through the back of the superintendent's belt. Stunned by the ambush, his belt suddenly a tourniquet around his midsection, Welter's head plunged forward, his legs swung up from behind, and the cranes' cable carried him aloft. Legs kicking, arms flailing, he rose into the chill air. Welter twisted and wrangled, yelling with wretched alarm, "Pierre! Pierre! Make them put me down. What the hell's going on here?"

"You're being hung in real-life effigy," Fritz shouted up to him.

Welter's protests came in clipped wheezes. Twenty feet in the air, he yelled down to the crew with choked gasps. *"You can't ... do this ... to me, you ... bastards. Wait till ... Rudy ... finds out ..."*

"Rudy knows all about your hanky-panky," Jericho shouted to him. "The ol' whore dogs smelled a rat, Welter. It was only a matter time before we'd grab it by the tail. We plan to stand here and watch you swing till you either freeze to death or die of starvation, whichever comes first."

Grumpy shut off the rig, climbed down, and stepped back for a more satisfying look at *Wicked Dick* oscillating in half-circles high above. "I think I'd like it better if he figures out a way to unhook his belt."

With that, the men went back to work.

"How long do you intend to leave him up there?" Pierre asked.

"Overnight, at least," Fritz said, an amalgamation of contempt and oppugnancy, resolution and contentment welded to his smirk.

Every half hour or so throughout the afternoon, one or more of the men came out of the barn to check on Welter. Red-faced from a combination of breathlessness, blood rushing to his dangling head, and a whipping wind, *Wicked Dick* seldom made another peep.

When the crew piled into the Buick and drove away at five o'clock, only a pinch of pink left in the purple sky, Gulliver asked the Grump if he thought Pierre would be able to start the crane and lower Welter to the ground.

"I don't know if he can run that rig or not, but unless he knows how to hot wire it like I did to drive it down to the barn, that back-stabbing super had his last supper last night."

"Could he die before we get back in the morning?" Weepy wanted to know.

"I heard the weather forecast on the radio after lunch," Grumpy said. "I might have suggested winching him down if it wasn't for the warm front moving through. It could go up to fifty degrees overnight. The dirty dog won't die, but he'll learn one helluva lesson."

When the Buick was out of sight, Pierre climbed into the cab of the crane. He soon discovered there was no key to start it and climbed back down. "I'll go for help," he shouted up to the limp body swinging from the hook.

"I can't wait for that," Welter said, his voice betraying early-stage asphyxia.

"I've got an idea," said the Frenchman. He walked up the hill, drove his car down to the site, and emerged with a length of rope.

With extraordinary daring, Pierre climbed onto the top of the crane, threw his legs over the long metal arm pointing horizontally into the darkness, and shimmied along on his butt until he reached the end. He tied the rope off there and dropped the other end to the ex-super. Weak from his ordeal but encouraged by the Frenchman's bravado, Welter jerked his torso to swing toward the rope. A minute later he was able to reach out and snare it. He lashed the end around his feet, grabbed the rope with both hands to pull himself upright, then climbed, inches at a time, the short distance to the end of the crane's projection arm. Pierre shimmied backwards to give the man enough room to throw a leg up and over the arm. With the modicum of strength remaining in his wracked body, Welter heaved himself onto the arm and hugged it tight.

Pierre shimmied forward, reached out to find Welter's legs, then his buttocks, then his belt. He turned the hook sideways, pushed it free of the belt, and let it fall with the cable. "Be real careful, Richard. It's a long drop from up here."

Both men shimmied backwards, precariously gripping the cold metal of the crane's boom with their thighs and their hands.

When one of Pierre's feet finally touched the body of the crane he dropped down. "We're there, Richard. You've only got a few feet to go. Get a good hold and let your legs swing down. Your feet will feel the track. If you want to relax a minute, I can get the flash light out of my car so you can see where you're landing."

"Don't bother," Welter said. "I think I'll be all right."

When Welter jumped down from the track he collapsed into a sitting position and stayed there for several minutes. Pierre paced back and forth nearby.

Still sitting, "That was incredibly courageous of you, Pierre."

"I probably wouldn't do it again."

"I could have been up there all night. I might not have survived. Can you believe those guys hung me out to dry like that?"

"I'm still trying to get it through my head that you were hanging *them* out to dry."

"They're barbaric, Pierre. A bunch of sick-os. Look how they treated those men the unemployment agency sent here to help them out. Good-for-nothing degenerates, that's what they are."

"Good for nothing? Take a look at this job, Richard. Sure they're crude. But the truth of it is they didn't need any help. I can tell you this; every time I showed them how to do something I never had to think about it again. They built this horse barn right. The whole project went off without a single hitch, two days ahead of schedule. And below budget, since we didn't have to hire a lot of other workers. Jericho's recruits did it righteous, just like he said they would. And if everything goes okay tomorrow, we'll be getting a decent bonus."

Welter got to his feet and rubbed the parts of his midsection where his belt had dug in the deepest. "It isn't over yet, Pierre. Roger Framingham happens to be an agent with the State Attorney General's office. We'll see what his report has to say."

"Roger's fulltime with us, as of this morning. He quit his state job. There may not even be a report. Or if there is, it'll clear these men of any wrongdoing. Roger says he's never had so much fun his whole life. Heck, I can say the same for me. And we owe it all to Jericho's dog soldiers."

Welter was shocked to hear about this turn of events. "Roger quit his state job? You've gotta be shitting me."

Pierre stepped up to his former boss in the moonless night and poked him in the chest with a stiff forefinger. "I don't have to shit you, Welter; you stink bad enough as it is."

With that, the Frenchman got into his VW and drove home, fighting the urge to apologize to himself for his heroic act.

Thirty

Tuesday morning everything seemed to go in slow motion; Fritz saying it reminded him of his last two weeks in Vietnam. Not a lot got done, which might have been okay except that it took so long. Hammer a few nails here. Screw a few screws there. Chuckle at a pointless comment, pretending to find its humor. Boredom, suddenly, was a serious threat.

There were no more boards to saw; only hardware to install. Little screws in little holes twisted into smaller holes. Line it up, inspect the fit, and screw it in. The horse barn, now, was all about marking time, marking time. It was, in a word, maddening.

No one had questioned how it was that a half-frozen, down to his last breath, flaccid with hopelessness, physically beaten and emotionally flagellated *Wicked Dick* wasn't hanging from the crane's boom when the crew arrived Tuesday morning. After the fact, nobody cared. The high-minded scalawag had been beaten by his own weapon; behind-the-back intrigue meant to discredit with low-minded humiliation prompted by mid-level scorn. Welter was easy. More importantly, his demise was overshadowed by the greater events of Walter's critical condition and Remington's desolation.

Toward the end of the horse barn's long day, the dog soldiers had, in many ways, triumphed. All but the final touches remained to complete the project, to include the final inspection and Wednesday's clean-up. Welter was history. Roger was marginalized, having found himself in love and then, via bizarre but deeply satisfying events, having found himself. *Ohh Pee-errh*, who never spoke of his valorous deed to the men who would either approve or reprove it – possibly both – was also, in many respects, a new man. But it was, indeed, a long day. And it wasn't over. For Fritz Swilling, an angry warrior resolved to a lofty mission, there was unfinished business.

Not long after the flatbed arrived at four o'clock to haul the crane away, the owner's arrived in three government sedans. They stood next to each other on the bluff for a few minutes admiring their barn, shook each other's hands, then walked down and asked for Gulliver to take them on a tour.

Gully expounded ad nausea about the care, precision, and perfectionist pride that had, along with high quality materials, expert craftsmanship, and sound economics, given rise to a magnificent barn that would soon be home to Arabians and quarter horses, Morgans, palominos, and paints. He walked astride the owners, who were mesmerized by his blue ribbon discourse.

The sole female owner, however, was either distracted or taken by Box Car. Standing outside stall seventeen, she whispered into his ear, *"You're covered with hair"*.

Box moved his heavy head back for a better look at the refined lady who was fifteen years his elder if she was a day. "Yes," he said. "Yes I am."

The woman smiled and posited a follow-up question in a suggestive tone. *"Everywhere?"*

"All over my body."

Gulliver's entourage, enraptured by his flamboyant gesticulations, walked into the tack room. The inquisitive middle-aged woman tugged at Box's sleeve for him to stay put. When the others were out of sight, her smile widened and her eyes gleamed with anticipation, "Even ... *even on your buttocks?*"

"Of course. I'm an animal. The only animal with no hair on its ass is a baboon. Do I look like a baboon to you?"

"I didn't mean to insinuate ..."

"My ass is covered with hair." Box reached for his belt. "Here, I'll prove it."

She quickly seized the wrist of his zipper hand. *"Oh my, no. Not here."*

Box leaned closer to her. "You just give me the word, lady, and this furry ass of mine is all yours."

The woman blushed. Overcome, she swallowed with obvious difficulty; whether from nervousness or excitement Box wasn't sure. "We should catch up with the others," she said.

"Please picture, if you will," Gulliver stated with ebullient flair, "this spacious tack room adorned with a full complement of bridles and bits, crops and caps, English saddles and western saddles, grooming sponges and currying brushes. Why it's enough to inspire another Flicka or Fury, Silver or Trigger."

Gulliver motioned toward the center ring with a sweeping wave of his arm. "Who's to say that one among the equestrian riders who will canter here, who will trot and jump and halt, who will ride in rhythmic cadence with her noble steed, graceful and disciplined, won't someday represent our proud country in the Olympic Games?"

With that, the owners and the dog soldiers launched into enthusiastic applause.

Each of the state officials walked up to Gulliver to shake his hand or to pat him on the back.

"Well done," said one.

"Magnificent presentation," said another.

"Inspirational beyond belief," said the lady.

"You're so full of it those robin's egg eyes of yours have turned dog-shit brown," Jericho said when he and Gulliver were out of earshot.

The owners walked around the outside of the barn posing for photographs from various vantage points. Gully snapped off a few shots of them in front of the entrance.

By the time they were leaving, Jericho had cajoled them into attending a gala celebration of the barn's completion at his place Friday evening.

Twilight folding into darkness, the men untied their nail bags, put away their tools, and trudged up to the Buick to head for *The Man's Bar*.

Remington was already three sheets to the wind when they walked in. If Wynona had been there, Rem was too blotto to recognize her. For the first time in years, he poured quarter after quarter into his favorite pinball machine and lost every game, mostly because of tilts from clumsy play.

Weepy stayed out in the car wolfing reefer. Gulliver picked a partner and sprinkled the shuffle board with saw dust. Fritz climbed onto a bar stool between the Bork brothers.

Fritz's mood was not conducive to witnessing a spectacle of condemnable pig-outs. Grumpy, to his left, chowed down the first of seven pickled sausages arrayed like saw logs next to his beer mug. Box Car, on his right, popped open a jumbo bag of *Wise* potato chips and began a ceaseless crunching interrupted only by long swigs of draft beer.

After twenty minutes and three beers, Fritz was astonished to see that Box had eaten the entire bag and had ordered another. "Ludicrous as this may seem, Box, the food we used to get in K-rations didn't add up to the amount of crumbs in your beard."

"That's what it's there for," a nonplussed Box Car calmly stated, "to collect my next meal."

"Do you realize how much grease you've just consumed?"

"Not enough, apparently, or I wouldn't have ordered another bag."

Fritz turned to Grumpy. "Those things don't make you sick?"

"Wouldn't matter if they did. I love these babies."

"But they've been floating around in a monstrous jar of vinegar for months. You may as well stab a fork into those Siamese twins the carnies cart around in a jar of formaldehyde. What's the difference?"

"I prefer vinegar."

"But those putrid sausages are dripping with it."

"That's what makes them taste so good."

"Didn't you hear what the doctor said about Walter's diet? All that vinegar he's been getting from pickled tripe, from bottle after bottle of olive juice, from dill pickles and sweet pickles, from pickled eggs and pickled cocktail onions has turned his stomach into one big blister. Blood is leaking through his veiny bag like a fucking sieve."

"Vinegar's good for you."

"Too much of it isn't."

"My grandmother used to spoon it to us, along with some honey."

"Honey is just another form of sugar. Vinegar is pure acid."

"Get off my back, Fritz. I don't eat near the vinegar Walter does. I don't drink fifteen cups of coffee a day like him either. And I damn sure don't eat *Zero* bars or tons of aspirin all day long. I'm not Walter, goddamnit."

"Fine. But that hardly means you and your odious brother over here aren't a couple of witless slaves to the sinister junk food industry, just like everybody else."

"Go tell it to the Marines. I'm minding my own business, trying to get drunk."

Fritz slammed his fist on the bar. "You're going to die a young man, Grumpy! All those French fries and double cheeseburgers, popcorn and Twinkies, milk shakes and soda pops, slushies and corn chips, donuts and frosted cupcakes will take your sorry ass to an early grave, watch and see. But you won't just die of a sudden heart attack or stroke, of pancreatic cancer or lymphoma; your bloated cadaver will float down the river of horrors stocked and dredged by the high-salaried thugs who adopt their deadly directives in the boardrooms of the murderous food cartel. And you won't understand what's happening because you refuse to listen to me. *You refuse to heed my warnings, Grumpy,* and because of that, you're a walking dead man."

"You're insane, Fritz. You've lost your marbles. The war did a bigger number on you than you realize. If you don't get off the subject, I'm going to order five more of these fat little devils and devour them right in front of you."

Half an hour later, Remington staggered to the bar for another roll of quarters and another Jack Black. "Where's the eldest Swilling?" he asked the Box. "I don't see him in here."

Box stared into Rem's glossy red eyes. "I'm surprised you can see anybody in here. How long do you intend to stay drunk?"

"Until the hangover finally wins. Where the hell's Fritz?"

"He took off ten minutes ago."

"D'he walk home or head to another bar?"

"I don't know and I don't care. That schizoid war nut went into another one of those wild fits of his about sugar and shit – something about an army of trucks delivering slow death to the gaping maws of the mindless bourgeoisie and how something needs to be done about it before it's too late."

Rem grabbed his drink and the fresh roll of quarters. Despite his two-day bender, he was remarkably lucid. "Fritz has been on the razor's edge lately. I'd like to be worried about him – he's capable of just about anything in this frame of mind – but I got my own problems. To make matters worse, the only booze that sickly albino has in his apartment, which smells like rotten tomatoes, is vodka. *I hate vodka.* It's only saving grace is that it's got alcohol in it."

Typically, Gulliver walked from his apartment to Box's before daybreak, as did Fritz, and the three would wait for Remington to pull in ahead of Grumpy and Weepy. Then they'd pick up Walter. Wednesday morning, there being nothing left to do at the horse barn but walk around picking up scraps of boards and other debris and tossing them into Jericho's truck for kindling, the crew didn't mind waiting a while for Fritz to show up. But he didn't. Half an hour had passed when Box suggested they drive to Fritz's apartment.

Gulliver climbed the stairs and knocked on the door. There was no answer. He knocked again. No answer. He pounded on the door and hollered for his brother loud enough to wake up every tenant in the building. Gulliver discovered that the door was unlocked. He walked in. Fritz was not there. It was hard to tell whether he'd slept there since he never made his bed. On his way out Gulliver checked the refrigerator: a carton of cottage cheese, two apples, a grapefruit, broccoli and celery in the crisper, a jug of water, and two quarts of beer. It irked him not to find something hypocritical to use against the hypercritical anti-junk food fanatic.

"He's not up there," Gulliver told the others. "I have no idea where he could be."

"Great," said the Grump. "The last day on the job and Fritz is nowhere to be found, Walter's in a hospital half dead, and Rem's on a wicked bender. How did it come to this?"

Roger was up on the roof helping Pierre with the cupola and Jericho was sitting in his truck in front of the barn's entrance when the depleted pack of dog soldiers arrived an hour late, Rem too drunk to bring with them.

Weepy made an observation on the way down to the barn. "I can't imagine what the hell I'm doing here. I took my equipment home last weekend."

"Today's clean-up day," Grumpy said.

"But I can't stand picking up after myself, much less cleaning up after a bunch of ol' whore dogs."

"Did you honestly think, on the very last day at the horse barn," Gulliver asked, "that any of us expected you to work?"

"No I did not. So let me repeat: why am I here?"

"To be a part of history," Gulliver said. "To savor the moment. To put an exclamation point at the end of a profoundly absurd statement. To avoid missing out on any last minute act of insanity that any one of us is all too capable of performing."

"And to sing *Hello Dolly*," Grumpy said, "with or without your guitar."

"You have to have a horn to do *Satchmo*. How many times do I have to tell you?"

"You'll change your tune," Grumpy said, "when I grab Jericho's gun out of his pants and aim it at that blocky skull of yours, you pecker head."

Jericho got out of his truck and railed Box Car about the crew being late. "And besides that, where the hell is everybody?"

Gulliver explained. "We left Rem at Walter's because he's virtually incoherent. We're not sure if the albino is dead or alive but we plan to pay him a visit on our day off in either case. And the jackass jarhead disappeared."

"What do you mean, disappeared?"

Gulliver explained. "I mean he's gone. It's my way of indicating we can't find him. It portends the possibility he vanished, flew the coop, went poof, vacated. Or, if you'd listened, *dis-a-fucking-peeeered*."

"But I want him at the party."

"Why?" Grumpy asked. "Nobody else does."

"Remember the mysterious Marsha who came prancing in here trying to pass herself off as a horse woman; the one who showed up the party, then came back here to get Fritz to give her the lowdown on *Butt Fuck*?"

The men nodded.

"I found out from Roger that she works at the Washington County *Chronicle*."

"She's a reporter?" Gulliver asked.

"That's right."

"I'll be a monkey's uncle," Box said. "Walter was right after all."

The men stared at the *Missing Link* for a moment, unable to argue with either remark.

"I planned to call her at the paper and invite her to the celebration," Jericho said, "in the hopes she'd finally take Fritz with her when she left. But hey, I don't have to worry about getting rid of him if he already got rid of himself."

"He'll show up when we least expect it," Grumpy said. "What else did Roger have to say?"

"About what?"

"About him spying on us all this time. About the investigation he's been conducting without knowing we knew. I was thinking maybe I'd get to see my brother in handcuffs."

Box chuckled. "Roger'd better have a few good men with him if he plans to throw the cuffs on me."

Jericho stepped away from the barn to survey the roof. "*Hey, Fartingham*, get your ass down here and tell us what happened with your investigation."

Roger slid on his heels and haunches down the tin roof to a ladder leaned up against the side of the barn and climbed down. He was all smiles. "What would you like to know?"

"Is my brother going to jail or not?" Grumpy asked.

Box gave the Grump a decisive shove. "If I'm going to jail, we're all going to jail."

"Nobody's going to jail," Roger said. "Nor will there be a civil suit. Not that you hounds aren't guilty of infringing upon the civil rights of just about everybody who came onto this construction site during the last three months. It's my professional opinion that you didn't directly violate them in a manner grievous enough for a court to be convinced that irrefutable irreparable harm was caused to your easily exploited victims."

"Is that the long way of telling us there won't be any charges filed?" Grumpy wanted to know.

"That's what I'm saying."

"If that's the story, what the hell good are you?" Grumpy inquired with unexpected ire.

"I don't understand what you're saying," Roger said. "I conducted a thorough investigation. My findings exonerated you."

"What am I supposed to do with all the write-ups I've got stuffed in my glove compartment? You mean to tell me I did all that work for nothing?"

"What write-ups?" Roger asked, completely baffled.

"Every time one of these men got out of line I made a note of it. I was hoping I'd get a chance to hand them to you before you finalized your report but the wild goose chase didn't turn out like we wanted. And then you went and resigned."

"I never had an assistant on this job," Roger said.

"I'm a sworn-in deputy sheriff over in Chittenden County," Grumpy explained.

"He parks cars during fair time," Gulliver clarified.

"Are you telling me you were hoping to rat on your own friends?" Roger asked, still trying to grasp Grumpy's point.

"Look, I didn't play favorites. When *Butt Fuck* first got here Walter was too sick to do it down and dirty so I climbed up on a stack of boards and gave it a shot. Turns out I can't dance for shit. I had no choice but to write myself up. How's that for being objective?"

Roger scratched his head. "My report's been filed, Grumpy. You boys flirted with disaster, time and time again, I won't say you didn't. Neither will I say that a pretty darn good case couldn't have been made against you. But I came to realize that all of your shenanigans, at the end of the day, were nothing more than gross insults, low-brow character assassinations rooted in a sense of humor that's reprehensible, detestable, and downright nasty. But not so bad as to warrant criminal indictment or civil action. Taking a page from Welter's book, you're off the hook."

Box raked a clubby hand through his beard, a flurry of potato chips spilling out. "If that's the case – the fact that there isn't one – I'd like to offer you a personal invitation to the celebration at Jericho's Friday night."

"Thanks. I wouldn't miss it," Roger said.

"Will you be coming with Mabel?" Gulliver asked.

"You betcha. She's the love of my life. Confidentially, the reason I've been a bachelor this long is because women can't get past my nose. To them, it's a deformity that outweighs certain other attributes I possess. After a while I got self-conscious about it. My mammoth muzzle always got in the way of a serious relationship. Then I found Mabel, a down to earth goddess with a deep appreciation for my titanic trunk."

"Sounds like a love story for mucous membranes," Jericho said, howling.

With that, the dog soldiers sniffed around the barn for odds and ends, joked about their pranks and capers and callous name distortions during the construction of the horse barn, raised grave doubts about the albino, exchanged wagers on how long Rem's drunk would last, and debated the whereabouts of the infuriated war vet.

Pierre finished the cupola and broke for lunch a half-hour after the others had walked up to the bluff. The only remaining task was to christen the barn with the weathervane.

Box rolled down the window as the Frenchman approached. "Jump in the Buick. Jericho and Roger are in here having lunch with us."

Pierre obliged, Box sliding over to Rem's customary position in the middle.

As Pierre opened a black lunch box worn to a dull silver along its ridges from years of daily use, Box peeked inside. "Got any interesting fruit in there?"

"My wife doesn't put bananas in any more."

"I don't care what your wife does in her spare time; I was hoping you had an extra apple, a tangerine maybe."

Pierre stared at the Box. "It never stops with you guys, does it?"

"Where do you go after this?" Gulliver asked. "Grumpy has twenty dollars says you move up to Welter's job."

"I don't think so," Pierre said. "I wouldn't mind working inside more, especially with winter knocking at the door. Rudy needs somebody who's good with estimates. That's not my forte."

"You never have much to say," said Jericho, "but when you do, I notice you like to throw some French into the mix."

"You use French too, whether you know it or not."

"No I don't."

"I beg to differ."

"Beg all you want. I don't use French words."

"What's your favorite saying?"

"You mean, 'That's the beauty of it?'"

"Do you think the word beauty is an English word?"

"Of course."

"It's French, my friend. The English language owes its remarkable range and flexibility, its richness, its nuances – there's another one right there – to the French language."

"Good thing Fritz isn't here," Box said. "He'd challenge that contention."

"He would lose," said Pierre with understated confidence. "This entire project is heavily imbued with words derived from the French language; words you mistakenly think of as original English."

"You're going to have to explain that one," Roger said.

Pierre closed his eyes to think a moment.

"Who takes a nap *before* they eat?" Weepy wondered aloud.

"I'm not napping," said Pierre. "I'm trying to come up with a short tale to illustrate my point."

"Apologies for sabotaging your reverie."

The Frenchman closed his eyes again. A moment later, "*Voilá.* I have it."

"We're listening," Gulliver said.

"A contract was signed at a bargain price and laborers were hired at a fair wage to build a horse barn out in the country. Great skill was used to measure and saw and nail while one played music, one was a spy, one was struck with a malady, and one went nuts about sugar. The job commenced with a real guarantee but with no regard for authority. Fools were forced to defend their honor. Obedience was sacrificed to self-righteous nobility. Though accused of many injustices, the dog soldiers were acquitted instead of arrested to complete the stables and enjoy the fruits of their labor; which proves that virtue is all about money."

Jericho was not impressed. "That's a neat recap, *Moan Sewer Pee-errrh*, but I didn't hear one French word in all that tortured verbiage."

"There was an abundance of French words in that ridiculous little story," Pierre responded.

The gunslinger demanded an accounting. "Which ones!"

Pierre laid his head back on the seat and closed his eyes, trying to remember them in chronological order: "*contract, bargain, price, laborers, wage, country*. Those were all in the first sentence. Let's see now: *skill, measure, music, spy, malady, sugar*. I have to think a second: *commenced, real, guarantee, regard, authority*. What else now: *fools, forced, honor, obedience, sacrifice, nobility*. Then came: *accused, injustices, soldiers, acquitted, arrested, complete, stables*. And finally: *fruits, labor, prove, virtue, money*. I bet you guys were thinking all those words are pure English. They're not. Every one of them was taken from the French. You owe those and at least eight-thousand others to William the Conqueror."

Gulliver, a word-worker himself, wanted to know how Pierre knew all that.

"I'm working on my masters in philology."

"What the hell is that?" Grumpy asked.

Gulliver intervened. "He loves literature and learning. He's into etymology, lexicology, morphology, syntax, phonetics, semantics; he's a potential polyglot."

Bridled with contempt, Jericho stuck out his tongue with boorish innuendo at the smug Frenchman.

Gulliver wasn't finished. "It turns out Pierre was not only guarding his glossological gift for gab, but also his virtuosity as a cunning linguist."

Precisely at two o'clock, Pierre finished securing the weathervane to the cupola. Straddling the roof's ridgeline, he stood and raised his arms to the sky, glorying in the barn's completion. The crew, bored into slovenly mulling during an hour of restless anticipation, roared to life with hoots, whistles, and applause. They slapped backs, drove meaningful punches into arms and midsections, rooted, snorted, and stomped. The construction of the horse barn, at long last, was an accomplished fact. The crew's histrionic barnyard hoopla was vindicated, their roughhouse achievement a shining spike of overbearing confidence, their triumph a brutal historic pounding by the sledge hammer of egregious conduct; a job, well – done.

When it came to celebrations, there was never a better time than the present for the dog soldiers. Grumpy wheeled the Buick into the parking lot at Walter's to pick up Remington and head for *The Man's Bar*. Surely he'd be teetering on the edge of an apocalyptic hangover by now and was in need of rescue.

Gulliver knocked on the door of the apartment and waited. There was no answer. It felt like déjà vu when a second knock yielded no response from within. But wait. Someone was inside. He could hear strange noises. It had to be Rem. Not surprisingly, given a repeat of the morning's events, the door was unlocked. Gully stepped inside. He could hear his brother behind the door to the bathroom. What he heard sounded like a sputtering engine. He paused to consider whether his search had gone far enough. But no, that wasn't it at all. There was a husky heaving to the noise. He inched closer to the door and listened intently. For a moment, there was no sound at all. Then it started again. Gulliver realized his brother was crying. No. It was worse than that. What he heard, distinctly now, was a baleful sobbing. He rapped on the door. "Hey Rem! You okay in there?"

"Go away."

"It's me, Gulliver."

"I said *get the fuck out of here*."

"Rem, c'mon. Tell me what's going on."

"You don't want to know."

"I'm going to stand right here until you come out."

A moment later, "The door's not locked."

Gulliver opened it. Remington was sitting on the throne with his pants up. His head was in his lap. When he looked up, Gully could hardly recognize him. Rem's face had been put through a sausage grinder, blotched with swollen reds and streaks of white, and soggy with tears. His eyes twitched, stinging too much to fully open them.

"Jesus, Rem. What the hell happened?"

Remington rubbed his eyes and tried to stand. Gulliver went to him, held him upright, and the two staggered out to the kitchen. "It's over there," Rem said, pointing to some papers sitting on the table next to Walter's typewriter.

"What is?"

Remington, pickled by alcohol and weak with anguish, could only point.

Gulliver helped him into the chair and picked up the papers. At the top of the first page the names *I. M. Hornblower & G. Willikers* were written in elaborate script, under which was a Burlington address. He turned to Rem. "A law firm?"

Remington nodded and drove his fists into his eyes, falling forward with a choke and a sob.

Gulliver read down the page. "She's filing for divorce?"

Rem whimpered and choked.

Gulliver read the second page ... *nonsupport* .. yeah, yeah ... *thinks only about his cock* ... big deal .... *addicted to gambling* ... blah, blah ... *infidelity.* "Shit, you're not allowed to go inside your own house?"

Rem rolled his head in emotional distress, digging his fists into his eye sockets.

Gulliver read the final half-page, an elucidation of pre-hearing conditions, the most devastating coming at the end. "You mean to tell me you're not allowed to see your own daughter?"

Remington threw his head back and wailed in agony.

Gulliver had to think hard about what to do next. Finally, "Can I pour you a drink?"

Rem nodded and sniffled. "I'd like that."

"Holy shit," Gully said, glancing at the kitchen counter and seeing three bottles of Jack Black; one full, one empty, another more than three-quarters gone. "I thought you said Walter only had vodka in this place."

Rem tried to collect himself. "I paid a cab driver twenty bucks to hit the package store."

"Good idea. Listen, the others are out in the car. What do you want me to tell them?"

"Tell them to get the fuck out of here. I want to drink alone."

"You want me to leave?"

Rem dropped his head to his knees again, then nodded.

"You going to be okay?"

Rem didn't answer.

"Will you get too drunk to find Walter's bed?"

Again, no response.

"We finished the horse barn, Rem."

Rem mumbled something.

"One helluva saga, wouldn't you say?"

Rem looked up. "I could give a shit less."

"Yeah. Right. Sorry to mention it. We, uhm, we're going to head over to *The Man's Bar* now to, uhm, you know, celebrate. Will that bother you?"

Rem did not respond.

Gulliver spotted a glass near the sink with two fingers of hooch still in it. He topped it off and brought it to the table. "Here's a fresh one for you. Look, do you want me to go see Sibyl? Try to talk some sense into her?"

Rem didn't answer.

"Yeah, you're right. It's past that."

Grumpy laid on the horn.

"Okay then, I guess there isn't much more I can do here."

Rem did not respond.

Gulliver closed the door to Walter's apartment. He walked outside, Rem's sobs fading. He felt helpless. Maybe the best thing for him, as well, was to get dead drunk.

The news that Sibyl had filed for divorce didn't take any of the dog soldiers by surprise. But it put a damper on their celebration, if not their drinking. By eleven o'clock, Gulliver, Box Car, and Grumpy staggered out of *The Man's Bar* and climbed into the Buick where Weepy, stoned to the rafters, had his head cocked to one side and was plucking listlessly at random guitar strings.

Dropping each man off, Grumpy offered gruff reminders that he'd be picking them back up at eight o'clock in the morning to pay Walter a visit.

Thirty-One

Gulliver climbed into the blue cruiser, groggy and indecisive. "What should we do Grump? Rem might be worse off than Walter. Do we check on Rem before seeing Walter, skip Rem for the Walter visit, check out Walter and then see Rem, or …"

"Whoa," said the Grump. "You're not doing my hangover any good. I gave everybody the schedule last night. I'm picking up the Box after you, then we get Fritz, then we grab Weepy on our way through Winooski, and we go straight from there to the hospital. You know as well as I do Rem'll be too fucked up to go with us."

Moments later, Grumpy laid on the horn. Box came out and they drove to Fritz's. Gulliver climbed the stairs and knocked. Like the morning before, there was no answer. He turned the door handle. It wasn't locked. Inside, there was no indication Fritz had been home. The bed sheets appeared to be ruffled in the same manner. The items in the fridge were exactly as they had been; two full quarts of beer the most telling clue. Gulliver scratched his head. The last time the eldest Swilling vanished without a trace he'd taken off to Dallas, hunkering down in a friend's apartment with his guitar and virtually never coming out for an entire year, writing songs that he never played for anybody. It didn't make sense that Fritz would do something like that again; not without getting his last paycheck.

"He's not up there," Gully told the Bork brothers.

"Maybe he's at the hospital," Box said. "He's always at odds with the albino but he does have a soft spot for him."

It took Weepy a minute to come out to the car, Grumpy laying on the horn the entire time.

The foursome, slowed by hangovers, picked up their pace walking through the hospital lobby, aware that Walter may have been transferred to the morgue. In the elevator, Weepy wept.

"You shouldn't expect the worse," Gulliver told the sorrowful entertainer.

"I know. I can't help it. That's how my mind works. I had a dream last night that Walter's hair fell out. If you think he looks pitiful with white hair you should see him without it."

The elevator opened on Patrick 3. The last time they'd seen their fallen comrade he was unconscious the entire time. The scene that greeted them at the door to his room was more than gratifying. Walter was sitting up in bed spooning the last of his tapioca pudding. One of the two IVs had been removed. A monitor blipped his pulse at 62 and his body temperature at 99. Walter lit up like a thousand watt bulb at the sight of his friends. Placing his spoon on the serving tray, "I thought you guys had forgotten I even existed."

"That's a worthwhile thought," Gulliver said. "Unfortunately, it isn't possible. One doesn't soon forget a ghoulish freak like you."

Weepy leaned over the bed and hugged the albino like some dog lover whose runaway pet had finally come home.

"Careful, Weepy; you're smothering me."

"Has Fritz been in here since the last time we visited?" Box asked.

Walter was bewildered. "You've already been here to see me?"

"Sunday," Gulliver said. "We watched the Giants' game right here in your room. Fritz was with us. The next day he had a deeply corrugated corn cob stuck up his ass. We haven't seen him since."

"I haven't seen him either," Walter said. "But then, this is the first time I've seen any of you. I came out of the fog around three o'clock this morning. I had no idea where I was. When I tried to get out of bed I realized I was tethered to a bottle of saline. Then I reached down to discover a tube shoved up my dink. Talk about a rude awakening!"

"What's it feel like?" Weepy was curious.

"I don't want to go into it," Walter said. "By the way, did Rem make a piss stop down the hallway or is he with Fritz somewhere?"

"Rem's at your apartment," Gulliver said. "I've got bad news on that score."

The comment startled Walter. "Did that sonuvabitch drink all my *Pepto*?"

"No. But he did polish off your vodka."

"That isn't so bad."

"Sibyl threw him out. Not only that, she had divorce papers served on him at your place after she figured out that's where he was. And that isn't the worst of it. He's restricted from going anywhere near his house and he's not allowed to see Bea."

Walter stared at his empty tapioca dish. "I guess I could see this coming. Not being able to see Beatrice, *jeepers*; that must be crushing him."

"He went on a wicked bender Sunday; right after Sibyl gave him the heave-ho. I did a double take when I saw him. He was four-fifths done his fourth fifth. I imagine he'll keep putting the sauce to him. Those divorce papers stung him deep, especially the part about his little honey bee."

"What's the status on the horse barn?"

"It's done. The Frenchman put the weathervane on yesterday afternoon. We're here this morning because we got the day off. Tomorrow too, not counting the party at Jericho's starting around five. Think you'll be out of here by then?"

"I hope so. I feel pretty good. But, of course, the drugs they've got me on might have something to do with the mild euphoria I'm experiencing."

"Your doctor told us you'd been bleeding pretty bad inside."

"He says I still am, but the leaks are getting plugged one by one."

"Make sure your doctor knows you can't miss the celebration," Grumpy said. "According to Jericho, that's when Rudy's going to hand out our bonus checks."

"I'll tell him, as long as I know I'm not going from here to the party and then to jail. What's the deal with Roger's investigation?"

"He's one of us now," Gully said. "He handed in a report that completely absolved us of any wrongdoing. Then he quit his job with the state and took a job with Rudy. He's been giving the goddess a nose job ever since."

Box happened to look up and see a news bulletin on the TV, which was tuned to Channel 3 but with the volume turned down. "I wonder what that's all about. Looks like a bunch of local cops and a small army of state troopers caught somebody up on the Power Dam Bridge. Mind if I turn it up?"

"Go ahead," said Walter. "Could be interesting."

"Good thing we took the Winooski route," Grumpy said. "Traffic is backed up all the way to the Five Corners in one direction and half way to Williston in the other. Film crews are set up with tripods all over the place."

"Maybe the bridge is about to collapse," Weepy suggested.

"That ain't it." Box said. "A minute ago they showed a guy straddling a girder at the very top. I can't believe he made it all the way up there. It might be some lunatic threatening to jump off."

In the newsroom at the Washington *Chronicle*, Marsha got up from her desk and walked over to the small television that sat on a table outside the editor's office. Regular programming had been interrupted for a breaking news report of a man perched high atop a large green structural steel bridge spanning the Winooski River between Williston and Essex Junction. One of Green Mountain Power Company's generating plants was nestled against a shoulder of the massive structure. The nutcase sitting at the highest point of the bridge's impressive arc, legs dangling, one arm raised in a fist, the other pointed at the people below and jabbing in their direction with perfunctory zeal, looked vaguely familiar.

A moment later, a more powerful camera zoomed in. Although the angle precluded a truly definitive look, Marsha recognized enough of the man's features to hit the panic button. She bolted to her feet with a rush of adrenaline. She flung open the editor's door. "I'm off to Chittenden County. A potential suicide victim is up on that huge bridge in Essex."

"Our coverage area is restricted to Washington County," the editor said. "Seems like you're always going after big stories. Weekly newspapers don't care about them. It's not what we do."

"I understand that. But this happens to be somebody I know; a person I believe it's possible I might somehow care about."

"Either you do or you don't. Why the ambiguity?"

"Because I don't know him well enough to know."

"Are the obits ready to be type-set?"

"Yes. I put them in my out-tray."

"And you're not after a story that doesn't pertain to us?"

"No. I'm not. But I have reason to believe I may be able to talk the man down, assuming I can get there before something goes terribly wrong."

"Okay. Good-bye. Don't drive too fast."

"Turn it up," Grumpy said. "I can't hear shit."

The men were riveted to an interview a reporter was conducting with a policeman.

"This is Mylar Persimmons reporting to you live at this very moment from the Power Dam Bridge where I'm talking with Chief of Police, Mortimer Winkins. Chief Winkins, tell us what's happening here today."

"Can I go back to last night? That's when it all started."

"Fine."

"We got a number of phone calls throughout the night from truck drivers claiming they'd been shot at going through this bridge."

"*Shot at,* chief? That's a serious allegation."

"I'm just telling you what they said."

"Fine. Please go on."

"The night dispatcher didn't pay a whole lot of attention to the first call, figuring the problem was a couple of kids up past their bedtimes pecking rocks."

"Then what?"

"I'm trying to tell you."

"Yes, of course. Go ahead. Don't let me interrupt."

"You keep taking the microphone away."

"I'm not here to argue with you, chief. Please go on with the story."

"Anyway, about an hour later another call came in."

"Another truck driver?"

"That's right. You gonna let me talk?"

"Yes, by all means. Please continue."

"As I was trying to say, the first call we got was from a driver delivering pastries to all the mom and pop groceries around here; you know, cream-filled moon pies, frosted cupcakes, devil dogs – the kind of stuff mothers pack in their kid's lunches."

"Fascinating."

"The next call we got was from another delivery guy. This man was dropping off boxes of snack foods to local stores."

Standing on either side of Walter's bed, the dog soldiers snaked their eyebrows at each other.

"In other words, chief, a pattern was developing."

"At that point, we didn't know if it was a coincidence or what."

"Soon enough, however, all of your uniformed men descended on the scene."

"Not right then. The dispatcher was still considering it might be some kids chucking rocks. We've had that happen any number of times, but usually during the summer months or come Halloween. Once colder weather sets in, things usually quiet down in good shape."

"Understood. In the meantime, how many uniformed officers did you have on duty."

"One. Problem was, at that particular moment he was way the heck over on Sand Hill Road sneaking up on a car parked in the woods."

"Investigating a stolen vehicle?"

"No, checking out a suspicious lovey-dovey couple parking. In a situation like that, you want to make sure the guy ain't too old for the girl, if you know what I'm saying."

"Let's get back to main story, chief, if you don't mind."

"I'm trying to tell you we didn't have a cruiser anywhere near the problem area as things began to unfold. It wasn't a major problem; we can get from one place to another pretty fast, not having to obey the speed limit like everybody else. But it was a logistics issue that we had to sort out."

"So the dispatcher radioed the officer after the second call, I presume."

"Not yet. The dispatcher was tossing the rock throwing theory around in his head when I'll be damned – *woops*; excuse my French – if a third call didn't come in."

"Chief, excuse me."

"What's the problem?"

"You never told us specifically the type of goods the second driver was delivering."

"Oh. Right. His product line was mainly cheese twists, popcorn, pork skins, potato chips; items of that nature."

"More junk food, in other words."

"I don't want to stand here being the judge of what folks eat. Far as I'm concerned, one man's poison is another man's ambrosia."

"Well put, chief. You say there was a third call?"

"This particular gentleman was very irate. When the dispatcher told him it was probably some kids hitting his truck with rocks, he said 'no way in hell' – *his* French, this time – that he'd been in the Vietnam war and he could pretty darn well tell the difference between a gunshot and a stone if one or the other smacked against his truck."

"And what was this driver delivering?"

"You know those small pies you can buy for fifteen cents?"

"Yes."

"Those. Nowadays, they got blueberry, apple, cherry; I don't know what else."

"I'm sure we're all familiar, chief. Is that when the dispatcher finally let your uniformed officer know there was trouble brewing at the Power Dam Bridge?"

"I was getting to that part."

"Continue, please."

"Officer Singleberry was just about to shine his light into that parked car up on Sand Hill when he thought he heard the radio back at the cruiser cutting in and out, which of course annoyed the hell out him, close as he was to catching a guy red-handed with some local …"

"You're straying again, chief."

"Oh. Right. *Sorry.* Anyway, from the time it took the officer to get from one place to the other, risking his life clocking damn near a hundred on the IBM road, I'll be damned if the dispatcher hadn't gotten two more calls."

"From drivers of delivery trucks?"

"You guessed it."

"Junk food again?"

"Let's go with snack food."

The local radio stations were also covering the event. Marsha picked up WJOY's signal on the Bolton Flats. There was a lot of static interference but it sounded like a radio news reporter was setting up an interview with a state trooper. On the other side of Jonesville, the signal getting clearer. Marsha turned up the volume.

"Trooper Colder, have you been able to get a make on the sociopath up there?"

"You mean do we know who the man is?"

"Okay, yes."

"No."

"There's been some mention of gunfire. Does he have a weapon?"

"We're not sure."

"Can you tell us whether or not he's threatened to jump?"

"Not to my knowledge."

"I'll take that as a no. Is a plan being formulated to get him down from there?"

"Not that I know of."

"Is there anything else you can tell us?"

"No."

"Thank you, Trooper Colder. You've been very helpful."

Realizing that every on-duty state policeman was at the Power Dam Bridge, Marsha drove thirty miles an hour over the speed limit. On a long straightaway between Richmond and Williston, she leaned over, flipped open the glove compartment, pulled out her press pass, and placed it on her lap. She would pin it to her coat when she reached the scene of her friend's irrational stunt.

At the Mary Fletcher, the dog soldiers watched intently for a good look at the animated bridge psycho, but the camera crews were unable to get a decent shot of him. Nevertheless, they could see that the man wore blue jeans and sneakers. That's what Fritz wore at all times, during all four seasons, no matter what the weather. The Marine Corps field jacket was another tip off, as was the straggly beard and shoulder-length hair. Walter and his visitors didn't need to hear about delivery trucks being fired upon to know it was the eldest

Swilling up there.

"Hey Jericho, come in and see what's on the TV," Deirdre hollered into the garage.

"I'm busy," he hollered back.

"Looks like you're not the only gunslinger 'round these parts. Some guy's up on the Power Dam Bridge shooting at trucks going through."

Jericho dashed into the house. "Really?"

"See for yourself."

Jericho plopped down in his easy chair. There must have been sixty cops in blue or green uniforms milling around, some of them carrying foghorns and calling up to the weirdo perched fifty feet above them shaking his fist and hocking spit.

"This is better than a Yankees-Red Sox game," Jericho told his wife.

The Channel 3 reporter conducted a number of other interviews, but nothing of substance was added to Chief Winkins' comments. The identity of the man on the bridge, who continued to yell and point and occasionally spit at the crowd beneath him, was, the authorities said, still unknown.

"What's the forecast?" Walter asked.

"I say he never comes down," Gulliver said.

"I was talking about the weather."

None of them knew, but the implications were clear. Rain would make the iron bridge extremely treacherous. If Fritz lost his grip sliding down, he'd go too fast; or worse, fall to one side or the other. An icy rain, a frequent occurrence this time of year, meant he'd surely fall to his death. Snow would likely produce the same result.

"We should get over there," Grumpy said.

"They won't let us anywhere near the action," Gulliver said.

"But you're his brother," Weepy said. "They'll let you through."

"What good would that do?" Gulliver asked. "Fritz won't listen to me."

"Sooner or later, he's going to fall," Grumpy said. "You mean to tell me we're just going to stand here and wait for it to happen?"

"Would you rather watch a ballgame at the stadium or on television?" Gully asked no one in particular. When no one answered, he did. "*On TV*, of course. That's why they have blackouts. They have to force people to go to the ballpark because they know damn well people'd rather watch the game from the comfort of their own home, where they don't have to deal with ridiculous traffic or push through huge crowds at the turnstile or pay a fortune for a ticket; where they can listen to the play-by-play, *unless it's Curt Gowdy*, and where it doesn't take anywhere near as long to go take a whiz. By the same logic, watching Fritz's game from right here in the comfort of Walter's hospital room makes a lot more sense than fighting all that traffic to get to the bridge. Besides, when Fritz spits I'm the one who gets hit more often than not."

Gulliver had a good argument. Weepy's only real reason for wanting to go was to smoke a joint on the way over, so he could be in a much looser mental state for this nerve wracking drama. Box Car figured he wouldn't be allowed to drink beer in the company of all those cops any more than he would at the hospital, so why go to the trouble. Grumpy relented primarily because he didn't want to miss anything during the time it would take to make it all the way to the bridge. And Walter, tethered to a bottle of saline at one end and a bed pan at the other, had no other choice. Furthermore, he didn't want to face catastrophe alone, should the crazed leatherneck do the unthinkable.

One of the cameras zeroed in on a woman pleading with a group of Staties. "Isn't that the phony horse woman?" Box asked.

The others nodded, wondering what she was up to.

A moment later, having pocketed some device that a trooper had handed to her, she was scaling the arc of the bridge.

One of the camera crews hastily broke down equipment and reassembled it in a location better suited to capturing her daring climb.

"What the hell is she thinking?" Grumpy wondered aloud.

"She's got bigger balls than I have," Weepy said.

"I thought I spotted a press pass pinned to her coat," Walter said. "That confirms she's a reporter."

"You called that one," Box said. "Jericho found out she works for a weekly in Washington County. This isn't the kind of story a small paper covers."

"I think she's smitten by the eldest Swilling," Gulliver said. "Must be all that subtle suavity of his finally won her over."

"Hold your horses everyone," Walter said. "She stopped half way up."

"She made the mistake of looking down," Weepy said. "Now she's paralyzed with paranoia; like I am just watching her."

"If Fritz could see how she's clinging to that girder, it might be enough to bring him down," Gulliver said. "Even the real horse woman doesn't hold on that tight."

"How would you know that?" Grumpy wanted to know.

"None of your goddamn business," Gully said.

"Look, she's regained her courage," Weepy said, "scrambling up that slab of iron like a circus performer."

"She's a regular monkey," Box said.

"Curious analogy for you to make," Gulliver said.

The TV screen went to another camera that was focused on the psycho. Fritz was leaning to one side, watching the woman climb toward him. He was yelling something to her but his words were inaudible. By his gestures, it looked like he was telling her to go back.

"Deirdre. *Deirdre.* Get in here," Jericho shouted toward the kitchen.

"Has he jumped yet?" she asked.

"You're not going to believe who the guy is on the top of that bridge."

"They've identified him?"

"No. But I have."

"What makes you think you know who it is, Sherlock?"

"The field jacket he's wearing. *And don't get smart.* The sneakers. His dungarees. That wild hair whipping around."

"Fritz?"

"You betcha. Know how else I know?"

"You tell me, Perry."

"He was shooting at delivery trucks. *I said don't get smart.* At first they thought it was three or four truck drivers. Now they're coming out of the woodwork. So far they've counted eighteen trucks shot at. Police chief says half a dozen drivers claimed they were fired on by an automatic weapon."

"According to you, they're not legal."

"They're not. But that crazy jarhead stole one from the Marines just before he mustered out. He's got an M14 he can flip right to auto; unload a whole clip in a couple of seconds. Makes me wish I was up there with him. Of course, if it wasn't for me there's no way he could have pulled this off in the first place."

"Oh? And what do you have to do with it?"

"I'm the one who gave him the bullets."

"Well aren't you the perfect accomplice, sitting safe and contented in the comfort of your own living room fifty miles away watching the sick-o you armed to the teeth scare the bejesus out of people?"

"I had a hand in it. That's good enough for me."

"So tell me, Paladin, have they shown the rifle?"

"Not yet. *Aren't you the smartass today?* Must be he's got it laid down up where he's sitting. I expect him to pick it up any minute now and empty a magazine on all those pigs down there."

"He wouldn't do that. He's a sitting duck."

"Yeah but Fritz is like a fisher cat, bad tempered and unpredictable. He's liable to do just about anything."

"Look, there's a woman up there, inching her way toward him. I suppose you're going to tell me you know her too."

Jericho leaned forward in his chair, squinting for a better look. "Damn it all to hell, Deirdre, put some popcorn on. This could get interesting."

"You know who she is, don't you?"

"Yup. She's the horse woman Fritz fell for."

"Let's hope you got the tense right," Deirdre said, heading back into the kitchen.

"What are you doing up here?" Fritz asked, his tone matter-of-fact.

"I don't want you to jump," Marsha said, her voice edgy.

"I have no intention of jumping."

"You don't?"

“No. What made you think I’d jump?”

“I’m fairly certain that’s what everybody thinks.”

“Not the people who know me. Dying is an interesting phenomenon. As far as I’m concerned it can’t happen soon enough. But that doesn’t mean I’m suicidal.”

“What do you intend to do, then?”

“I’m not sure. I did what I wanted to do. Now that I did, I don’t know what I’ll do now.”

“You’re not worried about falling?”

“No. I love heights. How about yourself?”

“I’m scared to death.”

“Then you shouldn’t be up here. This is no place for someone who’s afraid of heights. Then again, you’re a reporter. You’ll do anything for a story.”

“That’s not true.”

“You’re not a reporter?”

“Yes, I am.”

“But you’re not up here to do a story?”

“No.”

“I don’t get it. Why are you up here?”

“Fritz, I think it’s high time I told you that I think about you more than I would have thought.”

“Why?”

“I don’t know. I guess because I lead a dreadfully boring life full of boring people. You’re the most unusual person I’ve ever met. I mean, look what you’re doing right now. It’s the complete opposite of boring. Besides, I’ve never had anyone come on to me the way you do. It’s disarming, in a pleasantly dramatic sort of way.”

“Thanks.”

“Speaking of which, they said you might have a gun up here; possibly an automatic weapon, which isn’t legal.”

“You think I give a shit about the fucking law?”

“You see? A boring person wouldn’t think that way.”

“Thanks again.”

“So where’s the gun?”

“*Ahhhhh,* so that’s why you climbed up here, to confirm that I’ve got an automatic weapon.”

“No. Darn it, Fritz. I’m risking my life to be with you. Can’t you see?”

“I’m trying to understand.”

“A lot of delivery truck drivers allege they were shot at when they drove through this bridge. Some of them say the gunshots were from an automatic rifle.”

“They can’t prove it.”

“If you threw your rifle in the river they’ll just send divers down and find it. Even if they can’t match your fingerprints, you’re the only possible suspect.”

"They won't find any automatic rifle in the river."

"Where else could it be?"

"Confidentially?"

"Of course. Even if I *was* doing a story I would keep that information in the strictest confidence."

"I'm not sure how many trucks I shot at. Twenty, maybe. I used an M14 that I stole from the Marine Corps. They've got all they need, what with no wars going on right now. M14s break down into a lot of different pieces."

"Divers are sure to find most of them."

"No they won't; magazines and empty .308 shells with no prints, but not an automatic rifle. Here's the secret. I never shot at tractor-trailer trucks. I figure they carry furniture or building materials, appliances or carpets, mattresses and box springs. You never know what's in there, but I gotta think it's mostly consumer durables. I only shot at small delivery trucks, the ones I knew were transporting evil to the mindless masses."

At the hospital, the men were sitting on both edges of Walter's bed, arms folded on their chests.

"This is beginning to get boring," Box said.

"What the hell could they be jabbering about for so long?" Grumpy asked.

"I think she's scared shitless and Fritz is trying to talk her down," Weepy said.

"They're in love," Walter said. "They're having a lover's spat."

Gulliver had his own take. "As we know, Fritz is haunted by what he sees as a vicious conspiracy among the big-time food producers, the beverage behemoths, the fast food chains, and, ultimately, the pharmaceutical industry. Turns out the devious plot he imagines sugars all the way down to bakers and snack food companies at the local level. It's eating him up so bad he's finally had to take his concerns outside our little circle. We've all had a belly full of it by now, but in his mind, these nefarious enterprises need to be brought to justice for poisoning us with toxic fertilizers and deadly dyes, with lethal fats and disease-causing artificial flavorings. He's explaining his theory to her. You gotta hand it to him. He knows she's an enterprising reporter. First he makes himself the center of attention, then he convinces her to tell his story to the world. It's brilliant."

The men considered Gully's postulation, waiting impatiently for the next shoe to fall.

"I think Walter's right," Weepy said. "They're in love. At some point, she talks him down. He gets arrested. His story is told, but only by the local media. The wire services never pick it up. Years later, he's released from jail. By then, Marsha is somebody else's chickadee. Despite his spectacular crowing, Fritz will have laid a goose egg. And take a gander; it isn't golden. It's a big fat zero, the scoreboard's symbol of impotence. *Goose egg. No score.* That cockamamie rooster is wasting the best opportunity he'll ever have to get in her nest."

"The only thing I can surmise from that convoluted diatribe is that you're brimming with pessimism," Gulliver said. "And a bit confused about gender, I might add."

"Okay, but that's the most optimistic scenario I can come up with."

"And just so you know," Fritz said, "I didn't aim to hurt anybody. I was simply sending a message. From here, it was easy to drop one piece at a time onto the tops of the tractor-trailers. You can't imagine how I hated to let that scope go. If it hadn't been for you, I might have forgotten to get one. Beauty of it is, my M14 will end up in four or five different states. Some of the pieces won't be found for years. And when they are, they'll be pitted and rusted; trash for the nearest dumpster. Those idiots plotting my rescue and demise down there won't be able to prove anything."

"That strikes me as rather brilliant."

"Trust me. I know what I'm doing."

"But I don't understand what the message is."

"They're killing us, Marsha. One bite at a time, they're destroying us."

"Who is?"

"The food cartel. They're in cahoots with fast food restaurants unfurling all over the country like fiddleheads around a swamp."

"That strikes me as rather poetic."

"Somebody has to call attention to this insanity. Cancer, diabetes, coronary artery disease; most of those are because of the food we eat. It's getting worse all the time. If something isn't done about it, half the country will be obese before the turn of the century."

"You really believe that."

"Don't you? You seemed to indicate you're enlightened about proper diet."

"My focus is vitamins and minerals, amino acids and oligosaccharides. But yes, I eat mainly nuts and berries, fruits and vegetables. For protein, I eat lots of yogurt, fish twice a week, and skinless breast of chicken. I seldom have red meat, and when I do, I make sure it's the leanest cut – when I can afford it."

"I knew it. I just knew it."

"Knew what?"

"That you're the woman of my dreams."

"*Oh Fritz.* Let's get to know each other better. We could start a health food store together. I'm tired of working at a weekly newspaper. It's boring. I'm ready for a new challenge. With your hatred of sugar and junk food and my knowledge of micronutrients, we could have a thriving business."

"I'm not much of a businessman but I am interested, especially about us getting to know each other better. I think you'll find me to be rather suave."

"Did you feel that, Fritz?"

"Feel what?"

Marsha looked up. "It's starting to rain. We should climb down."

"They'll arrest me."

"You can't sit up here the rest of your life."

"Do you think they got my message?"

"I think you sent a mixed message. But listen, they gave me this." Marsha pulled a walkie-talkie from her coat pocket. "Here. The Chief of Police has the other one. Maybe you can strike a compromise."

"I'm not one to compromise."

"Did you hear that?"

"Hear what?"

"The rain. I think it's turning to ice. It's pinging against the metal."

Fritz held a hand out, palm up. "You're right. You'd better go back down."

"What about you?"

"I don't know. I have to think about it."

"Please, Fritz. Talk to the chief or climb down with me."

"I don't want to be arrested."

"But they can't prove anything. You've disseminated the evidence all over the country."

"That's true."

"I can't imagine what they can charge you with. Is it illegal to climb a bridge?"

"Not to my knowledge."

"Feel the bridge, Fritz. It's already wet. It'll ice over in no time. We'll plunge to our deaths. Let's climb down."

"I'm thinking about it."

"Please Fritz. You've sent your message. They can't charge you with anything. There's no reason for you to stay up here."

"I said I'm thinking about it. Give me a minute."

"The rain has turned to sleet, Fritz. Please. What can I say to convince you to climb down?"

"Tell me you'll go to Jericho's party with me tomorrow night."

"Yes. Yes I will."

"Let me have a word with the chief. You go ahead. That is, in arrears."

Marsha handed Fritz the walkie-talkie, clutched the metal rail with wet hands and trembling thighs, and pushed herself backwards. "Don't talk long. The bridge could ice over any minute."

"This is Fritz to the big chief. You copy?"

"This is Chief of Police, Mort Winkins. Who are you?"

"I'm the guy on the bridge."

"*I know that.* What's your name?"

"Fritz Swilling, United States Marine Corps."

"You're a Marine?"

"I was. I got out not too long ago."

"Honorable discharge?"

"That's right."

"War veteran?"

"South Vietnam; Quang Tri Province."

"I was a Marine myself. WW Two."

"*Semper fi*, chief."

"Well I'll be damned. *Semper fi* right back at you, you goddamn leatherneck."

"You planning to arrest me if I come down?"

"Yup. Got all kinds of things we're gonna charge you with. You planning to cooperate?"

"No."

"This bridge is about to ice over, son. Rain first. Then sleet. Then snow. That's the forecast. Rain didn't last too long before it went to ice. I figure the snow'll start any minute. You'll freeze up there or you'll slip and fall. Either way, you're dead."

"I don't want to be arrested."

"Uh-huh. Say, is that the reporter I see getting ready to slide down this end?"

"Should be. She's the only other person up here."

"What's it going to be, jarhead? Jail or death?"

"We Marines are always faithful to each other, right chief?"

"*Ah c'mon now*, you can't lay that trip on me."

"Why not?"

"It ain't fair. Listen up, grunt. Being arrested ain't so bad."

"It isn't?"

"Nah. You get three square meals a day, your own bunk, lots of regimented activities, and plenty of buddies to shoot the shit with. Just like in the Corps."

"You're right, chief. The bridge is getting icy."

"By the way, what the hell have you got against delivery trucks?"

"Do you realize what they deliver?"

"Food, from what they say."

"Pies? Cupcakes? Cheese curls? Greasy potato chips? You call that food?"

"If it's any consolation to you, that lady reporter made it down okay. Sounds like she wants one of us to go up there and save you. *Ha-ha.* That's a laugh."

"You don't care if I live or die, do you chief?"

"Haven't given it much thought. Tell me, you trying to be some kind of health food martyr?"

"You can't prove I shot at any trucks, chief."

"Why don't we leave that up to the courts?"

"There's no evidence. I don't have a gun."

"That's *rifle*, son. Marines don't use the word *gun*. Weapon. Piece. Rifle. Those words are okay for you to use. But not *gun*, damnit. You oughta know that."

"Fine. I don't have a rifle."

"What'd you use to shoot with?"

"Who said I did any shooting?"

"We got somewhere near twenty trucks with some pretty deep pock marks."

"Must've been kids throwing rocks."

"You know, that's what the dispatcher was thinking."

"You should promote him to detective."

"You could've tossed your piece in the river. Divers'll find it."

"They'd be wasting their time, chief. The more reasonable deployment of resources is to go find those rock throwing kids."

"You mind telling me what the hell you're doing up there if it wasn't to shoot at delivery trucks?"

"I do this all the time. I like heights. Compared to Vietnam, it can get pretty boring around here. Climbing this bridge is a real thrill. If it hadn't been for those kids throwing rocks, nobody would have noticed me."

"Well all right then, c'mon down and we'll sort this all out."

"*Semper fi*, right chief?"

"Yeah, yeah. *Semper fi*."

"Look," Walter said. "He's going down."

"He's going down all right," said Grumpy. "Soon as he hits the ground they'll slap the cuffs on him."

"Where's his gun?" Box was curious.

"Knowing Fritz," Gulliver said, "he ditched the evidence."

"Either that or he knew the weather forecast," Weepy said. "He did his dastardly deed, laid his weapon down on the top of the bridge, hung out till the authorities showed up, kept them at bay till the rains came, then slid down when the rain turned icy, knowing they couldn't climb up to retrieve it."

"Shit, they could fly a chopper over the bridge anytime they feel like it to see if he left a rifle up there," Box said.

"I say he threw it in the river," Grumpy said.

"He couldn't chuck it over near the falls from where he is," Walter said. "If he could have, finding it might not be easy. But the water isn't turbulent near the bridge. Divers would spot it no problem."

"They'd work the dam to calm the water under it, making it easy for divers," Gulliver said. "We're not giving Fritz enough credit. Anybody whose crafty enough to have an automatic weapon – it's not like you can buy them anywhere; they're illegal – is crafty enough to get rid of it in a way that would be almost impossible to trace."

"How?" Grumpy asked.

"I don't know," Gully said. "I'm not particularly crafty."

"Without a weapon, there's no evidence they can link to him," Box said. "Any charges they file won't stick."

"I hate optimism," Weepy said. "There's no glory in it."

"He's under arrest, look!" Jericho yelled to his wife. "I'll be damned if he didn't turn himself in. What an inglorious ending to a promising event."

"What were you hoping for, that he'd either jump or fall off the bridge?"

"Not necessarily. I expected him to climb down sooner or later. I was just hoping he'd fire off a few rounds before he did; *pop, pop, pop*."

"What do you suppose he did with the gun, throw it in the river or leave it up there?"

"If it was me, once I'd had my fun I would have broken the M14 all the way down and tossed the pieces one by one onto the tops of tractor-trailer trucks going through the bridge. Before long, that rifle would be in four or five different states."

Deirdre considered the scenario. "Yeah, that's what he did. Sick minds think alike."

Thirty-Two

"You boys are going to have to leave now," said the man in the white coat flipping through the paperwork on his clipboard."

"Visiting hours over with, doc?" Grumpy asked.

"No. We've got to prep Mr. Birdsong for surgery."

"Surgery?" Walter wailed.

"*'Fraid so.* Tests we got back from the lab indicate the internal bleeding hasn't completely stopped. We need to go in and find out why."

"But I'm getting better without surgery," Walter said. "In fact, I've never felt this good my entire life."

"That's the morphine drip. Remarkable substance. Not only does it eliminate pain, it creates a euphoric state. No wonder it's illegal."

The men shuffled around, gave the albino pats on the head, and advised him to hold himself together and to put his trust in professional hands. Box told him somebody'd come by to bring him out to Jericho's for the celebration.

"Don't leave me," Walter screeched in desperation.

"We're not allowed in the operating room," Gulliver said.

A nurse came in and injected something into Walter's arm. "But I don't want to go under the knife," he pleaded. "They're supposed to stop the bleeding, not start more of it."

"It's a normal reaction he's having," the doctor said, his voice reassuring. "Pay no attention. We hear this all the time."

"Is the surgery dangerous, doctor?" Weepy wanted to know.

"Surgery of any kind is dangerous. But we have no reason to believe he won't pull through without any complications."

Walking to the elevator, the men were mum. Inside, Box pushed the down button, emitting a sad grunt. Weepy used his thumb and index finger to squeeze tears from his eyes. "Who would you rather be?" he asked. "Walter, Fritz, or Rem?"

"There you go again," Gully said. "Your mind not only goes to the worst possible situations, it debates which one it likes best."

If there was a surgical procedure capable of cutting emotional pain out of a man's mind, Remington Swilling, beset by grief and guilt, despondency and self-loathing – his bi-cameral mind unable to cope with the inflammation of distress and the dry ice of depression – would have handed over the scalpel and tongs himself, entreating a team of psychosis-trained surgeons to warm his cold despair and cool the heat of his anxiety, to extricate his misery and suture shut the horrifying chasm of his sense of loss.

"I think he's experiencing delirium tremens," Weepy said, "the way he's laying there with his knees scrunched up, convulsing uncontrollably."

The men were standing in the doorway of Walter's bedroom, Remington oblivious to their presence.

"You really think so?" Grumpy asked.

"I should know. I used to get DTs all the time before I switched to drugs."

"See if you can talk to him," Box said to Gulliver.

Gully went to his brother, knelt by the bed, and gently shook his arm. "You need to snap out of it, Rem. While you're at it, you might think about giving up the birds. Your cock is what got you into this predicament."

"Don't tell him bad things," Box scowled. 'You'll only make him feel worse."

"He's got a point," Weepy said. "The exhilarating violence of a couple of bandy roosters going at it could prove to be his only salvation. Unless I can get him to share a reefer with me."

Gulliver stood up, staring down at his brother with forlorn in his eyes, along with the dull spark of contrition. "You're right, Box. I lost my head there for a second."

Grumpy left the room and came back with a full bottle of Jack Daniels. He left again and came back with five plastic tumblers. "Let's get drunk with him."

"That's more like it," Box said, grabbing the fifth and a tumbler and pouring himself a drink. I'll be able to deal with this better after a couple of these."

Grumpy and Weepy hoisted Remington up into a sitting position, propping two pillows behind him. Gulliver brought a tumbler of Jack Black to his brother's lips and encouraged him to imbibe. "Here you go, Rem. Just what the doctor ordered."

There was no indication Remington recognized anybody, though he nodded and sipped, sipped again and took in a deep breath, his eyes making an effort to open.

"See there?" Box said. "He's coming out of it. We probably saved him from a killer hangover."

Grumpy left the room several times, dragging kitchen chairs into the bedroom.

The men sat and drank and waited, Gulliver occasionally leaning over to give his brother another sip.

His tumbler half drank, Rem's lips moved.

"What's he saying?" Grumpy asked.

"No words came out," Gully said.

A moment later, Rem spoke. "Lemmeseebee, Swillaby."

"What was that supposed to mean?" Weepy asked.

"I couldn't make it out," said Gulliver.

Rem spoke again. "Wona neez my bo ninner dens my risses."

"He's fucking delusional," Box said.

"He's speaking in tongues," Weepy said.

"I can't understand a word he's saying," said Grumpy.

"Something about Wynona needing his bone in her, against his wishes; that's my guess," Gulliver said.

"You should have been a cryptographer," said Weepy.

"Miz bee mos a ball. Neeseebee in sool. Preez. Prelly preez, Sillybull."

"What'd you come up with there?" Grumpy asked Gulliver.

"Went right by me that time. Too many syllables."

"I think he's begging to see Beatrice," Box said.

"Out of the question," Gulliver said. "Court order won't allow it."

Two sips later, Rem slumped forward, passing out.

"I wouldn't wish sobriety on anybody," Weepy said, "but it might have helped in this case. What do we do now?"

Gulliver and Grumpy moved Remington into a more comfortable position and pulled the sheet over his shoulders.

"Let's head over to the jail," Box said. "Looks like Rem'll be out of it for a while."

"What do you mean we can't see him?" Gulliver asked the man behind the caged window.

"For one thing, visiting hours are over. For another, a new inmate isn't allowed visitors the first twenty-four hours. Come back tomorrow."

"What time are we supposed to come back? And who the hell are you, the Wizard of Oz?"

"*Don't get smart.* Let's see. Swilling, Fritz. Fingerprinted at … okay … mug shots at … let's see … final paperwork … here it is; process completed at 6:30 pm, about an hour ago. One full day means you can't see him tomorrow either. Visiting hours end at five. Come back on Saturday."

"He's going to miss the party," Grumpy noted.

"What's he charged with?" Box asked.

"Let's see. Abuse of public property. Disturbing the peace. Threatening law enforcement officers. Armed assault on commercial vehicles. *Whoa.* This fellow could be here for a spell."

"They set bail yet?"

"Let's see. Yup. Twenty-thousand dollars."

"That's absurd," Box said. "For climbing a fucking bridge?"

"That does seem high. If he can afford a good attorney, I'd suggest he get one. Public defenders aren't too good at getting bail reduced. Come to think of it, they aren't too good at public defending."

Back in the Buick, Grumpy fumbled to put the key in the ignition. Exasperated, he turned to his riders. "This has been one long hellacious day. The only way I can think to end it is at *The Man's Bar*."

His suggestion met everyone's approval and the crew headed back to Essex.

Later, taking a long pull from his first beer of the night, Grumpy slammed his mug on the counter and looked at his companions with conflict in his eyes. "Makes it hard to celebrate, doesn't it? Fritz gets thrown in the slammer. Walter goes under the knife. And Remington may as well blow his brains out, for all they're worth. How did it come to this?"

Grumpy might have asked himself the same question late the following morning when he got a call from Remington that he couldn't begin to understand.

"Okay, Rem, you just hold tight. I'm on my way over there."

Grumpy found his friend staggering around the kitchen. Remington must have gotten some sleep during the night; some of what he said was intelligible.

"You want to go to Bea's school, is that what you're saying?"

Rem leaned over the table, stiffened his arms, and plugged his fists on either side of Walter's typewriter to steady himself. "I gotta see her, Drump. Sheeee'z ebbryting do me."

"I know. I know. You know you're not supposed to do this, right?"

Rem nodded, drool dripping from a corner of his mouth.

"She's at school, you say?"

Rem nodded again, reaching a hand up to wipe away the spit.

"Okay then, let's go."

Forty minutes later, not wishing to call attention to themselves, Grumpy parked the Buick against the curb alongside a chain link fence outside Bea's school. "What do we do, sit here and wait for recess?" Grumpy asked.

"Okay," Rem said.

"You sure you want to do this?" Grumpy asked. "You could end up in a jail cell next to your brother."

"Frississ … Frississ is in … is Frississ in …?"

"That's right. Fritz is in jail."

"Wha' for?"

"It's a long story. You wouldn't remember if I told you."

Rem laid his head back on the seat and was snoring within thirty seconds.

Nearly two hours later, Grumpy shook him. "Wake up. Rem, wake up. I see a thousand kids running out into the playground. Maybe Bea's one of them."

Rem shook his head and rubbed his eyes. "Where are we?"

"We're at your daughter's school. You wanted to come here to see her, even though the divorce papers say you can't."

Rem stared long and hard at the Grump, trying to understand what the man had said. Then he turned his head and looked through the high fence. A minute later, he opened the door, staggered to the fence and yelled. "Honey bee. Honey bee. Daddy's here. Daddy's here."

In the midst of a throng of children running in circles, a little girl stopped and looked toward the fence. Rem continued to yell and wave. Beatrice stepped away from the others. She shielded her eyes from the sun for a better look and saw that her father was calling to her. She waved her arms frantically and ran toward the fence, fell down, got back up, and ran again. *"Daddy. Daddy. Daddy."*

Remington dropped to his knees and pushed his fingers through the fence to touch his daughter's hands. The sight of her made him cry. "Oh Bea, my beautiful Bea, Daddy loves you so much."

"I love you too, Daddy." Bea squeezed his fingers with both hands. "Where have you been, Daddy? You never come home any more."

"Daddy has to work, sweetie. Are you okay?"

"*Uh-huh.* But I miss you all the time. When will your job be done?"

"I don't know, honey bee. Soon, maybe. It'll all be over soon and I'll be with you forever."

Beatrice let go of his fingers and jumped for joy. Then the bell rang.

"I have to back inside, Daddy. Can I see you again later?"

"Maybe, sweetheart. I need to talk to your mother."

"She's mad at you."

"Yes, honey bee, I know."

Bea turned around to see the other kids filing back into school. "I have to go now."

"I know, sweetie. I just wanted to see you for a minute. You make me so happy. I love you, Bea. I love you so much."

"I love you too, Daddy." With that, Bea turned and ran.

Remington clutched the fence, choking back tears. Suddenly, Bea turned around and ran back to him.

"Daddy, daddy. Before I go in, will you make your eyes dance for me? Please? Pretty please?"

Rem smiled. He blinked the stinging salt from his eyes and opened them as wide as he could. It took all of his concentration to make his eyes begin to jiggle. When the pupils began to skip and stutter, Beatrice giggled, jumped up and down, and clapped her hands with joy. "It's magic, Daddy; it's magic."

When he regained his focus, Bea was half way across the playground, the last child to go back into the school. Rem slumped to the ground and wept. Grump reached under his armpits, lifted him up and helped him back into the car. "C'mon Rem, we'd better get out of here before a school official sees us."

Rem sobbed all the way to Walter's apartment.

Grumpy helped him get back into bed. "Think you'll be up for going to Jericho's party later?"

"Bring me some Jack Black," Rem said.

Returning with a fifth, Grumpy asked again.

Rem took a big swallow, wiped the back of a hand across his mouth, and nodded.

"Okay. I'll come by with the boys in about three hours."

No sooner had Grumpy stretched out on his living room sofa in the interest of accumulating energy for the party when the phone rang. He let it ring for a long time in the interest of avoiding any more problems, but whoever was on the other end was winning the battle of patience. Then too, three of his closest friends were in dire straits. If there was any more bad news, he'd hear about it sooner or later anyway.

"This is Grumpy."

"I've got some good news on two fronts." It was Gulliver calling.

"Great. It's been nothing but bad news since the weathervane. Shoot."

"First, I called the hospital and they patched me right through to Walter's room. Unlike one lazy bastard I know, he picked up the phone on the second ring."

"How'd he sound?"

"Like the old Walter."

"Doesn't sound like much of an improvement."

"He told me he feels like a million bucks. Says he wouldn't miss the party for anything in the world."

"Think they'll let him out so soon after they opened him up?"

"That brings me to the second front. Fritz called from the correctional center."

"Don't call it that. It's a fucking jailhouse."

"I'll say this, Grump; you've got the best nickname of anybody I know."

"What'd he have to say?"

"Marsha's putting up bail. Her bank confirmed that a money wire was sent for the full amount."

"She's got that kind of money?"

"Apparently, her folks are loaded. *Filthy rich*, according to Fritz. Her father's a big shot lawyer and her mother's on the board of a Wall Street investment bank. Fritz says if he can bend her ear he might be able to put the capital squeeze on Kellogg or Sara Lee."

"You'd think he'd learn."

"He's fanatical Grump, you know that. Always was, always will be."

"Go back to Walter."

"Right. Fritz has no idea how long it'll take to process out of jail, so he doesn't want us to wait for him. He says Marsha is emotionally sapped from everything that's happened, to include resigning from the paper this morning. She doesn't want to drive all the way to Burlington just to turn around and rush back to make Jericho's party. So she sent extra money for Fritz to rent a car."

"What's all that got to do with Walter getting out of the hospital right after surgery?"

"Fritz is going to drive over there and sneak him out."

"What if Walter's feeling great because his brain is saturated with morphine? For all we know, leaving the hospital could be the worst thing for him."

"Walter's psyched about the celebration. He says Fritz can take the IV bottle off the stand and Walter can tuck it under his arm like a football. They'll tell the nurses they're going for a walk, then jump into a warm car that Fritz'll have waiting near the front door. After the party, Walter can ride back with us. We'll drop him off at the hospital and he can apologize for taking such a long walk."

"Why can't Fritz bring him back?"

"He's hoping Marsha will take him with her when she goes home."

"The whole thing sounds harebrained to me. I don't like it."

"Seems plausible enough to me. Ten to one Fritz walks into Jericho's house with that ghastly ghost hanging all over him."

"Those sound like good odds. Let me think about it."

"What's the verdict on Rem? Are we taking him with us?"

"I told him we would. I was with him earlier. We drove out to Bea's school."

"He was coherent?"

"Barely."

"Did he get to see Bea?"

"Yup. She was overjoyed. Saddest thing you ever saw."

"I'm confused."

"Bea was thrilled as all get-out to see her dad. Went nuts when he did his rapid eye movement for her. But Rem was broke up over it. Cried like a baby all the way back to Walter's place. Hard to believe Sibyl is doing this to him. I know how much he loves his cock, but he needs to realize how it's come between them."

"The way I see it, the whole thing was up in the air until he succumbed to Wynona. That's what clinched it."

"It's all about his bets on the birds, Gully. Rem's no angel – same goes for the rest of us – but he's lost a small fortune at those cock fights. Twice now Sibyl has had to take out equity loans on the house to pay off his gambling debts."

"Who knows, Grump? Maybe the drastic action Sibyl has taken will convince Rem it's high time he put his cock down."

"If it doesn't put him over the edge first."

When Fritz walked into Walter's room, two doctors, three nurses, and a Catholic priest were hovering over the albino's bed.

"What the hell's going on?" Fritz asked, his stomach diving.

One of the doctor's came over to him. "I'm afraid you can't be in here."

"Why not? What's happening?"

"Are you next of kin?"

Fritz hated lying. It wasn't easy to do at the police station and it wasn't any easier here. He peered over the doctor's shoulder, swallowing hard when he saw Water's resting eyes and ashen face. His mind fired a flurry of synapses reenacting one particular night when he broke a beer bottle over Gulliver's head. Shattered glass flew in all directions. Blood streamed down

Gully's face. Others were injured too. Jericho had been thrilled to extract shards from his bleeding cheek. Walter was horrified to see blood trickling from his shoulder. Fritz's forearm was deeply cut. He could picture the albino shrieking in protest when he rubbed his bloody arm onto Walter's open wound. *"Stop that, Fritz. I have no interest in being your blood brother."*

"Yes. Yes I am," said Fritz. "I'm his brother."

The doctor looked down at the paperwork on his clipboard. "Says here Mr. Birdsong has a mother living with a sister in Arizona. We're trying to get through to them now. There's no mention of any other immediate family member."

"How can that be? We're … we're *brothers*. Honest."

The doctor stared into Fritz's sleet gray eyes. Neither pair would give the other the satisfaction of blinking.

The doctor looked again at his papers. "We have a phone number for his mother and another number for someone in Washington County, a Mister Jericho Laramie."

"I'm not surprised. He'd want Jericho to know if … if … the worst should …" Fritz swallowed hard. "Can I ask a question, doc?"

"Sure."

"What's the priest doing here?" Fritz asked.

"According to his records, Mr. Birdsong was raised Catholic."

"He's not a religious man. That's something his brother would know."

"I see. Consider, however, that a man on his death bed might do a little soul searching; perhaps experience a change of heart."

Fritz grabbed the doctor's shoulders and shook them. "Did you say *death bed*?"

"Oh my God, I'm sorry. During your brother's surgery, we were initially quite pleased that the holes and tears in his stomach from a number of rather nasty ulcers seemed to be on the mend, so to speak. Then we discovered a serious complication."

"Life threatening?"

"Oh my God, I should say. Do you know anything about diverticulitis?"

"Not much. A problem in the intestines?"

"Many of us get it as we grow old. We seldom see it in a man of Mister Birdsong's age. His diet, certainly, was a mitigating factor."

Fritz grabbed the doctor's shoulders again. "Just tell me what the hell went wrong!"

The doctor shrugged Fritz's hands from his shoulders. "I'm trying to be courteous. Please show some courtesy in return, if it's not too much to ask."

"I'm sorry, doc. You said Walter – my brother – is on his death bed. Look, I didn't come here in the best condition myself. The last twenty-four hours have not been easy for me."

"Fine. Let me explain. When the walls of the intestines become weak they can fissure. A pouch – it's called a diverticulum – is created. Sometimes, especially if there are many diverticula, an infection can develop. Perforations can occur. When a blood vessel in a pouch bursts, there's bleeding. If the infection spreads into the abdominal cavity, we have a condition called peritonitis, which can often be – and in this case certainly is – *fatal*."

"Walter's going to die?"

"I'm sorry. We've done everything possible to stop the bleeding. We failed. It's just a matter of time now"

Fritz's face stopped. He felt a wave of nausea sweep over him. His knees buckled.

The doctor glanced over his shoulder. *"Some help here?"*

A nurse quickly positioned a visitor's chair behind Fritz. He collapsed onto it. He looked up at the doctor. "How much time?"

"We can't say. Could be minutes. Could be hours. Certainly not more than a few hours."

"I need to talk to him."

The doctor walked over to Walter's bed, briefly discussed Fritz's request with the other doctor, then walked back. "Okay. We don't see what harm it can cause. There's nothing more we can do other than monitor his vital signs. That can be done from the nurse's station."

"Thanks, doctor."

"I think it would be wise if Father Howell spent a few minutes with him first; then you can have whatever time is left."

"Walter should be the one to say whether or not he wants to be given last rites. Is he able to speak?"

"Remarkably, yes. I must say, morphine truly is a wondrous substance, albeit illegal."

"Does he know there's a priest here?"

"I'm not sure."

"Let me talk to him first, doc. I'll tell him about the priest."

Again, the icy eyes were compelling. The doctor had a quick word with the others and they left the room.

Father Howell positioned a chair outside the door, sat down, smoothed his vestments, placed a black book on his lap, and folded his hands over it. He swiveled and looked into the room. "The message from our heavenly Father is not lengthy, but it is important. I'll sit here till I'm wanted. Don't wait too long."

Fritz stood up, stared at his emaciated friend, moved his chair to the bedside, sat on the edge of it, and stroked the albino's arm. "Can you hear me, Walter? It's Fritz."

Walter nodded. One of his eyes partially opened.

"Can you talk?"

"I think so," Walter said.

The response brought a smile to Fritz's funereal face. "Do you know where you are?"

Walter nodded. He reached for Fritz's hand and squeezed it with weak fingers. "I'm dying."

Fritz dropped his head. He looked up, tears welling, and put his other hand over Walter's bony fingers. "We all are, Walter. We all are."

Walter did not respond.

"Is there anything I can get you?"

The albino's words came slow. "You're here, Fritz. That's good enough."

Not one to cry, tears trickled into his beard. He swallowed, unable to speak.

"Is the party tonight?" Walter asked.

"Yes. Yes it is."

"Guess I'll miss it."

Fritz dropped his head again. He removed his hand from Walter's to rub the tears from his eyes.

"Say hi to everyone for me."

"I will, Walter. You know I will."

"We did a good job … on the horse barn."

Fritz smiled. "We sure as hell did. We'll remember it for a very long …" Fritz swallowed the last word, upset with himself.

Walter closed the eye. His gray-white tongue traced his top lip.

"Can I get you some water, old buddy?"

Walter moved his head slowly, indicating no.

Moments passed. Walter's fingers were losing their grip. Fritz leaned toward his face. He could hear faint raspy breathing. "Are you sure I can't get you something?"

Walter's eye half opened. "Did I see a priest … or was that … my imagination?"

"You must've told them you were Catholic. You know how Catholics are; they like having priests around."

"He wants to give me … last rites, Fritzie. Or why … why would he be here?"

"Should I tell him to leave?"

"No. I might want to find out … what it's all about."

"It's a celebration of the promise Jesus made, that we will have abundant life."

Walter seemed to gain a modicum of strength by these words. "But I haven't had an abundant life. I won't even make it … to the celebration."

"I got into the Bible pretty deep once upon a time, Walter. If I remember right, it was James who said, 'The prayer of faith will save the sick person'."

The end of Walter's tongue peeked through his cracked lips, then retreated. "If you say so."

"The priest will anoint your palms and your forehead with some kind of oil. It's a sign of Christ's healing presence."

Walter was getting weaker by the minute. "Worth … a shot, I suppose," he said, his voice fading.

Moments passed. Fritz didn't know what to say next.

Walter's dry lips trembled. "I thought … I thought I'd be afraid … to die. I'm not though. Not really."

Fritz admired Walter's courage but the words tumbled in his stomach and wouldn't stop falling.

"I've had a good life, Fritz. The best ... friends ... a man could ask for. I don't think I did anything wrong ... you know ... to piss off the gods."

"No. No you didn't, Walter. If there's a heaven ..."

"You think there is one?"

"I don't know, Walter."

"I hope not."

"Why's that?"

"Sounds boring. Clouds. Harps. Fat little angels ... flying around."

"But if there's a God, you'll get to see him."

"Maybe. I'll bet the priest ... will ask ... if I believe Jesus Christ ... is my Savior."

"Do you?"

"How should I know? I like the guy ... and everything. He reminds me of us. Always breaking the rules."

"Yeah, you've got a point there."

"He was a carpenter, you know."

"That's what they say."

"I wonder if he ever built a horse barn."

"Or a camel barn," Fritz said.

A smile tugged at the corners of Walter's parched mouth.

Long moments passed. There was almost no strength in Walter's fingers. The rasp in his breath was barely audible.

"Can I get you anything?"

There was no response. Walter's heart rate, according to the monitor, was 36. Twenty minutes earlier, it had been 44.

"Want me to send the priest in?"

Moments passed. Again, no response. Fritz choked on his grief. Through a haze of tears, it looked like Walter was trying to muster one final erg of energy to nod his head.

Another moment passed. Fritz released Walter's hand and stood, pushing the chair away with the back of his legs. *Don't wait too long*, he said to himself. Don't wait too ...

With the stealth of a spirit, Father Howell was standing next to him, opening his black book over the albino's motionless body.

Fritz placed his hand lightly on Walter's forehead. It was pasty and cool. He thought he detected an eye trying to open but he couldn't be sure. Suddenly, the pounding in Fritz's chest was calmed by solemn resolve. The bedraggled iconoclast leaned over his dying friend, the palm of his hand pressed more firmly to his forehead. His voice, gentle but strident, seemed to lord over the priest's low chant. "I have to go to the celebration at Jericho's now, Walter. I guess, for you, the fun is over. But we had a glorious time. The horse barn stands as a symbol of our irreverence. We not only built it right, we built it righteous."

Fritz lifted his hand, lingered for a moment above his friend's floury face, then slowly stepped away. At the door, he turned for one last look. Were Walter's eyes partly opened? The priest was dipping his fingers into a small bowl.

Thirty-Three

After his body and mind shut down without warning in the late afternoon, Remington groped for a sense of presence, propping himself up between Grumpy and Box Car. A fifth of bourbon, two-thirds full, jostled and sloshed between his legs. His consciousness flagged. His head fell, then snapped back. He looked left to find the Grump, right for the Box. Seeing them both was oddly reassuring.

Gulliver was glum in the back seat. It was satisfying to have finished the horse barn, but ever since the placement of the weathervane everything had become directionless. At the moment, he was in no mood for a celebration.

Weepy sat in Fritz's customary position against the other door plucking his acoustic, humming a haunting tune.

"I know that song," Gully said. "What is it?"

"If you know it, you don't need to ask."

"Don't play games with me; I'm not in the best of spirits. Any second now I might slide my ass over there, wrap you in a vicious headlock, and start pounding away with unmerciful rage."

Weepy tapped gently on his guitar, as one would burp a baby. "I'd rather you not." He strummed a few solemn chords, then stopped to sniffle, his head on his chest.

"What're you crying about now?" Gulliver asked.

"I can't help it. All I can picture is that diaphanous disaster in the hospital room; how fragile he looked. How pitiful."

Remington craned his neck. The garble of his speech seemed to be clearing up. "Sing it, Weefy. I wannoo hear it."

Weepy hoisted his heavy head and wiped the tears from his face. His voice was mournful as it rose and fell:

We skipped the light fandango
Turned cartwheels cross the floor
I was feeling kind of seasick
But the crowd called out for more
The room was humming harder
As the ceiling flew away
When we called out for another drink
The waiter brought a tray

And so it was that later
As the doctor told his tale
That his face, at first just ghostly,
Turned a whiter shade of pale

Even Box Car, not one to choke up, stared out the window, his anxious hand a squeegee running through his beard.

"You sure we got enough to drink, Deirdre?"

"That's your department. I'm in charge of the food."

"I'm not sure about the others, but those dog soldiers can put it away."

"I don't care if they can eat a horse, we won't be running out of food."

"I'm not talking about food. I'd be surprised if any of them ate. I'm concerned about running out of booze."

"That's insane. You bought three bottles each of every spirit there is, plus ten cases of beer. We're expecting seventeen or eighteen people, not a hundred."

"Maybe. But I won't be happy until everybody's dead drunk and passed out cold."

"Aren't you the perfect host!"

Pierre and his wife Lorraine were the first to pull into the driveway. It was already dark at six o'clock. Jericho walked into their headlights, directing them to a specific spot on the lawn. "No, no, no," he shouted. "Park that stupid beetle over here, you dumb Frenchman. I've got seven or eight vehicles to park tonight. Don't clog up the goddamn driveway."

"Your friend seems a little edgy," Lorraine said when she and Pierre stepped out of the car.

"You should try working with him. When he's not slicing you to ribbons with knifing comments, he's threatening to shoot you in the head. This is as calm as I've seen him."

In the house, the foursome said their hellos; Deirdre hugging Lorraine, Jericho giving Pierre a friendly punch to the ribs. No sooner had the Frenchman dipped a corn chip into a bowl of salsa when Rudy drove in with his wife, Melanie.

Jericho ran out to the yard, instructing the general contractor to park his truck next to Pierre's bug.

"I was hoping you wouldn't be able to find the place," Jericho said as a welcoming gesture. "But since you did, step right in and pop yourselves a couple of cold ones."

"Your friend is rude," Melanie said to her husband during the brief walk to the house.

"You should try dealing with him over the phone. I'd rather take a stroll through a minefield. What you heard was his sweet side."

"Make yourselves t'home" Deirdre said to the new arrivals. "The table's full of food; everything from Swedish meatballs to porcupine balls, cheese balls to melon balls. We've got French bread with hot cheddar fondue, a pork roast, racks of lamb, bacon-wrapped scallops, a kettle full of corn, and two skillets of fried smelt. Over at the other end you'll find relish trays, six different salads, and four platters of breads: raisin, zucchini, banana, and pumpkin. There're five different chips for seven different dips. We've got three trays heaped with cold cuts, two platters of raw veggies, and a mountain of sliced turkey. And that's before I bring out all the desserts."

"Pay no attention to her," Jericho said. "The kitchen counter's got more booze on it than any bar you've ever been in. Half a dozen coolers on the floor are full of beer and I got more in the basement. Nothing ruins a good drunk like food."

Pierre nibbled his chip apologetically. He wasn't much of a drinker, but he had a big appetite and he'd skipped dinner to make sure he and his wife made it to the party on time. He hadn't seen this much food since three churches in Randolph combined parishes one Saturday for a nickel-a-dip supper that featured eighty dishes on twelve long tables. Before it was over, he'd spent almost ten bucks and swore he'd never take another bite of macaroni salad the rest of his life.

"I don't see any boudin," Lorraine whispered to him.

"I don't either, but that's about the only thing missing. Just to make Jericho happy, I'm going to pour myself a scotch and soda. You want anything to drink?"

"Since when are you a scotch and soda drinker?"

"It's all I can think of. Maybe I'll like it."

"Suit yourself. Get me a tall glass of bourbon, no ice."

Roger and Mabel showed up at six-thirty, pulling in a few minutes ahead of Marsha.

The parking lot attendant was doing a fine job lining up vehicles in a semi-circle on one side of the lawn. "Hey Roger," he shouted. "Whatever the women want to do is fine with me, but as far as the men are concerned, *yard pissing* is in effect."

"I can't use the bathroom?" Roger asked, sliding out of the Lincoln.

"No. The house is fed by a natural spring handed down by my ancestors going all the way back to when we grabbed this land from the Indians. It's down to a trickle this time of year. When you go in make sure you tell Rudy and Pierre; it'll save me from having to make an announcement."

Roger stroked his gallant nose with an apprehensive smirk, but he was all smiles when he walked by the gunslinger. "We've got great news."

"Good for you, Rammaham. I don't want to hear it. Hey Mabel, I didn't mean to exclude you. If you're wearing a dress under that coat with no skivvies, feel free to parade your ass out here anytime you feel the urge. This lawn's the size of a small pasture. Pick out a good spot, spread 'em wide, and let it flow."

Mabel lowered a Marilyn Monroe wink of her right eye at the gracious host, leaning toward him with the headline, *"I missed my period."*

Jericho's mind locked up, a congratulatory remark out of the question.

His first thought was, *hear the news*, dog soldiers; you've got yourselves a great sorrowful mystery. Beside himself with evil joy, he relished the distressed confusion this was sure to bring.

When Marsha stepped out of her car alone, Jericho's mind unlocked. "What's the deal? I thought you were coming with Fritz. Is he out of jail or not?"

"He is but he wanted to stop at the hospital and see the albino. The last I talked with Fritz he was hatching some crazy scheme to sneak Walter out so he won't miss the party."

"Makes sense. Walter can tuck his IV solution under his arm like a football and jump in a warm car with it still hooked up. Only problem is, Fritz doesn't have a car. Must be he and Walter are riding with the Grump."

"Fritz rented a car."

"Big mistake. *Oh, be big ... Whoa.* Fritz can't drive for shit. Walter's in grave danger."

"Too late now. They're probably on their way."

"I'd be surprised if they make it. More'n likely they'll be wrapped around a tree before they hit Waterbury. Go ahead inside and drink up."

Jericho paced around the yard. So who in the world is it, he asked himself. Grumpy? Weepy? Roger? Wouldn't surprise me if Gulliver got into the act, knowing him. Not the Box, though. Who'd risk offspring with the *Missing Link*?

Jericho saw three sets of headlights snaking up the dirt road toward the house. It looked like a small motorcade, the cars moving at a snail's pace, bumper to bumper. Not surprisingly, they were state vehicles.

What the fuck's the story here, he wondered. Here we are celebrating the completion of the horse barn, the greatest construction project since Noah's fucking ark, and the crew responsible for all the bulling and jamming, the men I recruited, aren't even here. What if they don't show up, the bastards? Be just like 'em.

"No, no, no, over here, you dumb sonuvabitch," the mad attendant barked. "You – *no you* – park right next to that one. What is it with you people? You're acting like the three blind mice." Jericho waved his arms frantically. "Can't you get organized, for chrissakes? Pull in here. No, no, no. *Over here*."

"Sorry if we screwed things up," one of the owners said after closing his car door. "We're used to having our own parking spaces. We know right where they are, down at the capital."

"Does this look like the capital to you? All you had to do was follow my directions."

"I'm sure that's true, but we're not used to following directions. We're used to giving them."

"Yeah, yeah, yeah. You're a bunch of big shots. *Oh, please* ... Listen, the last time I had a big-ass party here – *please be big for me* – it was like a demolition derby; everybody hauling ass at the same time, drunker'n loons. I want everybody on one side of the lawn facing the same way. You'll be less likely to run into each other once you're too drunk to drive. Besides that, I'm running out of room. I'm expecting another car; two, if a miracle happens."

The owners shook Jericho's hand with great exuberance and walked toward the house.

"Hold up a sec," Jericho called after them. "I invite you to do anything you feel like doing tonight – in fact, the worse your behavior the better – but I do have one rule. *Yard pissing* is in effect. Except for you," he added, pointing to the female owner. "You can use the bathroom."

"Thanks," she said.

"One more thing. Pay no attention to all that food my wife's got set out. Head straight for the booze on the kitchen counter. Drink righteous and don't stop till it's hell to pay trying to find your way home."

Jericho had placed a cooler outside just for himself. Grabbing a beer, he resumed his pacing. It must've been Grumpy, he was thinking. He's the one who had the most shots at it. Be better if it was Weepy, though. Good lord, how he'd bellow then. 'Course, Gulliver ain't a bad bet either, that sly devil. And what if it is Roger? It would serve him right. He was an underhanded watch dog right up until the end.

No sooner had Jericho given up hope when the Buick barreled onto the lawn, skidded to a sideways stop, then backed smartly into one of the last remaining parking places.

Jericho crushed his empty can of beer and tossed it in the air behind him. "Now that's how it's done, goddamnit. What took you boys so long?"

"We had to pull over a bunch of times for Weepy to puke," Box explained.

"He's drunk already?"

"No. He's worried sick about the albino."

"Fritz has probably spirited Walter out of the hospital by now," Jericho said. "It'll be a godsend if they make it though, what with Fritz driving. But we won't let that stop us from getting this little hootenanny off the ground."

Pierre was sitting in a chair near the door sipping his second scotch and soda and rifling bacon-wrapped scallops into his mouth like raisinettes when the crew walked into the house.

Each man grabbed a scallop from the Frenchman's plate, walking past without acknowledging him.

Box surveyed the expansive table of food.

Gulliver waved to his adoring fans in the adjoining room, then mixed himself a rusty nail at the kitchen counter.

Grumpy poured a rum and coke before dragging a kitchen chair and Weepy's amp into the living room, trying to get on the entertainer's good side in case he took requests.

By the time everyone made sure they all knew each other, Marsha having to remember more names than anyone else, Weepy was plugged in and ready to sing. "Does anyone have a song they'd like to hear?" he asked the crowd.

"You're taking requests?" Grumpy asked.

"Not from you," Weepy said.

Jericho, a devout Stones fan, shouted in from the kitchen, "How about a little *Sympathy for the Devil*?"

Eager to get his mind out of Walter's hospital room, Weepy gave his guitar a final tuning, cranked his amp, and sang with the kind of passion that only agony conveys.

Please allow me to introduce myself
I'm a man of wealth and taste
I've been around for a long, long year
Stole many a man's soul and faith
And I was round when Jesus Christ
Had his moment of doubt and pain
Made damn sure that Pilate
Washed his hands and sealed his fate
Pleased to meet you
Hope you guess my name
But what's puzzling you
Is the nature of my game

Much to Grumpy's infamous chagrin, Weepy continued to take requests. Deirdre asked for Cocker's version of Cohen's *Bird on a Wire* and she got it. The female owner wanted *Norwegian Wood* and Weepy sang it for her. Gulliver requested Dylan's *Like a Rolling Stone* and the request was honored. Box had to have The Trogg's *Wild Thing*, and that's what he got. Mabel wanted to hear another Dylan number, *It Takes a Lot to Laugh, It Takes a Train to Cry*, and that's what she heard. Lorraine asked for *Hang on Sloopy* by the McCoys and Weepy reluctantly complied. But when Grumpy wanted Satchmo, Weepy balked.

Jericho had to be forceful, steering each man other than dog soldiers, who knew the rule, away from the bathroom and out to the lawn. After two hours of heavy drinking, all of the men were in compliance.

Jericho kept his beer outside in the cooler. He wanted to keep an eye out for Fritz and Walter. Reaching for another, he noticed Marsha standing by her car. He walked over to her. "You never know with Fritz. Sometimes he comes through when you least expect it."

"What if he got caught trying to leave the hospital with Walter and they took him right back to jail."

"Nah. He'd be allowed one phone call and this is where he'd call. Deirdre never fails to hear the phone ring. If Fritz had phoned she'd have said something. My guess is it's taking longer than he thought to get the albino out of there. Come on back in and drink. It'll do you good."

"I'm already tipsy from three drinks."

"You've only had too much to drink when you don't know you've had too much to drink."

At the front door, Marsha walked in when Grumpy was walking out.

"Time to drain the lizard?" Jericho asked.

"What's it to you?"

"I've got a little something you may want to hear."

Grumpy walked to the far corner of the house. "I'm listening."

"Mabel's pregnant."

"How the hell would you know?"

"Missed her period. She told me when she first got here. I happen to believe you're the father."

"First of all, just because she's late with her period doesn't mean she's pregnant. Second, I'm not the only suspect."

"Yeah, but you have to be at the top of the list."

"No way."

"Why not? You shooting blanks?"

"Must be. I've been with lots of loose women over the years. I'm as careless as they come but I've never knocked anybody up."

"Over the years? You may look like you've been around for half a century, but you're nineteen."

"I don't take any precautions and nobody's gotten pregnant; must be I'm sterile."

"Horse shit. You've been lucky, till now."

Grumpy zipped up. "That's my story and it's as good as anybody's."

Jericho howled. "You're worried about it aren't you?"

"Of course I'm worried about it, you dumb shit. I may or may not be at the top of the list, but I'm damn sure on it."

"Just as long as you're a nervous wreck, that's all I care about."

"You're a sick puppy, Laramie."

"Thanks. Let's go in and get Weepy to play some more Stones."

"I want to hear Louie Armstrong."

"You might be nineteen, Grumpy, but you're the oldest man I know."

"That's right. I'm so old I'm impotent."

"Nobody's buying that either."

Inside the house, Weepy had just gone on break.

"I wanted something from *Sticky Fingers*," Jericho told him.

"I need a breather," Weepy said. "I'd like to walk around; talk to people."

"Hold up a sec. I'm outside this whole time worrying my ass off about Fritz and Walter – they're three hours late – and just when I decide to come in and make one simple goddamn request, you put down the guitar to get up and mingle? You're a horse's ass, O'Toole."

"You get to see a lot of things when you sit where I sit. I want to find out what they're all about."

"Like what?"

"Like one of the owners, a lady of some refinement I might suggest, reaching inside Box's shirt a few minutes ago to rub his hairy chest. Like Remington, sloshed to the gills, telling Lorraine and Melanie about his prize cock. Like Mabel dancing only to slow songs. Why isn't she wearing her muumuu?"

"You think those are good enough reasons to take a break?"

"I'd also like to get a drink; go outside and toke up."

"You want to drink?"

"Yeah."

"Forget I said anything. Get your ass in the kitchen and pour yourself a stiff one. I'll meet you outside for a couple of hits."

A few minutes later, one of the owners went to Weepy's microphone and gave it a couple of thuds. "Excuse me. Excuse me please."

It took several minutes for the room to quiet down, with the exception of Remington who kept babbling to no one in particular.

"Ladies and gentlemen, I have an announcement to make."

Jericho and Weepy were outside abiding by house rules, passing a joint back and forth with their free hands. "One of the owners is in there shooting his mouth off about something," Jericho said. "You want to go back in and listen to him?"

"No. While everybody else has been drinking, I've been working. I'd like to see if I can't catch up in the next half hour. This killer weed oughta help."

Remington noticed that his audience of two had turned its attention elsewhere. His mind found Beatrice; the image of them together at the park making him happy, the sight of her on the other side of the school fence making him distraught. His head fell into his hands and he wept.

The announcement was beginning. "We, the owners of the horse barn, would like to extend our heartfelt gratitude to all those who made it possible. Our inspections surpassed our expectations. The final product is, without question, outstanding; the finest structure of its kind in the entire state of Vermont."

A round of applause filled the room.

"I don't know where in the world Rudy found such a wonderful crew to build our barn. These tireless laborers, with their foreman, Pierre Toussenant, performed, in our opinion, courageously and without complaint even when nasty weather the past month or so made things extremely difficult. The horse barn is truly a thing of beauty.

"But it's more than that. The horse barn is, in a word, *ideal*; a symbol of uncommon effort and accomplishment, of striving and achievement, of valor and rectitude. Our horse barn, today and for the ages, stands as a monument to harmony in the workplace, a shrine to the ideals of selfless dedication and noble purpose. It is, by any measure, an erection we can all be proud of."

Again, a rousing applause ensued, though it was somewhat spattering since Grumpy, Gulliver, and Box, having quickly tired of the speech, were in the kitchen mixing drinks.

"*Ah-hem.* Now then, I would like to announce that on Monday morning, we, the owners, will be sending a letter to the National Builders Association nominating Rudyard Appling as our candidate for the prestigious award of Vermont's *Builder of the Year*."

Those remaining in the room shook Rudy's hand. Rem, sitting on the floor between two chairs, sniffled and wept. "Oh, look at him!" Melanie said to Lorraine. “He really is overwhelmed by all this.”

Fritz, at long last, paid his tab and climbed down from the stool. He had stopped at a bar on the outskirts of Montpelier, unable to face the group at Jericho’s in a state of sobriety. It took three shots of tequila and seven beers for him to feel up to the task. Back in the rental car, he turned the ignition, made sure the heater and the radio were still off, gripped the steering wheel with determined hands, and asked himself an important question: can I remember the way to Jericho’s?

An hour after the owners’ announcement, despite large dents made in the cornucopia of food, dangerous levels of alcohol consumption took charge.

Asking everybody to come into the living room, Rudy went to the microphone and announced that the horse barn crew would be getting bonuses for finishing their quality work ahead of schedule. He’d expected to pay out the equivalent of two weeks base salary. However, Roger had not cashed any of his checks since double-dipping would have been unethical. Rather than book the booty to profits, Rudy was using these unexpected funds to boost the bonuses. With that, he handed out checks, giving Fritz’s and Walter’s to Jericho for later distribution. The dog soldiers applauded Rudy’s generosity. Gulliver leaned toward the Box to confide that he planned to spend his bonus on an African safari.

Moments later, Weepy again took requests. Upon finding out that the middle name of one of the owners was Louis; Weepy honored the man’s request for *Hello Dolly*. Grumpy sang along with jaded delight.

Mabel began dancing to the faster songs, joined in the center of the room by Roger, Deirdre, Melanie, and Lorraine. Rudy huddled in a corner with the two male owners, debating prayer in school. Marsha sat flush-cheeked on the couch, woozy from her fifth drink, worrying about Fritz. Pierre sat in a comfy chair drinking his seventh scotch and soda, trying to console Remington. The female owner was stalking Box Car all over the house, even accompanying him outside when it came time for him to obey Jericho’s golden rule. Gulliver and Grumpy stood on either side of the kitchen counter pounding libations and discussing the sorrowful mystery. Jericho darted from his bedroom to the kitchen table where he had removed many of the dishes, replacing them with a grand assortment of his prized weaponry.

Remington had become inconsolable. He was guilty of infidelity. His wife was divorcing him. He could see his daughter only at the risk of being arrested. Now that the horse barn was finished he had no source of income. Unbeknownst to Sibyl, he had gotten threatening phone calls about his mounting gambling debts in the weeks preceding the Wynona incident. And his cock had been all but beaten to death the last time out. His world had almost completely disintegrated.

“Cheer up,” Pierre told him. “You still have your friends.”

"They can't bring my little honey bee to me. They can't pay off my debts. And they can't make Wynona go away. I need to talk to Walter. He'll understand. He knows all about misery. He's been living with it all his life. Walter is the only one I can turn to. I love that man, Pierre. Do you hear me? I love that man."

"I know. Would you like a drink? I'm going to try and find the kitchen for another refill."

Remington held up his fifth to the light. "I got almost half a bottle left."

Pierre left the room and Remington crawled on all fours over to Weepy, somehow making it across the room without spilling a drop.

"Is there something I can play to make you feel better?" Weepy asked.

"Beatles. White Album. Lennon. *Happiness is a Warm Gun*."

In the kitchen, Jericho held a pistol to Grumpy's head. "I'd like to ask you to come over to the table and admire my guns." He waved the pistol at Gulliver. "You too."

Winchesters, Remingtons, and Colts – more than a dozen rifles and pistols – were laid out next to the fondue pot, the relish trays, and the cold meats. "What do you gentlemen have to say about these beauties?" Jericho asked.

"I'd say they sure are beautiful," Gulliver said.

"Me too," said the Grump.

"That's all fine and dandy, but I want you boys to pick out the one you like the most. Then we'll go outside and do some shooting."

Remington beat the floor with his bottle while Weepy sang:

> *... I feel my finger on your trigger*
> *I know no one can do me no harm*
> *Because happiness is a warm gun*
> *Yes it is.*

While Gully and the Grump admired the guns and considered their selection, the door opened. Fritz staggered in. Marsha walked into the house behind him, her cheeks drained of their flush by Fritz's news.

"Where the hell have you been?" Jericho asked. "And if it's not too much to ask, where's the goddamn albino?"

"I'm afraid I've got some bad news."

"I'm sure of it. Simple as the job was, you couldn't figure a way to sneak him out."

"That ain't it."

"You had an accident somewhere along the way and Walter ended up in some other hospital."

"Will you let me talk?" Fritz shouted.

"As long as I'm holding a gun and you're not, seems to me I'm the one deciding who does the talking around here."

"Walter isn't going to make it."

"What the hell does that mean?" Grumpy asked.

"Expiration. The final demise. Grim Reaper. Total cessation. The black horse. Complete biological necrosis. Knocking on heaven's door. What I'm trying to tell you is that everybody's favorite ghost is exactly that."

Remington heard Fritz's voice at the end of *Happiness*. He reeled and lurched his way into the kitchen. "What'd I hear you say about Walter?"

"He took a turn for the worse," Fritz said. "The doctor told me Walter's intestines looked like a colander, leaking blood all over inside. He said they couldn't do anything about it, that it was just a matter of time."

Rem stumbled over to Fritz and shook his brother's shoulders with frantic urgency. "*Tell me he's still alive.* Tell me Walter isn't dead, for chrissakes."

Weepy caught part of the discussion and entered the room to hear more.

"By now, I don't know," Fritz said. "But I'd say the situation is all but hopeless."

Weepy swooned, grabbing the kitchen counter for balance. "Walter's dying?"

Fritz looked at his friends, at Marsha beside him, at Deirdre standing in the doorway to the living room, at Pierre's face pasted to the dim light behind her. "When I left the hospital a priest was at his bedside reading him the last rites."

"Should I call the hospital?" Deirdre asked.

"I gave them the number here," Fritz said. "When it's over, they'll call. Must be Walter's hanging on longer than expected."

The news hit Remington and Weepy hardest. Rem collapsed in a kitchen chair, the last of his disintegrating world shattering into sharp shards inside his head. Weepy stumbled over to him, knelt by his side, and wailed in agony.

Fritz and Marsha turned to walk back outside. Box and the female owner were frozen on the other side of the doorway. Deirdre relayed the news to those in the living room. Jericho placed his pistol on the table and joined Gulliver and Grumpy at the kitchen counter. Drinks were poured.

An hour later the death vigil continued. The horse barn celebrants, despondent or sympathetic, drank with unremitting abandon. Gulliver pleaded with Weepy to pull himself together enough to go back into the living room and play. "C'mon, O'Toole. It'll change the mood. At least until the call comes."

In the other room, Rudy and two of the owners were discussing various social ills. Pierre sat like a morose Buddha on the couch, Lorraine encouraging him to take the last swallow of his eighth scotch and soda. Roger sat in the comfy chair with Mabel on his lap, her legs bared to the moon and dangling with racy grace over the arm of the chair, her hand caressing his nose with long loving strokes, her eyes a blue million miles.

Outside, Box Car and his refined lady groped each other in the front seat of her car. Items of clothing were flung toward the back seat. Box was a bit uncomfortable with this captivating divergence from Walter's plight, but he relented. He feigned kissing, which freed him to emit beastly groans while she tugged at the fur on his shoulders, ran her fingers through the thicket on his chest, and stroked the shag carpet that covered his navel.

Three cars away, Marsha was trying to take Fritz's mind off his friend's imminent departure. They kissed tentatively and engaged in tender petting, the way young lovers do when every touch is a nervous exploration of uncharted territory.

In the kitchen, Remington sat at the ravaged buffet table absently scanning the array of gleaming weapons, his tortured mind trying to cope with the burden of what he knew.

Gulliver, Grumpy, and Jericho belted drinks as if it was last call, numbing their sensitivities to the inevitable.

Weepy sang the blues.

Roger, a man of unusual strength, climbed out of the chair, the equine goddess limp in his arms. With no one's apparent notice, he carried her outside to the privacy of his cavernous Continental.

Deirdre, positioned by the phone, left for the kitchen when Melanie joined Rudy in a benign argument with the owners over the separation of church and state.

"Jericho," Deirdre shouted toward the counter. "What's with all the guns?"

"Before Fritz got here we were on our way outside for a little target practice."

"Are these guns loaded?"

"Some are. Some aren't. I happen to know which ones, but I'm not about to tell you."

"You should put these things away before somebody gets hurt," she said, stalking back into the living room to sit near the phone.

Remington had only vaguely noticed the guns until Deirdre drew his attention to them. After three more swigs of Jack Black, he reached a hand onto the table and touched several of them with excited apprehension.

"Excuse me, gentlemen," Gulliver said, leaving Jericho and the Grump to have a word with his distraught brother.

Outside, Fritz and Marsha were letting their newfound intimacy take them where it would; all the way.

Within minutes of climbing into the Lincoln, Mabel was in full giddy-up while Roger hung on for dear life.

Both couples were too engrossed in their own private worlds to hear Box Car growl into the shameless night, *"all aboard ... all aboard."*

Gulliver came back to the counter. "I figured out what Rem needs."

Grumpy thought he had too. "Visitation rights and zero gambling debts wouldn't hurt."

"I can't do anything about those things," Gulliver said.

Jericho was next to visit the sullen Swilling. As if to satisfy a profound secret wish, Jericho picked out a gun with his friend's name on it and placed it in his hand. "You can't always get what you want," he said, "but if you try sometimes, you just might find, you'll get what you need."

Remington took the gun and stumbled out the door onto the lawn.

Weepy was into a Doors' song:

Cancel my subscription to the Resurrection
Send my credentials to the House of Detention
I got some friends inside

The face in the mirror won't stop
The girl in the window won't drop ...

The phone rang. Deirdre picked up the receiver.

The prevalent sound outside was the squeaky springs of three bouncing cars.

Grumpy, Gulliver, and Jericho poured fresh drinks.

And Weepy sang:

Before I sink
Into the big sleep
I want to hear
I want to hear
The scream of the butterfly ...

Deirdre looked confused. "Could you repeat that?"

Remington walked in tiny circles on the lawn in front of the cars.

The three men at the counter downed their drinks and poured another round.

In Burlington, Sibyl heard a scream.

And Weepy sang:

I hear a very gentle sound
Very near yet very far
Very soft, yeah, very clear
Come today, come today

Three cars rocked with passion in the desperate night.

Sibyl ran to Bea's bedroom.

Deirdre plugged her other ear to hear better. "He said what? Jesus came to his bedside and placed a healing hand on his head?"

And Weepy sang:

Save us!
Jesus!
Save us!

Remington went round and round in endless circles, finally falling to his knees in the center of the lawn. He rocked gently, holding the gun, like a baby, to his heart.

"What is it Bea? What is it?" Sibyl cried.

"It's daddy. It's daddy, mommy."

"What do you see, sweetie. Tell me."

"Daddy's looking at me. But his eyes, mommy. Daddy's eyes ..."

Gulliver left the kitchen counter to go outside and find his distressed brother.

Grumpy poured another drink.

Jericho picked up a gun from the table and went to the door.

And Weepy sang:

So when the music's over
When the music's over, yeah
When the music's over
Turn out the lights
Turn out the lights
Turn out the lights

Fritz reached around the steering wheel for the switch to the headlights. "What the hell is he doing?" Remington was kneeling on the lawn, the barrel of the pistol in his mouth.

"Say that again," Deirdre said. "He said Jesus talked to him?"

Roger forced a slower pace when the headlights shined on Remington lurching forward. What's he doing, he asked himself. *Praying?* To get a better look, he flashed the Lincoln's headlights on the supplicating Swilling.

"What about his eyes, sweetie? Tell me."

"They were dancing, mommy. Daddy's eyes were dancing. But they stopped. Daddy's eyes stopped, mommy. I didn't want them to but they did. They stopped and then they stared at me, mommy. They stared at me and stared at me."

And Weepy sang:

Well the music is your special friend
Dance on fire as it intends
Music is your only friend
Until the end
Until the end
Until the end!

What the fuck is Rem doing? Box wondered. *Retching?* He reached around his convulsing hair-brained lady and turned on the headlights.

Gulliver walked slowly toward his brother.

Deirdre hung up the phone and looked at Pierre. "The nurse said Walter told her a bearded man appeared to him in a dream, laid a hand on his head and said something righteous, something glorious, something like, *bless you, my son; it's over!* Walter believed he was being saved."

The bouncing cars went motionless, the breathless attention of three enraptured couples riveted to the man kneeling on the lawn in the beams of three sets of headlights.

Gulliver knelt down in front of Rem, a breath away.

A voice, mysterious and sincere, its identity hidden, its message clear, spoke from the shadows falling across the battlefield of Remington's mind: If there is a place in the fast space and timeless silence between the trigger's click and the hammer's strike, this is where eternity lives; a place where horror and happiness are one, where need begs decision, where torment and solace draw swords, where madness and reason collide, where punishment's rewards loop in zany flight like moths to the fire. Look! Look into the hot red of the deathless night. See the frenzied wings sparkling like euphoria, like dread.

A gunshot rang out.

Six riders of the night held their collective breath.

Gulliver inched closer to his brother, head to head, knees to knees.

Jericho held the barrel of his pistol close to his mouth and blew away the smoke.

Gully took the gun from his brother and tossed it aside. He leaned back and breathed deep. With the full force and weight of his surging body he rammed into Remington's chest. Rem fell back, his arms straightening, his fists digging into the ground behind him. He righted himself, found his balance, then charged hard into Gulliver's midsection, determined to make the feather's fly.

"*Mock the cock*," Fritz shouted. "That's what he needed."

Sibyl hugged Beatrice. "Daddy's all right, sweetie. Daddy's all right."

Grumpy came to the doorway and stood next to Jericho, Weepy weeping behind them. "How did it come to this?" Grumpy asked.

"It's all about shock value," Jericho said.

"Could'a fooled me," said the Grump.

Jericho slipped the gun into his pants. "That's the beauty of it."

I know I dreamed you a sin and a lie
I have my freedom but I don't have much time ...

Wild horses couldn't drag me away
Wild, wild horses, we'll ride them someday

Rolling Stones

Epilogue

A thick layer of low clouds suggested worse, but there was only an annoying drizzle. A horse show was in the offing. Pickup trucks, with or without horse trailers, were pulling in at a steady pace; as many as ten or twelve during the past half hour.

Determined equestrians prodded their horses backwards down metal ramps, uncertain hooves tapping an awkward dance on the slippery planks.

Those who boarded their horses at the barn lugged saddles and tack inside. A few of them paused at the dark gaping entrance, perhaps in awe of its immensity, then tromped off to their respective stalls. We could hear the excited animals snort and stomp at the sight of their owners approaching.

Sobering fragrances of wild flowers, herbs, and self-seeding weeds blended with the wet bouquet of fresh horse shit, infusing the gray air with intoxicating country perfumes.

My eyes rose to the far hills beyond the weathervane. Despite the dimmed light, Vermont's fulgent foliage retained its radiance, peaking in full fall glory. In the poignant stillness of an isolated moment, my sense of time's unforgiving pace was piqued by the inertia of the stoic rooster and the heroic horse; arrogant with purpose, impossibly oblivious, heading their separate ways.

Going back thirty years, my friend and I had been sitting on the bluff trading horse barn stories for the better part of three hours, reliving an inglorious history, joking and laughing till it hurt.

The teeming scene below, pullulating with chestnuts and sorrels, palominos and paints, was a peculiar dichotomy; a bizarre vector of kinship and detachment. Our affinity for the horse barn, not the least lessened by the years, seemed utterly estranged from its actual purpose. There were no horses here when the barn was ours.

We stood and stretched our limbs. We walked down the bluff, veering across a small pasture that glistened in the rain. We disappeared into the woods.

Early in the barn's construction, unaware that a *Port-a-Potty* would be delivered to the site, we had each taken a discarded section of treated beam, carved our initials near the tops, and pounded them into the ground. The posts had marked our *squatting zones*; each set a safe distant apart near the edge of the forest.

Over time, trees had encroached onto the pasture. Walking deeper into the woods, our heads down in meticulous search, ten minutes elapsed before one of us spotted a marker; a stubby block badly decomposed.

"Can you make out the initials?" my friend asked.

"Not really."

"Looks to me like *FS*.

I squatted to inspect the carving more closely. "Could be. I can't really tell."

There had been nine posts; three for the Swilling brothers, two for the Bork boys, and one each for Jericho, Walter, Weepy, and Pierre. We found two lying on the ground twenty feet apart in the late stages of decay. We couldn't decipher the initials on either.

On the way back up to the bluff my friend asked if I remembered the name of the state investigator.

"Of course. Roger. Roger something-or-other."

"Farmingham, as I recall."

"He had one helluva schnoz."

"Mabel was certainly taken by it."

"You ever hear much about them?"

"It's been a while. They moved out to Missouri not long after the wedding. As far as I know they're still there. Rudy stayed in touch for a while."

"That's right. Long enough to solve the mystery. I'd give anything to have been a fly on the wall when she delivered."

"Seeing those pink eyes must have raised a red flag."

"They had to suspect something."

"Once the hair came in white as snow there was no denying it."

"Fascinating how the boy followed in his father's footsteps."

"Rudy says his articles have appeared in dozens of newspapers and magazines. I forget the name he goes by."

"I heard that his *nom de plume* is Speilvogle."

"That's it. *Birdsong*, in German."

We climbed into my friend's truck, lingering half a minute to watch the riders work their horses. Coolers and grills had been carried into a concession area. Judging booths were set up. There were microphones and speakers.

My friend perused the proceedings as if peering through a fog. "Things were a lot different back then."

"I'll say. Back when nothing was politically correct."

"Not for us, anyway. My wife says we were a bunch of misogynists. You agree?"

"We might've argued the point at the time; but sure, some of us were."

"Social misfits?"

I laughed. "I'd like to think we still are."

Horse Barn

"Would you do it again?"
"Not a chance. The horse barn was a once-in-a-lifetime experience."
"But worth it?"
I looked at the riders walking or trotting their horses. "Yes. Yes it was."

Acknowledgements

Engineered to be a risible fictive, *Horse Barn* is based on an actual event. Many of the characters are histrionic adaptations of real persons; others, creations of the author.

I owe more than thanks to Sam Haskins; a diehard Vermonter, high-strung dogmatist, and devoted family man. If not for Sammy, this hysterical – nay, historical – watershed saga could not be told.

My wife, Merry, gave critical reads to *Horse Barn* and, not surprisingly, made many corrections and suggestions that improved the story's accuracy and readability. More importantly, Merry created the conditions in Costa Rica that allowed me to write it. For that, my gratitude to her is exceeded only by my love for her.

Billy Ward, the funniest and most insightful person I've ever known, brought more to the writing of this story than any other person. The corner post of my inspiration, Billy was my primary advisor throughout.

My thanks to Mike Sullivan; a critical thinker and prolific reader whose wit and humor are the golden shoes of a thoroughbred. Sully's counsel convinced me to groom out the snarls and braid the tale tighter.

Finally, a note of special thanks to Andy Rudin; catalyst, friend, and technical advisor. It was Andy's winning bid and crazy bet that corralled us all in the winners' circle.

CPSIA information can be obtained at www.ICGtesting.com
Printed in the USA
LVOW07s0624080914

402903LV00012B/143/P

9 781602 640085